D
an

NIGHT'S RECKONING

For over a thousand years, the legendary sword Laylat al Hisab —the Night's Reckoning—has been lost in the waters of the East China Sea. Forged as a peace offering between two ancient vampires, the sword has eluded treasure hunters, human and immortal alike.

But in time, even the deep gives up its secrets.

When Tenzin's sire hears about the ninth-century shipwreck found off the coast of southern China, Zhang Guo realizes he'll need the help of an upstart pirate from Shanghai to retrieve it. And since that pirate has no desire to be in the middle of an ancient war, he calls the only allies who might be able to help him avoid it.

Unfortunately, Tenzin is on one side of the globe and Ben is on the other.

Tenzin knows she'll need Ben's keen mind and political skills to complete the job. She also knows gaining Ben's cooperation won't be an easy task. She'll have to drag him back into the darkness he's been avoiding.

Whether Ben knows it or not, his fate is balanced on the edge of a thousand-year-old blade, and one stumble could break everything Tenzin has worked toward.

Night's Reckoning is the third novel in the Elemental Legacy series, a paranormal mystery by Elizabeth Hunter, *USA Today* best-selling author of the Elemental Mysteries.

PRAISE FOR ELIZABETH HUNTER

[Hunter] writes mysteries that, beyond vampires and elemental powers, capture a human truth brought into perfect focus not despite the paranormal elements but because of them.

— KENDRAI MEEKS, BESTSELLING AUTHOR OF THE RED HOOD CHRONICLES

While the treasure hunt is very entertaining, it's the emotions between these two, what's being said and left unsaid that is very powerful. ...this is Elizabeth Hunter at her best.

— NOCTURNAL BOOK REVIEWS

Ms. Hunter delivers. Every. Single. Time. I have the majority of her books and I am in awe of every book that she has penned and every book she has brought to life and here it is no different.

— KATE'S CORNER

PRAISE FOR NIGHT'S RECKONING

The writing is flawless and has a certain beauty to it and the characters and plot pull you into this amazing and utterly unique world. I just can't get enough.

— Jeri's Attic

Night's Reckoning is a brilliant, complicated story. I am certain that I love Elizabeth Hunter's soul and talent, because I just read something golden and rare. Bravo, Ms. Hunter. Bravo.

— Mac's Meanderings

Night's Reckoning is a fast-paced pageturner that kept me on the edge of my seat. I read the book in one sitting I couldn't put it down.

— KDRBCK

I finished this book in one evening, even though I didn't want it to end. The world and characters Elizabeth Hunter has created are one of the most developed I've ever had the pleasure of reading.

— Carla, Goodreads

NIGHT'S RECKONING

AN ELEMENTAL LEGACY NOVEL

ELIZABETH HUNTER

Cover: Damonza
Content Editor: Amy Cissell, Cissell Ink
Line Editor: Anne Victory
Proofreader: Linda, Victory Editing

Recurve Press LLC
PO Box 4034
Visalia, California
USA
ElizabethHunterWrites.com

GLOSSARY

Alitea—*former island of the Greek immortal court, seat of the newly formed Council of the Ancients, which comprises Saba, Arosh, Kato, and Ziri; largest seat of power in the Mediterranean Sea, Europe, Africa, and Western Asia*

Arosh—*fire vampire, age and origin unknown, ancient king in Eastern Europe/Central Asia, sits on Council of the Ancients, consort of Saba, former rival of Zhang Guo*

Benjamin Vecchio—*human, midtwenties, born in New York City, antiquities dealer, antiquities locator, adopted nephew of Giovanni Vecchio*

Cheng—*water vampire, born late eighteenth century in Guangdong, current governor of Shanghai, entrepreneur, former pirate, Kadek's sire*

Chloe Reardon—*human, midtwenties, born in Los Angeles, dancer, romantic partner of Gavin Wallace*

Emil Conti—*water vampire, born second century BC in Rome, governor of Rome, sire of Ronan*

Filomena—*water vampire, born in Naples, age unknown, governor of Naples*

Gavin Wallace—*wind vampire, born in Scotland, age unknown, entrepreneur, currently based in New York City, romantic partner of Chloe Reardon*

Harun al Ilāh—*fire vampire, origin and age unknown, master of damascene steel and glasswork, deceased*

Jinpa—*human, midseventies, born in Tibet, servant of Tenzin*

Jīnshé—*boat, a scientific research vessel out of Shanghai*

Jimmu—*water vampire, age and origin unknown, immortal lord of Japanese archipelago*

Johari—*earth vampire (formerly a water vampire), born in Zanzibar, daughter of Saba*

Kadek—*water vampire, born in Indonesia, sea captain, son of Cheng*

Kato—*water vampire, born in Greece, age unknown, sits on Council of the Ancients, grandsire of Giovanni Vecchio*

Laylat al Hisab—*the Night's Reckoning, a sword made in the ninth century by famed fire vampire and swordsmith Harun al Ilāh*

Mr. Lu—*human, Kadek's second-in-command, day captain of the Jīnshé research vessel*

Penglai Island—*immortal island in Bohai Sea, seat of the Eight Immortals, largest seat of power in Eastern Asia*

Professor Chou—*human, university professor in charge of the underwater archaeology team*

Qamar Jadid—*ninth-century Arab dhow carrying ceremonial gifts from Arosh to Zhang Guo to finalize the Treaty of Kashgar*

Saba—*earth vampire, born in Ethiopia, age unknown, eldest known immortal, "mother of vampires," current queen of Alitea, Johari's sire*

Sina—*water vampire, age and origin unknown, ancient queen of the South Pacific Sea*

Tai—*wind vampire, age and origin unknown, son of deceased Zhongli Quan, current servant of Zhang Guo*

Tenzin—*wind vampire, born approximately five thousand years ago in Central Asia, former assassin, former mercenary, former military commander, daughter of Zhang Guo*

Zhang Guo—*wind vampire, born over five thousand years ago in Central Asia, eldest of the Eight Immortal Elders of Penglai Island, Tenzin's sire*

Ziri—*wind vampire, born in North Africa, age unknown, sits on Council of the Ancients*

For the Readers
who have stuck with me
through fire and water
valleys and mountain tops,
this book is for you.
—EH

WIND SPEAKS

You say you want to know me.

I don't think you do.

I am old.

You don't want to know the things I have seen.

Have you watched a tree grow from seed to leaf? Days and nights passing as you rest in a shadowed place. Light and dark flickering by like one of the film reels you love to watch. Have you seen this?

I have.

I am as old as the wind I walk upon.

I am a mother. A daughter. A sister to murdered kin.

A friend. A lover. An enemy.

A hero?

I have been a hero and a villain in the same moment. If you grow old enough, you might understand what that means.

I dream in a tongue that died a thousand years before time was counted. I no longer count time. It is meaningless. There is only the light and the dark. Hot. Cold. I am a creature of sense.

A murderer.

A liar.

A thief.

I hold myself subject to no man's law. The laws came after me. There is only one law I recognize.

I survive. I protect what is mine.

You say you want to know me. Maybe you do.

Do you want to see rivers change course? See mountains fall and islands rise? Do you want to see waves of humanity ebb and flow as civilizations grow? When they die?

Both are equal in my eyes.

Humanity grows like a canyon cut by rivers of blood and conquest. Leaders rise and are swept away. I have seen it. I will see it again.

Are you sure you want to see it?

It might make you mad.

I have been mad. It was... freeing.

I have been mad and wise. One is only a shadow of the other. I have been fueled by rage and love in the same breath.

When I choose to breathe.

I have loved. And love has made me mad.

I have loved, and the loss of it made me rage.

I have killed those I loved.

Love is more dangerous than madness. More fickle than rage.

Love.

The Greeks had many names for it. Foolish humans divide everything, as if the dissection of an emotion will let them understand its power.

Love is larger than their divisions. I have loved. I will love again. There is only that. The love I hold has lasted as I have. It lives in my blood.

Don't pretend to understand, human. You cannot.

We are immortal. We are the elements. Earth. Water. Wind. Fire.

Other.

We are born of them. We feed on them. We return to them when our bodies are slain. That is our eternity. We will be born again.

You say you want to know me, but what do you want to know?

I have killed thousands of your kind.

Thousands.

Did you want to know that?

I cannot hide among you. I don't even try. If you met me, I would only be a shadow that your brain chooses to forget. A trick of the darkness. I am only known to those whom I choose. I lie when it suits me. I might be lying now.

I probably am.

You want to know what I see when I look at him?

I see a shining boy with shadows in his eyes. A shallow pool that grows deeper with every footstep. One day he will be infinite.

You see only the edge of a shadow of who he will become.

Do you see visions?

I do.

Don't pretend to understand. You're lying now. Like me.

You say you want to see a happy ending, but what does that mean for me? I have no ending.

You say I deserve to find love?

I don't.

Love has been handed to me, and I threw it away. I deserve nothing.

Do I want it?

I take what I want.

You say you want to know me. I don't think you do.

I am not what you can understand. The span of your life is a speck of dust in the wind of my existence. I exist outside this world. They call me a wind-walker. There is truth in that. The wind travels over the world untethered. It has many names.

Zephyros.

Vardar.

Taku.

Bora.

Mistral.

Nashi.

They are all the same air. Like me. I am all of them and none of them. I chose my name.

Tenzin.

Holder of teachings.

I will choose another someday when I am tired of this one.

I have had many names.

Mother. Daughter. Sister. Lover. Friend.

I am all of those, but none of them define me.

Maybe you do understand.

No.

The truth is not always beautiful
nor beautiful words the truth.
—Lao Tzu

B en was expecting the punch, but that didn't make it hurt any less. It landed on his jaw, snapping his head back. His skull cracked on the edge of the metal chair where they'd tied him up.

He was sitting in an old warehouse on the run-down edges of Genoa, taking their vicious punches with his ears open, ignoring the taunts of the humans around him. The men had grabbed him when he'd been snooping around the warehouse near the railroad tracks.

Exactly as he'd planned it.

One vampire stood with the humans, silently watching Ben as he tried to ignore her. The humans he wasn't worried about. The vampire was another story.

"I hear she keeps him on a tight leash," one of the men said. "I'm surprised he got this far out of Napoli."

The vampire was female and petite. In Ben's experience, a vicious combination. She stared while Ben tried to look beaten and miserable.

"Poor boy." Her voice purred. "Little puppies who wander too far get kicked by the bigger dogs." Her voice was a whisper that begged for his attention, drawing him in, seducing him, exactly as she wanted it to.

Ben narrowed the one eye that wasn't already swelling shut and concentrated on the pain to resist the lure of her voice. Hits to the face he'd put up with for the job. Kicks to the ribs were hardly anything new. But if the vampire touched him, she would be able to use *amnis*, the electric current that gave her elemental power and control over humans if she wished it. Ben would do nearly anything to escape his brain being messed with. It had happened before, and he wasn't a fan.

He'd been told he had natural resistance to amnis, but resistance wasn't immunity.

"What does Piero want with him?"

The vampire's purring voice turned hard. "Shut your mouth if you want to keep your tongue, human."

Ben tried to see which man was talking. It was the bombastic one, the tallest in the group with three days' worth of beard and a sweat-stained polo shirt clinging to his chest. The man had fists the size of Iberian hams, and they felt just as solid.

It didn't matter. *Piero.* Ben had a name. One down, one to go.

The human puffed out his chest and angled his shoulders back. His chin went up. "I don't work for you."

"You stupid mortal," the vampire muttered. "Of course you do."

"Piero gives me orders. I don't even know why he brought you to Finale—"

The man's voice cut off with a strangled gurgle.

And a place. The corner of Ben's mouth turned up. That was quicker than he'd thought. *Gotcha.*

The humans in the gang started shouting at the vampire, who released the man's throat from her iron grip and let him slide to the floor.

Ben silently released his wrists from the restraints he'd loosened an hour before, minutes after they'd tied him up. The humans weren't very good with knots.

As the men shouted at the small vampire in defense of their friend, Ben moved, slipping from his bonds and easing into the shadows between stacked pallets in the warehouse. The whole place smelled of sardines and motor oil, not a good combination.

"Stefano, where's the kid?"

More shouting in loud Italian. Their accents didn't sound like Genoa. Much farther south if Ben had to guess. Not Naples. Sicily? Calabria maybe. His client would want to know. The vampire wasn't Italian. Ben was guessing French.

As he crept away, he listened for her movements. She was the only one who presented a real threat. The floor was cold against his feet—hard-packed dirt with cracked concrete near the door. They'd taken his shoes, and he had no idea where they'd put them.

"You idiot!" another yelled. "Piero is going to take your balls!"

"He's a skinny foreigner. Find him, you shit! He can't have gotten far."

Ben slipped into a shadowed corner and climbed up the plastic-covered pallets, clinging with his fingertips and toes to the edges of the wrapped cans and waiting for the first man to come to him.

A dark-haired human looked into the narrow corner but didn't notice Ben halfway up the wall. He turned around, and Ben immediately fell on his back.

Ben locked his elbow around the guy's neck and slapped a hand over his mouth to block his muffled yell. Once his mouth was covered, Ben chopped the edge of his hand against the man's throat in a swift slicing gesture, bringing him to his knees and driving the breath from his lungs.

Ben released his hold, and the choking man clutched his throat as Ben quickly drew his fist back and aimed for the temple. His fist made contact, the man's head snapped to the side, and he fell in a solid thunk.

Ben quickly rifled through his pockets, grabbing his wallet and the knife and gun in his waistband. He felt for an ankle holster but didn't find one.

Shoes? He needed shoes.

Damn. This guy's were too small.

"Topo, where are you?"

"By the door!"

"Luca?"

Nothing.

Ben looked at the man he had to guess was Luca. He'd wake up eventually, and he would deserve the massive headache.

Now with one hundred percent more weapons, Ben crawled on top of the stack of pallets and surveyed the warehouse. His head was throbbing, but he needed to eliminate the human threat and avoid the vampire.

He'd have to climb down eventually to reach the door. He crawled over two more stacks of pallets and dropped to the ground. Three more humans and he'd have a clear shot.

The second man nearly walked into Ben. He turned in to the alcove where Ben was waiting and his eyes widened, but Ben put the knife to his throat before he could yell.

"Shhhh." Ben put a finger to his lips. "The baby's sleeping."

The man cocked his head, confused. "Wha—?"

Crack. Another fist to the temple. Another snapped neck, and the human fell to the ground with his eyes rolling back.

And his shoes were still too small. What was with these people? Did they all have miniature feet?

Ben kept the knife out. There were three more wandering around, not counting the vampire.

Where was the vampire?

He had the door in sight when he nearly ran into two of the men. One reached for his gun, but Ben kicked it before the man could raise it. He muttered a curse and reached for his knife while Ben dodged the other man's grasp.

They weren't expecting Ben to be so fast. They thought they'd wounded him. They'd thought he was broken.

Gotcha, suckers.

Silence was useless now. The men were shouting as he fought them off. He grabbed the unarmed man by the shoulders and brought his face down to his knee. Ben felt the spurt of blood from the man's nose.

The scent of blood lay like bitter copper in his mouth. His own skin was broken. One man rolled on the ground, holding his hand to his face as blood poured out, and Ben turned to the other man, who was now a little more cautious. It was the original ringleader, Stefano, whose throat was still red and raw from the vampire grabbing him. He was bent to the side, still limping.

His voice was hoarse. "Who are you?"

Ben touched the corner of his split lip and flinched. "No one important."

Before Stefano could ask another question, Ben brought his foot up and swiftly kicked him in the gut, knocking the man to the ground. Then Ben walked over and kicked Stefano's temple, snapping his neck to the side and making his eyes roll back.

Ben examined the two men on the ground. Making a swift decision, he grabbed Stefano's shoes and slipped them on his feet, leaving the laces untied. They were a little big, but they were better than nothing.

He ran for the door. He was nearly home free when the vampire appeared.

She appeared a few yards away from Ben, moving so quickly he nearly didn't see her. She stomped her foot on the ground and a crack split the floor. Ben's foot fell into the earth and he felt the pulse of power as the dirt tightened around his ankle.

Earth vampire. He added that to the file.

"Hey there." He kept his knife out and reached for the gun he'd slipped in his pocket, never taking his eyes off the vampire walking toward him. "Ben Vecchio. How you doing?"

"I know who you are." She wasn't angry. She was curious. Her head was angled to the side, and she examined him like normal people examined an interesting specimen at the science museum.

"I'm just trying to get out of here," Ben said. "I have no desire to start a fight."

"You've already been in one." Her voice was still barely over a whisper, and Ben was starting to wonder whether she had some physical disability that affected her voice.

Contrary to human mythology, changing into a vampire didn't cure all your ills. It didn't make you younger or heal anything other than the most recent injuries. If you were missing an arm before you turned, it was still going to be gone. If you were deaf as a human, you'd be deaf as a vampire. Nerve damage could be cured, and immortality fixed all but the most severe eye problems. But a damaged voice? You'd live with that for eternity.

"I'm not looking for a fight," he repeated. "I just want to go home."

"Do you?" She met his eyes and her fangs fell. "And who would miss you if you didn't go home, Ben Vecchio?"

He raised the gun. "I don't know you. I am a human under vampire aegis. We have no quarrel. Let me go."

Her mouth was halfway between a smile and a pout. "If you're under vampire aegis, you should know that gun won't do anything to stop me."

"I know if I hit your spine, you'll be out of commission until nightfall tomorrow." He glanced at the ceiling. "You'll be safe in here. I won't even have to feel guilty. No direct sunlight. Whoever might find you during your day rest, that's not my problem, is it?" He really wished Luca'd had a semiautomatic he could steal, but he was still a decent shot with a revolver. "I'm an excellent shot. You don't want to take a chance. Let me go."

She smiled. "I'm not going to kill you. I was simply curious."

"Oh?" He kept the gun trained on the vampire's neck as she moved.

"Curious what she sees in you."

Fuck. Ben knew exactly who *she* was and just the reminder pissed him off. He cocked the gun. "Let me go."

"I don't poach." She came closer. "But I wonder if a taste—"

The gun went off and her long hair blew back. Ben could see a red line where the bullet had passed by her neck.

"Back off," he said in a low voice. "I won't miss again."

"You didn't miss that time. Interesting." She blinked and smiled fully. "I do understand what she sees in you, Benjamin Vecchio."

Without another word, the vampire ran out the door and Ben heard it creak from the swift gust of air.

And his foot was still stuck in the ground. "Really?"

Wiggling it back and forth, Ben managed to work it out, but only because Stefano's shoes were bigger than his foot. He left the right shoe stuck in the ground and limped to the door.

Ben was almost there when it swung back, revealing a thin man leaning against the wall, pointing his gun at Ben with a shaking hand.

Ben glared at the man. "You really want to do this?" He raised his revolver and the man lowered his gun.

"No, I don't—"

"Are you Topo?"

The man nodded.

Ben kept his voice low and walked toward him. "Okay, mouse, the rest of them are out. The vampire's gone. You want me to punch you or shoot you?"

The blood drained from his face. "Are those my only options?"

"You think your boss is gonna be satisfied if you just run?" Ben nodded over his shoulder. "She knows you were here and walking when she left."

Topo's face crumpled. "I guess... shoot me. Left leg?"

Ben had been certain the man would go for the knockout. "A bullet? You sure?"

The man pointed to his eyes. "The doctor, he says if I take any more punches, I could lose an eye. I used to be a boxer."

"That sucks."

Topo shrugged. "It's only a nine millimeter."

"Still a bullet, man."

Topo hesitated. "Maybe... you could break a few ribs?"

It was a solid option. It wouldn't put him completely out, but with enough bruising, his boss would believe Ben got past him. After all, he'd already taken out all the other brutes.

"If you're sure."

Topo put the safety on his gun and tossed it to the side. "Yes."

Ben didn't hesitate. He smashed his fist into Topo's ribs, punching him until the man was falling to the ground and Ben's fist felt like hamburger.

Damn. He really wished he'd just gone with the bullet like Topo wanted. His knuckles would take weeks to heal.

Ben finished Topo off with a swift kick to the side. He looked at Topo's feet and bent over. "Hey, mouse?"

Topo could only blink. He was gasping for breath.

"I hate to do this, but I'm gonna need your shoes."

2

Ben was holding an ice pack to his face when he contacted
Fabia on screen chat. "Hey."

"*Cavalo!*" She leaned toward the camera. "What happened
to you?"

"The other guys look worse." He shifted the ice pack.
"Okay, probably I look worse, but they have concussions.
Doesn't matter. I got the info. Let Filomena know I'll be down
in Naples tomorrow night. Going to sleep, and then I'll catch
the train in the morning. I'll have to check the schedule because
I can't remember when—"

"Ben, you need to see a physician. Come back to Rome and
I'll call Dr. Mariano."

He winced when he shifted. He hadn't broken any ribs, but
his face and his hands were battered. "I promise it looks worse
than it is. Nothing broken. My feet are a little torn up, but I
finally found shoes." He glanced at Topo's shoes, which were
sitting by the door. "Actually, after I clean them up, I might keep
them. They're really well made."

"What are you talking about? Have you lost consciousness

at any time in the past few hours? I'm worried about you falling asleep by yourself. Do you want me to come get you?"

"I'm fine." He reached for a cotton ball and dipped it in disinfectant before he dabbed his lip. "I'm going to clean up, take a nice long shower, and then I'll feel better after some sleep. I'm in a secure place. I just wanted to call you because my phone got smashed and I knew you'd be worried."

"I am worried. About your health." She frowned. "Do you at least have a spare phone?"

He held up his newest burner. "Yep."

"Set an alarm and call me in three hours." She held up a hand. "Don't argue. You've been punched repeatedly in the head, and I'm a doctor."

"You have a PhD in archaeology. That doesn't make you a doctor."

"Do you want me to call Angela?"

He glared at her. "You'd better not."

If Fabia called her aunt, Angela would call *his* aunt and then Ben would be harassed from both hemispheres.

"Call me in three hours," Fabia repeated. "Then you can go back to sleep and call me in another three. Otherwise, I'm driving up to Genoa to get you right now."

"You know, this is why we never got together. You're a worrier."

She raised an eyebrow. "Really? *That's* why we never got together? Are you committed to that story?"

"It's not too late." He blew kisses at the camera. "I know you find me irresistible." His right eye was completely swollen shut; his lips were cracked and bleeding. He had a dark bruise blossoming on his left cheekbone.

"Oh yes," she said. "Irresistible. That's definitely the first thing that comes to mind. I'm worried about brain damage. Clean up, get some sleep, and call me in three hours or so help me, I won't call Angela, I'll call someone *else* I know you're avoiding. Chloe has her number."

He glared at the screen. "Over the line, Fabi."

She looked chagrined. "Ben—"

He snapped the laptop closed and shoved it away. Then he set the alarm on his phone for three and a half hours and carefully walked to the narrow shower in the apartment bathroom. He kept the lights off, left the hall door open, and turned the water to lukewarm. After stripping off his clothes, he walked in and immediately forgot his irritation with Fabia in a wave of pain.

Everything hurt. The cuts across his skin. His muscles. His fists. He soaped up and washed the blood, oil, and grit from his body. The worst was cleaning his feet. Not only were they cut and sore, he had to bend in half to wash them. He nearly lost his balance so many times he ended up sitting on the floor of the shower, gingerly picking gravel from beneath the skin and being happy he was currently living alone so no one else could see his humiliation.

After he'd gotten his feet clean, he stood and leaned his head against the tile, letting the hard spray of water pound against his back, soothing a little of the ache.

I don't poach.

His fingers touched the fang marks on his neck. They were too faint for human eyes, but vampires would see them. See the vicious, uncontrolled bite of a vampire in bloodlust. See the carefully healed scars she'd sealed with her own blood.

I do understand what she sees in you, Benjamin Vecchio.

She wasn't gone. She was never gone. Except that she was. She was a gaping hole in his life, and nothing he did seemed to fill it. Not fighting. Not work. Not travel. Not drinking.

Worse than that, there were letters. Three of them were sitting in the kitchen in Rome, carefully addressed to him and bearing the seal of the Eight Immortals on Penglai Island in China.

He couldn't bring himself to open them. He'd been hiding in Rome for the past four months, dreading a return to an empty apartment in New York. Chloe was gone. Tenzin was gone. Chloe was at Gavin's, and he wasn't sure where Tenzin was. All he knew was that she was probably keeping tabs on him.

Infuriating vampire.

It had been six months since he'd seen Tenzin. Six months since she'd run away from whatever twisted relationship they'd been falling into.

Ben didn't know what the letters from Penglai were about. He didn't want to know. He knew he should open them, but he didn't want to deal with whatever inevitability he'd be faced with once he did. And every night that passed, it grew a little bit easier to leave them hidden away.

HE WAS CHANGING trains in Florence the next time he managed more than a cursory check-in with Fabia.

"Did you tell Filomena I'm on my way?" A mother and child passed him. The little girl's eyes went wide while the mother carefully looked away. "I want to get this job done with and get back home."

Ben knew he still looked frightening, but he'd used a little of the theater makeup Chloe had taught him how to apply in New York. He could at least pass without people gawking and staring.

"Her Majesty said she'd meet you at 'your spot'—her words not mine—at eleven o'clock tonight. Do you know what she's talking about, and does that give you enough time?"

"Just a sec." Ben flashed his ticket at the conductor and

boarded the first-class compartment for the final leg to Naples. He quickly found a seat near the back corner by the window. He stowed his bag in the overhead compartment and took a seat before he answered. "That's plenty of time." He tipped his head back and leaned against the seat. "I'll get there a little after seven. And I know where she'll be."

"How long are you staying in Naples?"

"That depends on how friendly Filomena is."

"Ben, be serious."

He smiled. Then he winced. His lip was still really painful. "I'll leave in the morning. I miss my bed."

"Do you have accommodations in Naples arranged?"

"I have a place." While Chloe acted as his general assistant and human external hard drive in New York, Fabia had taken over his life in Rome. She was between jobs at the moment and wasn't teaching at the university this semester, so she had the time and Ben needed the help.

He'd been contracting for short jobs with various friends and vampire allies for the previous few months. Taking time off from treasure hunting and lying low was a good idea since the last heist, which he and Tenzin had gotten away with in Puerto Rico.

It made sense for him to stay in Europe while North America cooled off a bit. He'd annoyed more than a few vampires in New York and Puerto Rico. Plus he could avoid being in his and Tenzin's empty apartment in SoHo if he was hopping around Europe.

He'd spent some time in England, a little in Scotland with friends, but Rome had always felt like a second home. His uncle was Italian and had houses in Rome and Tuscany. The Vecchio private library was in Perugia. He'd grown up spending as many holidays in Rome as he did in Los Angeles. When life got complicated, Italy was where he ran to.

And life felt... very complicated at the moment.

Fabia said, "Call me when you get to your hotel after you're finished with Filomena tonight."

"Will do."

"Don't forget you have a meeting with Ronan on Friday evening."

He had forgotten about the meeting. "About?"

"He didn't say and I didn't ask. I assumed you knew."

Ronan was working directly for Emil Conti, the vampire in charge of Rome. He'd grown up with Ronan, both kids raised in the vampire world. Of course, no two families were exactly alike. Ronan's parents were human, and Ben's were vampires. And Ben was determined to remain human while Ronan had turned under Emil Conti's aegis two years before.

Ben glanced around at the relatively deserted compartment and lowered his voice. "So is Ronan fully non-bitey at this point?"

Fabia laughed. "I ran into him a few weeks ago when I was out with friends. Other than being a bit paler, he's exactly the same Ronan."

"I shaved my beard. Think he'll still hit on me?"

"I think his partner might object to that."

"I didn't know he'd paired up." Ben smiled a little. "Good for him. He's a solid guy. I still have no idea what he wants to talk to me about. For some reason, I thought he just wanted to hang out."

"When he called, I got the impression it was for business reasons."

Ben shrugged. "Then I'm sure he'll tell me on Friday."

"Could be something like what you're doing for Filomena."

"Could be he wants to know *what* I'm doing for Filomena."

"That's also possible."

Ben wouldn't tell. He was charming enough to avoid giving

answers he didn't want to give, and protecting privacy was one of his hard-and-fast rules. Unless someone gave him a reason to spill secrets, he was a vault.

"Fabi, I'm gonna hang up. I'll see you tomorrow."

"Don't forget I need to hear your voice tonight."

"I won't forget." He ended the call and closed his eyes as the train pulled out of the station.

A normal person might think Fabia was being overprotective, but all her requests were standard safety protocol when living in the vampire world. Call when you finish the meet. Call when you're locked in safe for the night. Daylight was for moving. Nighttime was for caution.

Of course, most humans never had to worry about any of that. Most humans knew nothing about the shadow governments, immortal politics, and twisted economy of the vampire world. They didn't know that thousand-year-old immortals walked among them when the sun went down. They didn't know that world events were often subtly shifted depending on the whim of an earth vampire in Greece or an immortal council outside Beijing.

There was no reason they *should* know. The majority of vampires didn't kill to drink blood. Killing was inconvenient and, frankly, a waste of natural resources. All but the most sociopathic of them drank from unwitting humans or cooperative ones they employed for that specific purpose.

Vampires couldn't exist without humans. Not for sustenance and not for business. Ben was evidence of that. He'd been adopted by a vampire when he was only twelve years old, and he'd been under Giovanni Vecchio's protection and working for and with him ever since.

Did Giovanni love Ben? Yes.

Did Giovanni also expect Ben to send emails for him when

he couldn't figure out how to work the voice-controlled computer in his office? Also yes.

Then again, most kids had to deal with parents who didn't understand technology, so Ben couldn't complain too much. Of course, human parents wouldn't fry electronics if they got too close to them, but that was mostly a fire vampire problem.

The train to Naples took nearly three hours, so Ben took a nap in the afternoon sun beaming through the window and woke a little before seven feeling refreshed. He patted his face with cool water in the bathroom and took stock of his injuries.

It wasn't the worst he'd ever looked, but it was close. Most of the time when he had cuts or open wounds, Tenzin would heal them with some of her blood. Humans couldn't ingest vampire blood unless they were nearly exsanguinated and on the edge of death. But vampire blood could heal open wounds. It could hide bite marks and help bruising along.

He dabbed a little concealer over the worst of the marks and let his dark hair fall over his swollen eye. His olive skin had grown darker since he'd been in Italy. He'd been spending as much time in the sun as he could, partly for safety and partly to remind himself he was human.

Human. Not vampire.

He stared in the mirror, the eyes staring back at him blood-shot from the violence they'd seen.

Persian eyes. Tenzin had told him once that he had Persian eyes. He didn't even know what that meant.

Ben had dark brown eyes rimmed with thick lashes. Regular brown eyes. Olive skin. Dark curly hair. His blood was an even mix of Lebanese and Puerto Rican, which meant when he was in Italy, he blended in just fine. He blended in through most of Europe, the Middle East, and both Americas. Ben liked blending in. It made work much easier.

He walked back to his seat and gathered his belongings just

as the train came to a stop. Most of the compartment was filled with tourists from all over the world. American. African. Asian.

A group of college-aged girls from China rushed past him, their happy chatter informing him they were excited about seeing Pompeii. Ben smiled and kept walking. He'd never seen Pompeii, but he'd met people who were alive when Vesuvius erupted. That had to count for something.

He walked outside Napoli Centrale and looked for a cab. He had less than three hours before he met with Filomena, and he still had some research to do.

3

Filomena, vampire governor of Naples, met Ben at a small restaurant near the waterfront on the Bay of Naples. It was hidden down an alley near the Castel dell'Ovo and specialized in a particular kind of fried fish that Ben loved.

Since Filomena was governor partly because of actions spurred by Ben and Tenzin several years before, Ben felt safe with her even if Fabia worried.

She was sipping a tall glass of prosecco when Ben arrived. He bent down, kissed both her cheeks with his cracked lips, and sat across from her.

Filomena's eyes went wide. "How many were there?"

"Six and a vampire."

She pursed her lips. "In that case, you're looking good."

"Thanks." He paused while the waiter set down a glass of prosecco and a small tray of crostini. "You're looking gorgeous. Of course, you always look gorgeous."

She glanced down at her pale blue blouse and silk scarf. "Thank you."

It was the absolute truth without a hint of flattery. While

most vampires tended to have above-average looks—immortal creatures of the night did like pretty things—Filomena was a true beauty. She'd been turned in her late thirties if Ben had to guess. She was tall for her age and had long wavy hair the color of dark caramel. Her features were dramatic, and her cheekbones looked as if they'd been carved from marble.

She'd propositioned Ben more than once. He'd always been tempted, but he'd never given in. Sex with vampires was complicated. Sex with political vampires? Even more so.

"So?" She waited for him.

Ben picked up a menu. "Do you mind if I order? I skipped lunch because I had to transfer in Florence."

"So you were in Tuscany?"

Ben waved over the server, who'd been hovering just out of earshot. "Have you tried the pasta with sea urchins? How is that?"

Filomena spoke directly to the waiter. "Tell *il mostro* that this man is my guest and he's hungry. He eats everything—make him something I would like."

The server nodded. "Very well." Then he took the menu from Ben's hands with a slightly apologetic smile. "*Signore.*"

"Sure," Ben said. "What she said." He leaned back in his chair, stretched out his legs, and crossed his ankles. "*Il mostro?*"

"The chef is a monster, but he's a talented one. This is where I come when I want to eat human food." She sipped her wine. "So, you were in the north?"

"I was in Genoa."

"The smugglers are in Genoa. That makes sense."

"But his headquarters aren't there."

She lifted an eyebrow. "Where then?"

Ben paused. "They obviously have an office of some kind in Genoa, but the headquarters of the operation is in a little town called Finale Ligure. It's west of Genoa in Savona, about halfway to France."

"I know that place." Filomena narrowed her eyes. "Why would their headquarters be in such a place? That's a seaside resort. It's for tourists."

"Probably because he's an earth vampire and he's from there." Ben opened his tablet and flipped it over so she could see the grainy picture Ben had found. "Piero Caviglia. Or at least that's my best guess about who Piero is. I asked around with some trusted sources. He's loosely under Emil Conti's aegis, but only very loosely. He was more connected to Conti's wife. After she died, he worked with Jean Desmarais for a time, but of course—"

"Poor Piero," Filomena said. "His benefactors seem to have a habit of dying."

Jean Desmarais had been killed rather famously for working with the old Athenian court, who were trying to addict vampires to an Elixir that eventually killed them. The old Athenian court had been wiped out by the resurgence of four ancient vampires on a small island called Alitea, and anyone connected to Elixir was eliminated. If this Piero had survived, he must have kept his nose relatively clean.

"He's an opportunist," Ben said. "Works in Liguria and the south of France. I don't think any of his missteps in Naples have been intentionally aggressive toward you. I think he's looking for work and he's stepping on toes. It might be deliberate, or your ships might have been in the wrong place at the wrong time. If you approach him right, he'd be likely to make amends and it could be beneficial to you."

Her eyes cut to him. "Why do I need a clumsy immortal from Savona?"

"He's connected loosely to Rome, and more importantly,

he's in the north." Ben shrugged. "I'm just saying that you're very powerful, very influential *here*. But your reach only extends so far."

Filomena's eyes were guarded. "I have no desire to rule Italy."

Liar.

"Who said anything about ruling?" Ben put on his shocked face. "I know how deeply Naples and Rome are bound together. Sister cities, if anything."

Filomena's eyes danced with unspoken ambition. "Exactly."

"I'm only speaking of business," Ben said. "Building a business alliance with someone from the north could be beneficial to you both."

"Hmmm." She crossed her legs, drawing Ben's eyes to one of her best features. "Do you have a report for me?"

He handed over a folder. "Of course."

"I'll look it over. You might be right."

"It happens occasionally."

"More than occasionally. I'll make sure your fee is transferred in the morning." She tapped the edge of her empty glass and the server was at her side, filling the glass to the brim. "Nice work, Ben."

"Thanks, Nena."

She smiled at the old nickname. "It's been a couple of years since you called me that."

"Has it been?"

She leaned forward, rested her arm on the table, and stroked a thumb over the corner of his unswollen eye. "I see it now."

He captured her hand and dropped a kiss on her wrist. "See what?"

"The man you'll be. Are you so determined to leave us, *gigio?*"

21

He smiled. "Do you know how many times I've answered this question?"

"Maybe that means you should rethink your answer."

"Nena—"

"You could stay here if you wanted. Human or vampire. You're always welcome in Naples, Benjamin. I could use a man with your skills and your confidence."

The corner of his mouth turned up. "You scaring your employees again?"

She shrugged. "Half of them are mice. Useful mice, but still. I need people I can trust. People who will tell me I'm taking the wrong step. If you worked for me—if you were sharing my bed—I would trust you."

"Do you want an employee or a lover?"

She frowned. "Why should I have to choose?"

Ben laughed and knit her fingers with his. "The food here takes a long time."

"It does. I wanted you to myself for a while." She squeezed his fingers. "Have you heard from her?"

He opened his mouth. Closed it. "I can't say."

"You won't say."

He rubbed his hand over the scars on his neck. "It's complicated."

"Of course it is. For you. Is it complicated for her?"

His smile was rueful. "That's an excellent question."

"I am not being harsh. I am acknowledging her years."

Ben knew Filomena wasn't criticizing. She would never judge Tenzin. From what Ben could tell, Filomena wanted to be Tenzin when she grew up.

"You mean am I really all that important to someone who's been around for..." Tenzin's age was a secret, and Ben wasn't going to change that. "... for as long as Tenzin has lived? I can't tell you that. We're partners. We're taking a break right now for our own reasons, and I don't make a habit of predicting the future. Or talking out of turn."

"Understood." She smiled. "But you're not free to take other jobs?"

"I took a job for you, didn't I?"

"I'd hire you on a far more permanent basis, Benjamin. Just keep that in mind as you bounce around the world." She leaned forward. "As long as I'm the governor of Naples, you will always be welcome here."

"Thank you. I don't take that lightly."

"And you are sure you don't want to come work for me?" She ran the point of her shoe up the back of his leg. "I can promise a very generous benefits package."

Ben smiled as he looked at the curve of her leg. "I have no doubt."

"Don't say no," she said. "Say 'Not now, Nena.'"

"Okay." He looked up slowly. "Not now, Nena."

She nodded. "Fine."

His food finally came, a small mountain of delicate pasta heaped with seafood of all kinds. Fish, shrimp, clams, and calamari. "*Grazie.*" He pushed the bowl toward the center of the table. "You're going to help me eat this, aren't you?"

"Of course." She picked up her fork and spoon. "Are you hungry?"

"Always."

"Then I'll have the chef make you a dessert as well. After all, I still owe you one."

He shook his head. "You don't owe me anything."

"Don't be careless." She met his eyes. "I don't offer favors lightly."

"Good. Neither do I."

❧

BEN ARRIVED in Rome before noon the next day. He caught a taxi to the Pantheon and walked a few blocks to Residenza di Spada, his uncle's home in the city. He turned his key in the massive door that faced the road, only to have the latch click and the door swing in, revealing Fabia behind it.

"You didn't call me!" She was dressed in a summer dress and sandals. It might have been fall, but it was still warm for most of the day. "I told you last night I'd pick you up."

He slung an arm around her shoulders. "I didn't want to ride on the back of your scooter from Termini."

"I can drive, you know. There's a car here."

He shrugged. "Easier to take a cab. I'm fine."

"You're injured." She turned his chin to the side. "I cannot believe you haven't been to see the doctor."

"It's better than it was."

"Which makes it even more horrific that you didn't go. Dr. Mariano is coming this afternoon."

He groaned. "Seriously, Fabi, all I want is a nap."

"So take a nap. And then Dr. Mariano will check you out and I won't be as much of a pest. Also, Chloe has been trying to call."

He checked his watch. "I'll call her tonight."

"Also..." She ushered him into the kitchen and nudged him toward a kitchen chair. "There is more mail."

He cut his eyes toward the counter where she stacked the mail. "What is it?"

"Chloe forwarded some things from New York. And..." She glanced over her shoulder. "There's another one."

Another envelope from China.

His expression hardened. "Just put it in the drawer."

"I'm not putting it in the drawer, Ben." She grabbed two glasses from the cupboard. "That is formal correspondence delivered by courier. It screams 'Dangerous Vampires Wrote This—Don't Ignore!' Don't you think you ought to—"

"I'll open them when I feel like it," Ben said.

She filled both glasses with water. "It's been six months."

"And she hasn't called me once. She hasn't sent me a message." Ben walked over and grabbed the manila envelope with the New York return address. The thick linen envelope with a wax seal went in the drawer with the others. "*This* is not from her."

Fabia waved at the counter. "You don't think those letters are from Tenzin?"

"I think they're formal communication from the Eight Immortals on Penglai Island. Which is not a letter from Tenzin."

"Isn't her sire one of the Eight Immortals?"

Ben sat back at the counter and opened the envelope from Chloe. "Yes."

Fabia put a glass of water in front of him along with two pills. "Take these. You're splitting hairs. She might be trying to communicate through her father."

"Why would she need to do that?" He threw the pills in his mouth, letting the bitterness dissolve on his tongue for a second before he swallowed the water. "Tenzin has my phone number. My email. My address here and in New York. She knows how to reach me if she wants to."

"Maybe..." Fabia shrugged. "I don't know."

"And I do. The reason she'd communicate formally through her father—whom she does not get along with, by the way—would be to create a *formal* obligation instead of a personal one." He started sorting through the envelopes Chloe had forwarded. "She wants me to pay attention to her, but she doesn't want to apologize for running away. I know how she works. I'm not falling for it."

Fabi watched him, gathering envelopes as he tore through his mail. It was a mix of personal and professional. A few letters from Cormac, the vampire in charge of New York. One from his uncle with updated pictures of Sadia, his new sister whom Giovanni and Beatrice had adopted the year before. He handed the picture to Fabia, who stuck it on the refrigerator next to all the other pictures of the little girl.

"She's getting so big," Fabia said.

"I know." There were charity solicitations he'd have to sort through. A gallery opening for a friend. "I need to get to LA soon."

"Christmas, maybe?"

"They'll probably come here."

Ben sorted the mail from his life in New York and tried not to think about how many of the letters he wished he could ask Tenzin about. He wanted to show her the pictures of Sadia. He wanted to take her to the gallery opening. Did she want to donate to the New York Restoration Project? Probably. He had no idea.

"What happened between you two?" Fabia asked for the hundredth time.

"I was honest. She wasn't," he muttered. "I'm not apologizing for being honest, and I'm not going to come running because she summons me. If she wants to call me or write me, she knows where I am."

"She doesn't think like you, Nino. She doesn't think like anyone else."

He set down the mail and looked up. "You know what? She knows what risk is. If she wants me to pay attention to her, she can stick her neck out and apologize, just like I stuck my neck out with her."

Fabia didn't say a word. She walked over, put her arms around Ben, and hugged him.

Ben took a deep breath and hugged her back.

"I don't know exactly what happened, but I know you miss her," she said. "I'm sorry."

He felt his heart crack. "Why didn't I fall in love with you?"

Fabia pulled back and winked. "Careful what you wish for. I can be a monster too."

4

L ately, video calls with Chloe were inevitably interrupted
by a cat.

"Down, Pete!" Chloe nudged aside the lanky feline that had
taken over her life. "Sorry about that."

"No problem. As long as I don't have to watch Gavin
rubbing up against you, I can put up with Pete." Ben couldn't
stop the smile when he saw Chloe on the screen. He might have
been a cranky bastard lately, but if anyone could lift his mood, it
was Chloe. "How've you been?"

"Good. Better than you, judging by that face. I think you
need to leave Italy. You seem to be getting beat up a lot."

She was sitting on the floor of Gavin's penthouse, and he
could see the dark windows in the background, which meant
Gavin was probably hanging around somewhere. Ben had
waited to call until the morning in Rome so he could catch the
two of them at night. Once daylight hit, Gavin would be locked
in his day quarters and unavailable.

Ben gingerly touched his swollen eye, which was slightly
less swollen that morning. "It's fine. I needed some information,
and I played the easy mark to get it."

"If Arthur were here, he'd probably try to analyze your subconscious need for punishment and what that says about your current romantic life."

Gavin and Chloe had only been together a few months, but Ben's human friend and his vampire friend were making a relationship work. They both seemed happy. It was more than many couples managed.

"I have no romantic life. Next subject, Chloe."

"Okaaaaay," Chloe said. "Um... I'm auditioning for a new role in an off-Broadway show on Tuesday! It's not off-*off*-Broadway, so I'm making progress. Gavin thinks I'll get it for sure, but I keep telling him he's biased."

"He is biased, but he's right. You're going to kill it."

Her smile was wide and generous. "You two guys. For the record, Arthur also thinks I'll get it, and he's far more honest than both of you. Also, he knows the director."

"Well, there you go. If Arthur says you have it, then you have it. Say hi to him for me."

"I will." She made a face. "Why am I so surrounded by men lately? You know, I actually struck up a conversation with Novia the other night at the pub, even though I find her completely frightening and far too fangy for a casual friendship. I'm telling you, Ben, there is not enough estrogen in my life."

"Come to Rome. Fabia would love to meet you."

"She seems so great!" Chloe smiled again. "I want to meet her too. Maybe she can come back to New York with you for a visit." Chloe raised her eyebrows and rested her chin on her palm. "Maybe maybe? When you come home? Which will be soon? Right?"

Ben scratched his stubble. "Not just yet. I still have some... stuff to do here. Some stuff to work out."

The smile fell a little. "Have you talked to her?"

"No. Have you?"

Chloe shook her head. "She emailed me though. She wanted pictures of the roof garden."

That was news. "For?"

"She didn't say. Probably just to make sure I haven't killed anything."

"Huh." What was he supposed to think of that? Did that mean she intended to come back? That she still felt like New York was home?

Did he care anymore?

"Gavin had a meeting with Cormac the other day, and according to Gavin— Hey!"

A flash of red plaid covered the screen for a moment as Gavin Wallace sat on the couch behind Chloe. "Why are you sitting on the floor, dove?" His thick Scottish brogue was thicker when he was at home with Chloe.

"It's comfortable." She leaned against his legs.

Ben said, "Gavin, the last thing I need seared in my memory are your balls, so you better keep your legs together."

Gavin reached over and tilted the screen up. "There you are, Vecchio. Looks like someone used your face for a football. You must be making friends."

"Everyone here loves me. I'm getting job opportunities thrown at me left and right."

Chloe laughed, but Gavin's smile didn't reach his eyes. He knew Ben was telling the truth, despite the flippant tone.

Ben was the ward of two powerful vampires, had worked for years with an ancient and well-respected assassin, and had taken on numerous immortal clients successfully. He had money, power, good connections, and intelligence. Added to that, he could work in daylight and wasn't interested in becoming a vampire or moving up in immortal politics. For those of Gavin's kind, Ben presented a very attractive package as an employee.

"How's the Eternal City? The last time I was there, I was breaking your uncle out of prison," Gavin said.

"Rome is doing well. Emil Conti keeps things quiet. Business is good, and humans are all they've ever been. I'm meeting with an old friend who works with him tonight."

Gavin said, "Be cautious."

"Always."

Chloe said, "I'm going to get dinner before I forget completely. Gavin, do you want anything?"

He caught her hand and kissed her knuckles. "Nothing for me, dove, but a glass of Macallan if you don't mind?"

"No problem."

Ben waited until he couldn't hear her. "She still trying to avoid all the political stuff?"

"As much as she can." Gavin tilted the screen so he could see it better. "She's wading in the water at her own pace. I'm not going to rush her."

"If there's no need to, then don't."

Ben had been forced to jump headfirst in the deep end, but then, his uncle had always had very powerful enemies. Gavin owned bars and pubs around the world that were known as neutral ground in what could be a tumultuous immortal world. No one wanted to piss off the owner of neutral ground.

Ben asked, "How are things there?"

"Quiet." Gavin shrugged. "It's nice. Cormac has control of the city in hand. Officially, he and his brothers still share power, but in practice, he's the one in charge. Novia has corralled the younger immortals in the city. She's become something of an enforcer for him, but she's not reckless or impulsive."

"Good to know."

"You come up in passing, but no one seems too eager to have you back at the moment."

"So great to be missed." He drummed his fingers on his thigh. "Any rumors about Tenzin and me... on a break?"

"Is that what you're doing?" Gavin frowned.

"I have no idea." Ben stood and took the tablet with him as he headed out the door. "I need coffee."

"That daylight is quite brilliant, isn't it?" Gavin narrowed his eyes. "Have you redecorated the place?"

"Fabi made some changes when Angela retired. She's updated a few things. That's pretty much house rules. Whoever runs the house makes the rules. Unless it's vampire quarters, of course."

"Of course." Gavin spread his arms across the back of the sofa. "No gossip about you and Tenzin right now. The small angry one hasn't called you?"

"Nope."

"I've never understood your relationship."

"Join the club." He set his tablet on the kitchen island and grabbed the silver moka pot on the counter. He filled the bottom with water and added dark brown espresso grounds. "I don't want to talk about her, Gav."

"So you don't want to hear the rumors?"

He froze for a second in front of the lit range. "What rumors? You said no one was talking about us."

"No one is talking about the two of you, but they are talking about her. I do have clubs in East Asia, you know."

He felt his chest tighten up. "Is she in Shanghai?"

"She's in Shanghai. She's in Singapore. She's in Hong Kong. She's in Beijing. She's all over."

"So much for spending some time in the mountains," he muttered.

"Is that where she said she was going?" Gavin shook his head. "She's on the water, my friend. Someone reported she was inquiring about a boat."

He frowned. "A boat?"

Gavin shrugged. "Your guess is better than mine."

A boat? He had nothing. Ben had thought she'd gone to her former lover—or current lover, fuck if he knew—in Shanghai. But Cheng had boats. If she needed one, he'd give it to her. So why was she asking about boats?

Why do you care?

"Hey, Gav, I don't want to keep you. You probably have to get to work." He leaned on the counter while he waited for his coffee. "Thanks for the update. I appreciate it."

"I'm keeping my ears and eyes open." Gavin leaned forward. "I don't have many friends, but I count you as one of them. Plus Chloe loves you, and I love her. So try not to get yourself killed or maimed, will you?" The corner of his mouth lifted. "It pisses me off to see her cry."

"You're such a romantic." He waved. "I'll be fine. If I leave Rome, I'll let you guys know."

"Do." Without another word, Gavin turned off the screen.

SHE WAS LYING in his arms, her body lax against his as they lay in a hammock under the stars. The wind was warm, soughing through the palm trees overhead. He heard music in the distance, but he couldn't identify it.

Her voice whispered in his ear, an echo of the wind. "Don't leave me."

"I wouldn't."

"You will."

He shifted so he could look into her eyes. The deep grey had always confused him. Her eyes should have been brown. Sable. Mink. Some rich velvet tone that he could fall into.

But they were grey. Had they changed thousands of years

ago when her body had frozen in time? Had they turned the color of storms and clouds and the violent wind she controlled? He had never understood her eyes.

"Have you always been this way?" he asked.

She blinked. "You don't know me."

"I do."

"You don't." Her eyes were sad.

He felt the anger in his chest. "Don't pity me."

"You don't know me. You never did."

He sat up and she was gone. He stared at the ocean as the moon reflected off the water and the wind whispered overhead.

You don't know me.

BEN TRIED to wipe the dream from his thoughts as he sat at the bar in Piazza Trilussa. He was waiting for Ronan, who had grown up in Trastevere and would likely never reside anywhere else, even if he lived to be a thousand.

Ronan had always been a quiet man with an unobtrusive presence. That was until you noticed him. After you noticed him, he was impossible to ignore. As a human, he'd sauntered stylishly in the most current fashion, so effortlessly cool that both women and men were drawn to him like flies to honey. He lived on the edges of a party, waiting for people to come to him. And they did.

Ronan had practiced being not the most dominant personality in a room but the most intriguing. It didn't surprise Ben one bit that Emil Conti had offered to turn him into a vampire.

A few moments after eleven, his old friend appeared.

"Ben." Ronan held out his hand.

"Ronan." Ben stood and shook it.

"So formal?" Ronan smiled slightly, holding on to Ben's hand. "Be honest. Am I strange to you now?"

Ben shook his head. He didn't know what he was feeling, but he released Ronan's hand, leaned forward, and embraced him before he kissed both cheeks in greeting. "You will never be strange to me. At least, not any stranger than you were before."

Ronan smiled, carefully concealing his fangs if they were down. "It's what I wanted. I've known for a long time."

"Then I'm happy for you." Ben sat down and Ronan followed. "Are you enjoying wine yet? This is a nice white."

Senses were heightened once you turned from the mortal life to the immortal. Bland food and drink was the norm.

"Some red wine would be good." Ronan raised a hand and signaled a server to order another glass. "Did you order food?"

"A little," Ben said. "I wasn't sure what you had in mind for tonight."

Ronan was dressed in a soft grey-brown jacket that emphasized his blue eyes and dark hair. He wore a ripped T-shirt under his jacket and looked like he could go anywhere, from a club to a gallery to a quiet bookstore.

"I just wanted to meet with you," he said. "Have a drink. Catch up. You've been in Rome for months now, and I've run into Fabi a few times, but I keep missing you."

Ben smiled. "I've been working."

Ronan nodded to Ben's face. "I can see that."

"Trust me, I've heard all the jokes."

"I'm sure you have." Ronan's eyebrow went up. "I know you were down in Naples. I don't suppose you'd tell me why."

"No, but I appreciate that you're direct about asking." Ben waited for the server to set down Ronan's wine and the prosciutto-wrapped melon he'd ordered. "Help yourself."

"Thank you." Ronan leaned forward and picked up a fork. "I'm not going to be anything but direct with you, Ben. I've known you for too long to be anything else. I know you're a professional at keeping confidence. That's partly why Emil likes you."

"That's nice to hear." Ben took a bite and didn't offer anything. Ronan was here to deliver a message, and he'd listen.

"As long as your work for Filomena doesn't undermine Emil in any way—"

"It doesn't."

"Then we have no interest in her internal politics." Ronan sipped his wine. "You know, you were right to order a white with this."

"How are your parents?"

"Doing very well. My mother is partly retired now. She had the more stressful job of the two of them, so I was glad."

"She was a courier, correct?"

"Correct."

Ben nodded. Couriers often lived very dangerous lives, so for Ronan's mother to make it to retirement, she had to be good. "And your dad is in accounting?"

"Something like that. He's still working. And my mother has become an avid gardener."

"Really?"

Ronan cocked his head. "Avid, mind you. Not necessarily successful."

Ben smiled. "I'm glad they're doing well."

"She had a harder time with it than he did. With me making the change."

Ben looked up and caught Ronan's eye. "She's seen more."

"Yes." Ronan set his fork down and sipped his wine. "But they're both at peace with it. And they're happy I'm staying in Rome."

"I imagine so."

"You've been in Rome for some time now."

Ben smiled. "Don't worry. It's not permanent."

Nothing was permanent.

Ronan folded his hands. "It could be. If you wanted."

Ben finished the food and picked up his wine. "Do you think so?"

"Emil considers you part of the city." Ronan raised his hands. "Not in a proprietary way. He knows that you remain under your uncle's aegis, and he has no problem with that."

"Even if I were to remain?"

Ronan chose his words carefully. "Someone with your skills and connections is always welcome in a city if they operate in good faith. Which you are known for. Emil would be very interested in having you be part of his organization. No aegis. No allegiance. Just... good faith. You have a home here. You have friends here. You could stay in Rome, Ben."

The idea wasn't all bad. "What would I do for Emil Conti?"

Ronan shrugged. "What do any of us do, really? We make life move. With your skills, I imagine you'd be doing many of the same things you're doing now. Just with... more resources."

So Emil wanted him as a spy. Interesting.

"And of course I'm sure you'd continue working with your uncle. There would be no need to end your part in the family business."

And the "family business" was a little safer than the freelance work that Ben had been doing on his own.

He watched a group of young people pour out of a club on the far side of the Piazza. They were joking and laughing with each other. Shouting about going back to someone's house for drinks.

Ronan noticed. "You could have a life here, Ben. It would be exciting enough to keep your interest but settled enough to build something real."

Something real.

Something... settled. Or settled enough.

You don't know me.

It was the opposite of the life he'd been living. And... it wasn't unappealing.

"Just think about it," Ronan said. "This isn't a formal offer to accept or turn down. This is an idea from a friend."

"Just from a friend?"

Ronan smiled. "And from his employer who respects you a great deal."

"Understood." Ben nodded. "Thanks, Ronan. I'll think about it."

"Good."

5

Shanghai, China

Cheng spread a map of the coastline across the table. "The fisherman said the boat was a dhow, as was the *Qamar Jadid*. It would have stayed relatively close to shore. Traders during that period rarely risked sailing too far out."

Tenzin glanced at the area marked on the map. "The wreck isn't very close to the mainland."

Cheng looked up, his eyes alight with enjoyment. "Currents. Storms. All sorts of reasons it could have ended up there."

Tenzin tried to act interested, but she was bored. Bored in China. Bored with this treasure hunt. Just... bored.

Bored without him.

She told the voices inside her to be quiet. "If so many people have been looking for this shipwreck for so long, why is it just now turning up?"

"Because it's a big ocean." Cheng straightened and put his hands on his hips. "And even water vampires like me are not her master. If the ocean wants to keep a secret, it does."

He was a beautiful man. His black hair was longer than

Tenzin's now. It brushed his shoulders and fell in his eyes when he was distracted. He was dressed in what Tenzin thought of as his house clothes, loose fisherman's pants and a tunic that fell to his hips. He looked like a pirate, which made sense because he was one. Or he had been.

Cheng had a luxurious office building of his own in the Pudong district of Shanghai that housed the majority of his operations, but he didn't live there. He lived on a converted barge that floated off the coast.

While technically the council of the Eight Immortals where her sire sat ruled all of China, in Shanghai, Cheng was king. Any immortal looking to do business in the city or use its port had to get permission and pay a hefty toll to operate in Cheng's territory.

It was a situation the elders in Penglai had allowed to happen, even if they weren't thrilled with Cheng's power. He gave them lip service when they required it and they received a healthy share of his profits. In return, they left him alone. Mostly.

Cheng was in his element, grabbing this map and that chart, extolling the modern capabilities of the university research vessel he'd secured to allow them to search for the wreck of the *Qamar Jadid*.

You should care more.

The ship they were looking for had carried the *Laylat al Hisab*. The Night's Reckoning was a legendary sword. Tenzin loved swords. Finding it meant her sire would pay her an exorbitant amount of gold. This job involved gold and sharp things. She should have been thrilled to take it.

She wasn't.

Cheng was excited. "The optimal search window will open in three weeks after the last threat of storms has passed. I know you're waiting for your partner—"

"We need him."

"You *want* him, Cricket." Cheng crossed his arms. "We don't *need* him."

Tenzin lay back on the chaise next to the table. There were silk pillows against her back. The lounge was covered in rich leather.

She thought about the spare alcove in the loft apartment she shared with Ben. The two settings couldn't be more different.

"We need him." She leveled her eyes at Cheng. "Don't you trust me?"

The corner of his mouth twitched up. "Just exactly as much as you trust me."

Translation: a little bit and only within reason.

Cheng could always make her smile. They hadn't been lovers in years, but Tenzin would always carry affection for him. Long ago, he'd helped her feel desire again, shown her the male body could be an object of pleasure, not punishment. He was well built; his musculature was defined from his human years working on the sea. He could be a brutal captain when he needed to be. He could also be a playful lover and a loyal friend.

"I don't expect you to understand," she said. "But I expect you to trust me."

He walked to her and leaned over, bracing his arms around her shoulders. "Tell me why you wait."

"Because I have the time." She put her hand on his smooth cheek. "You are so young."

"Far older than him."

"I suppose so. But you and Benjamin share the same hunger. The same ambition."

Cheng glanced down at her. She wasn't wearing anything that would attract attention. Black leggings. A grey tunic. Still, when Cheng looked at her, she felt exposed.

"I have no doubt your human and I share some hungers.

41

The difference is, I am well practiced at sating hunger while he is a petulant child who pouts when a banquet is laid before him."

She shrugged. "He'll answer the letters when he's ready."

"And we're expected to wait until he does?" Cheng eased onto the chaise next to her. "I don't wait for humans."

"I wait for this human, and—if you want my help on this job —you wait for me."

He picked up a strand of her hair. "I do wait for you. I wait for you to consider my offer."

She looked away. "I have considered it."

"No, you haven't. Nothing in this life is permanent, Cricket. All I am asking is for you to try it. Try us. Consider what we could be together. Try us for a century or two. If we don't suit each other, then we part as friends, as we've always been."

Tenzin looked at the old-fashioned European wall clock mounted to the wall in Cheng's floating palace. In many ways, they *were* perfectly suited to each other. He expected loyalty, but not any human folly like love. He saw Tenzin for what she was. And what she wasn't.

He doesn't see all of you.

"I can't consider anything until this job is over." Tenzin pushed him away and stood. "We still need two more people. Our kind, not human."

"I have a couple of ideas about that. I'm waiting to hear back."

"Good." She walked toward the door. "I'm flying home for the night."

"Your room is ready here."

"I don't want it." She looked over her shoulder. "Thank you."

He said nothing, standing with one arm braced on the library table and the other fisted at his hip.

She nodded toward his shoulder. "You should have a parrot."

He frowned. "What?"

"To complete the pirate look." She pointed her chin at his shoulder. "A parrot for your shoulder."

He frowned. "I don't care for birds."

"Your loss." She left him in the study, walking up the stairs and onto the deck where she took to the air without another word.

He was crouched down in the courtyard, staring at the delicate creatures.

"You brought home birds. In a cage?"

"I know you don't like—"

"Caging birds destroys their nature, Benjamin."

"I understand that, but—"

"Birds in cages cannot fly. It is in a bird's nature to fly."

Tenzin flew until she reached the silent house in a water village west of Shanghai. She didn't visit often, but when she did, her sire inevitably showed up.

She saw Zhang sitting in the courtyard, feeding the koi that swam in the channels running through the house.

Tenzin landed and continued walking past him, holding up a hand when he opened his mouth to speak. "Give me a few moments."

Zhang Guo, eldest of the Eight Immortals, wind vampire of impossible power and sire of a single, deadly immortal child, shrugged his shoulders and continued feeding fish. "Fine."

The house was more like a compound. The front house and rooms were taken by Jinpa, the human woman who kept the house. She and her granddaughters lived in the front rooms. Tenzin walked across the courtyard and over a bridge, passing the gate that marked her private rooms. She opened the door and paused inside.

Moonlight shone through the alabaster windows high on the walls. Finely carved screens separated the two formal rooms that never received visitors. She walked through them and into her private library. In front of her, dim light shone through the four massive doors that had been a gift from her father. They were carved with two mythical figures entwined with each other, eternal and powerful.

The dragon and the phoenix.

"I told you I'd hurt you if you broke into my room."

"If we're comparing the situations, I'm not in your bedroom. And you're not naked. Are you going to take the knife away from my carotid now?"

"Your pulse isn't even elevated. That's rather extraordinary for a human."

"What can I say? I have interesting friends."

Tenzin stared at the screen until she felt her temper even out. She couldn't understand what she was feeling. For the past few months, she'd been repeatedly drawn into her memories, which annoyed her. She was a creature of action. She moved forward, not back. Memories of Benjamin were not welcome.

Do not waste your regret on the past.

She walked out of the house, across the courtyard, and into the kitchen. "My father and I would like tea."

Jinpa's granddaughter nodded. "Of course, Tenzin. I will boil the water now."

"Thank you."

Tenzin walked out of the kitchen and into the courtyard, taking a seat across from her father, who had placed a table in front of him and was setting out the wooden pieces for a very old game called they called *abachee* that was a little like human chess.

She picked up a piece. "Where did you get this set?"

"I carved it," Zhang said. "I thought you could keep it at your house."

His hands were smooth and strong. He might be an ancient, but he'd been turned in his prime. He was a handsome man with a noble forehead and long black hair, a full beard and mustache. His eyes were unlined, and his skin unwrinkled.

Tenzin hated that she looked like him, but unmistakable shared ancestry marked both their faces. Zhang had come from the same human clan Tenzin had. The girl she'd once been shared blood with the creature who had murdered her. And Tenzin's sire was the only one left who spoke the language of her dreams.

When she had dreamed.

"The light pieces are pear wood." Zhang held them up to the lamplight as Jinpa's granddaughter set down a tray of tea on the small table her sister had set out. "I like the finish."

"They're beautiful." Tenzin set out the darker pieces he handed her, placing the soldiers and swordsmen before the archers, horsemen, and the sun and moon pieces. "And this wood?"

"Zitan."

Tenzin looked up. It was the hardest and heaviest of woods. In some eras, zitan had traded for the same price as gold. "You honor me with this gift."

"You honor me by being my daughter," Zhang said. "Have you made any progress on the recovery?"

"The plans are coming along. Cheng says the best search window will be in three weeks' time." Tenzin glanced up.

Zhang answered her unspoken question. "I have not received a response to any of my letters."

Tenzin huffed out a breath. "I'm calling Giovanni."

"I ask that you do not."

"If you don't want me to *call* Giovanni, then I will write him."

"Or you could write to the human directly."

"No. Ben is being childish not answering your letters. That's not rudeness to me, that's rudeness to *you*. And the council. He should know better."

Zhang shrugged and made the first move on the board, as was his right as the eldest player. "He's human. And since when do you care about rudeness to the council?"

She ignored the question. "Ben is living in the immortal world. He knows more about protocol than most newly turned vampires." She moved her own piece in response to his.

"Since when do you care about protocol?"

"Since I want to use it to my advantage."

Zhang smiled. "At least you're honest."

It was amusing he thought she was honest. Tenzin and Zhang played in silence for three more moves, and Zhang took Tenzin's soldier.

"I want to meet this man," her sire said.

"Why?"

"You know why. Did you play at being naive with him? Maybe that is why he's angry with you."

"I am not going to talk to you about this." Tenzin imperiled a swordsman but did not take it.

"I respect his uncle." Zhang's tenth hand came, which meant that he could make two moves. He quickly stole one of Tenzin's archers and imperiled another. "How will you answer that?"

Tenzin stared at the board. Then she used her two moves to escape the trap he'd set and shore up the position of her most valuable piece, the sun god.

Zhang chuckled. "You're going to lose."

"Why do you say that?"

"Because you're playing defensively." He moved a horseman, the most flexible piece on the board, and imperiled her moon god. "You can't win in this game or this life by playing defensively."

"Maybe not win..." Tenzin stole a soldier from under his nose and rescued her moon god. "...but you might survive longer than your opponent."

"Survival *is* winning." Zhang moved his horseman again, this time nearly stealing her sun god. "Winning is survival. I want to meet this Benjamin."

"And yet you don't want me to write Giovanni."

"No, I do not." Zhang looked up. "Not when you can write to the man directly. Do not play defensively if you want to win, daughter."

Tenzin moved her moon god into position, blocking his swordsman and sitting at the feet of his sun piece. In two moves, she could win the board.

Zhang sat back, staring at the game, his eyes creasing in amusement.

"If you survive long enough, you always win," Tenzin said. "You taught me that."

6

Rome, Italy

B en stared at the letters in the drawer. He started to shut the door again when Fabia interrupted him.

"Please, for the love of God, at least get them out of my kitchen," she said, "so I don't feel like they're a time bomb waiting to go off."

Ben lifted a letter. "There's no bomb in here."

"I'm using metaphor. Didn't your American school teach you about that?" She walked over, snatched the four letters from the drawer, and shoved them at his chest. "Take them away. Every time I walk to this side of the kitchen, they threaten me with their importance."

Ben took them and stuck them under his arm as he reached for an orange. "I'm sure it's just Tenzin trying to get me to go do something or find something or clean up a mess for her *again*. And I'm taking a break, okay? I'm taking a break from her insanity."

"You're taking a break from responsibility," Fabia said. "Just open the damn letters and answer them. You can say no, can't you?"

The problem was, Ben was very afraid he wouldn't be able to say no. He didn't have the best track record of refusing Tenzin.

"I'll take them to my room," he said. "Happy?"

"Yes." She grabbed her purse. "I'm going to the market, and then I'm making a salad for dinner. It's too hot to cook."

"Bring me back a chicken burrito," he muttered.

"Ha ha." She rolled her eyes. "Actually, that does sound really good."

Maybe it was time to go back to California.

Speaking of California, he saw his phone buzz with an out-of-focus picture of his uncle. Ben raised the screen to his face and pressed Accept. "Hey! How's it going?"

Giovanni Vecchio, fire vampire, Renaissance scholar, and new father of a preschooler, appeared on the screen looking exhausted, which wasn't typical for an immortal creature of the night, but maybe was typical for a new parent.

"Ben, I heard something disturbing today."

"I have not been driving your car here, so I have no idea how it got that dent. I think it was Fabi, but I'm going to fix it anyway."

Giovanni frowned. "There's a dent on the Ferrari?"

Ben blinked. "Uh... no."

The Ferrari was a classic from 1968, and it lived in Tuscany. Ben couldn't control rocks that flew up from trucks, but he was going to get it fixed. Soon.

Giovanni narrowed his eyes. "Tabling the car discussion for now. I heard through very convoluted channels that you're ignoring a letter from Penglai Island."

"That's not exactly true." He was ignoring *four* letters from Penglai. "I have them, I just haven't had time to open them yet."

"Them?" Giovanni's eyes went wide. "Ben, what the hell are you doing?"

He sat on the couch in the living room and ran a hand through his hair. "Listen, I know this is just her trying to get my attention without actually talking to me, and I'm not going to play her games right now—"

"Benjamin." Giovanni's voice had fallen into "scary quiet" mode. It was a tone that often preceded fiery, burning kind of situations. It was a tone that was used so rarely Ben could count the occasions.

It was a tone that made Ben shut up immediately.

"The Eight Immortals are the most dominant vampire council in Asia," Giovanni said quietly. "They rule all of China, most of Korea, and much of the marine territory in the Pacific."

He took a breath. "I know that, but—"

"Shut. Up." His uncle's eyes were burning. "Have I taught you nothing? Do you realize that your aunt—my *mate*—is a scribe of the court? Do you know what that means? Do you know how this reflects on us? On *her*? As far as they are concerned, you are her *son*, Benjamin. And you are ignoring them."

Ben felt like he was about fourteen years old. He felt a rush of embarrassment combined with anger. "Do you know how long it's been since she—"

"I don't care!" Giovanni yelled before he threw the tablet down, and Ben heard shuffling and muffled voices in the background. A few seconds later, his aunt came on the screen.

"Hey." Beatrice's eyes were wide. "What's going on? Why are you angry? Why is he being all steamy?"

Ben cleared his throat. "I'm not responsible for his moods, B."

"Excuse me?" Her voice was sharp. "It looks like you're both having temper tantrums. What is going on?"

"Someone on Penglai Island sent me a few letters. I haven't opened them. Did Tenzin call you guys?"

"I haven't heard from Tenzin. Why haven't you opened the letters?"

"So how did he hear about—"

"Why are you avoiding the question? He had a meeting with Ernesto earlier tonight, but I hardly think Tenzin would send a message—"

"No, she wouldn't." Everything clicked at once. "But Cheng and Ernesto constantly coordinate on shipping stuff," Ben muttered. "Which means she's probably in Shanghai, and she probably said something to Cheng, who said something to Ernesto, who said something to Giovanni."

Beatrice pursed her lips. "Vampire politics. Not as different from high school as you'd think, actually."

"I'm going to open the letters, B. I've just been—"

"Good. Full stop. Don't say anything else to me right now. Open them and answer them. Ignoring formal correspondence like that makes me look bad and makes you look like an irresponsible kid. Which you're not. You may think that's unfair, but that's the way it is. Part of my status depends on showing respect to scary people. And you may not find Tenzin scary, but the entire rest of the world does, especially those elders. So buck up, buttercup. Answer your mail and stop avoiding your responsibilities."

Ben knew she was right, but he didn't have to like it. "I'll answer the letters."

"Today."

"Today." He let out an angry sigh. "You know, I didn't ask—"

"No, no, no, no," Beatrice said. "Don't piss me off, Ben. This is the way things are. If you're going to be in this world—"

"Well, maybe I don't want that anymore!"

Beatrice was silent for a long time. "Okay," she finally said. "Talk to me."

Ben stood and walked toward the stairs. "Maybe I don't want to be part of this anymore. You know, I could stay here. Stay in Rome. Find a job here working for... I don't know. I have money I've earned myself now. I could take some time and... I don't know."

"Calm down," Beatrice said. "Just talk to me."

"I could go back to school." He felt his throat getting tight. "Get a normal job. Live here with Fabi. Go to the beach and get a tan and sleep at night like a normal fucking human, you know?"

He walked into his bedroom, shut the door, and locked it. Then he sat on the bed, still holding on to the phone and his aunt's image, six thousand miles away.

"I'm listening," Beatrice said.

He took a hard breath. "I don't know if I want to live like this anymore." His voice was quiet. "I don't know if I can."

Beatrice waited to speak for a long time. "Is it because she's gone? Be honest."

"I don't know." He shook his head. "I can't keep living in this... limbo. Not knowing who or what I am. Not knowing what I am to her." He shook his head. "I can't. It's not fair." He laughed a little. "I know life isn't fair."

"Life isn't, but you get to pick who you allow in yours," Beatrice said. "She's our friend, Ben. And our ally. Whatever happened between you two—"

"I don't want to talk—"

"Whatever *happened*"—Beatrice said again—"is between the two of you. You have to do what's right for you. Giovanni and I, we're going to love you no matter what. Our relationship with Tenzin doesn't depend on you. And vice versa. She's our friend, but you're our kid. Even though you're not a kid anymore." She poked at the screen. "Is that white in your beard?"

"Ha ha." Ben rubbed the stubble that had grown out the past few days. "If I'm going grey, it's her fault."

"That wouldn't surprise me." She took a deep breath and let it out slowly. "She's not an easy person to love."

"I don't..." He swallowed hard. "It's not that."

"Are you sure?"

She was feeding from him, and it was no gentle bite.

It was pleasure. It was pain. It was heaven and hell and she was drinking his blood and he wanted it. He wanted her to devour him. One hand moved from her ass to her breast and he squeezed. He swept his thumb over her erect nipple and turned his head so she could go deeper. His other hand gripped her hair, pulling her mouth from his neck. He could feel his flesh tear, but he ignored it, dragging her bloody mouth to his.

"Whatever it is," he said. "It's not love. I've seen what you and Giovanni have. It's not that."

"All relationships are different, Ben. Don't compare yourself to us. That's not fair to either of you."

He pressed his fingers to his temple. "It doesn't matter what I want, does it? Not really. She's the one who ran away, and she's the one who gets to call me back. She holds all the cards right now, and she knows it. It's all about winning with her, and she won't stop until she's got me under her thumb."

Beatrice said, "I know it feels like that, but don't forget that you have your own reputation to carry. I know you've been working for Filomena. And for Emil. Don't forget your power, but also don't forget your responsibilities. Open the letters. Answer them and make all the right noises about apologies. Deal with whatever comes after, but don't make yourself look like a petulant child. Understood?"

"Understood." He looked up. "I really love you, B."

"I really love you too." She smiled. "You'll make it through this."

"I know." He shut off his phone and tossed it on the bed.

Then he sat down at his desk, found the first letter from China, and broke the seal.

FABI FOUND him in the courtyard after the sun had set and his hand was sore from using his very best handwriting. Of course, the wine was helping with the sore hand.

"Hi." She leaned against the archway leading from the street. "So you are very drunk."

He leaned back in his chair and swapped out the vinyl on the old phonograph he'd found at a shop in Naples. "Not too drunk to change the record, and that's what counts."

"You were cutting back." She walked over and lifted the record sleeve. "What got you feeling sentimental?"

It was a blue sleeve with an old jazz recording. "As Time Goes By" was echoing off the stone walls. Ben stood and grabbed Fabia around the waist. "Put the groceries down. Dance with me."

She smiled and set her bags on the cobblestones. "Oh, Nino. What was it this time?"

"Can't I just want to dance with..." He took a deep breath to steady himself. "...a beautiful woman? Who lives with me... but refuses to kiss me?" He ducked his head down to meet her eyes. "You used to kiss me."

She put her hand on his shoulder and wrapped an arm around his waist. "When we were teenagers. When we were still figuring out what went where."

"Maybe I'm still figuring out what goes where," he said. "You could give me lessons."

"Oh no." She laughed. "I have no interest in a man who is very obviously in love with someone else."

He swallowed hard. "I'm not in love with her."

"You don't think so?"

"No." He took a deep breath. "And even if I was... it's not healthy."

"And I'm not your cure." She gently pushed him away. "Let me get you some water. You need to sleep."

Ben stood in the middle of the courtyard, staring into the blue-black sky as a heartbreaking trumpet solo floated through the air. "I thought love was supposed to make you feel good."

"Oh, Ben." Fabia sighed. "I wish that were true, but it's not. Elias and I are proof of that."

Ben forgot about his own dysfunctional heart and looked at Fabia. "Elias was an idiot."

"No, he was just normal. And I'm not."

Fabia and Elias had made it for three years before the necessary secrets of Fabia's life had alienated her boyfriend, who had no idea that vampires existed. Fabia had let Elias move on without any of the answers he begged for, even though she loved him desperately.

"You could have told him." Ben walked over and put his arms around her. "I trusted him. Giovanni trusted him."

She spoke in a quiet voice. "He wouldn't have wanted to know."

Ben had nothing to say to that, because that was simply the way it was sometimes. Some people didn't want to know. Some people wanted to live simple lives, and Ben couldn't fault them for that.

"Would you rather not know?" he asked. "If you had the choice?"

Fabia wiped her eyes. "Sadly, I would never choose ignorance. If there's a thing to be known, I want to know it. That's probably why I spent so much time in school. I'm a glutton for knowledge."

"Yeah. I get that." He swung her around as the song changed to a quicker tune. "You know, who gets to say what's normal and what's not? I think we're very normal."

Fabia laughed through her tears. "Oh yes. So normal."

"What? Why are you laughing?"

"Did you finally open the letters from the scary thousand-year-old vampires in China who want to hire you for something? 'Cause, you know, that's a very normal thing to do."

He nodded slowly. "Right. About that. What do you know about maritime archaeology?"

She frowned. "I did part of my graduate studies in Calabria mapping the wrecks in Crotone. You know that. I love diving."

"Are you still certified?"

"Yes." She narrowed her eyes. "Why?"

"How hard do you think it would be to find a house sitter by next week?"

7

Beijing, China

"Sir?"

Ben woke when he heard the flight attendant's voice.

"Sir, we are approaching Beijing. Can you please bring your seat upright?"

Ben nodded wordlessly and pushed the button to shift his seat. He'd slept all the way from Abu Dhabi, settling into a business class seat next to Fabia, who'd gazed at everything with wide and wondering eyes.

She was reclined next to him, her sleep mask pushed up and her short, pixie-cut hair mussed. "That was the most comfortable flight I've ever taken." She stretched up and out. "I am ruined for economy class."

"Really?" The corner of Ben's mouth turned up. "Want to know how much the seats cost?"

"Please no." She took off her mask, rubbed her eyes, and yawned. "I'm just going to pretend that I'm living in a dream right now. I refuse to spend thousands of unnecessary dollars on a plane seat when that amount of money could get me a Prada handbag."

Despite working for her uncle, Fabia didn't travel much. And while she made a good income between the university and Giovanni, she didn't have time to spend it. Convincing her to come to Beijing as his assistant was surprisingly easy. Especially when he told her they'd be going after a ninth-century Arab shipwreck.

The plane touched down in China, and they started to gather their things and make preparations to exit the cabin.

"You're sure this visa is legal?" Fabia muttered. "I've never heard of one going through that fast. When people from the university have to travel—"

"They go through normal channels," Ben said. "Not... other ones." He glanced at the people around them, none of whom were paying attention and none of whom assumed Ben could speak Mandarin. Which he could.

Thanks to Tenzin.

"The visas are fine," Ben said. "Trust me. And trust Emil. It was his liaison who arranged everything."

"Okay." She didn't look reassured, but then Fabia disliked taking anything on faith. It was what made her such a good friend and an excellent backup. "If you trust them, I will."

"It'll be fine." He knew they were being watched. There would be a court representative meeting them after they retrieved their luggage, but they'd be under surveillance the moment they stepped off the plane. Ben was an invited guest of the elders of Penglai Island. Nothing about this visit would be routine.

"Have you been here before?" Fabia asked.

"China? Sure."

"Not China," Fabia said. "The... other place."

Penglai Island. Ben shook his head. "I've only heard stories."

"Pictures?"

"Not allowed." He took Fabia's hand and followed the signs toward immigration and customs. Before he could reach the line, he noticed a solemn Chinese man in a very nice suit trying to catch his attention.

Ben paused, recognized that the suit was far too expensive for a government employee, and walked over.

"Mr. Vecchio." The man spoke with a crisp English accent. "If you'll follow me, we can expedite your and your guest's entry."

"Thank you." He followed the man toward the diplomatic entrance.

Their guide opened his wallet and showed the official his credentials. The official narrowed his eyes, looked Ben and Fabia up and down, then nodded. He pointed toward a desk where an attractive, smiling woman sat behind glass.

She examined their passports and visas, then she nodded and said, "Welcome to Beijing" before she motioned them toward the exit.

Ben continued following their guide toward the baggage claim, keeping Fabia's hand in a firm grip.

"That was fast," she said in Italian.

"Yes, it was." Even faster than Ben had expected. He felt visible. Conspicuous. There were so many eyes on him it made his skin itch. So many cameras. So many observers. "But hey, we're not standing in that hours-long line."

"I'm in a dream, remember?" Fabia quipped. "There aren't any hours-long lines in dreams."

Ben smiled and saw the sign for the luggage claim.

Their guide looked over his shoulder. "If you'll give me your claim tickets for the baggage—"

"I need to see your real credentials," Ben said quietly. "Before we give you anything."

The man stopped and turned. "Of course." He handed Ben his wallet and a sealed letter from his inside jacket pocket.

Ben recognized the seal of Zhang Guo because he'd seen it over the years on letters sent to New York for Tenzin.

Interesting.

The letters weren't from the court as a whole. Nor was their escort. That would be a different seal. This seal was Zhang Guo's personal one, and the letter was written in a familiar flowing hand.

> *Mr. Vecchio,*
>
> *I trust you are asking for Andrew's credentials before you leave the airport. Mr. Leu has been a friend for seven years and will be escorting you to Penglai and informing you on all matters of protocol pertinent to your comfort.*
>
> *Formal introduction to the court will occur when you reach the island. If you have any questions, Andrew will be happy to answer them. You can depend on his discretion as he reports only to me. No one else.*
>
> *Welcome back to China, Mr. Vecchio. I look forward to meeting you.*
>
> *His Excellency and most supreme elder,*
> *Zhang Guolao*

Ben took the letter, folded it, and slid it into his messenger bag. "Thank you, Andrew."

"Of course, Mr. Vecchio." He turned to Fabia. "May I take any of your luggage, Miss Salvadori?"

Fabia looked at Ben, who nodded in reassurance.

"Thank you." She handed over her carry-on bag, keeping her purse tucked under her arm. "I'm looking forward to seeing more of Beijing."

"We'll be proceeding directly to a private airport for your next flight," Andrew said.

"Oh." Fabia looked deflated. "Wait, a private airport?" She frowned. "I thought the island was only accessible by boat."

"It is." Andrew followed Ben over to the luggage belt, which had started moving. "But it is a short flight from Beijing to the coastal city where we will catch the boat."

Ben said, "Don't forget how huge this country is." He saw Fabia's bag, grabbed it, and handed it to Andrew. "How big is the plane?"

"I assure you, it is very comfortable."

"Cool." Ben spotted his bag, and that was that. They hadn't packed heavily. Giovanni and Beatrice had already arranged for formal clothes to be taken to Penglai for both Ben and Fabia since only traditional clothing was allowed on the island. Any other equipment they needed would be procured after formalities were over. "It's all good, Fabi."

"If you say so," she said, clearly not thrilled about getting on another airplane.

As Ben had suspected, going through the private airport was little more than driving into a hangar, hopping on a small jet, and sitting down.

"Oh." Fabia settled into the plush seat. "This isn't bad."

Ben smiled. "Yeah, it's easy to get used to this kind of air travel."

"How long is the flight?"

Andrew sat across from them. "An hour and a half."

"And then the boat?"

The man nodded.

"And then the island." Ben took the glass of sparkling water the flight attendant handed him. "*Xièxiè.*"

Her smile was sweet. "You're very welcome, Mr. Vecchio."

Like Andrew, her accent was English. "Is this Zhang's plane?"

"No," Andrew said. "It's mine."

"Huh." Interesting. "So you have other businesses than simply being Zhang's assistant."

Andrew smiled. It was subtle, but Ben noticed it.

"I have many businesses," he said. "Working for Zhang is my pleasure."

Ben was dying to know, and Zhang said he could depend on Andrew's discretion.

"Do you know Zhang's daughter?"

Andrew's expression didn't change. "I do."

"Is she on the island?"

"She is."

Ben sipped his water and let it sink in. He'd be seeing Tenzin. That night. He'd be seeing her for the first time in months. He had no idea how to feel about that. He wasn't happy, and yet...

There was a buzz of anticipation in his blood, and it pissed him off. He didn't know what she was thinking or feeling. He didn't know if she knew he was coming.

She knew.

Ben hated that the only clearly identifiable emotion he felt was anticipation. He was hungry for her and angry about it. She was a drug. An addiction.

What did she want from him? Why had she insisted on his being there? Was it a control thing? Ben didn't know, and the more he thought about it, the more irritable he grew. It was probably a control thing. Tenzin played chess with people, and at that moment, Ben felt like a pawn.

"I'm not in love with her."

"You don't think so?"

He crossed his arms and thought about the job ahead.

Focused on that. It was a maritime recovery. Possible artifacts from the ninth century. He didn't know much more than that, but he could get excited about the job. He'd never done a maritime recovery before; it was one of the reasons he wanted Fabia along. It would be a challenge, but a good addition to his résumé.

Did he still care about his résumé?

Maybe.

Before long, they were touching down on another runway, but this time they weren't surrounded by city. Green fields stretched away from the windows, and Ben saw cars in the distance. They exited the vehicle and walked to the cars. Ben kept Fabia's hand in his the whole time, sensing her confusion.

It was a lot to take in, even for someone like him who was familiar with vampire protocol. The court of the Eight Immortals was probably the most formal Ben knew of.

"Any idea where we're going now?" Fabia asked in Italian.

Ben asked Andrew. "When do we meet the boat?"

Andrew opened the car door for them and motioned to the porters to put their luggage in the trunk. "The only boat that leaves for the island is piloted by a water vampire. We will leave when Myung is ready to take us. I have an associate waiting at the dock, and they will call when it has been sighted."

"So not until after dark at least," Ben said. "For now?"

Andrew nodded toward a hangar in the distance. "We have a reception area for you to relax. You'll be able to clean up and change there. A chef will prepare dinner for all of us."

Ben looked at Fabia, who nodded. "Sounds good."

"Thank you," she said. "I would definitely like to clean up."

The cars drove to the rounded hangar in the distance. When they arrived, another group of humans welcomed them and took their luggage. Ben saw a slim man standing to the side with two large garment bags.

"I see Mr. Huang is already here." Andrew nodded to the man before he ushered Ben and Fabia through the hangar door. "Mr. Huang is the tailor I recommended to your uncle. He has your formal clothing for tonight. More casual clothing will be delivered to the ship before we leave." He spread his arms to indicate the hangar, which had been transformed into a comfortable and modern lounge. "Until then, make yourselves at home."

~

It was ten o'clock when they boarded the boat helmed by a silent water vampire who looked barely legal to drive a car, much less pilot a centuries-old traditional Chinese sailing vessel.

Fabia was dressed in a richly textured green silk *chang-ao*, a traditional garment that folded across the front like a robe. There was delicate gold embroidery around the collar and the long sleeves, but other than that, it was simple. And very rich.

"You look beautiful." Ben helped Fabia up the gangway leading onto the deck. "Any problems with the outfit?"

"No." Fabia turned and smiled. "I love it. I much prefer this to the skintight formal wear expected in the Roman court."

Ben smiled. "Emil does like his modern Italian designers, doesn't he?"

Ben's black *zhiduo* was similar in style to Fabia's outfit but far more severe. The silk was thick and unpatterned. The garment fell to the floor and nearly covered the simple shoes he'd been given. Loose pants completed the outfit. He felt like he was walking barefooted and his movement was unrestricted.

Yes, far better than going into an unknown situation in a wool suit.

He racked his memory, trying to think of the symbolism of the two colors, but there was too much in his mind.

Andrew followed them, dressed in a blue zhiduo similar to Ben's. "The Penglai court is more traditional than the current Roman court, though of course all the elders are well-versed in modern conventions and manners."

"Of course," Ben said. He and Fabia took a seat on the forward deck of the ship while he watched their luggage being loaded. He kept his eyes on the locked laptop case that he normally carried himself. It would be impossible to keep it with him constantly, but having it out of his hands still made him itchy.

"Please remember," Andrew said, "you will not have any mobile phone service on the island. You are welcome to keep your electronics, but put them away. No photographs are permitted anywhere. There is no internet at all." Andrew smiled. "With all deference to our Irish friends, *Cara* is not welcome here."

Cara was the electronic voice of the Nocht system developed by water vampire Patrick Murphy's software company in Dublin. She was a modern, voice-activated assistant to vampires around the world who struggled to use modern technology because they usually shorted out electronics with their amnis.

Fabia's eyes went wide at the restrictions. "So no phones. No computers. Nothing?"

"I'm afraid not, Miss Salvadori."

Ben nodded. "Is there *any* communication off the island?"

"There is one landline you may use in emergencies. Other than that, if you must send a message to anyone, please contact me and I will arrange a courier."

The boat started to move, though Ben felt nothing. No wind. No motor. Fog grew thick around them, and they floated away from the land.

"Wow." Fabia looked around them. "It's cold. Beautiful, but cold."

"I was worried I'd be too warm in this." Ben remembered summer in Shanghai all too clearly. "But the tailor knew what he was doing."

They drifted silently through the water, moving fast enough that the wind whipped his hair around his face. Fabia tucked a blanket around herself and leaned into him.

"How long?"

It had only been fifteen minutes. Maybe twenty. But Ben knew without question. "Not much longer."

He could feel the energy like the draw of a great magnet. It pulled him.

She pulled him.

Ben saw the clouds thicken and gather like a layer of snow covering a mountain.

Fabia squinted. "What am I seeing? There's something there, but I can't..."

The water vampire in the bow of the ship heard her, turned, and lifted the corner of his mouth in a half smile. With a flick of his wrist, he tossed the fog back, revealing a massive, rocky mountain rising from the ink-black sea.

Golden lights spiraled from the base to the summit. Sharp points of light flickered in the darkness like stars fallen from the sky. As they approached the dock, Ben saw a horse cart and two carriages waiting, steam rising from the huffed breath of the animals while humans rushed around the platform, ready to greet guests.

"I feel like I'm in a movie," Fabia said. "A really fancy one that will probably get nominated for awards. The costumes are going to be epic."

Andrew smiled. "You're not far off, Miss Salvadori. Welcome to Penglai Island."

8

W ithin minutes, Ben and Fabia had left the ocean behind and were bumping up the cobblestone road to the Palace of the Eight Immortals. As they went higher on the island, the trees grew thicker. The scent of wood smoke and incense filled the air. After a winding journey, they stopped in front of a giant stone gate guarded by two lions.

Andrew descended from the carriage behind them. "Remember, both of you, I will be introducing you. Do not feel like you need to speak unless you are spoken to."

Fabia looked at Ben. "Will I—"

"I don't think so," Ben said. "I told Zhang you were my assistant."

"Good." Fabia's skin was pale in the flickering torchlight. "I'd just as soon remain a spectator to this movie, thank you very much."

They followed Andrew under the gate and up the stairs to a set of doors guarded by humans in brown robes. The doors were layered in gold leaf and decorated with brightly colored stones.

"This is quite the place," Ben said quietly. He was silently taking stock of everything he saw. It was perfectly preserved architecture from the same era as the Forbidden City in Beijing. Sloping tile roofs and intricately carved posts and lintels layered with rich colors to invoke a sense of grandeur. The first doors led to a second set of doors with even more gold and more gemstone mosaics.

Through the mosaic doors lay a formal courtyard garden lit with flaming torches and decorated with standing stones and trickling fountains. A lush green lawn led from the doors of the palace to the main hall.

"Welcome to the Palace of the Eight Immortals," Andrew said. "Here all elements exist in balance. The disputes of an empire are settled peacefully, judged by the eight wisest elders in history."

They walked through the courtyard and toward the steps to the main hall. Fabia was speechless behind Ben while Andrew narrated their journey.

"You are guests of the most supreme Elder Zhang Guo, master of air and battle. He is the founder and oldest patron of Penglai." He nodded to the garden they were walking through. "This area was planted by Cao, the youngest of the elders."

Earth vampire.

"It's very beautiful," Fabia said.

Ben was taking everything in. Every symbol, every color, every number. All had meaning. Nothing was chance.

Black. Giovanni had dressed him in black. Why?

They walked up the steps and toward a pair of monks who bowed low before they opened a pair of gold-covered doors. The gold wasn't leafed. It was layered and chased with the symbol of a giant dragon clutching a pearl.

"The doors are a gift of Elder Lu Dongbin, the current chairman of the council. The dragon, of course, is not a fire symbol here."

"It's a water symbol," Ben said. Water, like Giovanni's family.

"You are correct," Andrew said.

Black is a water color.

Though his uncle had been sired to fire, Giovanni was an anomaly. All fire vampires were. They spontaneously erupted like an immortal genetic mutation. No pattern. No prediction. Often they killed themselves at a young age. Only the strongest and most controlled lived to maturity. Giovanni had come from water, and any children he had would be sired to it.

Black.

The Black Tortoise.

Not a simple turtle, a warrior symbol and one of the cardinal points in the sky.

Black Warrior. Water.

It finally clicked in Ben's brain. Giovanni had chosen black so that the elders would be reminded who Ben belonged to in their world. Some might have been tempted to see him as Tenzin's human partner. Giovanni was reminding the elders— and reminding Ben—who he was.

He was Giovanni Vecchio's son.

Ben had been chosen and adopted by the immortal child of Kato, ocean god of the ancient world. Reared by an assassin, a scholar, and a scribe.

Ben lifted his chin as the doors swung open, and he walked into the Hall of the Elders of Penglai. Nothing could have prepared him for the sight.

Silver leaf coated the walls, and massive malachite pillars held up a soaring roof. The floor was pure white marble, and rosewood panels lined either side of the center walkway.

Ben kept his eyes forward as they followed Andrew.

Easily a hundred people filled the Hall, all of them turning their attention to the newcomers as the three humans walked by. There were vampires and humans buzzing around, whispering in ears and casting sidelong glances at the mortals who merited an invitation and formal introduction to the Hall.

And at the far end of the building, eight vampires sat on individual thrones, each reflecting a different geography or period. All were clothed in identical pure white, the color of death in Chinese mythology.

Because they are the masters of death.

Ben had memorized their names from books, but he couldn't place all of them. There was no illustrated directory of vampire royalty that could give him a clue. He guessed that the tall, thin immortal in the center of the group was Lu Dongbin, water vampire and chairman of the council. The vampire to Lu's right was the only woman on the council, He Xiangu, a legendary fire vampire said to keep a phoenix as a pet.

Ben could also identify Lan Caihe on the far right, the other fire vampire on the council and possibly the most enigmatic. Elder Lan appeared to be the youngest of the council, but they were actually one of the oldest. Giovanni had instructed Ben never to underestimate them. Lan was cagey and clever, a gender-fluid trickster who enjoyed a bit of excitement and was often the one to provoke the more serious elders.

The rest were mysteries Ben would have to discover another time.

As they reached the front of the Hall, Ben and Fabia halted behind Andrew, who nodded to a bearded vampire on the far left with waist-length hair who could only be their host, Zhang Guo.

He was clothed in white, but his robes reflected the style of the ancient Eastern Steppe. His features were Central Asian, like Tenzin's, though his eyes were dark. His skin was darker and his beard thicker.

Ben locked eyes with the immortal, refusing to look away as

Zhang took stock of the humans in front of him. His expression was unreadable.

He looks like Tenzin.

Or rather, Tenzin looked like him.

Ben hadn't been expecting that.

Was there a blood relation? Did they come from the same family? Ben knew so little about Tenzin's human life—he had no way of telling what her human relationship to her vampire sire might have been. Whatever he'd been as a human, as an immortal, Zhang was one of the most powerful presences Ben had ever felt.

The elder rose and said, "Welcome, Andrew Leu, my dear friend. It is always a pleasant sight to see you in our hall."

Andrew bowed deeply but did not angle his neck, indicating he was not Zhang's blood donor. "Thank you, Elder Zhang."

"Please introduce my guests."

"Honored Zhang Guo, esteemed elders of the Hall, I present to you Benjamin Amir Santiago Vecchio, adopted son of Giovanni Vecchio. He is a friend of Rome and Master of Iron in Lothian."

Zhang Guo looked directly at him. "Welcome to Penglai, Benjamin Vecchio."

Ben finally spoke. "Thank you, Elder Zhang. It is my honor to be here."

Where was Tenzin? Was she watching? There were too many vampires in the Hall, and he couldn't sense her. The press of amnis was too strong.

Andrew continued. "It is also my pleasure to introduce Fabiana Teresa Salvadori, human scholar under the aegis of Giovanni Vecchio. She is a friend of Rome *and* an assistant professor of archaeology and art history."

As Ben's eyes furtively scanned the Hall, a pleasant murmur of approval surrounded him. He had to stifle a smile. Apparently being a scholar of Rome was far more agreeable than being a sword master in Scotland.

Where was she? She had to be here.

Elder Zhang said, "Welcome to the great hall, Miss Salvadori. Scholars and teachers are always welcome in Penglai."

Fabia's face was pleasantly flushed, and her voice was barely audible. "Thank you very much."

Andrew bowed again. "I thank the elders for their attention and ask if there is any assistance I can offer at this time as a friend of the court."

"There is not," Lu Dongbin said. "Thank you, Mr. Leu."

A subtle murmur rose in the Hall, and Ben saw attention had already drifted away from them. This was a busy place, and they were three humans who were guests. No one was going to halt their evening to make a fuss over them.

Andrew turned and motioned them toward the back of the room with raised eyebrows.

"That is all," he whispered. "You are introduced. We must go."

Ben looked over his shoulder one more time to see Zhang speaking to someone just beyond a screen to his right.

For a moment he saw her, and she saw him.

A flash of red silk, a pair of grey eyes, and a second later, Tenzin was gone.

WHY HAD he brought the Italian girl?

A sour taste filled Tenzin's mouth as she paced in Zhang's antechamber. Her fangs nicked her bottom lip and she tasted blood. Why had Ben brought that woman? Zhang's letter hadn't asked for Ben to bring a team. It had asked him to come to Penglai. Him. No one else.

Zhang entered the room off the Hall of Elders where he met in private with petitioners or took breaks to meditate. The room had vaulted ceilings and windows to the outdoors, in respect of his element. When Zhang required her to be in the Hall, she most often remained here.

"Give him some time to settle in, then summon him to meet me," he said.

"Send a servant." She bit out the words.

"No." Zhang looked at her. "I have allowed you to set the terms of this assignment and have coerced your human to the island. I have already agreed to pay him an additional fee to what I am paying Cheng and you. But I am not your intermediary. Whatever conflict you have with this man, it is yours to settle. If you want me to hire him, you can bring him to me. You, Tenzin. Not a servant."

Tenzin's eyes flashed. "So pronounces the Great Arbiter."

Zhang's gaze was steady. "Should I fear your rage? Your condemnation? You have given me both." He spread his arms. "And yet I remain your sire. As I always will be. It would be wise of you to remember that."

"It would be wise of you to remember that it is your alliances that suffer from the loss of the Laylat al Hisab, not mine."

Zhang raised one eyebrow. "Do you have alliances? I thought your only loyalty was to yourself?"

Tenzin stepped toward her sire, spread her arms dramatically, and got down on her knees before she put her face to the ground. She pressed her forehead to the cold marble before she looked up with fire in her eyes. *"Aabmen."*

My father. The words he always longed to hear, spoken in the most patronizing voice she could muster.

Zhang smirked. "Never before has a bow held so much defiance."

She rose to her knees. "What other allegiance should I have, Father, but to myself and the few beings who please me? Have I not learned your lessons well?"

"I have learned to evolve," Zhang said. "Have you?"

Tenzin straightened her garments. "That would imply that I need to change." Like Ben and the Italian woman, she wore a traditional robe that wrapped around her body. Unlike theirs, hers had a square, notched collar like her father's.

"Don't you need to change?" Zhang's eyes had never looked older. "Don't we all?"

"I suppose that is a kind of wisdom, but it is not mine." She rose to her feet. "I'll fetch Benjamin. You want to meet with him here?"

"No, take him to my personal quarters. I want to put him at ease. I'll tell the servants to prepare a meal."

"He likes burritos," Tenzin said. "You can bribe him to do anything with spicy chicken."

Zhang frowned. "What is a burrito?"

"Never mind." She walked toward the panels that led to the garden.

"Tenzin."

She turned.

"Should I forget this quest?" he asked. "Find some other way to formalize peace with Arosh?"

Her father's eyes had lost the hard edge he wore in public settings, but that didn't make them any easier for Tenzin to read.

He was her sire.

Her murderer.

Her warden.

Her savior.

She could live in the space between truths because he was

the one who had led her there. She could be the hero and the villain in the same breath because she had learned it from him.

"We will find it," Tenzin said. "And then this ancient war will finally be over."

"But will anything change?"

"Does anything ever change?" She walked into the darkness. "Twenty minutes. I will bring him to you."

9

Fabia turned to him in the doorway of the lavish bathroom in their guest apartment and held up a hand. "I don't care what you do right now. I don't care where we are. I don't care which bedroom you take. They're both fine, and either will do. But right now you will leave me alone in this spacious and beautiful bathroom. You will give me silence and peace from your brooding. And you will not open this door for at least an hour."

Ben smiled. "I feel like you want some alone time."

"Out." She pointed toward the door. "I don't like spending this amount of time with anyone I'm not sleeping with, and I am definitely not sleeping with you. Go find a drink. Go find Tenzin, for pity's sake. But go away from here."

"Fine." He could use the bathroom in the reception area if he needed it. Penglai had what amounted to a small hotel on the second level of the island. It was where human guests, visiting scholars, and other mortals stayed if they didn't live in the monastery.

The highest level of the island held the halls and personal apartments of the Eight Immortals and their retinue. The second level was for visitors and scholars. The third and largest level—the one closest to the ocean—was the monastery and human village.

Taoist monks were the guardians of the island, and if they did not allow you access to the immortals, you would not pass. Priests and their families lived and worked among the others on the island, farming, building, and generally serving the immortals who had made it their home for over a thousand years.

As Ben strolled through the manicured gardens that covered the second level, he saw many monks and priests dressed in brown, black, and saffron-yellow robes, going about their evenings. Some were serving in the great hall. Some would be serving visitors. All were quiet, pleasant, and nodded to Ben as he passed.

He'd taken off his formal zhiduo and put on the more casual clothing that had been delivered to their guest quarters. His tunics and pants were all in shades of black and grey, and Fabi's were in various shades of green. Nothing fancy. Everything comfortable and practical.

Ben found himself eased by the simplicity. Loose, comfortable clothing. Flat shoes. No one was competing about fashion here. There were no electric lights. Only torches, gas, and firelight. In the distance, he saw a group of humans and what might have been a few vampires practicing tai chi on a softly undulating lawn.

Yield and overcome; bend and be straight.

In the peace and silence of the night, he felt her approaching. She was in the air above him, hovering over the garden. Ben didn't have amnis. He didn't know how he could sense her, but he could. He'd been able to detect her for years. Some instinct at the core of his being recognized her presence drawing close.

"I know you're there," he said quietly.

A flutter of silk in the night.

Ben stopped at the base of a massive taihu stone, the twisting, pockmarked limestone pleasantly familiar from the Chinese garden at the Huntington Botanical Garden. Giovanni and Beatrice's house in California was only a few blocks from the Huntington, and Ben had grown up wandering among the stones and marveling at their height and age. He placed a hand on it and looked through the naturally formed crevices and holes.

She landed on the other side. Through the stone, he saw her eyes.

"Hello, Tenzin."

She said nothing.

Ben looked away. "I'm here, and I know it's because you want me here. So can you at least talk to me?"

"Why did you bring the Italian woman?"

Ben frowned and looked back at Tenzin, who was still on the other side of the taihu stone. "What?"

"Is something wrong with your ears?"

"Nothing is wrong with my ears." Was she serious? Ben crossed his arms over his chest. "I brought *Fabia*—who you've known for about seven years now, by the way—because she's an archaeologist who did postgraduate work on a dive in Calabria for two years and she's a certified diver."

"Oh." Tenzin flew up and perched on top of the rock. "That makes sense."

He looked up. "I thought so, yes."

He examined her in the torchlight. Her hair was a smooth sweep of black silk that brushed her chin, and she was still wearing the red silk robes from the Hall. Her skin glowed gold in the light.

I missed you.

You're so beautiful.

You make me insane.

"How were the mountains?" he asked quietly.

Her grey eyes met his and they looked a little sad. "I never made it. I stopped in Shanghai and Cheng told me about this job. I haven't been able to think about anything since."

"Really?" She hadn't thought about *anything* since then? Not him? Not New York? Not their fight? Or what happened between them in Puerto Rico?

"Yes, really."

Liar, liar, pants on fire.

Ben stuck his hands in his pockets and kept walking. If she wanted to talk to him, she could follow along.

She didn't follow, but she did fly to the next rock along the path. "My father wants to see you."

"Yeah, I figured that out after the fourth letter." He glanced sideways at her. "Thanks for that, by the way. Giovanni had a fun time chewing me out when he heard I didn't jump into service."

"What took you so long?"

How was it possible for her to piss him off so quickly? Ben stopped and waited for her to grow impatient enough to fly off the top of the rock. Within seconds, she flew down and stood in front of him. Ben glared at her, holding himself perfectly still.

"I said, what took you—?"

Ben's hand flew out and gripped the side of Tenzin's neck, pulling her toward him. A fraction of a second later, he felt her fingers digging into his throat. She was in his face, her fangs bared.

He waited, eyes locked with hers. The corner of her lip twitched in an instinctive snarl. Their bodies were so close he could feel the hair on his arms reach toward her. He could feel her cool breath on his lips.

"You left me." Ben drew the words out. Gave each one the weight it deserved. "You're the one who ran away."

He saw the battle in her eyes. She pushed back the predatory instincts and her fangs shrank back. They didn't disappear; they never disappeared.

She swallowed, but she didn't let go of his throat. "I wrote you letters."

"They were from Penglai."

"Don't be stupid."

He shoved her away. "What do you want, Tenzin?"

"Come to my father's quarters," she said. "He wants to brief you about the job."

Of course. The job. The only reason he was there.

"Fine," he said. "Does he want Fabi there? She asked for some time alone to chill out."

"Is she working for you? Or is she an independent contractor?"

"I'm paying her to be my assistant on this."

Tenzin shrugged. "Then it's up to you. You don't *need* to bring her."

"Fine." He started walking. "I know you know where I'm staying. Meet me at the front gate in ten minutes."

"I always know where you are."

Ben turned and a bitter smile crossed his lips. "That's creepy, Tenzin. Just so you know, that's something a stalker would say. Don't be a stalker."

She narrowed her eyes. "I only stalk people when I want to kill them."

He pursed his lips. "Again, very creepy. And also kind of proving my point."

Ben turned around and kept walking back to his room. Tenzin hovered in the air over him. He heard her fly away. Then she flew back. She landed on the path in front of him. She didn't look at him, but he heard her words perfectly.

"I would never kill you, Benjamin." Her voice was so soft it was barely audible. "I would sooner kill myself."

Without another word—before Ben could even open his mouth—she disappeared in the night.

~

"The Fire King and I were always rivals." Zhang sat on a low cushion at the head of a long table laden with food. "Arosh sent spies to my court. I sent spies to his. We fought sporadically for thousands of years."

"What did you fight over?" Ben took two slices of duck from the platter that was held out to him. Fabia, sitting next to him, also took two.

When he'd returned to the rooms and told her where he was going, she'd insisted on accompanying him. What had she called herself? A glutton for knowledge?

"We fought for all the reasons empires have always fought. Land. Human capital. Wealth. Knowledge."

"Knowledge is power," Ben said quietly. He didn't know how many times his uncle had drilled the idea into him.

"What do you hold in your hands?"

"It's a book."

"No, it's knowledge. Knowledge humans and immortals have pursued for centuries. Knowledge they kill and die for."

"Die for a book?*"*

"It is not a book."

"Right. It's knowledge."

"And knowledge is power. Do you understand?"

"Yes, we fought for power." Zhang took a drink of red wine from a glass goblet. "But in the end, Arosh and I fought because it was expected. Our people expected it. Our courts expected it. We had warriors, armies, advisers who expected it."

"And then one day," Tenzin said. "You didn't."

Ben watched Tenzin sitting to the left of her father's seat, across from Fabia, who sat at his right. Tenzin kept her eyes trained on her dish when she wasn't quietly instructing the servants in the room.

Commander of the Altan Wind.

Ben would bet money that Tenzin had been one of those people expecting her sire to continue fighting. Had she been disappointed when he stopped? Relieved?

Fabia asked, "Why did you do it?"

"Why make peace?" Zhang smiled a little. "I wanted to live a balanced life. Penglai Island already existed, but for thousands of years I had led a dual life. I flew to one court and made war while in the other I tried to promote peace. On Penglai, I had built a place where the wisest could be consulted so that humans and vampires no longer had to suffer blood and combat over conflicts that could be resolved with conversation. But I was still holding on to some of my territories with an iron fist."

"And now some of those territories are lawless," Tenzin said quietly.

"When they want peace, they will find it."

"Or Arosh will rise and make the decision for them."

Zhang stared at Tenzin, but Ben couldn't understand the look they exchanged. He didn't understand a lot of things about their relationship.

Zhang turned to Fabia. "I built Penglai because I wanted a place where scholars were respected and honored. For thousands of years, vampires collected human scholars for our courts, human poets and artists to amuse us, but we had none of our own." He shook his head. "What a waste. So many artists, poets, and scholars turned into immortals and then forced to be warriors when they only wanted to create."

Tenzin said, "But isn't there an art to war?"

Ben said, "Sun Tzu would say yes. But he'd also say that it is better to win without fighting. You could win hearts through poetry that you could never win in battle."

Zhang said, "An excellent point, Benjamin."

"I suppose Sun Tzu might say that." Tenzin smiled. "But I'm alive and he is dead. So you should probably take that into account." She twisted a long string of noodles around her chopsticks. "Zhang made peace with Arosh because my father was running out of good generals and he convinced his people that it made more economic sense to settle things with alliances rather than armies."

"There was that as well," Zhang said. "Whatever our reasons, we both wanted the fighting to stop. I sent emissaries to the Fire King's court. He sent some of his own back with mine. We negotiated for decades."

"Decades?" Fabia's eyes went wide. "*Decades?*"

"It isn't that long," Tenzin said. "Decades mean little to beings as old as Arosh and my sire."

"We finally settled at the beginning of the ninth century. We had signed treaties and exchanged hostages—"

"Hostages?" Fabia said. "You kept hostages?"

"During negotiations, one of Arosh's children came and stayed in my court as a gesture of good faith."

Ben looked at Zhang. "You only have one child."

"Arosh annoys me," Tenzin said. "Luckily, his palace was comfortable and he was rarely in residence. His harem kept me very entertained."

"The only thing left to do was a ceremonial exchange of gifts," Zhang continued. "I sent a caravan of silk, jade, and porcelain to Arosh. He was to send me a sword."

Ben said, "The Laylat al Hisab."

"The Night's Reckoning, a saber of unmatched beauty and strength," Zhang said, "made by the most famous swordsmith in immortal history. A vampire who lived in Arosh's territory, though never under his aegis."

"Harun al Ilāh," Tenzin said.

Ben didn't think he'd ever seen Tenzin speak of anyone with the awe with which she said Harun's name. "Who was he?"

"The sword master of Durūz." Zhang motioned for a servant to come closer. "Can you bring bowls to wash our hands, please?"

"Of course, master."

"Harun al Ilāh was a fire vampire." Tenzin's eyes glowed with admiration. "A legend. Not as old as Arosh, but still very ancient. An artist who did miraculous things with metal and glass. I have only one piece of his, a dagger. I treasure it. It is my personal dream to own one of his swords."

"They are sold for millions of American dollars," Zhang said. "*When* they are sold, which is only once every few centuries. It is not the cost that is prohibitive. Most vampires would never part with a Harun blade since so few remain now that he is dead."

"He is dead?" Fabia said. "But he was a vampire. What happened? Why would anyone kill an artist who was so well-respected?"

"He wasn't killed." Zhang turned his attention to Ben. "The Laylat al Hisab was one of his final creations, making it that much more valuable. In a letter to his wife, he said it was the most beautiful sword he had ever created, and the strongest."

"Damascus steel?" Ben asked.

Zhang nodded.

"No wonder they go for millions."

Fabia frowned. "They make Damascus steel now, don't they?"

"It's not the same," Tenzin said. "They have re-created it to a point, but nothing will ever match true Damascus steel, and Harun was its master."

Zhang continued. "The Laylat al Hisab was sent on a ship called the *Qamar Jadid* along with other riches from Arosh's palace, but none of it ever reached Penglai Island. A storm drove the ship off course, and it was lost. Until last year, we didn't even have a rumor of where it might be."

"Even from water vampires?" Ben asked.

"Not even them. And I sent many to look for it. And without the sword..."

"The treaty was never formally complete," Ben said. "You and Arosh have been in a cold war for centuries."

"Not exactly," Tenzin said. "Until Giovanni went to Rome and revealed the truth about Kato, the whole vampire world had assumed Arosh and Kato killed each other in the ninth century."

Ben's mouth dropped open. "That's right. Up until... what? Ten years ago? This was a dead issue, so to speak."

Fabia frowned. "What happened ten years ago?"

Zhang said, "The origin of the Elixir virus was revealed in Rome by Ben's uncle, your patron, Giovanni Vecchio. In the course of that discovery, it became known that Kato and Arosh had not killed each other, as the entire immortal world had believed. They were in hiding because the Elixir had broken Kato's mind and Arosh guarded him."

"So you thought Arosh was dead for a thousand years," Fabia said. "Which would mean the war was over. No need to recover the treaty sword because no treaty was necessary."

"Until Arosh came back to life," Ben said. "Meaning the war did too."

Zhang dipped his fingers in the rose-scented bowl of water one of his servants held for him. "Which is where you and Tenzin must play a role, Benjamin Vecchio. Arosh and I will jointly fund this recovery effort so that we may finally settle this. Cheng is the one who first heard of this shipwreck that matches details of the wreck of the *Qamar Jadid*. It is in territory where he has deep influence. He will be granted a rich finder's fee, but this sword is beyond priceless at this point. Many would kill to recover it. I need someone I can trust in Shanghai."

Ben nodded at Tenzin. "Your daughter?"

"My daughter cannot accomplish this on her own," Zhang said. "We are of the air, not the water. I need humans who know things. Humans I can trust."

"I get the feeling," Ben said, "that you don't trust many, human or vampire."

"I trust my daughter," Zhang said. "I trust your uncle and aunt. So if you will agree to take this job, I will trust you."

Ben leaned against the back wall after washing his hands. "The price is negotiable, but I'll be fair."

"I expect nothing less."

"Fabia comes with me." Ben watched Tenzin, and if he hadn't known her so well, he would have missed her reaction. It wasn't a flinch. More like a minute twitch around her expressive mouth.

"Your assistant is welcome. I will be sure to make that clear with Cheng. Also know that Mr. Leu is aware of your role in this enterprise. If you have questions during the course of your work, you may contact him."

Tenzin made a sour face but said nothing.

"I accept." Ben watched Tenzin. "Tenzin and I will find the Laylat al Hisab, return it to you here in Penglai, and your long war with Arosh will be over."

10

Taking the high-speed rail line south to Shanghai was about as different as you could get from flying into Beijing and taking a secret plane to a secret boat to a secret island in the Bohai Sea.

They'd spent one more night and day in Penglai, scouring the library and learning everything they could about Harun the sword maker and about Arab sea routes in the ninth century. Commerce across the Indian Ocean was thriving in those centuries, and sea trade was a vital artery.

Ben and Fabia left the island on the last ship before dawn. They spent much of the day in Andrew Leu's hangar before they headed back to Beijing to catch the bullet train.

They left Beijing in the afternoon and arrived at Hongqiao Railway Station after dark. The entire trip had only taken four hours.

"Where are we staying?" Fabia asked.

"Tenzin said Cheng would send someone to meet us."

"Didn't you say Tenzin has a house in Shanghai?"

"Outside it, yes."

Ben scanned the crowd for a familiar dark head of hair and a taciturn expression. If he had to guess, Cheng would send Jonathan, his right hand when it came to anything business related. Jonathan was British and his humor fittingly dry, though the man was a water vampire.

Fabia hooked her arm through his as they walked through the crowd. "I'm guessing from that chilly *au revoir* you and Tenzin exchanged that things have not been settled in any way. Are you two going to be able to work together without violence?"

"That's always the question, isn't it?" He spotted a tall, pale figure in the distance. "There. I see him."

Ben walked through the crowd and nodded at Jonathan, who spotted them and walked their way. His hands were in the pockets of his ever-present trench coat, and a thin red scarf hung around his neck.

"Good evening, Ben." Jonathan didn't extend a hand. His gaze fell on Fabia and immediately warmed. "You must be Miss Salvadori. I am Jonathan, Cheng's manager. It's my great pleasure to meet you. I hope your journey was pleasant."

Fabia brightened. "It was, thank you. The train was very comfortable."

"I've heard that it is." Jonathan extended a hand. "May I help you with your bag?"

Ben said, "You never offered to help me with mine."

The hooded eyes barely glanced at him. "You're not a renowned marine archaeologist, are you, Ben?"

Ben loved poking the overly formal Englishman. "I'm also not as cute as Fabi, am I? That's it, isn't it? Are you discriminating against me because I'm not as pretty?"

"That goes without saying." The corner of Jonathan's mouth turned up in a barely perceptible smile. "Miss Salvadori—"

"You can call me Fabi." The smile was in her voice.

"Fabi," Jonathan said. "Is he as annoying in Rome as he is

when he travels? Or is he one of those Americans who simply becomes irritable any time they leave Los Angeles?"

Jonathan pronounced it Los *Angeleeez*, which was just begging Ben's fist to hit his mouth.

"Tenzin and I have been living in New York. Not Los Angeles."

Jonathan glanced over his shoulder. "Not recently. She's been here."

Oh, Jonathan definitely needed to be punched.

Fabi put a hand on Ben's arm. "Ben's been so busy in Rome, I don't think he's had time to be irritable."

Bless you, Fabi.

"Busy?" Jonathan walked out of the station and toward a black car that was waiting in the private car lot. "I trust we'll be able to keep him occupied here as well. It might even keep him out of trouble."

"Are you sure you're not confusing me with my partner?" Ben asked. "I'm usually the one cleaning up the trouble, not starting it."

Jonathan switched to Mandarin once they were seated in the car. "Are you going to tell me what's going on between the two of you? Or should I just be ready to duck if blades start flying?"

Ben answered in Mandarin. "It's none of your business. We'll keep things professional."

"Since when does Tenzin keep anything strictly professional?" Jonathan's tone was derisive. "By the way, your Mandarin is excellent. It appears that shipping-vessel ploy worked."

Ah yes, the infamous container ship that Tenzin had stranded Ben on after his junior year of college. "Just don't try it again. I'm meaner than I used to be."

"Yes, I can sense that."

Jonathan didn't appear to be joking, which made Ben wonder.

Was he meaner? Was he harder? He tried to remember the boy who'd met Jonathan the first time. The first time Tenzin had dragged him across the ocean on a quest. The first time she'd double-crossed him and claimed it was for his own good. The first time she'd shown a hint of awareness of him as a man and not simply Giovanni's nephew.

The years piled on top of each other like storm clouds gathering. Ben felt old. Weary. He watched the city lights of downtown Shanghai speed by as their driver worked his way through traffic.

He was richer than he'd been at twenty-one, but what else had he accomplished? He'd finished a bachelor's degree. Started a business... of a sort. He'd made alliances and built a reputation.

And it was all in the vampire world.

"You'll be staying in secure rooms at Cheng's compound for the rest of the week." Jonathan switched back to English. "The research vessel is still gathering supplies, so that won't leave until Monday."

"Oh!" Fabia smiled. "So we'll have time to explore Shanghai? We didn't have much time in Beijing."

Jonathan's smile was indulgent. "Of course. Cheng's city compound is centrally located. You'll be able to explore the city tomorrow. In fact, after sundown, I'd be happy to give you a tour myself."

Fabia was all smiles. "Thank you. What a lovely offer."

"You're very welcome."

Ben rolled his eyes. Jonathan being charming just felt wrong. "Hey Jonathan?"

"Yes, Ben?"

"Are you going on the ship with us?"

Jonathan's smile fell. "No. Cheng decided he'd rather have me back here looking over things in the city. You'll meet your other team members later tonight."

"Team members?" For some reason, Ben had imagined that he, Tenzin, Cheng, and Fabia would be working alone.

"The *Qamar Jadid*—or the ship we think is the *Qamar Jadid* —has been lost for a thousand years. You're going to need help to find it, recover it, and document the historical significance of the find."

Fabia smiled. "I'm thrilled to be a part of this."

Jonathan said, "I understand you're an avid diver."

"Yes. I love it."

"Did Ben tell you I'm a water vampire?"

"He didn't. So no scuba equipment necessary for you?"

He shook his head. "I look forward to seeing the updates. I'm sure this recovery will be fascinating. It's rare to find a vessel of this age that appears to be intact."

"What kind of pictures have they taken?"

"Only the most rudimentary." Jonathan leaned back into the plush leather seats. "But you'll see more tonight when you meet the team. Cheng will show you everything."

THE BUILDING where Jonathan drove them looked like a luxury residential tower in the Pudong neighborhood of Shanghai. They pulled into the basement and were waved into a deserted parking area under the building near a sleek silver elevator.

Jonathan got out and instructed the valets who opened the doors to take Ben and Fabia's luggage to the eighth floor. Ben kept his messenger bag with him, and Fabia kept her purse and carry-on bag.

As their luggage was whisked away, Jonathan led them to

the elevator. "You'll have the use of this car while you're here. Fabia, the driver doesn't speak English or Italian, so if you need an interpreter, simply call the front desk and request one."

Ben sent Fabia a quick text. *Talk to me before you do that.*

Fabia glanced at her phone and nodded.

Jonathan continued. "I'll show you to your rooms, but traffic was a little heavier than I'd expected. Will you need much time to refresh yourselves? Cheng will have a meal prepared when you arrive at the meeting, so there's no need to eat."

Fabia said, "If that is the case, I don't need much time. Would a half an hour be too much?"

"Not at all," Jonathan said. "Ben?"

"Half an hour sounds good to me."

"Excellent. I'll come gather you at eleven thirty."

The building might have looked typical from the outside, but inside, it was the picture of luxury. The elevator had a padded velvet bench, rosewood paneling, and framed art on the walls. The carpet underneath their feet was plush.

When the elevator doors opened, Jonathan walked them down a wide hall with views of the city through a wall of mirrors. He paused in front of two carved wooden doors and handed over two hotel-room-style card keys.

"Your rooms are adjoining. There are multiple locking systems for security when you are inside. There is also a directory of building services on the desk. A full-service kitchen, spa, and fitness center are available twenty-four hours for your convenience." He looked at them both, but mostly at Fabia. "Is there any other way I can be of service?"

"I don't think so," Fabia said. "Thank you."

"You are most welcome. I'll see you in half an hour."

Ben slid his key in the lock. "I think someone has an admirer."

"Oh?" Fabia gave him a sidelong glance. "I think someone has a chip on his shoulder."

Ben and Fabia both opened their doors. Within seconds, Ben was opening the door between their rooms. A moment later, Fabia opened hers.

"I don't have a chip on my shoulder," he said.

"You like this city. You've told me a hundred times. And yet you've been sucking on a lemon from the time Jonathan picked us up at the station."

"I just... don't normally stay here."

"You mean with Cheng."

"Yes, I mean with Cheng." Ben ran a frustrated hand through his hair. "I don't like him. I don't like her being with him. I don't like that he's in charge of this. I don't like that I'm apparently taking orders from him. I mean, what is that about?"

"It's called being part of a team, Ben. Every team has a leader. It's the only way anything gets done."

"So why is he the leader? Why not Tenzin?"

Fabia rolled her eyes. "One"—she stuck out a finger—"I believe Zhang said he's the one who found this wreck, or found evidence of it."

"Fine. Yes." Ben crossed his arms.

"Two"—she continued putting up fingers—"he's a water vampire. You're not. Tenzin's not. It seems obvious to me. Three, it sounds like he's put a team together and acquired a research vessel. Maritime recovery is specialized work. The one who puts the tools together gets to be in charge. Those are the rules. Those are *always* the rules." She reached up and pinched his earlobe.

"Ow!"

"Grow up. Cheng isn't your competition. If Tenzin has feelings for him, then you don't want to have a relationship with her. That would be foolish. If she doesn't have feelings for him and the two of you actually stand a chance at anything approaching a normal relationship—which I still have very strong doubts about—then he's no threat to you. According to you, she's had him. If she wanted him, he'd still be hers."

"Maybe Cheng ended it," he muttered.

"Would he still be alive if he'd done that?" Fabia asked. "That's a serious question, by the way. I have no idea what Tenzin would do if someone broke up with her."

"Okay, probably not." Ben rubbed his ear. "Why are you so mean?"

"Because you are so thickheaded." She marched back to her room and closed the door. "I'm taking a shower and changing. Unless you want to scare her with your smell, you should too."

11

Tenzin watched Ben as he entered the room with Fabia. The two of them moved similarly. She hadn't noticed that before. They had a similar gait and pace. A consequence of growing up in comparable homes or something deeper?

Cheng glanced up from the plans he was scanning at the conference table. "Good. They're here." He looked at her from the side and his voice dropped. "You wanted him here. I don't want any problems, Cricket."

"There won't be."

"The woman is a good addition to the team. I looked over her résumé. She'll be an asset."

"That's what he said too."

"Did you talk to him in Penglai?"

"Yes." They hadn't talked in the way that Benjamin wanted, but Tenzin was still deciding what to do about that.

"Good." Cheng flicked his portfolio closed. "Then there should be no problems."

She looked at him innocently. "Are there ever?"

"Yes." The corner of his mouth twitched. "Always. That's why you should move here. You need a keeper."

"Do you think so?" How amusing. "And you think you'd like the job?"

"I've told you before. The offer is open."

Tenzin turned back to Ben, staring at him with no pretense of hiding her gaze. "No," she said. "You and I only get along for short periods of time, Cheng. We're too much alike."

"Do you think so?"

Not really. She and Cheng were as different as water and wind. Still, it was good to humor him, and she didn't want to say no too often. Doing that might create resentment, which wouldn't serve her purposes.

Cheng examined Fabia. "The archaeologist is attractive."

"She is. The short hair suits her." Tenzin fingered the shorn hair at her own nape. She liked the velvet thickness of it. Liked the sensation of running her fingers along the edge. She enjoyed the swing of cool silk along her jaw when the blunt edges of her hair touched her skin. The tactile pleasure of it fed a growing hunger that lurked on the edge of her consciousness. She didn't examine it; it was a hunger and she fed it.

She hadn't told anyone—not even Chloe—that she'd returned to New York a month before and asked Breanna to trim it for her. It had grown out too much, and Tenzin wanted the velvet feeling back.

Cheng had noticed the newly trimmed hair, but he hadn't asked. Jonathan told her short hair made her look like an adult and it was about time, which made no sense to her at all. She'd been an adult for thousands of years.

Cheng glanced at the old pocket watch he kept with him. "Kadek and Johari should be here in a few minutes."

Tenzin glanced at Ben. He was looking at her. Looking away. Looking at Cheng. She'd rarely seen him so uneasy. He usually blended in wherever he went. "Let them eat before the other vampires get here. Humans can become uncomfortable if they are the only ones eating in a room."

"Good idea." Cheng rose and walked over to Ben and Fabia, playing host for the humans, getting them food and drink to put them at ease. Chatting in that easy way he had with mortals. Tenzin remained at the end of the conference table, paging through a book she'd already read from cover to cover.

The New York penthouse had been the same when she visited. Her roof garden hadn't died, though it wasn't thriving the way it had been when she was tending it. Her loft in the apartment was free of dust and smelled as fresh as when she'd left it months before. Ben was the only one allowed in her alcove, which meant he'd been cleaning it in her absence.

Tenzin couldn't decide what she wanted to do about New York. Or about Ben. She hated to feel surprised, but he'd surprised her in Puerto Rico when he told her he remembered what had happened in the caves. She'd thought he'd been too rattled from blood loss to remember the passionate kiss. The biting. The... other things.

She didn't often lose control. Not anymore. She'd felt like an animal after the cave-in, which was not a memory she enjoyed. She was angry that he remembered her weakness.

As for what he'd told her before she left, his words were seared in her mind.

> *"Tell me this has nothing to do with me. Look me in the eye and tell me this has nothing to do with you and me and what happened in that cave and what's been happening for months —for years—now between us."*

He'd called her a liar when she told the truth. Losing control in the cave was one thing. What had been growing between them was entirely different. Tenzin didn't know what he wanted from her, which left her out of sorts, because she'd always known what Ben wanted.

He wanted respect. He wanted to be rich as well, but he mostly wanted respect.

When had it started to change? When had *he* started to change? Ben wanted different things now.

It was so... irritatingly human. Ben really needed to become a vampire. It was past time. The sentimental attachment to mortality no longer served him.

Cheng had remained at Ben and Fabia's end of the table after servants brought platters of food and silently departed. He mostly paid attention to Fabia, leaving Ben to shoot Tenzin unspoken questions with his eyes.

This guy? Ben glanced at Cheng. *Really?*

Tenzin shrugged. She trusted Cheng in most things. When it came to dealing honestly with her in business, she trusted him implicitly. Cheng was too afraid of her to cheat.

Ben looked irritated. Did he think she and Cheng had become lovers again? Was he... *jealous?*

Perhaps he was jealous.

"We're not having sex," Tenzin said from across the room. "If that's what you've been thinking."

Ben nearly spit out the water he'd been drinking. Cheng looked over his shoulder, his eyes narrowed. Fabia let out a laugh, then clapped a hand over her mouth.

"Thank you for the clarification," Cheng said. "Did you mean with me or him?"

Tenzin frowned. "Both. Or neither. I'll include Fabia in that too. I'm not having sex with any of you."

Ben wiped his mouth. "Good to know we're all clear on that."

"Thanks, Tenzin," Fabia said. "I'll try not to be too disappointed."

"Good."

Ben rose and walked over to Tenzin, leaving his plate of food half-eaten. "Can I talk to you outside please?" He paused by the table, grabbed her hand, and nearly dragged her onto the balcony.

Tenzin let him. He clearly needed some air.

There was a wide terrace that overlooked the skyscrapers of the Pudong. Black glass doors slid open with the touch of a button.

Ben walked to the far end of the balcony and dropped her hand to run agitated fingers through his hair. "What the hell, Tenzin?"

"I don't understand why you're irritated. I thought you might have imagined that Cheng and I—"

"Maybe." His eyes narrowed. "Maybe I thought that."

"So." She spread her hands out. "Now you know we are not. You have no reason to be jealous."

"I wasn't jealous of Cheng." Ben spat out the words.

Tenzin narrowed her eyes and noticed the flush in Ben's cheeks. "I think you were."

"I'm not." He crossed his arms. "I'm not jealous of him. That's ridiculous. I don't want his life. I have no interest in being some... modern pirate businessman with hundreds of servants and—"

"I assumed you were jealous of Cheng because he and I were once lovers and you and I are not." She frowned. "I didn't think it was those other things."

Ben kept his arms crossed over his chest—a defensive human gesture—and remained silent. She tried to read his face, but he'd become nearly as accomplished at hiding his true thoughts as his uncle was.

"You left me," he said quietly. "I was honest with you, which wasn't easy. I was expecting you to be angry. I was prepared to fight with you—God knows it wouldn't be the first time—but I was prepared for that. Instead, you just... left."

She shook her head. "That had nothing to do with—"

"Bullshit."

She glanced back at the conference room. "Do you really want to talk about this now?"

"Should we schedule an appointment instead?"

Tenzin nodded. "Yes. That is a good idea."

He dropped his arms. "I was being facetious, Tiny."

"I don't know why you'd make a joke about that. It's a good idea."

He took a deep breath. "Okay, I can't believe I'm doing this. What's your schedule like tomorrow night?"

She frowned. "Very busy. I need to fly to my house tomorrow night."

"For?"

"There's a book in the library I think might be useful."

"What about? Most of your books in the Shanghai house are European."

"I know, and there is an Italian one about the glass trade that I think might prove useful, but I can't remember where it is."

He narrowed his eyes. "Does it have a blue dust jacket?"

"Yes!"

"Take me with you and I'll help you find it. I think I know the one you're talking about."

"I was going to fly."

He shrugged. "So? Fly me with you."

She looked him up and down. "You're large."

"Are you saying you're not strong enough to do it? You going to drop me?"

If you continue to be this irritating, maybe. "No."

"So take me with you. We can look for the book and have our... meeting at the same time."

Talking while occupied in some other task did have its advantages. If Ben brought up things she didn't want to talk about, she could distract him. She was very good at distracting him.

"Fine." She walked back toward the doors. "I'll take you tomorrow. Now come meet the team."

～

BEN SAT BACK at his seat and picked at the remnants of food left on his plate while Cheng introduced the two other vampire members of the team.

"Kadek is one of my oldest sons," Cheng said. "He is an experienced sea captain and will be in charge of the *Jinshé*. He will also be coordinating with the crew from the university. Our client, Elder Zhang, was quite adamant that he wanted more than a direct salvage operation and was interested in scholars documenting this historic site, which is why we will have the university research vessel and not a smaller ship."

Fabia raised her hand. "For the purpose of clarity, are Ben and I considered part of the vampire crew or the human crew in this context?"

"Vampire," Tenzin said. "Kadek's men have been integrated into the human crew of this vessel—"

"Really?" Ben interrupted. "How did you manage that?"

The dead stare Cheng and Tenzin gave him was enough to shut him up.

"Okay then," he muttered. "Carry on."

Cheng continued. "It is enough to say that we have functional control of the ship. Kadek's first mate will be in charge of the humans during the day. I am the leader of the night team, Miss Salvadori, and you are a part of that."

"Thank you." Fabia folded her hands on the table. "That

more than answered my question."

"Kadek?" Cheng sat and gave the room over to his son.

Ben examined Kadek. He was a stocky, dark-skinned vampire who appeared to be from Southeast Asia. His hair was shorter than Cheng's, cut with military precision. He had a barrel chest and a face marked with several long scars near the chin.

"It's nice to meet all of you." Kadek stood and looked around the room. His accent was heavy but understandable. "Miss Salvadori, I'm very pleased we have at least one other person on our team who knows what kind of recovery we're looking at. Though I have worked many salvage operations, the academic aspect of this job is new to me and my team. Your expertise will be valuable."

"Thank you," Fabia said. "I can't make any predictions—not knowing more about the site—but I can offer general ideas."

"Understood," Cheng said. "Still, it will be good to have our own academic." He turned to the fourth vampire in the room, another person Ben had never met. "The final member of our team is new to all of us, but we are grateful she is able to join us from her home in Alitea. Johari, your recommendations are unparalleled. Welcome to Shanghai."

The woman who rose was tall, slim, and carried herself with preternatural grace. She was also stunningly beautiful. Her hair was trimmed close to her head, emphasizing a graceful neck. Her skin was a medium golden brown, and her eyes were a multicolored hazel with thick lashes.

Ben couldn't shake the feeling that he recognized her energy, but he had no idea why. He'd never met her before, never even been to Alitea.

Johari said, "Thank you, Cheng. And thank you to everyone for your welcome. I'm currently in Alitea, but I am a native of Zanzibar."

Cheng said, "Johari is well-versed in Arab trade routes through the Indian Ocean, but she also brings a particular gift with her elemental ability."

Ben watched Johari, whose face was inscrutable. "Why did you move to Alitea?"

She turned her fascinating eyes on him. "I was infected with Elixir. Saba cured me. I am her daughter now. Earth is my element."

Ben thought he might know just why Johari could be so damn valuable. "You weren't always an earth vampire, were you?"

Zanzibar was an island off the coast of Tanzania. A place rich in trade with a long history of human cultures intersecting. Islands like that often attracted water vampires.

She cocked her head. "I was not. My first elemental ability was water."

I'm sorry. Ben didn't say it, but he thought it.

Those with Elixir poisoning could be cured by Saba, the mother of the vampire race, but in doing so, they were forced to leave behind whatever element they had controlled and take on Saba's amnis, which was tied to the earth.

Ben couldn't imagine what it would be like to lose an elemental ability and then have to take on another. His aunt's element was such a deep part of who she was, losing her connection to water would be traumatizing. Tenzin was so connected to the air and the wind—losing that might be the one thing that could kill her.

"Fortunately," Johari continued without flinching, "this has given me unique skills that my new mother has often found useful. I am an earth vampire who moves comfortably underwater. I have no fear of it. In fact, I enjoy being in the ocean very much, even though I now draw my amnis from the earth."

Which was not typical for most earth vampires, who would

feel disconnected in the ocean. Johari was a brilliant addition to the team.

Fabia sat up straight. "You'll be able to move the sand and mud on the sea floor." Her mouth dropped open. "That's incredible. That could change everything."

Johari smiled. "I'm glad you think it will be of help."

Cheng stepped forward, and Johari took her seat again. "Johari and Kadek's skills will be invaluable to this recovery. We won't have a final location until we can search the area, and we're still waiting for the human crew. Tonight I think we should share a drink and get to know each other a little more. We'll be in close quarters on the ship."

Fabia raised her hand. "For the purpose of clarity, I am in favor of a drink, but I am not in favor of *being* a drink."

Cheng smiled. "Noted, Miss Salvadori. I believe we might order some wine."

"Speaking of drinks," Kadek said. "What will be the policy on the boat?"

"Preserved blood only," Cheng said. "If you want fresh, feed before we leave port."

Kadek wasn't pleased. "There will be more than enough humans—"

"Who are guests of the ship." Cheng added something quietly in a language Ben didn't speak.

Kadek fell silent, but Ben could see him brooding.

"Preserved blood," Cheng said. "And blood-wine. We will bring stores of both. We'll be too far offshore to hunt, but those who are diving will need to be mindful to keep their amnis fed."

Kadek looked like he wanted to speak, but he pressed his lips together and said nothing.

Interesting.

Ben would have to keep an eye on that.

12

Ben met Tenzin on the same balcony where he'd left her the night before. She wore her usual uniform of black leggings and a loose black tunic. This one was sleeveless and bared the smooth curve of her shoulders, the subtle muscles in her arms, and her delicate wrists.

Had he ever dismissed her as anything but utterly beautiful? If he had, he was a fool.

She was standing on the edge of the balcony, looking outward at the city. Fog drifting in from the ocean hung over the lights downtown.

"It's a good night for flying," she said.

"How long will it take to get there?" Ben was wearing a pair of grey linen pants and a black T-shirt.

She glanced at him. "With your weight added, maybe half an hour."

"I forgot how close it is."

"Yes."

"Why aren't you staying there?"

She turned her dark grey eyes up to him. "Is my presence here distracting?"

"Just wondering why you trust Cheng so much."

"My day chambers here are very secure. And you know I don't sleep."

He lifted his hand and ran his palm over the nape of her neck and the shorn black hair on her neck. It was soft. He wanted to put his mouth on her neck. Wanted to run his lips along the curve of her ear.

You want to bite her.

Was it payback or something more?

Tenzin's skin prickled in the darkness. "I flew to New York a month ago so Breanna could cut it."

"It looks great." He ran his fingertips up her neck. "I was in Rome a month ago."

"I know."

"Can you see the bruises?"

"Yes. They're faded, but they're there. Who put them on you?"

He shrugged. "No one important."

She didn't question him further. If she truly wanted to know, she'd find out.

"Should we go?" Ben left his hand on her neck. Tenzin didn't push it away.

"Yes." She slid an arm around his waist. "Hold on to me. Like you're hugging me."

Are you trying to torture me? "Okay."

Ben put his arms around Tenzin and immediately felt her power rising. The air around him moved, teasing over his skin like a curious cat winding through his legs.

"It won't feel like we're going fast," Tenzin said.

Ben felt his feet leave the ground and pushed back the panic instinct that wanted to rise.

"We're not flying against the wind but with it." Tenzin's mouth was close to his ear. "If I were too close to other elements like water or earth, lifting you would be difficult."

He clung to her, but she held him tight. He felt cushioned in a bubble of air.

"Up here," Tenzin said, "nothing interferes."

They rose up and over the roof, quickly rising into the dense blanket of fog.

"It's not flying." Her breath whispered against his neck. "We're simply asking the air to move us."

Ben looked down. Tenzin was in his arms, and they were moving through the air. Fog whipped past them, curving around the bubble of air that carried them.

"It loves you," Ben said.

"Yes." She smiled, letting her eyes close. "It knows me."

I know you.

His heart twisted in his chest. "Have you decided what color you want to paint your loft? Chloe wanted to call painters next week since we're both gone."

"No." Tenzin frowned. "I'm not sure... We'll talk about it at the house."

I'm not sure I'm coming back. It didn't need to be said. Ben knew she was having second thoughts about working with him. It was the only thing that gave him any kind of hope. If she truly didn't care, she'd abandon him without a backward glance. The fact that she was being evasive was probably the most positive sign he could hope for.

"Almost there," she said.

"Good." *Not good.* Of course, she still had to fly him back. "Tenzin, did you bring a backpack?"

"No, but you left one in your room at the house."

"I forgot about that. I'll grab it when we land."

Was this what needed to happen? Should he just pretend nothing had taken place between them in Puerto Rico? Move on? Forget what her mouth tasted like, what her body felt like? Forget that she'd writhed over him in pleasure, making his body ache and tripping her from hunger into pure bloodlust.

She is perfectly content with denial.

It shouldn't have surprised him, but it did. A little.

If Ben pretended nothing had happened and simply went back to the way things were, Tenzin would follow his lead. He could have his life back, have his friend back. He would never taste her mouth again. Never know what it would be like to sate her hunger. But she would be back.

Could he do that? Did he want to?

Ben felt their descent. The distant lights of Tenzin's small water village became visible through the fog. Dark channels cut through warm yellow lights and bobbing fishing boats.

They landed in the courtyard of the water house, and Ben immediately recognized the scent of the tangerine tree. Heavy fruit hung on the branches of the small tree in the center of the garden plot that lay in the middle of the courtyard.

She made sure their feet were on the ground before she released her arms from around his waist. "There. You've flown."

"Thank you." He didn't want to take his eyes off her. If he looked away, she could disappear.

She narrowed her eyes. "What?"

"Flying is much better than sitting in traffic."

"Is that the first time you've flown?"

He shook his head. "Gavin."

"Ah." She turned and looked around the courtyard. "I didn't tell Jinpa I was coming. I don't think she'll have any food prepared."

"Don't bother Jinpa. I ate before we left." Ben glanced around the courtyard. It had been over a year since he visited, but it was exactly as he remembered it. "Want me to make some tea? I remember where the kitchen is."

"Don't be ridiculous. I may not value convention, but you're still a guest in my home. I'll make the tea." She pointed toward the gate leading to her private quarters. "You go to the library."

"Thanks."

He waited in the courtyard, watching her walk away.

Tenzin turned. "Did you need something else?"

So many things. "No. Tea will be great."

BEN WAS KNEELING on the library floor, pointing his phone flashlight at the shelves when the light flipped on. He looked over his shoulder to see Tenzin walk in, holding a tray with two steaming cups on it.

"Light is helpful."

"I forgot you had electric lights in here." He switched off his flashlight.

"Lights." She walked to the wall and used a stylus to punch a button. "And an air conditioner."

"It's not that hot."

"Doesn't matter." She appeared to be fiddling with the settings. "It should always be on. This place isn't like my library in the mountains. It's humid here. The books and scrolls will mold if the air conditioner doesn't run. I'll have to make sure Jinpa is checking it."

Ben whistled slowly. "I don't want to know how much it costs to run AC all year round in this heat and humidity."

She set the tray of tea on a low table. "That's why I steal things, Benjamin. I have to take care of my books."

"Are you making a joke?"

"It has been known to happen."

Not often. Or at least not intentionally.

He turned back to the shelf, which he could now see definitely didn't hold the book on the history of glass. "Why are we looking for a book about glass when the thing we're looking for is a sword?"

"Because"—she picked up a cup and sipped her steaming tea—"I think it's likely glass would have been on board the *Qamar Jadid*. Harun had a glassworks that exported colored glass for use around the world. He had colors no one else had developed. If he sent a ship full of gifts, he would have included glass."

"Wouldn't the glass have broken by now?"

"It depends on what he sent. If it was shipped in ingots— which would be likely—those are solid chunks of melted glass. More like rocks than anything breakable. Which means they would also be easy to see." Tenzin looked up. "Do you see why I might want to learn more about glass?"

"Yes." A single question had been plaguing him for days. "Tenzin, this sword is important, but why is it *this* important? Why is your sire bothering with all this after so many centuries?"

She opened another book but closed it quickly. "Those around both Arosh and my father have been increasing pressure on them. Some in Penglai think Arosh must have imperial ambitions after so long living quietly. They think the pushback about infrastructure in Central Asia has sparked antivampire sentiments among human authorities. Zhang's people have been whispering about it. Arosh's people probably have too." She lifted her hands and pantomimed chatting motions with her fingers. "Blah, blah, blah. So much talking."

He couldn't stop his smile. "And you think finding the Laylat al Hisab would settle this conflict?" Ben shook his head. "I don't know. I think every now and then, vampires just like a fight."

"You're not wrong." She moved to another shelf. "But for

once it appears I'm playing the peacemaker. A war serves no one right now, and it risks our exposure. The balance of powers has shifted since Saba razed Alitea and rebuilt it. We're contending with a surge in human technology that threatens us." She shook her head. "War would be disastrous right now."

It was moments like this that reminded Ben she was thousands of years older than him. Half the time, he felt like the adult in the room, guiding Tenzin through one of her fits or confusion about the modern world.

But he hadn't seen millennia. He hadn't led soldiers into war or negotiated peace treaties. He hadn't watched human empires rise and fall. Tenzin had.

She put one book back and reached for another. "Despite all the current risks, some of my kind would risk exposure to exert power. And history proves that it's easier to start an old war than justify a new one. We need to make sure they can't get a foothold in this if we want them to avoid bloodshed."

"Do you?" Ben glanced at her. "Want to avoid bloodshed, I mean?"

Her voice was quiet. "I've had enough blood for some time."

Ben closed a book and set it on the floor. "Speaking of blood—"

"I shouldn't have bitten you, and I have already apologized for it. What more do you want?" Tenzin's eyes pierced him. "Seriously, *what do you want?* I've been trying to figure it out for months."

"What do I want?" Ben struggled to find words. "I want... I want you to acknowledge what's there, Tenzin."

"What's where?"

"Between you and me!" He moved his hand back and forth. "This thing between us."

"This *thing?*" She set down her book. "You mean what? Attraction?"

"Yes!"

"Fine." She narrowed her eyes. "You and I are sexually attracted to each other. I am attracted to you. You are attracted to me."

"Yes." He swallowed hard. "We are. And it didn't happen because of one kiss in a cave when you lost control. The thing in the cave happened because that attraction was already there."

"I agree. Chemical reactions between people occur. I am not immune to these. If anything, I am more susceptible to these forces because my senses are more responsive than yours."

"Exactly." *Wait, what was she saying?*

"So, I have acknowledged that we are sexually attracted to each other." She had the nerve to look baffled. "That is what you want?"

"Not just that." He stood and started pacing with his hands on his hips. "It's more than attraction."

"Why do you think that?"

"Because you have feelings for me!" He spat out the words. "And I have feelings for you."

"Of course I do."

Ben closed his eyes. *Don't say it. Just don't say—*

"You are my *friend*, Benjamin. I don't grant that title lightly."

And she said it.

"I know I'm your friend." He took a deep breath. Fine. If she was going to go that patronizing direction... "You know, Giovanni is your friend."

"He is."

Ben walked closer to her. "Beatrice too."

"Yes."

He stood in front of her, his hands stuffed in his pockets so he couldn't grab and shake her. "So, just out of curiosity, have you ever sucked on either of their necks so hard you wanted to rip their clothes off and have sex with them?" He lowered his voice. "Have they ever made you do that sexy-as-fuck grinding thing with your hips?" He bit the corner of his lower lip. "Just curious."

"Enough." She glared at him. Her lips were flushed and red. "We have discussed this enough. I think we should get back to looking for this book and focus on the job we agreed to perform."

"Your opinion is noted. I think you should tell me whether you've ever wanted to have sex with Giovanni or Beatrice."

"Does it amuse you to provoke me, Benjamin?"

"I haven't even started. How about Chloe? Gavin?" He leaned down. "Caspar, for that matter?"

She turned her back to him and faced the bookshelves. "I am going to look for the book. I am finished with this conversation."

Ben placed both hands on the bookshelf, caging her in, and leaned down to smell the delicate scent at her neck.

She growled his name in warning. "Benjamin."

"Tell me." He kept his voice low, watching as goose bumps rose on her skin. "Have you had that reaction to any of your friends? Or is it *maybe* just possible that something about me is different?"

He waited, his lips inches from her neck, watching her skin react to his presence. It was fascinating and sexy and infuriating.

"I told you I am done with this conversation," she said quietly. "Help me or don't. I told you what you wanted to hear."

"You only answered part of the question, Tiny."

"Back away."

"Fine." Ben straightened and took a step back. "Is the noodle place at the end of the block still open?"

If Tenzin was startled by the abrupt change of topic, she

didn't show it. "It should be. This time of year, all the noodle shops stay open late." She didn't look up from the book she'd pulled off the shelf.

"Good." He walked to the door. "I'm going to get some food. I'd ask you if you wanted anything, but God forbid you admit to being hungry."

"I'm not."

"Sure, Tenzin." He walked out the door. "Whatever you say."

Ben crossed the courtyard in long, impatient strides and grabbed a heavy key to the garden gate, not wanting to wake Jinpa or her daughters while they were sleeping.

God forbid she admit to being hungry. Or lonely. Or in need of anything she couldn't provide herself. Her ego was so massive Ben wanted to scream. He also had to recognize that her massive ego had probably been part of what kept her alive for so long.

Letting himself out, he turned right and walked down to the main thoroughfare where food stands and restaurant boats operated late into the night. There was a noodle soup he loved that he'd only ever had in Tenzin's village, and even if he wasn't hungry, he got a bowl when he could.

Ben crossed the arched stone bridge and walked toward the line of restaurants. It was only when he was walking down the other side that he realized he was being followed.

13

Ben crossed the bridge and immediately ducked into an alley running parallel to the main canal, curious how obvious they were going to be about following him. He heard one turn in to the alley behind him, but not the other.

He knew they were vampires from the way they moved. Not wind vampires though. Something else.

Were they following Ben or Tenzin's human? He walked to the end of the alley and turned left, joining the scattered crowds going home after late dinners and drinks.

The water town was a tourist attraction, not only for foreigners but Chinese tourists as well. He saw newlyweds in bright matching outfits, a few American backpackers, and slick Eastern Europeans wearing leather coats in the dense humidity.

The second vampire was back. Ben glanced over his shoulder, and both of them looked away quickly, but not before he caught their eyes.

Who do you belong to?

He crossed a series of stones laid carefully across a small canal and walked against pedestrian traffic, dodging slow-moving scooters and carts. He stopped and took a selfie in front of a shop, holding up his fingers in a V sign as he searched the area behind him.

There you are.

He snapped several pictures of them before they caught what he was doing.

Oh, you don't look happy, do you?

Ben slipped the phone in his pocket and kept walking. He passed the cluster of restaurants and clubs. He walked past a small marina with bobbing dark vessels. He turned left into another alley and immediately looked up when he saw the dead end.

Excellent.

The walls of the shops were made of stone. With an ease born of hours of parkour training, he climbed the wall and waited for the vampires to turn the corner.

They walked around the corner casually, two friends out for a stroll. They didn't hurry, but they did stop short when they realized the dead end was in front of them but no human was. One walked to the end of the alley and hopped up to peek over the old wall.

Nope.

The other side was nothing but water.

They exchanged a few quiet words that Ben didn't catch before one of them looked up. He caught Ben's eyes peeking over the edge of the building. Ben lifted his fingers and waved. Then he shot up and over the far side of the building.

He leaped from the roof of one building onto another. He could hear the vampires following him, and he didn't stop.

Ben suddenly wished he'd spent more time exploring this town and less time napping and enjoying Jinpa's cooking while they were there. The line of buildings ended in another waterway. He looped his arm around a rainspout and swung over the edge, bouncing from one wall to the other in the narrow alley until he landed on his feet.

He ran, dodging thinning traffic and leaping over narrow waterways. He quickly passed the business center of town and found himself in a deserted residential section with narrow canals and fewer pedestrians.

Shit.

The vampires were gaining on him, running just fast enough to pass for human while still outstripping him. As soon as there were no humans around, they'd drop all pretenses.

Which was... now. *Shit.*

Ben saw the blur to his left as one vampire raced in front of him and blocked his path.

He stopped in his tracks, panting. The vampire blocking the pavement in front of him stood calmly, his hands on his hips.

Ben looked over his shoulder. The one behind him stood with similar posture. Neither of them looked willing to budge or negotiate.

Ben nodded and turned his attention to the vampire in front of him while still keeping one ear attuned to the man behind him.

"How can I help you guys?" Ben had a knife in his boot. He always carried one there. Of course, a knife only took you so far with vampires.

Neither of them said a word.

"Great," Ben said. "So you're the silent types, I guess. Strong silent types? I don't know." He shrugged. "Kind of over-rated, if you ask me."

The vampire in front of him cocked his head.

Ben switched to Mandarin. "Who sent you?"

Nothing. It was like talking to two robots.

Were they robots?

Ben asked, "Have you been sent from the future to kill me or protect me?"

His breath was back. Stalling them had been good. He waited for the vampire in front of him to move, all while anticipating an attack from behind.

"I'm not here to make trouble," he said. "I'm here with Ten—"

"We know who you're here with." The voice speaking Mandarin behind him was frighteningly close. "Vecchio."

"That's Ben Vecchio, by the way." He lowered his voice. "Not Giovanni. Just in case you were pissed off at my uncle and not at me."

"You think I cannot tell the difference between a human pest and a vampire assassin?"

"I wouldn't want to presume." Ben waited. The vampire was coming closer. Ben wasn't a threat, so he wasn't walking silently. "If you just tell me what you want, we can all save some time. What do you think about that idea?"

"What we want?" The vampire in front of him finally spoke. "That is simple, Mr. Vecchio. You need to leave China."

Ben let his head fall back. "Shit. I hate it when you guys want something I can't give you." He looked back to the first vampire. "I mean, maybe that's the people-pleasing thing Chloe gives me a hard time about. I like making people happy."

"That's good to hear." That voice from behind him was awfully close. Just... very, very close. Too close. "You can make us happy right now. We might even... What's the American phrase?"

The vampire in front of him grinned, and Ben saw his fangs were fully extended. "Grab a bite to eat?"

"Yes, that's the—"

It happened too fast for the vampire to finish his sentence.

Before either immortal realized it, Ben had ducked down and spun to the side of the vampire behind him, grabbed the ten-inch knife from his boot, and locked his arm around the immortal's neck.

Without hesitation, Ben plunged the knife into the vampire's neck, angling it through the soft tissue and stopping just short of the man's spine. Arterial blood sprayed everywhere, but Ben didn't flinch.

The vampire in front of Ben rushed toward them, but the vampire in his arms shouted in protest and raised both his hands.

"Think again." Ben wiggled the blade. "I'm very close to making him as mortal as I am."

The vampire stopped, keeping his fangs bared, but he came no closer.

"You know"—Ben spoke softly—"I really hate doing shit like this. One, it's messy and I'm wearing light-colored pants. I know. Shortsighted of me. Two, I'm here working for kind of an important person, which means I'm going to have to report all this to him. And I really hate giving oral reports. Ever since ninth grade speech class. Did you ever have to take that?"

Both vampires were silent.

"I'm going to assume that's a no."

The vampire in his arms tensed.

"Ah." Ben wiggled the knife. "Really bad idea, dude."

The water in the canals around him started to churn.

"Water vampires," Ben said. "Okay. That answers one question. Who sent you?"

Neither one of them said a word.

"Here's the thing." Ben spoke into the vampire's ear. "I'm going to have to let you go at some point, or I'm going to have to kill you and take my chances with your friend. I'm guessing you're super pissed off at me right now on several levels, so I'm leaning toward killing you. I don't have a lot to lose." He could feel the blood dripping from the vampire's neck onto his hand and down the front of his shirt. "I'm Tenzin's partner, and whoever your boss is, she can probably kill them. And she will. Also, I really don't want to end up dead, which is likely going to happen if I let you go."

Barely contained fury rolled off the man in his arms. It was one thing to have a knife through your throat and touching your spine, it was another to have that knife be wielded by a human.

Ben looked at the man's partner. "I mean, you tell me. I'm guessing you don't want me to kill him—or maybe you do. I don't want to assume shit about your relationship. Just know that if I have to do that—"

Ben's words cut off when a dark shadow swooped through the air. The vampire blocking the sidewalk wavered for a moment, his mouth gaping, before a line of blood appeared at his neck. His head fell to one side. His body to the other. His head rolled and then splashed with a solid thunk in the canal.

Shit.

Ben pulled his knife out and shoved his hostage away. "Seriously?" he yelled into the air.

The vampire he'd been holding spun and slapped a hand over his bleeding neck, lunging toward Ben. Ben kicked out and clipped the man in the head, snapping his neck and making the vampire crumple.

Vampires wouldn't die unless you severed the spine, as Ben had been threatening to do, but snapping it would still render them useless until their bodies could regenerate the nerves, which could take hours.

The black shadow swooped down again, snatching the limp vampire from the sidewalk and disappearing into the darkness like a nocturnal bird of prey.

"That little shit!" Now they would never know who sent them.

Infuriating. She was absolutely infuriating.

Ben walked over and kicked the body of the remaining vampire into the canal. The head had already sunk. He dipped his knife in the water and dried it on his black T-shirt before he turned and walked back toward the house. He was going to have to go through the middle of town with a shirt covered in vampire blood. Glancing down, he realized it hadn't reached his grey linen pants.

At least there was that.

~

HE REACHED the garden gate and knew Tenzin was already in the compound. Steeling his expression, he unlocked the door and marched into the courtyard, already wondering just how much a ride share back into the city would cost.

"Every time," he growled at her. "Every single fucking time I'm trying to question someone—"

"They were going to kill you." Tenzin stood in the moonlight, her arms crossed and her face set in an obstinate mask.

"Did you not see the giant knife I had in the bastard's throat?" Ben stripped off the bloody T-shirt and tossed it on a garden bench. It was starting to dry and stick to his skin, which was just... gross.

Ben strode toward Tenzin. "I had a ten-inch hunting knife pressed to his damn spine, and you decide to—"

"You weren't going to be able to kill both of them." Tenzin looked up at him, her face still unmoving, though Ben could feel the fury vibrating off her. "Not both of them, Benjamin."

"But I might have gotten away, and I might not have had to kill either of them," he hissed. "And now we don't know who sent them. Did you ask for references before you killed the second one?"

"Don't be ridiculous."

"Then don't be so damn shortsighted!"

Her eye twitched. "You're calling me shortsighted?"

"Yes, you act on impulse. Every single time. If someone is after me here—"

Without warning, she rose up, hooked her arm around his neck, and locked her mouth on his.

Ben didn't think twice. He didn't care if he was furious with her. His body didn't care at all. He wrapped both arms around her torso and pressed her close, locking them together in the darkness.

Her mouth was ferocious. He cut his lips on her fangs and she sucked his tongue in her mouth, drinking him in. Her amnis rose, dancing over his bare skin like icy rain. He held one arm around her waist and gripped the back of her head in his hand, trying to control the violence of her kiss.

It was impossible.

Tenzin released Ben as abruptly as she'd taken him, but not before she'd sunk her teeth into his bottom lip, piercing the skin and making him taste his own blood. She shoved herself away from him with inhuman strength. Ben was forced to let her go.

Her lips were bloody, her face was glowing, and her eyes were wild. "If someone comes after you, then I will kill them."

She couldn't blame it on bloodlust this time. She was fully herself, though she wasn't fully in control.

"Tenzin—"

"Don't." Her eyes shifted to wary and guarded in the space of a second.

Ben heard someone waking in the house. Lights switched on.

He stepped toward her, looking her square in the eye. "Tell them to go back to bed. Send them away."

She shook her head.

"This isn't friendship," he whispered. "Maybe you don't know what it is. Maybe I don't either. But I don't want to pretend anymore. You want to know what I want? That's it. I want us to stop pretending."

She faded into the darkness just as Jinpa turned on the low lights in the courtyard.

"Benjamin?" The sweet old woman recognized him and was unfazed by his sudden appearance, shirtless and standing with a bloody lip in the middle of the night. "What happened to your shirt?" She fussed over him. "Come in the kitchen. I'll make you tea."

He let her guide him into the kitchen, but not before he saw Tenzin on the far side of the courtyard, disappearing into the night sky.

"Sorry." He turned to Jinpa. "I needed a book from the library and ran into unexpected company."

"It's fine." She pushed him into a chair. "Sit. I'll get you some gauze for your lip. You have an extra shirt or two in your room." Jinpa looked over her shoulder toward the courtyard. Her eyes narrowed. "Are you alone?"

I am now. Ben cleared his throat. "Yeah. I'm staying in the city right now."

Jinpa knew the score. She raised a single eyebrow, shook her head a little, and turned back to the stove. "When you're ready to go, Mei can drive you back into town. She has a car now."

"Oh yeah?" He closed his eyes, took a deep breath, and prepared to catch up with Tenzin's caretaker. "How's she doing in school?"

"So well. She makes us all very proud. All the boys want to

marry her, but she says no. No boyfriend for her. School only right now."

"That's good. Good plan. Relationships are nothing but trouble."

Jinpa took Ben's chin in her hand and angled his face toward the light. "And how are you, Benjamin?"

He took a deep breath. "Oh, about the same."

14

Tenzin reached the balcony of Cheng's building a few minutes before midnight. She saw Cheng sitting in the corner, smoking a pipe he enjoyed from time to time.

She marched over to him. "Did you send men after Benjamin?"

He raised an eyebrow. "No."

She placed a careful hand at his throat. "Are you sure?"

Cheng was unfazed. "You have blood on your lower lip, Cricket. Is there something I should know about?"

"Ben was followed and attacked by my home."

His eyebrow went up. "Do you really think I'd be that stupid?"

"You can be unpredictable."

Cheng carefully removed Tenzin's hand from his throat and set his pipe on the table. "Unpredictable? Yes. But you are anything but unpredictable when it comes to that man, so I would be an idiot to try to harm him, even if I find him annoying."

They stared at each other for long, silent minutes.

Tenzin didn't see any deception in his eyes. Also, Cheng was right. Coming after Ben would be stupid, and he wasn't.

She backed away from him and jumped up to sit on the edge of the balcony. "Then who?"

"That's an excellent question. Harming your pet human—"

"He's not my 'pet human.'" She glared at him. "Do you really see him that way? Are you so blind? Do you not see his potential?"

"Potential is not reality." Cheng picked up his pipe and drew a long puff. "And I know he's not a pet, but I do enjoy the look on your face when I call him that."

She stared at the reflection of the skyline in the glass. "He says we aren't friends anymore."

"He said he wasn't your friend?" Cheng narrowed his eyes. "I'll be honest, that sounds very stupid. And unlike Ben."

Tenzin swung her legs back and forth. "It wasn't exactly that. He said, 'This isn't friendship.'"

"Oh." Cheng shrugged. "That's quite different."

"How?"

"You know..." Cheng smiled a little. "You've been getting better about reading human reactions—any reactions, for that matter—which is one of the reasons I've put up with your odd relationship with him. I think he's been good for you. But do you really not understand what he's talking about, Tenzin?" Cheng leaned forward. "Do you really? Or are you afraid?"

She stared at Cheng, who was coming far too close to being overly perceptive. "This isn't about Stephen."

"You don't think so? How about Nima? Is it about Nima?"

Tenzin couldn't say anything. A flood of anger washed over her. Anger at Nima. At her humanity. At her loss.

"Nima is none of your business," she said quietly.

His face softened. "You and I would never be what you and

Nima were, Cricket. My heart isn't built that way. But yours was once."

"You don't know how my heart is built. You don't know me as well as you think you do."

"Does anyone know you?"

Nima had. And she was gone. She was dead because she was human, and she'd taken Tenzin's memories with her into the darkness.

And now Tenzin was feeling inexplicable urges to bite Benjamin. She wanted to hurt him and wanted to lie next to him and absorb his heat. He distracted her and made her want things she'd forgotten. It irritated her, like the feel of an insect buzzing around her face. She felt more at ease when she was in his presence, and it made her angry.

You say you want to know me.

I don't think you do.

Her eternally silent heart had beat wildly for a few seconds when she'd seen the two vampires stalking him tonight. The sensation was physically painful.

You don't want to know the things I have seen.

Ben might have thought he had the situation under control, but she'd seen their body language. They weren't going to leave him alive. He would have been dead and gone because he was so infuriatingly *mortal*.

Tenzin hopped down from the balcony ledge. "Ben will be coming back in his own car. Make sure the valets are expecting him. And be thinking about who might want to hurt Ben. It's not my father, but it could be one of your enemies trying to hurt me through you."

Cheng shook his head slightly. "Or we could guess it's very likely that just as the man has allies of his own, he also has enemies. Did you think of that?"

"Of course I thought of that." But she'd dismissed it. Ben's enemies weren't likely to follow him all the way to Shanghai, and they weren't likely to know the location of her home. This was far more likely to have something to do with Tenzin, her sire, or Cheng.

"I'll let the valets know about Ben." Cheng looked up as she walked by. "Did you at least find that book you were talking about?"

She stopped in her tracks. *Shit.*

TENZIN WALKED out of the room and toward the balcony on the far end of the floor. She opened the door, closed it, and floated up to the small room that Cheng had customized for her. It was the only place other than her own home she was willing to stay while she was in Shanghai.

It was only accessible from the air and there was no door connecting it to the rest of the building, only a small hatch nearly invisible to anyone who didn't know what to look for.

Tenzin imagined it had once been a storage area or something similar, but Cheng had finished the walls with calming blue silk wall hangings and carpeted the small room with silk rugs before he blocked up the old doorway.

The single window in the room overlooked the Shanghai skyline. She could see the glowing lights of the Pearl Tower among the dozens of brilliantly lit skyscrapers that dominated the modern Shanghai sky.

There was no bed, but there were low, comfortable cushions, numerous bookcases, and bottles of blood-wine in an ornate wine rack in the corner.

She sat on a cushion facing the window and closed her eyes. If she paid close enough attention, she could hear the rush of traffic outside. Smell the brackish water of the river. She opened the window and called the wind to her, bringing the scents of the city and the night fog into her space.

The air in Shanghai stank of humans, car exhaust, and cooking fires. *Too many humans.* She would be grateful for the emptiness of the ocean.

Tenzin glanced at her black tablet in its thick, vampire-proof case. There was a holder mounted to one wall where she kept the machine, which was equipped with her favorite computer person. She'd met other computer people, but she liked Cara the best. She had a pleasant Irish accent and took orders perfectly.

Ben would sometimes get irritated with Cara, which was completely illogical. Cara did exactly what she was asked, as long as you asked correctly.

"Cara, wake up."

A pleasant computer voice responded. "Good evening, Tenzin. How can I help you tonight?"

"Show me Benjamin's location."

"Which device would you like to track?"

"His American phone." Ben often changed phones, but he usually carried his American one with him because that was the number Giovanni and Beatrice used.

Did he know she was able to track his whereabouts via their household network? Possibly. Probably not, or he would have turned off the tracking like she'd done with her tablet.

"Benjamin's device is traveling at forty kilometers per hour, eastbound on the G50 motorway near the G15 connection. Would you like to see a map of his progress?"

"Yes." Tenzin waited for the small blue dot to appear on the screen, and then she tracked it silently as it steadily made its way eastward toward the Pudong.

Millions of humans died in common road accidents. Thousands every day. Just because he'd never had a road accident didn't mean he wouldn't have one. If anything, it made it more likely to happen.

As she watched the blue dot make its way toward her, she thought about Cheng's irritating question.

Does anyone know you?

Sadly, her sire knew her.

Giovanni knew her. To a point.

Beatrice knew some of her stories.

And Benjamin...

You say you want to know me.

I don't think you do.

You don't want to know the things I have seen.

Benjamin saw what he wanted to see.

Mei's car pulled into the garage under Cheng's building, and Ben held out cash to Mei. "You have to take it."

The girl's fair skin flushed. "I told you it's too much."

"You woke up in the middle of the night to drive me over an hour into the city, and now you have to drive back. Take the cash. Buy gas for the rest of the school year. Go do something fun with your friends. Buy a hundred coffees."

"Ben—"

"Just..." He kissed the top of her head. "Take the cash please?"

She tucked it into her purse. "I'll give it to my grandmother."

"You better not." He got out of the car and opened the back door to grab the books he'd found in the library. One was the Italian glass book Tenzin had been talking about. The other was a museum publication on a Tang dynasty shipwreck. Both might be useful.

Ben bent down smiled at Mei. "Drive safely please. And text me when you get home. I put my number in your phone."

"Okay." She gave a little wave. "See you later, Benjamin."

The blue compact turned around in the parking garage, and one of the valets held the traffic for Mei as she turned back onto the city streets and headed home.

Jonathan greeted him at the elevator. "I don't suppose you found the book she was looking for?"

"I'm the nephew of Giovanni fucking Vecchio." He held up the blue-jacketed hardback. "Of course I found the book."

"Excellent." Jonathan pushed the button for Ben's floor. "I see you cut your lip."

"Shut up, Jonathan."

The vampire looked amused. "Just another..." He gestured to Ben's face. "...addition to the collection, I suppose. The rest of the bruises were healing. You were almost back to your normal visage. How common that would be."

Ben looked at the pale, acerbic vampire. "Do you practice being an asshole in the mirror? Or does it just come naturally?"

"Quite naturally, I assure you."

Ben got off on his floor, leaving Jonathan in the elevator. Tenzin would get the message that he had the book. If she wanted it, she could come to him. Until then, he was going to take a shower, ice his lip, and get something to eat since he'd never gotten his noodles.

Was he going to think about the fact that she'd kissed him and then taken off again? No, he wasn't. Ben was beginning to understand something. Something that had been clarified in the dark courtyard after she'd run away for the second time. Or was it the third?

Tenzin was just as confused as he was.

They'd had one relationship, and now it was turning into

something else. What it was, neither of them knew. But he'd be damned if he was the only one willing to bend.

Both of them would have to bend, or they would break.

Ben stripped off his clothes and got in the shower, washing away the blood flaking off his torso and avoiding his lip until he could get ice on it. Most of his wounds from the last job in Italy had healed, and he only had a few greenish-purple bruises left. He could probably use a shave, but he didn't feel like it. The darkening beard on his chin would hide some of the bruising from Tenzin's kiss, so he'd leave it for now.

He got out of the shower and glanced at the clock. Only two in the morning. She'd be awake.

She's always awake.

Ben wondered if Tenzin had taken any time to meditate since she'd left New York. Normally she needed quiet solitude at least a few days a week in order to keep steady. That could have been part of the edge he'd been feeling from her.

He wrapped a towel around his waist and walked out to the small kitchenette in his room to grab ice from the freezer. He filled a plastic bag and pressed it to his swollen lip just as he heard the knock on the connecting door between his and Fabia's room.

He unlocked his side and opened it. "Hey."

She glanced up and down. "Where were you?"

"I went to Tenzin's house with her to look for a book about Italian glass."

Fabia glanced at the ice on his lip. "So how was that?"

He lifted the ice from his mouth. "She bit me."

Fabia opened her mouth. Closed it. Then she shook her head and walked to the table. "I'm going to stop trying to under-stand your relationship."

"That's kind of my plan too." He pointed to the table. "Might want to look at that. Tenzin's pretty sure that there would have been glass ingots among the cargo Arosh sent to her sire."

Fabia flipped open the book. "It would definitely fit with trade goods coming from the Middle East and India during that era, so let's hope so."

Ben walked into his bedroom and grabbed a new set of clothes from his suitcase. "Why would glass be good?"

"Very easy to find. Wood rots unless it's covered by the right sediment. Metal degrades unless it's gold or silver. Porcelain lasts, but it can break and fall apart. Glass ingots are very durable. Archaeologists have found glass ingots in underwater wrecks going all the way back to the Bronze Age. Seawater is pretty vicious to most materials—though these are colder waters, so that's good—but glass lasts for centuries with very little degradation."

"So it'd be easy to see in photographs?"

"Not photographs." She made a frustrated sound. "I won't know what equipment we have until we get on the ship. Have you heard anything about what we're dealing with?"

Ben walked out of the bedroom clothed in a fresh T-shirt and a pair of jeans, rubbing a towel through his hair to dry it. "Cheng partnered with a university, so we're probably dealing with pretty fancy stuff. This isn't going to be a bare-bones operation. Imagine the nicest equipment you can get. What do you have?"

Fabia ticked off the options on her fingers. "Side-scanning sonar for sure, which would kind of be like an aerial photograph. You use sound to map the sea floor before you send divers down. Other than that... There are a range of devices at every price range, but most of them involve mapping with sound waves of one kind or another."

"Yeah, I don't want to know. But we can plan on the university crew probably doing all that, right?"

Fabia nodded. "I imagine Cheng will have them narrow the search site, but looking for glass ingots is a good idea. They're likely to have been in the same location as the sword."

Something was tickling the back of his mind. Glass. Degradation. Damascus steel.

"Just how gnarly is this sword going to be when we find it?" Ben asked.

Fabia frowned. "Gnarly?"

"Messed up. Rusted. It's Damascus steel, and steel rusts."

Fabia's expression fell. "Yes. In fact, steel rusts much more quickly in saltwater than freshwater. I'm afraid what we're likely going to find—if we find the sword at all—is the hilt only. The blade isn't going to be in any recognizable condition."

Ben shook his head. "So we're going through all this to find a gold hilt? Maybe? What's that going to do?"

"What do you mean?"

"I mean the Laylat al Hisab—this legendary sword—is gone. Why are we even looking for it?"

Fabia shrugged. "Even the hilt would be a symbol."

"Of a peace that's already there. I don't see Arosh attacking Penglai Island anytime soon."

"But that's not the point. Can the gift of a sword actually end a war? Of course not. But the symbol is important."

He muttered, "Maybe it's a symbolic sword for a symbolic peace."

She sent him a sideways glance as she flipped through the book. "Don't disregard symbols, Ben. Civilization was built on symbolic gestures."

He tossed his towel over a chair. "Symbolic peace. Symbolic gestures," he grumbled. "If you want to look at the symbols here, maybe the shipwreck was a symbol that Arosh and Zhang were never meant to be at peace. They're both ancient vampires, but they're from different cultures. Different mindsets."

Arosh was from the Mediterranean. Zhang was from China. He was from New York. Tenzin was from... probably some Neolithic archaeological site in Outer Mongolia. He had no idea. She probably didn't either.

And he was probably reading way more into this than he should have.

Fabia said, "I think the fact that both Arosh and Zhang have committed so much time and attention to this is proof that—whether they say it or not—they both want peace. They want the same things, even if the rest of the vampire world may seem to be against them."

Yeah, he was definitely reading way too much into all this. "I need to get some sleep."

Fabia closed the book. "Me too. Can I take this?"

"Tenzin hasn't come for it, and if she does, I'll tell her you borrowed it. Want to go to that maritime museum tomorrow?"

"Yes, definitely." Fabia tucked the book under her arm. "And you better not sic Tenzin on me. Just because you're not afraid of her doesn't mean that the rest of us aren't terrified."

"Please. She's a bird." Ben opened the door. "A small, vicious, angry bird. With claws."

Fabia paused at the door, looked up at Ben's mouth, and held the book out to Ben. "You know, on second thought, I'll look at it another time."

15

Three days later, they boarded the *Jinshé* just after dawn. It was a seventy-meter research vessel built in Shanghai and used primarily for climate research. It was also equipped with enough geophysical mapping equipment to make Fabia clap her hands in delight and was used jointly by several universities for large expeditions.

Ben didn't know how much Cheng had donated to the university, but it must have been a lot. He and Fabia stood on the dock, staring at the vessel. "This is way more boat than we need, right?"

Fabia nearly ran toward the gangplank. "I'm not going to complain!"

"Of course not, you archaeology nerd."

It was a clear day with bright blue skies and a warm wind whipping across the coast. On board were twenty academics from the university maritime archaeology research team along with a full crew of humans Cheng had brought from his own operation, Ben, Fabia, and four hidden vampires.

"And a partridge in a pear tree," Ben muttered.

Ben walked around the ship, familiarizing himself with the

layout and introducing himself to crew members. The university team was pleased to know the American spoke Chinese and could act as an interpreter for Fabia, whom they were all eager to meet. Many of them hadn't participated in an on-site survey before, and Ben spent most of their time during the day acting as Fabia's translator.

Their rooms on the boat were simple but sufficient. While all of the university crew had to share cabins, he and Fabia—and all the vampires, of course—had private rooms. His was the size of a college dorm room with a padded L-shaped ledge that ran along the far wall, providing a long, narrow bed while the short end of the *L* made a bench under the window. A desk sat on the opposite wall, and a small galley and bathroom were located on either side of the door.

There was a large galley on the main deck and a spacious dining area. Additionally, there were two conference rooms, one above and one belowdecks, closer to the diving equipment and remote-operated submersibles.

There was a game room and a library. There was even a pool, though Ben didn't know why that was necessary on a boat that would be going through one of the most beautiful oceans in the world.

Ben retired to sleep right after the midday meal, knowing that the *Jinshé* wouldn't reach the wreck site until the next morning but wanting to be prepared for a full night's work. He was on vampire hours now.

The sky was dark outside the window when Ben woke, and he immediately flashed back to the weeks he'd spent on the freighter years before. His bed had been too short, and he'd woken every morning with aching knees. This ship smelled better, was far more comfortable, and his knees weren't aching.

And, of course, Tenzin was in his quarters.

He didn't hear her. Didn't see her. Didn't know how she

always managed to pick his locks without tripping his alarms. But he knew she was in his cabin before he even opened his eyes.

"Did you forget everything we discussed about boundaries?" His voice was rough with sleep.

"I didn't forget the conversation. I'm just ignoring it."

Of course you are. He cleared his throat. "What are you doing in here?"

"Aren't you going to yell at me and kick me out?"

"No. I'm tired of fighting with you." *And I'm tired of missing you.*

"Good. You shouldn't fight with me."

"Sometimes that's easier said than done." He wouldn't open his eyes. He refused. If he kept his eyes closed, this might all be a dream.

"You called me a miserable little troll once. Do you remember that?" Her voice sounded amused.

"Do you remember trapping me on a freighter for weeks to escort your container of gold back to Long Beach?"

Tenzin had tricked him into being a courier for a treasure cache they'd transported from Xinjiang. He'd made good money off the job, gotten a lot better with Mandarin, and discovered what it meant to live off rice for six weeks.

"That typhoon in the Pacific was not my fault."

"Are you sure?" Could Tenzin cause a typhoon? Probably.

Her sigh was long and tortured. "I'm so bored."

He kept this eyes closed. "How is this my issue?"

"I'm usually not bored when we're working together."

"Not true. You're very easily bored," he said. "And you're easily amused. You're on a boat, Tenzin. Go swimming."

"I hate the water."

"Then go fly where no one can see you. Play dodge the seagull. Haven't you been tormenting Cheng? Isn't that enough for you?"

She didn't answer him.

Good. Ben didn't really want to hear about Cheng, even if Tenzin wasn't sleeping with him. Not that she slept.

She asked, "Are you going back to New York?"

"What?" Ben opened his eyes and saw her sitting on the bench under the window. Her legs were folded underneath her, and she stared at him with unwavering focus.

She asked again. "Are you going back to—?"

"I heard you the first time."

"And?"

"I don't know."

She nodded.

"Are you?" he asked.

"I planned to go back."

"When? A year? A few years? A dozen maybe?"

"I hadn't decided yet."

"That's kind of the problem, Tenzin." He propped himself up on his elbows. "I don't have a dozen years to hang around waiting for you."

"You could."

"No." He sat up all the way and rubbed his eyes. "I couldn't. Even if I was a vampire, I wouldn't sit around waiting for you to make a decision for twelve years."

She leaned her head against the wall and stared at the ceiling. "You're impatient."

"No, I'm just not a sucker."

A fine line formed between her eyebrows. "I don't know what that means."

He stood and walked to the small basin where he'd set his bottle of water before he'd fallen asleep. The sky was dark outside his porthole, but the air was still warm. He bent down and washed his face before he dried it and then grabbed his water bottle.

"That means that everyone humors you and lets you do whatever you want because they're all afraid of you, Tiny." He gulped down two swallows of water. "I'm not afraid of you. Maybe when I met you I was too young and stupid to realize you were scary. Maybe it's just something about who we are together. But I'm not scared of you."

"Not everyone is scared of me," she said. "Giovanni isn't. Cheng isn't."

"Yes he is." Ben chuckled. "Don't kid yourself, Tenzin. Cheng is as scared of you as anyone is. You both pretend he isn't so it doesn't get weird." He drank more water. "And Giovanni isn't actively scared of you, but he still gives you a wide berth."

She snorted. "He does not. He criticizes me all the time. Remember when he forced me to take that sociopath test?"

"Remember when you *killed one of his servants?*"

"That was three hundred years ago, and that man was a violent bully and a cheat. He needed to die."

"But you didn't explain that to Gio, did you? You just killed the guy and then let Gio stay mad at you for ages. He never took revenge for that. He never even challenged you."

"That doesn't mean I scare him."

Ben leaned against the small sink. "No. But Giovanni would never let his guard down around you. As much as you both care about each other, there will always be a wall."

"And you don't have walls?"

"Of course I do." Ben took a deep breath. "You just keep flying over them."

She floated over and hovered in front of his face. She didn't speak, she just stared at him. Ben took another drink of water, not once looking away.

"You're not scared of me," she muttered.

"Nope. If you wanted to kill me, you would have done it years ago." He reached up and tapped her nose. "Miserable little troll."

"My father isn't scared of me."

Ben cocked his head. "No?"

"Why would he be scared of me?" She narrowed her eyes. "He's my sire. He's more powerful than me."

"Fear isn't always about power." Ben sat down on the edge of the bench, took off the T-shirt he'd been sleeping in, and rifled through his duffel bag to find a new one. "Why did you come in here, Tenzin?"

"Because I'm bored." She flopped down on his bunk, lifting her feet in the air and touching her toes. "Why aren't you insisting on uncomfortable conversations? We've been talking for ten minutes, and you haven't brought up Puerto Rico once. Or what happened at my house."

Well, he couldn't say she wasn't direct.

Ben pulled on a fresh T-shirt. "I haven't brought any of that up because I'm thinking."

"About what?"

"Don't you know?" He looked up and stared at her until her eyes met his. "Hasn't your supernatural vision shown you exactly what I'm thinking right now, Tiny? Haven't you seen it all? Known it all? Doesn't history just repeat itself over and over?"

She narrowed her eyes. "Not always."

He slid over to her, on his knees beside her while she lay in his bed. "You can't see what I'm going to do, or what I want, because as many years as you've been alive, there's only ever been one *me*. There will only ever be one me."

Tenzin kept her eyes on him; her body was frozen.

The cabin was silent, but it wasn't. The boat creaked and rocked. Waves licked against its metal skin, and in the distance he could hear crew members shouting at each other while Korean pop music played in the galley.

"You want to know what I'm thinking about?" Ben reached over and tucked a piece of Tenzin's hair behind her ear. "I'm thinking about whether the conversation we *need* to have is one I even *want* to have."

"I see."

"I doubt it." Ben stood and held out his hand. "Come on. I think it's time to go up to the deck. Kadek will want to brief us on what they found today. Hopefully that will help with the boredom."

"FROM REPORTS we've received from our people"—Kadek was pacing in the conference room—"we know the search area is still undisturbed. Since we determined that the site could be the wreck of the *Qamar Jadid*, we've had immortals in the area watching it."

Johari, Fabia, Tenzin, and Cheng were sitting around the huge table, looking at the giant map Kadek had put up on the wall.

"Cheng told Zhang that the wreck was *likely* the *Qamar Jadid*," Ben said. "So don't we already know where it is?"

"Not exactly." The stocky vampire continued pacing. "The wreck was found by a fisherman. He identified it as a dhow. Said it was relatively intact. There were a number of other clues that led us to believe it might be Arosh's ship, but we don't know the exact site. The fisherman didn't have a GPS. He tried to find it again, he said, but he couldn't. He could only give us a general area. That is what we've been watching."

Ben asked, "And no ships have stopped?"

Kadek said, "Human ships have passed through, but none of

them have stopped or shown any interest in this particular reef. The area isn't popular with divers."

Cheng said, "The greater search area is spread over a number of miles. There are reefs and other formations, so we'll be using the sonar on this ship quite extensively at first." He looked at Johari. "I'm not sure if you'll be able to narrow that down or not."

Johari raised her eyebrows. "I've never done this specific kind of work before. I will be able to move the earth when we find the site—more delicately than the human equipment could —but I'm not sure I'll have a better sense for where debris is located or not. There's too much water."

Fabia raised her hand. "I think the best idea is still using sonar to get a better picture once we're in range. Using that, the university crew and I should be able to get a better map of where we need to concentrate our attention."

Cheng asked, "What about the submersibles?"

Tenzin was sitting between Ben and Fabia. "Are those the robots? Do they have remote controls? I could operate the robots."

"The submersibles are robotic," Fabia said. "I haven't looked at them yet, but in water this shallow, we'd probably use them as backup for divers. They can record video of any excavation, which creates a better record to study."

"Have you been out there?" Ben asked Cheng. "Personally?"

Cheng shook his head.

"So we don't know that this isn't a completely unrelated dhow that has no connection to Arosh." Ben looked across the table at Johari. "Wasn't the dhow the most commonly used ship during the ninth century for trade?"

Johari nodded. "It was. And while they usually kept close to shore, they could be blown off course by storms, just like any other ship. The water in this strait is not particularly deep. If there are reefs, they could have easily caused a wreck."

Ben said, "Cheng, you said that you had other evidence that it was connected to Arosh. Can I ask what it was? Why are you and Zhang so sure that this ship is the *Qamar Jadid*?"

"Because the fisherman found this." Cheng reached in his pocket and flipped a small orange block toward Ben, who caught it and opened his palm.

"That's the *Saēna,*" Cheng said. "The seal is carved carnelian. That icon is an early form of the Persian firebird."

Ben looked at Tenzin. "Is this Arosh's seal?"

She looked over his shoulder. "It's one of them."

Cheng said, "Arosh would have set that onto any boxes or chests that came from him. Sealed with wax and that carved seal pressed into the wax to prove that nothing had been tampered with."

Ben held the carved stone up to the light. The carnelian was striped and the finish was dull, but the image of the winged creature surrounded by two crescent moons was intact. "How sure are you, Tenzin?"

"Very sure," Tenzin said. "I knew the minute Cheng showed me. There may be other dhows that wrecked along the Chinese coast in the ninth century, but as far as I know, none of them would be carrying Arosh's cargo."

Ben flipped the seal back to Cheng. "Sounds good to me."

Fabia kicked his foot.

"Ow." Ben frowned. "What?"

"You didn't let me see it," Fabia said. "Don't assume."

Cheng smiled and passed Fabia the small bar. "You may keep it as long as you like. Take pictures, in fact. I don't think anyone has recorded it properly, and I'm sure both Arosh and Zhang would appreciate a professionally prepared report since they're the ones paying the bills."

Fabia smiled. "I'd be happy to do that." She turned to Ben and stuck her tongue out.

"Are you twelve?" He couldn't stop his smile.

"No, but you have no idea how many times I've wanted to do that to old, pompous professors over the years. This job is going to be so much more fun."

Ben saw Tenzin from the corner of his eye. She was watching Fabia with an expression he couldn't interpret. It wasn't calculating. It was... thoughtful.

He shouldn't be worried about Fabia, but when Tenzin turned her attention that closely to anyone, it warranted caution.

What's going on in your head, Tiny?

16

Tenzin did go out and play dodge the seagull when all the humans went to sleep, which was a game she'd never heard of before Ben had mentioned it. It was far more entertaining than she'd anticipated. Then she flew back to the coast and estimated how far she would be from her Shanghai house. A little over three hours if she was guessing correctly. Not bad, though if dawn was too close, she'd have to find shelter.

It felt good to orient herself over the vast ocean. It was necessary to know where your exits and safety points were at all times.

"How many exits? Come on, Tiny. How many exits?"

"None!"

"Wrong. Kick out the front window. One. Break open the side doors. Two and Three. Moon roof. Four. In this small a room, four exits are more than enough."

She'd been terrified riding in a truck for the first time. Bumping over narrow mountain roads in a vehicle that leaned and creaked. He'd forced her to ride with him since she'd dragged him to the far western edge of China on slightly false pretenses. She'd only gone along with it to assuage him. Then she realized that a vehicle could be a death trap, even for a vampire.

He'd reassured her by playing that silly exit game. Tenzin couldn't remember the last time someone had reassured her. She was not someone others reassured. She was the one they looked to when they were afraid.

And now she and Ben had been hired for a job that Tenzin might hate even more than the one they'd done in the caves in Puerto Rico. Water was not her friend. Diving in the ocean for amusement was not a thing she did. Large bodies of water were lovely to fly over but otherwise to be avoided at all costs. Being wet, even in rainstorms, sapped her strength and made her amnis less powerful.

So why had she taken this job? She could have told Cheng it was his own headache. She could have refused her father. She'd refused both Cheng and Zhang many times before.

You knew you could draw him in.

He can't resist a challenge.

It's the one thing you can give him. A challenge.

She ignored the annoying voices and started back toward the ship. Whatever had possessed her to take the job, she was committed now. She would find whatever was left of the Laylat al Hisab and return it to her father.

The Night's Reckoning.

She had to smile. It was an utterly extraneous gesture, giving a sword to Zhang. Somehow, that made Tenzin want it even more.

Also, she'd told Ben the truth. The vampire world had experienced upheaval before, but nothing in over a thousand years had shifted the power balance like Saba's takeover in the Mediterranean. The Council of the Ancients in Alitea was an unknown quantity. The last thing that anyone needed was Arosh and Zhang being pushed into a territorial war.

Of course—in Tenzin's opinion—certain parts of Central Asia could do with Arosh's firm hand, but no one had asked her, and she wasn't going to delve into politics. She'd been the general who had commanded her sire's forces in the past, and she had no desire to lead an army of immortals again. Especially not wind vampires.

Ben had an American saying that perfectly described the experience: *herding cats.* Commanding an army of wind vampires was like herding cats.

She spotted the lights of the *Jinshé* in the distance. It was easy to identify because of the helicopter pad, but descending to the ship put the scope of the undertaking in perspective.

Cheng was correct. It was a very big ocean.

Though the wreck was located in a busy shipping lane, they were still the only ship for miles around. They'd had to obtain all sorts of permits and licenses from the human government, but Cheng and the university had taken care of that. The only thing Tenzin had to worry about was finding her father's sword.

The search site was spread out over miles, and within that, they had to find the probably scattered wreck of a twenty-meter dhow that—in the best-case scenario—would be covered in sediment, otherwise very little would have survived. Their hope was that the ship had sailed during the tail end of monsoon season— when storms were less likely to hit—and had been struck by an unexpected typhoon. No one knew for sure if that was why the *Qamar Jadid* had never reached Penglai, but that was the suspicion. If a typhoon was to blame, the boat could have been covered in mud and other sediment kicked up by the storm, only now revealing its secrets a thousand years later.

According to Cheng, they *wanted* mud and sediment, other- wise the frame of the ship would be entirely gone and the treasures it had transported would have drifted away or been too greatly degraded.

The seal was hopeful. Kadek's survey was hopeful.

But they could use all the luck they could get.

Lying on her back in the warm breeze of the East China Sea, Tenzin stared at the moon, the full, round moon shining bright over the ocean and drowning out the light of the stars.

When she'd been alive, the moon had been her talisman. It was the guardian of the mother, bringing milk and blood in turn. Milk to feed the children and blood to seed new life. Like a woman's body, the moon was always changing. It was the heavenly breast. The rounded belly. The lover's cheek.

Tenzin stripped the clothes from her body and lay prostrate to the eternal moon.

Do you remember me?

The wind and the moon were silent.

I have not changed in many years.

Tenzin whispered an old song, one she hadn't thought of in centuries. A lilting chant she'd sung when her babies cried.

Do you remember me, Mother? My children have all left me. They are so long dead, they are the earth that fed the roots of ancient trees. My belly does not swell with life. My body is frozen as it was, and my eyes have seen centuries the way mortals see years.

The moon's soft light bathed her in the darkness, but the wind said nothing.

Do you remember my voice?

Finally she heard an answer on the wind, but it wasn't the holy song of a celestial god. It was the song of a girl carrying a baby on her hip, bouncing him by the cooking fire. It was the song of the wind through the grass and a stream trickling over rocks. It was the song of goats bleating, ponies stomping in the snow, and women and men laughing together.

Tenzin opened her eyes and held her breath, willing away the pain that speared through her shoulder. *Don't curse me with memories; I've given them to another.*

But the moon and the wind had gone silent again.

She turned back to the blinking, manmade lights of the ship and descended. It was getting late, and she was starting to see sunlight growing on the horizon. When she landed on the deck, she pulled her tunic over her body and retreated to the dark hold she'd claimed.

She didn't look for the moon again. Those searching for buried treasure in the daylight would have to find their own luck.

BEN WOKE WITH A HEAVY HEART, and he didn't know why. His body wasn't aching. His face felt better than it had in days, and he felt well rested. He glanced at the clock. Just past noon.

That meant he'd gotten over eight hours of sleep, which was hardly the norm.

So why did he feel so *heavy*?

He swung his legs over the side and sat up, stretching his body and rubbing his eyes. The boat's movement wasn't overly noticeable; it had been just enough to lull him into deep sleep the night before. When he looked out the window, he saw nothing but deep blue sea. He glanced down and checked the wake. They were moving, but slowly.

Ben smiled. "They're scanning for the wreck."

He rushed through his morning shower and headed up to the bridge. Kadek's day captain pointed toward the stern, so he followed the railing back until he heard Fabia talking to someone with a heavy Chinese accent.

"Do you see?"

"Yes." It was Fabia. "This is great. I can't believe how good this sonar is."

"The very best," the other voice said. "Most modern."

"I can see that."

Ben turned the corner and saw an open door and a room surrounded by windows. Laptop computers filled a table in the center of the room, but a dozen people were huddled around one screen, buzzing excitedly in Mandarin.

"Hey." He grinned when he saw Fabia's face. "Good news?"

"Ben, you won't believe how good this equipment is." Fabia motioned him closer. "We've already narrowed in on a reef where we think the ship probably is based on the fisherman's reports."

"Oh yeah?" He popped his head over the crowd and looked at the screen, which was various shades of gold, yellow, and black. "A reef?"

The scientist who'd been speaking with Fabia said, "If we are certain this is a ninth-century vessel, it is very likely that any exposed parts of the wreck would be covered in coral at this point. This is good."

Fabia said, "Coral will preserve the overall shape, though it might keep us from documenting some of the artifacts. So it's a mixed blessing."

There was more chattering about archaeological details he didn't try to understand, but Ben was encouraged. It sounded like locating the wreck might take closer to days than the weeks he'd been fearing.

He found his mind tripping to Tenzin. She didn't sleep. Where was she? Did she have space to fly around, or was she stuck in a tiny cabin and going crazy? He hoped she'd been meditating, but something about her demeanor didn't reassure him.

Not your problem.

He had to stop obsessing over her mental state. Tenzin didn't need him hovering over her, nor would she welcome it. She'd survived for thousands of years without him. She'd be fine.

"Fabia, can I talk to you for a minute?" He nodded to the back where a broad balcony looked over the stern of the ship.

"Yes, of course." She dragged herself away from the other scientists, her eyes still glued to the sonar screen.

Ben ushered her outside.

"What's up?" she asked.

He kept his voice low. "Can you tell how much they know about... all this?"

Fabia wrinkled her nose. "It's so hard for me to tell because I don't speak Mandarin. As far as I can tell, they think Cheng is an eccentric rich man. I don't know if they think he's a treasure hunter or a benefactor. They know I'm working with him, so they might be cautious around me."

"Right." Ben nodded. "I mostly want to figure out how forthcoming they'll be with us. I don't want anyone hiding information that we might need because they think we're looters wearing suits."

"I don't get that impression from them, but again, I don't speak the language. They've been pretty open with me, as much as language permits, and they seem to accept my credentials. They know I'm an archaeologist and art historian—I've been showing them pictures from my previous jobs—so they've mostly asked about that."

"Got it." Ben needed to keep an eye on the humans. He didn't need curious scientists poking around a ship full of vampires, and he also didn't need them getting scared off. "I'm starting to understand why Tenzin wanted me on this job."

"Why?"

"Because she needed a professional juggler," he muttered.

"Keep the vampires hidden. Assuage the humans' curiosity. Keep the job on track and make sure no one gets exposed or eaten."

Fabia nodded. "Those are all very necessary tasks, and I'm sure you'll be successful."

She was tapping her foot.

Ben smiled. "You really want to go back to the archaeology-nerd room, don't you?"

"Please."

He waved her toward the door. "Go. Keep your ears open for anything a professional juggler might need to be concerned about. I'm going to go check with Cheng's human crew on the bridge."

"Okay!" Fabia ran inside and immediately back to the sonar screen where another group *Ooooh!* had just arisen.

Ben walked around the top-deck conference room and back toward the bridge to check in with Kadek's first mate. The man had been introduced as Mr. Lu, and that's how Ben addressed him.

"Anything I need to know about?"

Mr. Lu answered in English. "I mapped out a search grid with the captain before sunrise, and we are sticking to it. The team from the university seems to think they have already iden-tified the wreck site, but we will cover the whole grid before we return."

"Have you been on salvage operations before?"

Mr. Lu nodded.

"So... do you agree with the university team?"

Mr. Lu shrugged. "I am not an archaeologist."

Ben lowered his voice. "No, but I'm guessing you probably know what you're doing as well as they do, or maybe more."

The corner of Mr. Lu's mouth turned up. "The site they identified was one I noticed as well." He pointed to a monitor near the wheel. "The resolution on this isn't as good as theirs, but I agree with them."

"Could you tell anything about the condition?"

"There's some coral, but I am guessing it's mostly sediment, which is good."

"That's what I hear." Ben looked around the bridge. "Anything you guys need? Any messages I should pass along?"

Mr. Lu shook his head.

"Any questions?"

"We have been warned about the forward hold, so my men have been avoiding it, but there are noises that the humans are probably going to notice." Mr. Lu glanced at him from the corner of his eye. "Does she sleep?"

Ah. So that's where they'd put Tenzin. "No. She doesn't sleep. Does the forward hold have access to the deck?"

"You have not been on ships very much, have you?"

"I was on a freighter once."

"This isn't a freighter." Mr. Lu barked directions at one of his men, and Ben felt the ship begin to turn. "Yes, the forward hold has deck access. I was told that was necessary for her. My men can avoid that area, but there are supplies stored there. We will need access at some point."

"Let me know when you need them, and I'll go with you. I really don't think you'll have an issue, but she may not like being disturbed, and I can distract her if she gets..." How to put it? "...cranky."

"Understood." Mr. Lu glanced at Benjamin again. "If there is nothing else, Mr. Vecchio—"

"Ben." He lifted his hand in a wave. "Nothing from me. I'll let you know tomorrow if there are any messages."

"Thank you." He glanced at the sonar screen. "We will be finished with the search grid by nightfall. Unless I see something unexpected, I anticipate they will dive tonight."

17

Ben followed a low thumping sound to the forward hold of the ship. He paused at the hatch, wondering if she was doing what he thought she was doing.

He unlatched the door and pushed it open, leaning against the hatch as he watched her.

Tenzin didn't sleep during the day like most vampires. It wasn't her age—Ben knew of other ancients who slept during daylight—it was just a quirk of her blood. According to Tenzin, she'd slept once and dearly missed the oblivion it brought, though she didn't miss the lack of control.

Beatrice, whose sire had shared blood with Tenzin, didn't sleep much either. Much of both Beatrice's and Tenzin's days were comprised of finding ways to shut off their minds. Meditation helped. Beatrice practiced transcendental meditation, yoga, and tai chi for hours. Music also helped. When Tenzin was at home, she used a loom and could spend hours on end weaving. Ben had come to recognize the rhythmic thump of her weaving comb like a kind of white noise in the background of his days.

She wasn't weaving this afternoon; she was playing basketball, or some version of it. The overhead of the hold wasn't two stories like their loft in New York, but there was a low hoop attached to one end of the compartment, and the familiar rubber ball thunk, thunk, thunked against the metal deck. Tenzin was standing at one end of the hold, bouncing the ball before she lifted it and sent it flying with her amnis.

Unsurprisingly, the ball flew through the air and hovered over the hoop before falling directly into the basket.

"That's not how you're supposed to play." Ben couldn't stop the smile that pulled at the corner of his mouth.

"I know that." She flicked her wrist and the ball rolled back toward her. "But if I play it the other way—"

"You mean the right way?"

"I don't subscribe to your narrow definition of sport." Tenzin waved her hand in a careless gesture. "What is the fun of playing if you don't win?"

Ben hopped over the threshold of the hatch and intercepted the ball before it reached her. He dribbled in place before he walked slowly toward the small half court that had been marked on the metal deck with duct tape.

"The fun is knowing you might not win." He stood at the foul line and lined up his shot. "You practice and practice more until you're the best you can be." He tossed the ball toward the basket.

The basketball flew in a perfect arc, nearly reaching the hoop before it stopped in midair, spun around, and flew back toward Tenzin.

"And you still might not win." She caught the ball and tucked it under her arm. "What's the point of playing the game if you can't control the outcome?"

He walked toward her, shoving his hands in his pockets to keep from touching her. She was wearing a pair of soft black leggings and a fitted tunic that bared her arms. Her skin nearly glowed in the dim light of the hold.

"Controlling the outcome would spoil the game."

"So the game is chance. Like dice or stones."

He shook his head. "It's not chance."

Tenzin bounced the ball. "Humans think that work and preparation can predict outcome."

"Can't they?" His uncle was a fan of both preparation and work. "Talent aside, the player who practices the most has an advantage."

"Who decides who may practice and who must work?" Tenzin said. "It's not always the players. What about players who don't have the same facilities? What about a player whose diet is poor, so they cannot build muscle mass as well as a better-fed player?" She bounced the ball toward him and Ben caught it.

"So you're saying who wins in basketball is whoever has the most advantages going in?" Ben bounced the ball back. "It has nothing to do with hard work and talent?"

"I'm saying that success is built by many factors, and most of them are out of yours or any mortal's hands." Tenzin bounced the ball twice before she sent it back to Ben.

"Chaos theory."

"In a sense." Tenzin walked toward the basket and threw the ball in a perfect arc, just as Ben had taught her. A foot above the rim, the ball stopped. "I practiced throwing the ball—"

"Shooting a basket."

She raised one eyebrow. "I practiced shooting a basket exactly as you taught me. I practiced many hours."

"And?"

Tenzin flew up to the basket and floated next to her ball. "I thought about strength and speed. About angles and velocity."

"And your shot will go in." Ben walked across from her. "Look at it. It's perfectly lined up."

Tenzin kept her eyes on Ben. She pursed her lips and blew

as she released the ball. The basketball, thrown slightly off trajectory from her tiny breath, hit the rim, bounced back and forth three times, tottered on the edge for a fraction of a second, then fell to the floor, never making it through.

"You blew on that," Ben said. "Doesn't count."

"It's the only thing that counts," she said. "A butterfly flaps her wings and all your preparation and work mean nothing."

"So what's the point of playing the game?" Ben asked, thinking about the perfect arcs he'd seen when he first walked in. "What's the point of any game?"

"The point," Tenzin said, "is winning."

"And if you can't win fairly, cheat?"

She landed on her feet. "Cheating implies someone else makes the rules, Benjamin. And I make my own rules."

"And expect everyone else to follow them too?"

"No. I expect people *not* to follow them. That's what I prepare for. The inevitability of human selfishness. A tornado of butterflies."

"Human selfishness? Not vampire?"

She smiled. "Our selfishness is the most human thing about us."

Ben's head hurt. "I hadn't planned to stay down here debating the ethics of cheating in basketball. But just be aware that the ball can be heard outside and at some point they may ask you to stop so they can listen. Please don't kill them when they do that. Also, Kadek's human crew will need to get at those pallets eventually." Ben nodded to the stacked provisions near the rear bulkhead. "So if I come with some extra humans, don't assume they mean harm."

"Fine." She walked back to the ball and started bouncing it again. "How goes the search?"

"They think they found it. Or at least part of it."

"The university people? Or Kadek's people?"

"Both I think."

She nodded. "Good."

"Who is Kadek?"

"He's a pirate, like Cheng. Only... not like Cheng. Cheng is mostly legitimate now."

"Mostly?"

She looked up. "Kadek takes care of the parts that aren't in the mostly."

"So he's a pirate?"

Tenzin shrugged. "Are we looters if we find a thing that belongs to a vampire and retrieve it, even if we ruin an archaeological site? Your Italian girl might say yes, but we've done that plenty of times. It all depends on how you look at these things. Kadek has done many recoveries. Much of Cheng's original wealth came from ships like the one we're looking for."

"Shipwrecks, you mean?"

"It's an easy way of picking up wealth when you're young and ambitious." She looked at him from the corner of her eye. "Not all of us have rich uncles."

"Ha ha. And Johari?"

Tenzin's demeanor immediately changed.

"Watch her," she said. "I don't trust anyone who changes loyalties like she has."

Ben scoffed. "She had to, Tiny. She was dying and she took Saba's cure. What else was she supposed to do?"

"Die." Tenzin tossed the ball toward the basket. It sailed through the hoop with a whisper. "That was her fate."

"Harsh."

Tenzin cocked her head. "We aren't really immortal, you know. Am I supposed to be horrified that she might only have lived five hundred years instead of a thousand? Or more?"

"So you wouldn't take Saba's cure if you had to?"

"Never." Tenzin rolled the basketball back to her feet.

"Denying my element would be denying who I am. But Johari did take Saba's cure, which means she values her life above anything else, which means we cannot trust her."

"But she belongs to Saba now."

Tenzin passed the ball to him. "Do you think Saba is an ally of anyone but herself?"

Ben frowned and squared his shoulders to the basket before he released the ball. "I thought... I don't know. I thought Saba was one of the good guys. Giovanni—"

"Giovanni didn't tell you she was good, did he?" Tenzin's laugh made Ben bristle. "Trying to define any of us as good or bad is difficult. With Saba, it is impossible." She flew to the ball and grabbed it.

Boy, you are faithful. Few know such strength so young. Go to sleep. Your time is not now.

She'd told Ben that once when he was young. Saba, the mother of vampires. Saba, the oldest of their kind. Saba, most ancient of earth vampires. She'd been the most beautiful woman Ben had ever seen, appearing out of the shadows like a goddess. She'd healed his uncle, brought peace to his aunt, and disappeared in the night like a thief.

In those moments when she'd spoken directly to Ben in the hall, she'd made him feel special. Like maybe everything in his life—the abuse, the violence, the loss—it had all been for something bigger than himself. That he could be—that he *was* something more.

Ben said, "If she healed Johari and sent her here, she must want to find the Laylat al Hisab too. You're being cynical."

"Of course I am." She flew up and perched on the edge of the basket. "Johari might be trustworthy, but there will be no assumption from me. Watch her and wait. Don't suppose that we are all working toward the same goal, Benjamin."

IT WAS nightfall the next time he saw her. They had returned to the wreck site that afternoon and performed something Fabia called a multibeam sonar that provided a better 3-D map of the wreck site before they dropped anchor. And while Fabia and the university team had plans to send down the submersible robot the next morning with some student divers, Cheng and Kadek had other plans.

The wreck was located on a relatively shallow shelf where a reef jutted upward from the ocean floor. The wreck of the *Qamar Jadid* appeared to be lying on its side, its bow overtaken by coral, with much of the wreck buried in sand or sediment.

Cheng and Kadek weren't as trustful of the sonar as Fabia and the professors were. They wanted to see for themselves. They stripped down to the skin on the top deck, leaving on nothing but short trousers. Cheng had a net bag attached to his waist like divers used to collect specimens, a slim black knife tied to his leg, and a determined expression.

"We'll go down first." He plaited his long hair into a single braid. "Before the humans. We'll be able to tell for sure once we're down there."

Johari asked, "Do you want me along?"

Kadek shook his head. "We're not moving anything tonight. We're just going to get the lay of the ocean floor. You may be comfortable in the water, but you don't draw strength from it like you used to. Save your energy for the heavy lifting."

Ben watched Johari's reaction, keen to discover any ulterior motive since Tenzin had warned him, but he detected nothing. Not agreement with Kadek's order. Not impatience. Not disappointment. Wherever she'd gotten her poker face, it was professional level.

The two water vampires dove over the edge of the boat and

disappeared into the darkness of the night sea.

Ben strolled over to Fabia, who was stationed at a mobile monitor of some kind, and bumped her shoulder. "Hey."

"Hey." She looked up. "You weren't around today."

He glanced at Tenzin, who was watching the surface of the water intently. "I was around."

Fabia followed his eyes. "Ah. And how is that going?"

He shrugged. "It's nothing. We're avoiding anything disagreeable right now."

"Avoidance. The strategy of every healthy relationship," she muttered. "How long do you think you can continue that?"

"Me? Maybe to the end of this job. Her? Probably another thousand years."

"She is such a vampire." Fabia picked up the microphone and spoke into it. "Kadek, can you hear me?"

Ben frowned. "You have a radio on him?"

"Uhhh." Fabia fiddled with some knobs. "Kind of? It's something we're trying. He can't speak to me because he doesn't have any air down there, but he has a camera and a waterproof whiteboard. The camera is not part of the Nocht system, so we will see if it holds up or if he shorts it out."

A flickering image came on the screen.

"Look at that." Fabia pointed to the screen. "Ben, are you seeing this? That's the ship. It's definitely the ship."

Ben leaned closer to the monitor. "It looks like coral and rocks."

It was hard to see anything in the darkness, but the narrow glow of Kadek's flashlight illuminated craggy shapes and shadows.

"No," Johari interjected. "I can see it. The coral is only on the surface." Her hand moved to the monitor, but she drew back when the picture began to flicker. "What did I do?"

"You're fine, you're fine." Fabia waved Johari's hand away.

"Just stay back and look." She clicked on the walkie-talkie again. "Kadek, can you point the camera down a bit?"

Ben asked, "What are you looking for?"

"That." She pointed to the screen. "Look at where it's lying. It's not sand; it's sediment. At least half that ship looks like it has been preserved in sediment, which means the oxygen won't have had a chance to work on it, which means we're looking at intact artifacts."

"That's excellent news." Ben looked at Tenzin. "Is sediment enough to protect steel from decaying?"

Tenzin looked skeptical. "Is it *magic* sediment?"

"No, Tiny, I'm pretty sure this is just normal sediment."

"Then no."

"Great."

Fabia brought the walkie-talkie up again. "Kadek, can you swim the length of the hull? Give us an idea how big it is?"

A few moments later, Kadek began to move through the dark ocean, the light and camera held in front of him, and Ben, Tenzin, Johari, and Fabia were able to see the full scope of the site they would be in charge of excavating.

"You know, twenty meters doesn't seem all that big when you're talking about it," Ben muttered. "But in reality—"

"It's massive," Fabia said.

"Is it longer than twenty meters?" Johari cocked her head. "Twenty-five perhaps?"

Fabia spoke into the walkie-talkie. "Kadek, how long is it? Over twenty meters?"

A hand moved in front of the camera and gave a thumbs-up.

"More than twenty-five?"

The hand turned the thumb down.

"Okay," Fabia said. "So between twenty and twenty-five meters, which fits what the sonar measured. I mean, the bow is pretty wrecked, so there's no way of measuring for sure. There could be a large amount of cargo in that space if enough of the hold was buried, but we won't know for some time. We're fortunate that it is not in deeper water."

Tenzin took a long breath. "How careful do we have to be?"

"Very careful," Fabia said. "This wreck is vital to creating a narrative of trade between the Middle East and Asia. It's part of the maritime Silk Road and—"

"Fabi, as soon as rumors about this get out," Ben said, "there will be looters every day and every night." He put a hand on her shoulder. "This isn't a flooded city or dock. This is literally a treasure ship, and everything in that cargo hold is probably valuable."

She made a small noise that sounded like a wounded puppy.

Tenzin said, "The only advantage we have is that we have both human and vampire crews. We'll need to work as fast as possible."

Johari concurred. "A find like this is like blood in the water for our kind. Unknown treasure that is less accessible to humans and without any official provenance? This wreck is worth tens of millions of dollars in immortal circles. That's a conservative guess."

Ben tried to reassure Fabia. "We're going to preserve as much as possible. We're going to give the university team access as long as we can. We're going to take tons of pictures and document everything. But the priority on this trip isn't preserving a shipwreck, it's retrieving a valuable artifact for its rightful owner. Don't forget that."

She bit her knuckle. "Ben, there's so much here. The ship, the artifacts, even the position and location of the wreck tells a story."

"And you and the university crew will be able to read that story. But we're taking the cargo out. We have to. Otherwise, it'll all be gone."

18

Cheng ran a towel over his hair, drying his long locks as Tenzin lounged on the small sofa in the captain's quarters, which had been retrofitted for vampire safety. She stared out the broad windows he could enjoy when he wasn't locked in the compact and lightproof stateroom he'd had customized for the journey.

Cheng definitely had the best view. Tenzin supposed those were the perks of paying for the expedition.

"I just received a message from Jonathan." Cheng tapped on the tablet lying on his desk. "Your father is at your house."

Tenzin sat up. "What?"

"He alerted Jonathan to his presence but said he wouldn't be coming into the city so..." Cheng shrugged. "There's not much I can do about it. We agreed centuries ago that your village west of the city is neutral ground between my territory and Penglai."

"Technically, all of Shanghai is in Penglai's territory."

The look Cheng sent her was unamused.

Tenzin lay back down on the couch. "I'm just saying..."

"You sound so American now."

"Do I?"

"Yes." Cheng stripped off his wet pants and put on a pair of dry trousers. "This job is going to be more complicated with the university crew."

"Meaning you can't just grab what you want and take off with it?"

"We never destroyed things." Cheng's voice was sharp. "Those ships are the graves of my allies and enemies. I do not desecrate the resting place of the dead."

"But neither were you going to let their riches rot beneath the waves." She swung her legs back and forth. "I don't suppose you set up a square-meter grid over it and meticulously documented every shell you found?"

"No, we did not." He pulled on a shirt and walked over to sit next to her. "Why is your father watching us, Cricket?"

"I don't know." She was tempted to fly back and find out but wasn't sure she wanted to spend the day in the same house as her sire. He always wanted to talk about her life. It was annoying. "I can call Jinpa."

"Jinpa won't know." Cheng lifted her feet and rubbed her ankles. "You didn't ask him to come?"

"Does that sound like something I'd do?"

"Maybe if you didn't trust those you were working with..." Cheng gripped her ankles in firm hands. "Don't you trust me?"

She pulled her feet back and sat up slowly. "Exactly as much as you trust me."

The corner of his mouth turned up. "So Zhang is there for his own purposes, whatever they might be."

"Maybe he just wants to get some peace and quiet from court life. You know he gets annoyed with how visible he is there."

"Tell the truth. If he weren't so committed to peaceful regional government, he'd go back to the plains, wouldn't he?"

"Of course he would. Why do you think he's been trying to convince me to take his place on the court for so many years?"

"You would never."

"No, and he knows it." She walked to the windows that overlooked an expanse of ocean. She could see the lights of the nearest island in the distance. "How are you going to keep others away? There's no chance we haven't been spotted."

"I have my people stationed on the islands around us," Cheng said. "They're keeping an ear out for rumors, and I've sent couriers to both Sina in New Zealand and Jimmu in Okinawa. Jimmu has already sent word back to Jonathan that he respects our claim on the wreck since we're working for Zhang. I haven't heard from Sina yet."

"I don't know her, but guessing by her reputation, she won't be interested."

"Agreed. She's too focused on what's happening with the humans in her area right now." Cheng followed Tenzin to the windows. "No one wants a war."

"Wrong," Tenzin said. "There are some who would welcome it. Some old powers who are hungry for the chance."

"Does that include you?"

Tenzin took her time answering. "A hundred years ago, I would have said yes. I was hungry for anything violent then."

"I remember."

"But not now. There are too many things that interest me in this world. I'd rather spend my time exploring it. There is YouTube now. You can learn anything from anyone. Anywhere in the world. And video games. I very much like video games. Especially the racing ones."

"You are a strange, strange creature, Cricket."

"Also, I really want to get to my mountains."

Cheng smiled. "Are you ever going to show me your secret retreat?"

"No."

"I think you would show the human."

Tenzin contemplated the idea. Would she take Ben to Tibet? Would she show him her refuge and the valley where she was worshipped as a god? The last human who had lived there with her had been Nima. The last vampire who had been welcome was...

No one. Though her father had found her there, he was not welcome. It wasn't his place.

Would she take Benjamin to her valley? Maybe.

She nudged Cheng. "Show me. I know you didn't come back from that wreck empty-handed."

Cheng couldn't suppress the smile. "Who, me?"

"Pirate."

He bowed. "I claim that title with pride." Standing straight, he motioned her to a bucket she'd spotted near the door. "I left it in seawater for now."

"Good idea." Tenzin walked over, and Cheng retrieved the bucket, placing it on his desk.

Tenzin peered inside. "Is that a storage jar?"

"A broken one." Cheng reached in and turned the jar on its side. "Look."

The bucket probably held ten gallons and the storage jar filled most of the space inside. An intact jar wouldn't have fit, but this one was broken in half, and what she saw inside spurred the familiar flutter of anticipation in her stomach.

"Cobalt glass," Cheng said. "Look at the quality."

Mixed with the silt-like sediment in the bottom of the storage jar were dozens of small, fine glass bottles in brilliant blue with gold decorations on the outside. They had probably once contained perfumes, incense, or spices. Most of them were in pieces, but half a dozen were intact.

"Some of them still have stoppers in them," Tenzin said. "The glass itself—"

"Priceless." Cheng ran a finger along one curve of a delicate bottle. "They were likely packed in straw or sawdust. It must have cushioned the pieces when the ship went down. Over time, the mud covered them and kept them in place."

"This was sitting on the bottom of the ocean?"

"We saw the edge of the storage jar sticking out of the wreck. We took it just to see."

"There will be more," Tenzin said. "Much more. If the wreck was covered like this, what will the condition of the treasure be?"

"If it's covered like this or even better," Cheng said. "Good. Very good. But it will all depend on how it was packed and what was packed. Anything wooden would be most vulnerable. Spices from India, cobalt dye from Persia, and incense from East Africa—which is what much of the shipment would have been —would be gone. But the glass... The glass will be preserved. Fine metals will survive. Gemstones and metalwork will survive. And Arosh would have sent all that."

Tenzin didn't even try to stop the smile. "This has been a good night."

BEN WOKE EARLY the next morning, eager to look at the wreck for himself. He'd learned how to dive in Italy with Fabia when he was in high school. He'd never enjoyed the feeling of claustrophobia the mask produced, so he didn't dive for fun. But he did know how to do it competently.

Fabia was already suiting up with four university divers when Ben arrived.

"I see I'm not the only one who's excited."

Fabia's grin filled the room. "Professor Chou will be sending down the submersible with us to record everything. It has the best cameras. But we'll be setting up reference markers by hand." She motioned to the divers. "This is... Let me see if I can remember. Lin"—she pointed to a young woman who waved —"and Delun. They're the most experienced divers on the team. And then there's Meili—did I get that right?" The other woman Fabia pointed to nodded. "And... Je-on?"

"Jian," the last man said with a smile as he strapped on his dive tanks. "Just call me Jon. Like the American name."

"Jon has the best English," Fabia said. "And we'll all be connected by radio."

Jon responded to Ben in Mandarin. "It is nice to meet you, Ben. Fabia says that you speak good Mandarin?"

"I do," Ben said. "Well, I speak like a sailor, but that's a long story."

All the student divers smiled.

"We'll have to hear it another time," Lin said. "We are so excited to see the ship now."

"Sounds great."

"You are ready," Fabia said. "So don't wait for us. I'll wait for Ben to suit up and we'll meet you down there."

Professor Chou stepped forward and spoke quietly to the four students who were diving. They all listened intently, but Ben couldn't make out what they were saying.

Fabia proceeded to hand Ben a wet suit and then shoved him toward a small compartment with curtains drawn over the windows. "Go. Get ready. I'm dying to get down there."

"Oh goodie. A wet suit." Ben was glad he wasn't sore anymore. Nothing was worse than trying to get on a wet suit if you were sore. Come to think of it, even getting one on when you weren't sore wasn't a picnic.

He stripped down to his underwear, turned the suit inside

out, and carefully worked it up his body. By the time he was ready, he could hear Fabia and Professor Chou outside, giving directions to Jon, who'd taken the submersible down with the university team.

"A little to the right," the professor said. "Yes, there." He flipped the microphone off. "This site is so impressive. I wish we had more time."

"Looters," Ben said, walking out from the closet. "I can feel them circling like sharks. On a site this shallow, we're going to have to work quickly. If you can get more divers, I'd call them."

The professor nodded. "I agree. I may have a colleague in Shantou. Will Cheng approve of my contacting him?"

Ben didn't want to step on Cheng's authority, but he figured he'd been hired for a reason. "Call him," he said. "The more divers, the better. Just emphasize that confidentiality is key and this is... an unusual job."

The professor nodded. "I have other colleagues I would contact if this was not a delicate situation, but my friend in Shantou will not ask uncomfortable questions if I reassure him."

"Thanks, Professor." Ben began checking the regulator that would make sure he didn't suffocate fifty feet below the surface of the ocean. "Fabi, you want to double-check my stuff?"

She walked away from the monitor. "How old are you again?"

"Old enough not to be overconfident."

It took over half an hour for Ben to prepare everything, but soon he and Fabia pushed away from the boat with the diving flag flapping in the cool breeze.

She pressed the button on her microphone. "Can you hear me?"

Ben pressed his. "Yes. Can you hear me?"

She gave him a thumbs-up before she dove under the surface.

Here we go.

Ben sank below the surface into the heart of the brilliant blue sea. Lower and lower he went until he could see the divers beneath him. All four were working around the wreck, securing brightly colored stakes in the ground and taking measurements with tape.

What had looked eerie and mysterious from the sonar pictures and the nighttime flashes from Kadek's camera looked far less ominous in the daylight, though it was no less fascinating.

"Are you going to be able to interpret for me while we're down here?" Fabia asked.

He pushed the microphone in his diving mask. "If we keep it simple, it should work. Are we all on the same frequency?"

"Yes."

The professor's voice came through the speakers next to Ben's ear. He spoke in Mandarin. "Excellent work. We are placing markers right now. We are limited on time, but we work this one like any other job. Be deliberate. Document everything."

Ben didn't know exactly what their method was, but all four divers were busily working in different corners with clear purpose. They were measuring and documenting on white-boards attached to yellow frames. They motioned back and forth to each other, mostly ignoring Ben and Fabia, who swam around the wreck, surveying it from a distance before they swam closer.

"It's remarkably intact," Fabia said. "Ninth century?"

"Yes."

"It looks much newer." She swam closer. "Arab dhow. I want analysis on that wood. I'm so curious where it was made."

"Wouldn't Arosh know?" Ben asked. "I mean, this isn't exactly like a normal dig. He probably has a manifest of everything he sent, along with the names of the captain and crew. We already know the name of the ship. We can check with him or Zhang if we really want to know, right?"

Fabia shook her head. "You know, sometimes I go months and months at a time forgetting how strange my life is, and yours is even stranger."

Ben smiled. "I'm just saying I know people."

They approached the ship, trying to stay out of the way of the university divers. Fabia pointed to a long line of coral stretching away from the wreck. "I think that's the mast."

"Let's go closer." Ben swam alongside the line of the broken mast. While the ship lay on its side, the hull was mainly intact. It appeared as if the entire boat had simply turned over, lain down, and sunk. "Storm maybe?"

Fabia touched her microphone. "Maybe. We are quite far from established shipping channels. The dhow would have been closer to the coast. If it was blown off course because of a storm, it could have been overcome by waves."

"Throwing the cargo overboard wouldn't have been an option," Ben said. "Not when you're carrying an offering from the Fire King."

"You're right." Fabia swam closer. "The top deck is completely rotted away down to the surface of the sediment. The hull is breaking apart. I can see storage jars inside."

Ben had researched as much as he could about Arab-Chinese trade in the ninth century, as well as the history of the dhow. The cargo on the wooden sailing vessel would have been packed in widemouthed storage jars and stowed belowdecks with ballast weights and provisions for the journey. The crew would have lived in tents or small shelters on the top deck, pulling into harbor at regular intervals to exchange goods, trade, and buy new provisions.

Dhows generally didn't stray far from the coast, so they

didn't have to carry provisions for weeks at a time. The amount of trade goods they could carry was impressive. While overland routes were limited by time and the amount a camel could carry, maritime trade was far more efficient.

Dangerous, but efficient.

Ben took everything in, noting the depth of the sediment, the condition of the jars he could see through the hull. He didn't have a camera with him, and he wasn't about to borrow the cameras of the university crew, but he noticed something almost immediately.

Something he didn't want to say over the radio.

"I wonder how many men died on this ship?" Fabia asked.

Ben swam toward her. "According to Cheng, the *Qamar Jadid* would have had ten crew members, but there's no way of knowing for sure. He said at least eight would have been needed to sail it."

"Ten men who never saw land again," Fabia said. "Ten men who died here."

Ben floated over the wreck in silence, thinking about those men. Thinking about drifting away in a watery grave, only to have humans and immortals arrive a thousand years later to salvage the cargo you sacrificed your life trying to deliver.

In the silent water, he felt their ghosts surrounding him.

19

Ben decided that the official discovery of the *Qamar Jadid* deserved a party, both for historical significance and to kill some of the tension building on the ship. Cheng's human crew needed to socialize with the university people, who needed to at least meet the vampires—even though they wouldn't know they were vampires—so they wouldn't become overly curious.

He planned the party for six thirty so the vampires could join the humans who weren't on duty. Some of the crew would be at their posts on the ship and some of the university crew would be monitoring the cameras they'd set up around the wreck.

Cameras that would be shut off as soon as the vampires started working, of course.

Meanwhile, Ben and Fabia were doing their best to decorate the mess hall with limited resources.

"I can't believe you ordered a cake to bring on the ship."

Ben set the frozen sheet cake on a table to defrost. "I've learned a few things about people in my many years on earth, Fabi. And one of them is that even enemies will sit down together if there's cake involved. If you add champagne into the mix, you get even closer to world peace."

"And you don't think we should save all this for the end of the project?"

"Absolutely not." They needed warmer relations now, before the university people realized that the vampires had already confiscated some of the artifacts.

He'd noticed the blank spaces immediately. There were naturally occurring blanks in any artifact retrieval. Things moved. They broke. If they were in the ocean, they drifted away.

But then there were new, obvious blanks.

Obvious blanks where storage jars—or the remains of them —should have been. The rest of the humans might not notice, but Ben had been around vampires too long not to be suspicious.

He wasn't happy about it, but he was trying not to overreact. Maybe Tenzin had an explanation for it. After all, it was her father's shipment. It would all belong to Zhang in the end.

But Zhang and Cheng had agreed to let the university to document the recovery. That was the only reason he'd been able to convince Fabia to come along. If the vampires were looting, that made Ben a liar.

Perhaps one of the storage jars contained artifacts that were evidence of vampire existence. That had to be it.

Fabia held up a long loop of bright blue rope. "I could print out some pictures from my phone and hang them on this for a banner?"

"Great idea." He was doing his best to draw a mural on the giant whiteboard at the end of the room. It was difficult when you only had black, red, and green to work with.

"Did you say the galley was making a special dinner?"

"Uh... kind of?"

"Kind of doesn't sound very special."

"They're making noodle soup."

Fabia narrowed her eyes. "Like the noodle soup they serve us every night? Don't get me wrong. It's good, but—"

"*Not* like the noodle soup they serve us every night." Ben turned around. "They are adding beef to the soup."

"Fancy!" Fabia grinned. "I can't complain. I was on a dig in graduate school where we had the same food at every meal. The food here is pretty decent, especially for a ship's kitchen."

"What was the food?"

"What?"

"The one you ate every meal?"

Fabia grimaced. "Boiled potatoes and gravy."

"And...?"

"That was it. No meat. No vegetables. Potatoes and meat gravy. I think it was beef, but I can't be sure."

"That... doesn't sound good."

"Yes, that is why I decided to concentrate my archaeology work in Italy." She winked at him. "We feed everyone well. Even poor students."

"Well, tonight we get noodle soup with beef." Ben bowed dramatically. "And cake."

"No champagne?"

"Beer will have to do."

She whispered, "And you can come to my room later for wine."

"Done."

By the time they finished with the mess hall, it looked... well, not beautiful. But festive wasn't too far of a stretch. There were bright ropes with pictures pinned to them all around the room, and Ben and Fabia had rounded up all the games they could find aboard the ship. Many decks of cards, one mahjong set from Mr. Lu, two boxes of dominoes, and a battered chess set borrowed from Professor Chou.

Around six o'clock the professor and his students began to come in, followed by some of Mr. Lu's crew. Since entertainment on board research ships was limited, the games were immediately picked up. Ben was pleased to see the crew and the research team mixing.

"This is good," Fabia said, sidling up to Ben with a beer in her hand. "You were right."

"I often am."

Cheng was the first vampire who showed up. He grabbed a beer, nodded appreciatively at Ben, and sat down at the mahjong table with some of his crew and two of the university team. A few minutes later, one of the crewmen stood and walked to the corner to turn the radio on. Immediately the sounds of Chinese pop music filled the room.

Johari and Kadek were the next vampires to arrive. The room went quiet for a moment when Johari walked in. She was the only African on the boat, and she was stunningly beautiful. Ben suspected she often made people stop and forget what they were saying.

Ben walked over immediately. "Can I get you a drink?"

Kadek abandoned them to join a table playing cards.

Johari looked around the room, then back at Ben. "Yes. I would like a beer."

"Of course." He drew her away to one of the tables with fewer people and pulled out a chair facing the room for her. Nothing that would expose her back to the room. The corner table would allow both of them to survey the crowd of humans and vampires.

Johari sat while Ben walked to the counter to get a beer from one of the tubs the galley crew had set out. It was a mixture of local beer with a few miscellaneous imports thrown in. Ben grabbed her a local brew.

"Thank you." She lifted it and waited for Ben to raise his own drink. "Cheers, Benjamin Vecchio."

"Cheers." He took a drink. "How do you say *cheers* in Zanzibar?"

Johari smiled suddenly. It was the first time Ben had seen it, and he couldn't deny it took his breath away. Her smile was like the sun breaking over the horizon.

She said, "I don't drink beer in Zanzibar."

"Ah."

"But cheers in Swahili is *afya*. Properly, it would be *maisha marefu*, which is a wish for long life—"

"Appropriate with your family."

Her smile softened. "No doubt. But with your friends you would say 'afya.' Which is like... good life. Good day."

He lifted his beer again. "Afya."

She clinked their bottles together. "Afya, Benjamin."

"Ben."

"Ben." Johari took the time to look around. "I cannot remember the last time I was invited to a party."

"So Alitea isn't the party capital of the Mediterranean, huh? That's it. I'm canceling the cruise."

Johari lifted an eyebrow. "It is not a vacation destination. My sire is very focused on bringing order to the eastern Mediterranean. She has little patience for festivities at the moment."

"I hear she makes a great cup of coffee though."

Johari swallowed a mouthful of beer. "Truly?"

"I've heard rumors. She *is* Ethiopian. Have you had Ethiopian coffee? It's amazing."

"That is true."

Ben saw Tenzin slip into the room. She approached Cheng

but didn't stop at his table. She slid over to Kadek's table and spoke to him for a moment. Made polite faces at the humans there. She grabbed a beer and leaned her back against the wall, searching the room. When she locked eyes with Benjamin, the hand holding her beer fell to her side. Her eyes went to Johari, then back to Ben.

Ben looked back at Johari. "So, was your first sire from Zanzibar?"

Johari's face froze.

"I'm sorry," he added quickly. "I didn't mean to be rude. It's none of my business."

"He was." Johari set her drink down carefully. "I am not offended. The question was unexpected. Once I traveled to Alitea, no one asked me about my past life. I was Saba's daughter. That was all."

"That's... I don't know what that is." He saw Tenzin leave the room from the corner of his eye. Which was fine. He wasn't going to chase her.

"It was not unexpected." Johari's eyes followed Tenzin. Looked back at Ben. "In a way, I was grateful for the opportunity to begin again. My sire is no longer living, and my brother did not agree with my seeking Saba's cure. So I have no family left at my home."

"I know that feeling."

"Do you?" Johari glanced at the door. "What is your relationship with Tenzin?"

Ben's eyebrows went up. "That's direct."

"You asked me a direct question. I was responding in kind."

Ben took a long drink of beer. Then he took another. "My relationship with Tenzin is... complicated."

"I see."

"I'm not sure—"

"Genuinely. I do understand." Johari picked at her beer

bottle. "I became a vampire because my lover was a vampire. That is the reason I chose this life."

"You did?" Ben blinked. "Where is he? Did he—?"

"He's still in East Africa." She kept her face neutral, but her fingers destroyed the label on her beer bottle. "We were together for many years, but we never mated. I didn't understand many things about this life then. Eventually we went our separate ways."

"I'm sorry."

She frowned. "It is the way of things, Ben Vecchio. A human lifetime is one commitment. An eternity is another."

Something in his chest hurt. Physically hurt. "Yeah."

Johari nodded. "I believe the purpose of this party is for us to meet the humans, correct?"

"Yes. Just don't refer to them as 'the humans' if you can help it. Makes it a bit less conspicuous."

"Then I will leave you and meet some of them." She stood. "I believe most of them have stopped staring now. I enjoyed our conversation, Ben Vecchio."

"Thanks. Me too."

Johari nodded and took her leave, approaching Cheng's table where he, a sailor, and two students were playing mahjong. Cheng stood and added another chair to the table so she could sit down.

Ben stood and tossed his empty beer bottle in the trash. He walked by Fabia, bent down, and said, "Don't forget to serve the cake."

"You're leaving?"

He pointed at the overhead speakers. "Getting some quiet. I'll probably be back, but for now I'll leave you in charge."

Fabia glanced at the door, then back at him. "Uh-huh."

"Don't make that face. I'm going out for air."

She cocked her head. "I guess that's one way of putting it,

considering she's—"

"Shut up." He stood and walked away. "Like I said, don't forget the cake."

Ben walked down the passageway and up the stairs, looking for fresh air and quiet. The fact that he found Tenzin perched on the railing when he arrived on the top deck was purely a coincidence.

"Hey." Ben waved a hand.

"Hello." She glanced at the lit windows. "It is a nice party. Gavin would be proud."

"I try."

She nodded and looked back over the wreck. "Are they working tonight?"

"I'm sure they will once the humans go to sleep."

"And you?"

He raised an eyebrow. "What about me?"

"Did you go down to see it today?"

"I did."

"And what did you think?"

He tapped his foot and looked over the water where the crew had set buoys to mark the rough perimeter of the ship-wreck. "Uh... it's a big waterlogged ship with lots of dirt and coral on it and theoretically some shiny stuff underneath all the dirt and sand."

She smiled. "There's shiny stuff. Trust me."

"Part of me just wants to dig in and damn the historical significance, and the other part of me wants to stay away completely. Usually when we go after stuff, it's just you and me on our own. We have a client. We have a goal. And we just go for it and make our own rules. This feels so..."

"Regulated."

"Exactly. And neither of us is a fan of rules."

"My father is a fan of rules," Tenzin said. "You should trust

Cheng. He's done many salvages like this. The Laylat al Hisab will be with the cargo."

"I'm sure you're right." Since she'd brought it up... "Speaking of the cargo—"

"We should dance." She hopped off the railing and walked to him.

Ben blinked. "I... What?"

She looked up with wide eyes. "Don't you hear it?"

He turned his head toward the open windows of the mess hall and heard the strains of "What a Wonderful World" drifting through the air.

He couldn't stop the smile. "There's a Chinese cover of this song?"

She stepped into his arms. "Ben, there is a Chinese cover of every song."

"Not every song." He put his arms around her. It felt easy. Friendly. Like it had been before everything changed.

"If there's not a Chinese cover of a song yet, give it another year," Tenzin said. "YouTube never sleeps."

"Maybe that's why it's your natural ecosystem."

Her eyes went wide. "You're right!"

Ben laughed and spun her around. The words were different, but the melody was the same. "Do you remember the first time we danced to this song?"

"In Venice?" She danced back into his arms and laid her head on his chest. "I remember. I remember everything."

His heart ached. "Do you?"

"With you? Of course I do."

Did that make it worse? He couldn't tell. He couldn't think. And for one night and one dance under a beautiful full moon, Ben didn't want to.

20

After the enjoyable night with the humans, the three diving vampires decided to take the rest of the night off. The party had produced an ebullient mood that spilled over the entire ship. Once again, Ben was proven right.

Cake. It was magic.

Cheng and Tenzin recruited some of the night crew and followed Fabia's directions, setting up the saltwater tanks that would be necessary to preserve artifacts until desalination could commence at the university. Kadek and Ben wrote out their own diagrams and survey maps of the wreck so Johari would know what she would need to do and where to focus once they started removing artifacts.

Ben went to bed a few hours before sunrise, eager to get some sleep so he could make another dive the next day, but he had a hard time relaxing. His mind was bouncing between the wreck and the crew. Between Johari's story of heartache and Tenzin reminding him about Louis. He kept replaying their dance in the moonlight. Over and over again.

There was something he'd forgotten. Something he'd meant to bring up, and then it slipped away...

"Speaking of the cargo—"

"We should dance."

Oh. Damn.

Ben sat up and his ebullient mood fled. "Nicely done, Tiny."

Of course she hadn't been feeling sentimental. Of course she wasn't reminiscing about Italy or their past. Tenzin didn't reminisce. She had sensed a subject she didn't want to talk about, and she'd dodged it by playing on his feelings.

Typical.

The realization turned his memories of the previous night bitter, but once again he'd have to get over it. It was Tenzin; he should have expected nothing less.

He'd bring up the problem with the cargo first thing in the morning. God knew she had nothing else to do during the day. Tenzin couldn't dive and she couldn't be out in the sun. It was pure luck they were carrying a bunch of academics who were completely focused on their work and ignored the mysterious woman in the forward hold who bounced a basketball for hours on end.

When he finally managed to sleep, Ben dreamed about dancing with Tenzin while sailors sank beneath the surface of the ocean. They danced across the sky while humans thrashed in the water beneath them and lightning struck the mast of a creaking wooden ship. They spun wildly in the tempest like a solitary twisting waterspout, consumed with each other and oblivious to the world around them.

One by one, the sailors' cries grew fainter and the sound of the wind grew. In his dream, their lips met, warmed by pulsing blood and hunger.

Then everything went silent. She floated away from him, releasing his hand.

He fell.

~

BEN DIDN'T WAIT LONG after he woke to confront Tenzin about the missing storage jars. He hadn't slept well, and he'd woken up annoyed that she'd used Louis to distract him from a conversation about the cargo.

He marched to the forward hold and opened the door without knocking. "Hey, Tenzin?"

She was lying in a corner of the room where she'd built a pallet for resting and meditating. Her eyes were closed and she appeared frozen. If he didn't know her, he would have thought she was dead.

"Tenzin."

Movement behind her eyelids.

"You're not sleeping, Tiny. And you knew it was me or you would have met me at the door with your fangs down."

Her fangs were always down. While other vampires could retract them to remain inconspicuous, Tenzin's never completely retracted. Her canines curved back in her mouth like raptor talons. He knew how sharp they were because he'd cut his lips and tongue when he kissed her.

"Tenzin."

Her eyes opened and she rose in one movement to fly at him. Gripping his shirt by the collar, she bared her teeth. "I. Was. Meditating."

Ben's pulse should have spiked, but it no longer did. He'd once been proud of that fact; now it disturbed him. Had he lost the ability to be shocked? Lost the ability to fear? He had become too accustomed to her quicksilver moods.

"I'd apologize for interrupting, but you very expertly distracted me from bringing this up last night, and I'm kind of annoyed."

"What are you talking about?"

"The cargo, Tenzin."

"What?"

"Okay, sure. You have no idea what I'm talking about." He took a deep breath and continued to ignore that she had her nails dug into his neck. "Cheng and Kadek have already stolen some of the treasure."

The corner of her lip curled up. "*That* is why you interrupted me? I knew that already. Cheng showed me the other night."

Ben didn't know what to say at first. "And... you just forgot to tell me?"

"Why do you need to know? It's a stunning collection of glasswork, by the way. If you ask nicely, Cheng might show it to you."

His jaw clenched. "So you're okay with this?"

"Ben, who exactly do you think is paying millions to fund this expedition? Cheng is. If he's going to take a small number of ninth-century Arab glass pieces to recoup his expenses, that is none of your business or mine."

"I believe your sire said he would be getting a generous finder's fee. I don't remember Zhang saying he could help himself to the cargo."

Tenzin rolled her eyes. "Details."

His patience snapped. "I was hired because your sire said he needed someone he could trust to oversee this job, and now Cheng is looting from the same ship he's supposed to be excavating."

"You were hired because I wanted you here, Benjamin. That's the only reason you were hired."

Her words hit him like acid burning skin.

"And Cheng isn't looting," Tenzin continued. "He's taking a commission from a ship he was hired to find and salvage. Do you know why he's doing any of this? It's a favor to me,

Benjamin." Her grip on his collar tightened. "Because I sure as hell am not diving under that ocean to salvage a shipwreck."

"The archaeology team—"

"Is a silk dress on a soldier," Tenzin said. "The archaeology team can document what they want—they're the reason we have this ship and this equipment—but they're not *needed*. Cheng is allowing them access because, despite what you might think, he actually cares about historic preservation and honoring the lost. He is not the bad guy, Benjamin."

The idea of it abraded his skin, but Ben had to admit she was partly right.

Cheng didn't need them. Cheng didn't need any of them.

He needn't have told Zhang about the wreck. He and Kadek could have looted every artifact from the *Qamar Jadid* without telling a soul. He could have put the Laylat al Hisab on the market and sold it to the highest bidder. The hilt alone would be worth millions.

"Why am I here?" Ben asked quietly. "If you didn't need me to coordinate between the two teams—if the archaeology team is just a silk dress on a soldier, as you put it—why was it necessary for me to be here? Why did you even want me on this job?"

"To make sure the humans understand their role."

"Their *role*." He let out a long breath. "I see."

"Do not bring this up to Cheng." Tenzin tightened her grip. "Or Fabia. Or the people from the university. Don't forget for a minute whom you're working for."

The back of his tongue tasted bitter. "I'm working for Cheng now?"

"No, you're working for me," she said. "And my father."

Ben felt small. Insignificant. Not her partner. He had never been her partner. They would never be equal. Maybe in his mind they had been, but never in hers.

Why am I here?

What am I doing?
What am I doing?

Ben stared into her beautiful, fierce eyes. Her grip didn't loosen on his collar, and her fingernails bit into his neck. Two things hit him in an instant, and all the anger, all the bitterness and animosity building in his heart, was washed away in a wave of sadness.

He loved her.

And she would never love him.

She wasn't capable of it. He wished it made him love her less, but it didn't.

Ben brought his hand up and tucked her hair behind her ear before he ran the back of his fingers down the curve of her cheek. She blinked, but her grip didn't loosen.

"You're so beautiful," he whispered. "Even when you're like this, I think you're the most beautiful woman in the world."

Her eyes narrowed, but she didn't speak.

Ben leaned forward and pressed his lips to hers. He slid his arm around her waist and pulled her closer. She froze, but Ben kept stroking her cheek when their lips parted. "I can't do this anymore, Tenzin. I won't do this anymore."

"What are you talking about?" Her voice was scary quiet.

"I mean I'm not willing to spend my life being at your beck and call. I thought we could be something different, but at the end of the day, you're always going to see me as your servant." He brushed his thumb over the small of her back where her shirt had ridden up, enjoying the buzz of skin contact while he still could. "I can't blame you for it. That's just who you are. And you're probably right. What you've seen in your life compared to what I've seen—"

"Benjamin—"

"This is not your fault. I'm not trying to lay blame. This isn't anyone's fault. Or maybe it's mine." He nodded. "It's probably mine."

"I do not consider you a servant."

"Of course you do. You always have. I just had... delusions of grandeur maybe?" He let out a bitter laugh. "You haven't changed. It's been ten years, and you haven't changed a bit."

Her eyes went wide. "You're wrong."

"I don't think I am," he said quietly. "But I'm not a kid anymore. I need to do something with my life. I need to *get* a life that's not yours. So I can't do *this* anymore."

He released her and she floated away, her face frozen in shock.

"I'll finish this job," he said. "You don't have to pay me. In fact, I don't *want* you to pay me. I don't want you or Zhang to pay me. Just... pay Fabia. I'll finish here, then I think I'm going back to Rome for a while. You can take your time getting your stuff from New York."

Her voice was wooden. "You're not going back to New York?"

He swallowed hard. New York was him and Tenzin. New York was their loft and their roof garden and bickering about weapons and training together and going out for noodles at midnight at the Tibetan place she loved. It was dancing when Louis Armstrong came on the radio and drinking whiskey at Gavin's pub after a midnight movie.

Ben said, "I don't think New York is for me anymore."

"You're not making sense," she said. "And I'm going to forget you said this, because you're going to regret it as soon as you walk away."

The smile he forced out hurt his face. "I'm not the one who walked away."

She had no response to that.

"'Tell me to send them away.'" He repeated words he'd

confessed on a rooftop in a drunken stupor. "You know I will. I always will."

Tenzin took a step back, her eyes fixed on his face.

"'Don't do this.'" He said the words he'd begged on the ship before she'd run away again. Run away from everything they'd lived through and survived. "I even said please that time."

All she could do was shake her head.

"Let's have one more dance when this is done, okay?" Ben cleared his throat and shoved his hands in his pockets. "When we find the sword, when we finish the job, promise me one dance before you take off, okay?"

Because if there was one thing he knew, she would always take off.

She said, "You're being foolish."

He backed toward the door. "And you're being patronizing. But I'm no longer surprised or offended by that." He took a deep breath. "It's okay. I'll see you, Tiny."

BEN LOCKED HIS DOORS—HE double set his locks—but he dreamed about her anyway. They were dancing in the alley behind the restaurant in San Juan. The warm tropical breeze surrounded them, wrapping around them as they held each other close. Music filled the air, and her arms were around his neck.

He felt her lips against his throat.

"I love you."

Her fangs pierced his skin and she drank from him. The euphoria was swift and overwhelming. He fell to his knees, weak from the pleasure of her bite. He gripped her harder, melding their bodies together. He gasped for air. He called her name, but she didn't release him. He felt the cobblestones under his knees.

"*I love you.*"

He gasped her name. He cried for more. He would give her anything. He would give her everything.

The cobblestones dug into his back. Blood dripped from the wound at his neck. He was bleeding everywhere. Blood leaked from his pores. It fell like tears from his eyes.

"*I love you.*"

TENZIN STARED at the churning wake behind the ship. She perched on the top railing near the radio equipment and the antennae for the bridge. The sun had set an hour before; Ben was sleeping somewhere. Kadek, Cheng, and Johari had started the recovery of Zhang's cargo.

"*I can't do this anymore.*"

He was a foolish, foolish human, and she'd have to be gracious when he realized how wrong he had been. She'd been wrong too. He wasn't ready. He wasn't nearly ready for the plans she had made for them. He would learn. He would come back. And she would forgive him.

Eventually.

"*You can't see what I'm going to do, or what I want, because as many years as you've been alive, there's only ever been one me.*"

He had surprised her. That didn't happen very often. She took to the air. She wanted to check on her father and her house. The rest of them could manage without her for one night.

Flying from the ship to the shore, she emptied her mind and allowed the air to fill her senses. She was surrounded by it, buoyed by the elation of space and the swift currents of wind. Even a rainstorm over Hangzhou didn't slow her down.

"You haven't changed. It's been ten years, and you haven't changed a bit."

"You're wrong."

That stupid, *stupid* man! Why were males such sentimental fools? Her sire. Giovanni. Cheng. All of them ruled by their hearts. Didn't they realize the moods of the heart shifted more swiftly than the wind?

"You never change."

The memory of another fight burst into her mind, and Tenzin stopped in midair, seized by the pain of memory. Nima had been in the garden and she had been weeping. Her eyes were red and her nose was congested. Tenzin had thought it was from illness. It wasn't.

"You never change." Nima's voice wasn't angry anymore. It was different. Softer.

Defeated.

"I am a vampire; I cannot change."

"I'm not talking about the outside, Xīngān. I am talking about who you are. Your mind and heart. I cannot spend eternity with someone who will never change."

"You would rather my love for you change like the wind? Like one season turning into another?"

Nima shook her head. "I will change and you will not. Then the person you loved will be gone, and you will leave. I will be alone. For eternity, I will be alone."

But she *had* changed. She had changed after Stephen was killed. She had changed even more when Nima died. And knowing Ben...

They were wrong. All of them were wrong.

Tenzin made it back to Shanghai in less than three hours. It was some of the fastest flying she'd ever done, and she didn't remember half of it. It was as if part of herself had moved through the air while the other was lost in memory.

You were.

You are.

You will be.

The whispers at the back of her mind were quiet, but they grew louder the more she thought about the past, which was why she did not think about the past. She thought about the future. She had made plans that included Benjamin. For now, those plans would be put on hold.

Don't think of it.

For now, she would focus on the job at hand, finding the Laylat al Hisab. Bringing peace to Arosh and Zhang and staving off a conflict she could feel brewing across the Old World.

She landed in the courtyard of her house and saw her sire sitting at a table, talking with Jinpa and drinking tea. He looked up and smiled when she approached.

"*Min zuvu.*" Zhang called her his little bird. "What brings you home?"

It was an endearment Tenzin had once used with her daughter, who had died from a fever before the age of three. She both hated and loved the term.

"A progress report." She wiped the pain of memory from her mind and sat cross-legged on the cushion across from Zhang. She waited while Jinpa fetched her a pot of tea. "And wondering why you are here."

"I feel I am needed."

"For?"

Zhang took a drink of tea while Jinpa poured Tenzin's.

"The Laylat al Hisab," he said, "was only ever a symbol."

"Symbols are important." Tenzin sipped her tea and nodded to Jinpa, who left for the kitchen.

"They are." He waited for Tenzin to set her cup down. "Who sent the earth vampire?"

Tenzin wasn't surprised he knew about Johari; she was surprised he didn't know who sent her. "Saba."

"Do you trust her?"

"No."

"Good." Zhang sat completely motionless. "She won't give you reason to distrust her until it is too late."

"It could be that Saba has relented."

"No. She never approved of Arosh's peace agreement with me. She believes too much peace is dangerous."

"Is she correct?" Tenzin thought about the lawless areas of Central Asia where there were constant turf wars between immortals jockeying for power, resources, and influence over human governments. "When you ruled in Kashgar, it was peaceful."

"Then there was war and Arosh ruled there."

Tenzin took another sip of tea. "Yet between those wars, there was extended peace, and both you and Arosh kept a watchful eye on those territories. Now no one pays attention to them and there is corruption, violence, and a constant immortal struggle for power."

Zhang sat motionless for a long time. "I will think about what you have said."

"You should," she said. "Progress on the shipwreck is going well. We have found the ship, and the humans have documented it. It will bring honor to the scholars at the university."

"That is excellent news." Zhang smiled. "I am pleased they will receive recognition for their work."

"So far there is nothing that would alert them to anything

being out of the ordinary. We do not have to worry. And Benjamin..." She surprised herself by stopping.

"What about young Vecchio?"

He is leaving me.

Tenzin swallowed the knot in her throat. "He is coordinating between the vampire team and the human one, smoothing relations between the two of them to make sure communication flows appropriately and the recovery is seamless. He organized a party on the ship for better relations."

"A clever idea. It seems he is an invaluable addition to the team," Zhang said. "You were wise to insist on his presence."

"Invaluable." Tenzin picked up her tea. "Yes, he is invaluable."

21

Ben watched Johari surface in the early-morning hours. The survey of the wreck had lasted three days while the human team took 3-D images of the wreck site and documented everything by video and photograph as well as sonar scan. Ben suspected that they had noticed various storage jars going missing from accessible parts of the wreck, but they didn't say a word.

There was nothing more they could document from images, so official removal of artifacts had finally begun, and Cheng had brought Johari down to the wreck to move the sediment as delicately as she could.

"What is it this time?" Ben called down while Kadek's men lowered a basket made for human rescue.

"Timbers from the hull," Johari said. "Are there tanks large enough?"

"Yep. Fabia will want to do wood analysis if she can." According to Fabia, letting any object dry out or shocking it with freshwater would cause damage, so it would be the job of the university to desalinate them properly. The holding tanks were only temporary.

What Cheng was doing with the artifacts he'd taken for himself, Ben didn't know, and he wasn't asking. He'd come to terms with his role for this job. He had given Zhang his word that he'd finish the job, so he would. Anything beyond that wasn't his concern. His job was to recover the sword or whatever was left of it and return it to Penglai.

That was it. And that would be the end.

He paced along the edge of the deck, enjoying the whip of wind across his chest. He'd been diving in the morning, taken a nap to recharge, and woken to find his cabin sweltering from an afternoon heat wave. He stripped down to a pair of board shorts and walked up to the deck to observe the vampires and take advantage of the breeze.

He hadn't seen Tenzin for two nights, and he hadn't looked for her.

Cheng's men used the crane to bring the long timbers up from the surface and onto the deck, shouting orders at each other while they worked. Ancient wooden pieces passed the modern metal hull of the research vessel. Boards that had been hewn in East Africa and had once sailed the ocean were loaded and handled like porcelain as the sailors moved them from the basket to the saltwater tanks.

Ben heard Johari dive again as Cheng surfaced. He was carrying two large storage jars in a bamboo basket. The area around him was glowing green from floodlights they had secured around the dive site.

"Hoist!" Cheng yelled, and the men came scurrying.

Ben walked over to see what they had already brought up. Fabia was overseeing the tanks, moving and bracing each jar with whatever she could find to keep it stable.

"How's it going?"

"I can't complain," she said. "They're moving fast, but they have an earth vampire who can literally move the sediment around each jar, so there's little to no damage. Look at this."

She pointed toward yellow tape that had been tied around the handle of one jar. "It has depth readings and measurements on it."

"What does that mean?"

"It means that once we collect all the data and the scans, we'll be able to match each jar to its location on the ship."

"Wow. So they're not just taking stuff out."

"They're documenting it. It's extraordinary. The most careful human excavation can't match these results."

Her confidence reassured Ben, who was trying to ignore Tenzin's warning about the earth vampire.

"Johari might be trustworthy, but there will be no assumption from me. Watch her and wait. Don't suppose that we are all working toward the same goal, Benjamin."

Nothing about the woman said she wasn't on their team. She was doing an extraordinary job with not a single complaint, unlike Kadek, who regularly grumbled about any task Ben asked of him.

Still, he couldn't criticize any of their work. The artifacts recovered were in better shape than he'd hoped, and the farther they went under the sediment, the better they'd been preserved. Some of the glass and metal objects looked like a simple clean and polish was all they needed.

Fabia had explained that they needed far more than that, but to Ben's eye, what they had found was extraordinary.

Storage jar after storage jar of intricate glass objects. Lamps and bottles. Bowls and platters. All in brilliant colors with gold trim and painted filigree. Silver plates and goblets. They hadn't found any gold yet, nor any jewels, but they'd barely started.

Ben was making notes about the artifacts already brought

up when Kadek climbed over the rail, following another basket of storage jars.

He took a towel from one of the crew, wiped off his face, and walked over to Ben. "Johari is invaluable."

"Good." Ben tucked his notebook under his arm. "So things are moving quickly?"

"If we had an earth vampire like her who could move that comfortably in water, we'd work every job twice as fast. Maybe three times. She can move the sediment without disturbing the visibility too. I don't know how she does that."

"She's the daughter of Saba," Ben muttered, watching Johari climb onto the deck. "I imagine Saba's daughters are taught very strict control over their element."

"She's powerful too."

"Her mother is an ancient."

"I suppose you're right." Kadek shook his head. "Nothing that looks like a chest so far. Nothing with dimensions like a sword. No glass ingots. I don't know why Tenzin was so fixed on them."

"We'll keep looking. You're still working on the first layer."

"True."

Ben said, "Any ideas how we're going to explain to the human crew how all this has been taken out without disturbance?"

Kadek laughed as he walked back toward Johari and the crew. "That's your job, Vecchio. I'll be resting by then."

"Thanks." Ben heard something flutter overhead and looked up.

Tenzin was perched on the top railing of the ship's measurement tower. He saw her hair moving in the breeze, but otherwise she was motionless.

Fabia looked up. "How's all that?"

He could be generous now that he'd come to a decision. "It's fine."

"Sure it is."

Ben had told Fabia he'd decided to return to Rome with her after the job finished and that he was seriously considering the job Ronan had offered working for Emil Conti. Fabia hadn't said much, but she'd nodded a lot and had looked skeptical.

Just like she was looking now.

Ben started taking notes again. "I know you think I'm not going to follow through, but I am. I'm done. I need to move forward."

"You say that," she said, "and yet I don't think either of you looks any happier or more relieved. Do you know Tenzin came and sat with me at dinner the other night?"

"What?" Ben looked up. "What did she say?"

"Nothing. Literally nothing. She just sat next to me and ate." Fabia shook her head. "It was strange."

Ben frowned and lowered his voice. "Was Johari around?"

"She and Kadek were talking about artifact removal at the next table."

He shrugged. "She was spying. It's what she does. She's suspicious of everyone."

"Then why didn't she sit with them? It wasn't exactly a secret conversation."

"How am I supposed to know what she's thinking, Fabi? I'm not her minder."

"Just don't expect the rest of the vampire world to understand that. You've been her partner for like ten years or something."

"That's nothing to them. And I wasn't her partner," he muttered. "Obviously."

"Oh, bullshit." Fabia measured the water levels in a tank that had just had new artifacts put in. "You have one fight—"

"It's not one fight. It's years of constant fighting. Constant bickering. Her constantly ignoring my advice—"

"And you ignore her advice too," Fabia said. "You're like an old married couple. I don't know what changed."

"Puerto Rico changed it." He shook his head. "I changed, and she won't. I'm human, and she's not, and I finally realized why this is all doomed to failure, so I'm cutting my losses and getting out."

Fabia was crouched on the deck, looking at a broken jar through the clear plastic. She looked up. "She has changed, Ben. You spend most of your time with her, so you don't see it. But she's changed. She's different now. She doesn't scare me anymore."

"She should."

Fabia snorted. "Now you just sound like an ass. You sound like the guy who breaks up with his girlfriend and then tells everyone she's crazy."

"You do realize—" Ben cut himself off. He knew Tenzin was mentally unstable, and she had been for years. She only had a tenuous grip on reality at times, and her moral code was forged in prehistory. But he didn't need to share that with Fabia. "Let's just focus on this. How much of the cargo would you estimate has been removed?"

Fabia shook her head. "Honestly, it's very hard to tell. If the ship was packed evenly—"

"Cheng said to assume that it was. Balance thing."

Fabia nodded. "That makes sense. Then I'd say that in one night, they've removed approximately a third of the remaining cargo." She stood. "Which is just... superhuman."

"Considering they are superhuman, that makes sense."

Her voice dropped. "That third is counting the parts that are not showing up in the official record, by the way."

Ben looked up from his notebook.

"Come on," Fabia said quietly. "I told you they were documenting the location of each jar. I can see the gaps. Did you think no one would notice? It was fairly clear that artifacts had been removed, even before they started the actual excavation."

Ben kept his voice soft. "I have been told that nothing of unique historical significance—"

"And do you believe them?" Fabia cocked her head. "Really? I mean, you're taking their word for it. How do you know that Cheng and his men—"

"Stop." Ben drew her away to a far corner of the aft deck where the wind carried their words away. "Okay, continue."

"How do you know that Cheng is being honest? He could have his own aims in all this."

"He was hired because Tenzin trusts him."

"And is that a good idea? Is he worthy of that trust? I am honestly asking because I do not know. You said that the loss of this artifact—this priceless sword—could mean war between the East and the West. Do we know that war would not benefit Cheng?"

Ben had been working on the assumption that Tenzin could trust Cheng, but maybe that was a mistake.

"I'm just saying," Fabia said. "I like Cheng. I like Kadek. Cheng is very charming and very respectful to me and all the human crew. And Kadek is gruff, but I've never felt unsafe with him. He's very competent. But if Penglai is involved in a larger dispute with foreign vampire powers, then they're not going to be looking his direction. That works to his advantage."

"So does Zhang owing him a favor."

"True." Fabia lifted her hands up. "I don't know, Ben. You know about all this far more than I do. I am just saying that if they're willing to hide some things, they could be willing to hide others."

"You're not wrong." Ben took a deep breath. "I need to talk

to Zhang, but I don't know how to get in touch with him. And Tenzin will be pissed off if I even imply I don't trust Cheng, because she'll see it as a personal insult."

"You can contact Zhang," Fabia said. "Call Andrew. The guy with the plane, remember? Didn't Zhang's letter say Andrew reported to him directly? Tenzin wouldn't even have to know if you didn't want her to know. Though if I were you, I'd tell her you were contacting—"

"I'll talk to Andrew first," he said. "Tell her later."

Fabia pursed her lips. "Whatever you think."

"You think I should check with her first?"

"That's not—"

"Not likely." Tenzin might think Ben was working for her, but that wasn't actually the case. He was working for Zhang. He'd given Zhang his word, not Tenzin. "Thanks for the suggestion, Fabi." He patted her shoulder. "I'm just relieved there's someone here I can trust."

BEN WAITED for daylight to call Andrew. He went up to the operations room where much of the university team had stored their equipment and borrowed one of the desks. The university team was on the deck, welcoming additional divers from a university in Shantou, who had arrived by helicopter that morning.

Ben had decided that unless Professor Chou asked about the rapid removal of artifacts, he would offer nothing in explanation. The students had oohed and aahed over the collection of storage jars secured carefully in tanks while they had slept. He was sure some of them wondered how the mysterious night crew worked so fast, but since all jars had been documented and marked with a location, they could say nothing. The work had been done to proper specifications.

He spun in the chair as the phone rang and watched the students and new divers chattering as they prepared for the day's work. Fabia stood at the railing with Professor Chou, probably detailing the steps she'd taken overnight. She might have been asking for more tanks from the university too. The ones on the *Jinshé* weren't going to be enough.

"Hello?" Andrew Leu's voice startled Ben out of his thoughts.

"Andrew, good morning. This is Ben Vecchio."

"I recognized your number, Mr. Vecchio. How may I help you? Is everything going smoothly on the ship?"

"Things are progressing very well, but..." How to frame this? Zhang must know that Ben and Tenzin weren't on the best terms. Maybe he should just throw it out there. "I'm going to be completely honest, Mr. Leu."

"That is always a good idea when it comes to Elder Zhang."

"I understand the ramifications of this job and how important the Laylat al Hisab is. I understand why Tenzin approached Cheng to complete this job. I also know they have their own history. For that reason—and I hope Zhang understands I am working solely for him in this matter—I would like to know if Zhang is aware that Cheng is reserving some of the wreck artifacts as his own. *Not* the sword, but other artifacts."

The line was silent for a long while. "I do not know the answer to that question."

"This may be customary or expected since Cheng is doing the work to retrieve the treasure. It may be something they have already discussed that I was not informed of. But since I am working for Zhang on this job, I wanted to speak to him about it directly."

"I understand, Mr. Vecchio. Thank you for contacting me in

this matter, and I will pass your question on to Zhang. I expect you will hear from him within twenty-four hours."

"Thank you, Mr. Leu."

"Call me Andrew," the man said. "I suspect we will be speaking again."

22

———

Something was wrong. Tenzin could feel it. She could sense it.

She roused herself from her daylight torpor and sat up. "Cara?"

The computer voice responded. "Yes, Tenzin."

"What is the time?"

"It is 6:30 p.m. local time."

The sun had been down for nearly an hour. She could hear the hum of human activity on the boat, the amnis of waking vampires, and something else.

"Cara, call Ben Vecchio."

A few seconds passed and Tenzin heard a phone ringing.

A second later, Ben's gravelly voice came on the line. "Tenzin, I'm slee—"

"Something is wrong on the ship."

His voice lost all annoyance. "What is it?"

"I heard something."

"Something?"

"Meet me in the hold." She rose to her feet and pulled on leggings, then slid into the flat shoes parked near the door and opened the hatch. After poking her head out, she scanned the area. She smelled humans. Other vampires. Engine oil. Blood. Seawater—

Blood.

Senses on alert, she stepped into the passageway and focused on the scent of blood. She was a vampire, and blood drew her even if it was old. This blood was not old. It was fresh, and it was human.

The passageway from the hold led her through the lower deck where storerooms lined either side. Footsteps approached from the top deck. They came down the stairs. Ben appeared, wearing basketball shorts, a T-shirt, and no shoes.

"Tenzin?"

She put a finger to her lips. She pointed to a storeroom door on the port side, and Ben walked silently toward her. She knew what they'd find before Ben pushed open the hatch.

The body was lying on the floor, the neck mangled and limbs splayed at unnatural angles. It was a young woman—one of the university divers—but Tenzin didn't know her name.

"Meili." Ben crouched down and put a finger to her neck.

"She's dead, Benjamin. I don't hear even a weak heartbeat."

"Dammit." He stood and gripped his hair in his hands. "Dammit! She was one of the first divers on the wreck. It was her first maritime site. She was working on her PhD. She learned to dive so she could complete her dissertation with original research."

Meili's eyes were wide and lifeless. She was also soaking wet. The seawater overpowered every other scent except the blood. Her clothes were soaked in it, as was her hair.

"Fabia is going to be heartbroken. She and Meili had already exchanged email addresses. Meili wanted to work on her English, and Fabi wanted to consult on her paper. Fuck, Tenzin, this is awful."

Tenzin had a difficult time feeling grief for most humans. Their lives were so short—it made little difference to her that this one had only lived for twenty-some years instead of eighty. Many humans received far less than that. But the violence of the young woman's attack *did* anger her.

"She wasn't attacked in her sleep," Tenzin said. "Her eyes are open."

"Whoever killed her probably used amnis."

Tenzin leaned against the bulkhead. "The list of suspects isn't long. It's not longer than one name for me."

Ben stood. "Who?"

"Johari."

"Johari?"

Tenzin shrugged. "Who else?"

"How about Kadek? Or Cheng?"

Tenzin cocked her head. *Really?*

Ben grimaced and shrugged. *Okay, probably not Cheng.*

He asked, "Can you sense any particular amnis on her?"

"No. Look at all the water. No scents are going to survive over that. Maybe a water vampire could get something, but I can't sense it."

"Okay," Ben said. "Why don't we call everyone down here and see what they say? Maybe Cheng will get something."

Tenzin raised her eyes. "You want to invite everyone down to a murder scene to see what they have to say?"

"It's not her murder scene. I guarantee she was killed somewhere else." Ben knelt next to her again. "How much blood is gone? Can you tell?"

"Does it matter?" Tenzin was disgusted by the waste.

It was completely unnecessary to kill a human to feed. No vampire, not even a newborn, needed that much blood. Sometimes, if a human had other health problems, the shock of blood loss could trigger a heart attack or stroke. And newborns often killed purely by accident because they could pierce arteries and didn't understand how to seal wounds. But there were no newborns on the ship.

Whoever had done this was careless, vicious, or both.

This human was no threat and had harmed no one. She was working for Zhang, and her safety should have been guaranteed by that alone.

"Sure, why not?" Tenzin said. "Call them."

~

JOHARI, Kadek, Cheng, Tenzin, and Ben stood around Meili's body. Ben watched all of them, but they were nearly impossible to read. The poker face had been invented by vampires.

Ben knew whom he suspected. Kadek's face was ruddier than normal, a clear signal that he'd fed recently. While all the vampires had all been instructed to feed on bagged blood for the duration of the job, Kadek had grumbled about it, complaining that they would be less effective if they couldn't feed from the ready supply of humans on the boat.

Now a human had been fed on and killed. Had she struggled? Had Kadek been afraid his amnis wouldn't wipe her memory?

Johari—the only other option in Ben's mind—was watching the body with more sympathy than he'd expected. Her eyes were trained on the young woman, and she nearly looked sad.

"Did she have a family?" Johari asked.

Ben said, "Yes."

"Very unfortunate." A line formed between her elegantly arched eyebrows.

"This is not good," Cheng said. "Kadek, you'll need to take care of this. She can't simply disappear or the humans will be distracted. They've made very good progress in the past week, and we can't interrupt that. Can you make it look like a drowning or shark attack?"

"Of course. I'll wait for Professor Chou to bring up her disappearance. Then we will conduct a thorough search before we find her body in the ocean."

Tenzin nodded. "The best solution."

"Agreed," Johari said.

"Wait a minute!" Ben said. "That is not the best solution." He looked around the room at the impassive immortals. "One of you did this. You can't just cover it up."

Kadek turned his eyes on Ben. "Are you accusing one of us?"

"Yes."

"Who?"

Ben looked at Kadek, not wanting to give away his suspicion if he was the only one who suspected Kadek. He turned to Cheng. "This was a human working under the protection of Elder Zhang Guo and you."

Cheng said, "I hired them. I never offered my protection. This is unfortunate, but—"

"Unfortunate?" He struggled to keep his ire in check. "Meili's death requires more than a carefully constructed cover-up. She was twenty-seven. She was the only child of her parents. The first in her family to go to university. This is more than fucking unfortunate."

Cheng nodded seriously. "I understand your concern, and her parents will be compensated for their loss."

"You're unbelievable."

Cheng narrowed his eyes. "What would you have me do, Ben Vecchio? I cannot bring her back from the dead. There is no court that will hear her case. That is not the world we belong to."

Tenzin spoke. "Cheng, I think we would all agree that you are the least likely to have killed this young woman. Do you—"

"Not even exempting yourself from suspicion, are you?" Cheng smiled. "You're one of a kind, Cricket."

Ben hated that Cheng called her Cricket. Absolutely hated it. But he didn't say a word.

"Why would I exempt myself?" Tenzin asked. "I have killed thousands. Why would any of you assume I *wouldn't* kill this woman? You all know my reputation."

The number shouldn't have shocked Ben, but it did.

I have killed thousands.

She'd been alive, at his best guess, between four and five thousand years. The idea of her killing thousands would be logical. She'd killed enemies, worked as an assassin, and been in numerous wars.

"You never kill without reason," Cheng said.

Kadek muttered, "Though her reasons don't always make sense to anyone but herself."

Tenzin cocked her head. "That's fair."

Cheng glared at his child and barked at him in a language that Ben didn't recognize.

"He has every right to resent me, Cheng." Tenzin knelt by Meili's body. "If we all agree that Cheng is the least likely to have killed this woman, we should all trust him to answer. Do you scent any immortal on her?"

Cheng crouched down across from Tenzin and picked Meili's body up. He was far gentler than Ben would have expected. He put his face in front of the bloody wound and inhaled deeply on both sides of her neck, both the bitten and intact sides.

"Nothing," he said. "She was killed recently and her body washed in the ocean. Other than that, I sense no trace of her killer." He rose. "Is there anything else?"

Ben said, "Yes."

Tenzin said, "No."

Ben turned on Tenzin. "Her killer is standing over her body right now."

"And we have no way of determining who it was," Cheng said. "Look around you, Vecchio. No one is going to confess, and I suspect we all have different suspects. Finger-pointing is useless. Suspicion without evidence is useless. Wasting time on an investigation is not in anyone's best interest."

Ben pointed to Meili's body. "It's in *her* best interest."

"She is dead." Cheng's expression held a hint of pity. "It does not matter to her."

"Her parents then."

Cheng spoke quietly. "No confession will bring their daughter back. And I promise you"—he cleared his throat —"that is the only thing they will want."

Tenzin put a hand on his arm. "Leave it, Benjamin. Her soul has left this body and will be born again. Nothing is ever truly lost."

"Unbelievable." Ben shook off Tenzin's arm and strode out of the room, leaving Meili with the uncaring monsters who had killed her. Maybe not all of them had drained her blood, but all of them were willing to let the perpetrator walk free.

He walked up to the top deck and searched for Fabia. She was sitting at a picnic table, drinking a glass of wine and showing notes to Professor Chou. She looked up as he approached.

"Ben!" She smiled brightly before she caught his expression. The smile fell. "What's wrong?"

He glanced at Professor Chou and quickly looked away. "I need to speak to you."

"Of course." She stood. "Professor, excuse us. This is likely something regarding the night crew."

Professor Chou smiled at Ben. "They are doing extraordinary work. I have never seen such precise excavation. Please give them our thanks."

"Yeah." The words tasted like sand. "I sure will."

He and Fabia walked to their spot on the aft deck where they could speak privately.

"I'm going to tell you something," Ben said. "And you need to not look upset."

Her face went blank. "Is it my family?"

"No."

She nodded.

"It's Meili."

Fabia's eyes filled immediately, and she blinked hard.

"She was killed earlier tonight. She was bitten and bled out. I don't know who, but I suspect Kadek."

Fabia struggled to speak. She was holding back tears and clearing her throat. "It... it can't be Kadek. He liked Meili. I saw them speaking a number of times."

"It has to be either Cheng, Tenzin, Kadek, or Johari." He glanced around, but they were still alone. "There's no one else."

"Another vampire—"

"That flew in and immediately gained Meili's trust before he drained her? This happened almost exactly at sunset."

"Tenzin—"

"She wouldn't do this."

Fabia spoke in a pained whisper. "I think you need to be honest about who she is, Nino."

"I'm not saying she's not capable of murder. Clearly she is. But why would she kill Meili?"

"Why would any of them?"

"Because they were hungry? To sabotage the job? To keep Cheng and Tenzin from finding the sword?"

"And you think Kadek would create this kind of trouble for his sire?"

"What trouble?" Ben heard people begin to call Meili's name. "They're going to look for her, Fabi. They're going to search the whole ship, and you can't say anything. You can't give anything away or you could be in danger."

"Is she just going to disappear?"

"No." He swallowed hard. "I promise. She won't be lost at sea. I promise, Fabi."

Fabia nodded, took a deep breath, and wiped her eyes. "Okay."

"Not a word," he said as they started back toward the operations room where lights were all flaring. "Not a single word."

BEN SAT on the top deck, staring toward the horizon as it slowly shifted from deep blue to pearly grey. He was smoking a cigarette when he heard her land behind him.

"When did you start smoking?"

Ben barked a laugh. "Tenzin, I picked up my first cigarette when I was nine. Maybe younger."

"It's a bad habit."

"I've had worse." He took another drag, enjoying the buzz on the end of his tongue. He didn't smoke much anymore, but if there was ever a night to fall off the wagon, it was this one. It was cigarettes or whiskey, and there were plenty of cigarettes on the boat and very little whiskey.

Cigarettes it was.

"The humans are sleeping now," Tenzin said. "Or they are in their cabins. I can't control whether they sleep or not."

"You used to make me sleep with amnis," he said. "Don't lie."

"Only when you were overtired."

"Don't ever use your amnis on me again."

"I won't."

Liar.

Ben stubbed out his cigarette and looked at her from the corner of his eye. "I called your father to tell him Zhang was taking a cut of the artifacts."

"How interesting." She seemed unconcerned.

"Andrew got back to me tonight. Zhang says that if you are unconcerned with the portion Cheng is taking, he is also unconcerned. He trusts your judgment."

"Good."

"So I guess I made myself look like an ass."

"No, you didn't." Tenzin sat next to him. "Zhang now knows that your professional integrity is more important than your loyalty to me. Well done. Very strategic."

"That's not why I did it."

"Which will impress him even more."

Ben looked at her. Looked away. "Does he know I'm quitting?"

"I didn't tell him what you told me, if that's what you're asking."

"I'm not going to change my mind, Tenzin."

"I believe you think that."

"Unbelievable."

She turned to face him. "You keep saying that word. Cheng is unbelievable. I am unbelievable. Why do you find us so unbelievable lately? Are you angry at us? Or at yourself for being one of us?"

"I am not one of you."

"In everything but biology," Tenzin said, "you are."

Ben rose and picked up the pack of cigarettes. "When are they going to find her body?"

"Just after daybreak."

He shook his head. "I'm going to bed."

"Sleep well, Benjamin."

"I stopped doing that about three years ago." He put another cigarette between his lips. "Just another bad habit I picked up hanging around the monsters."

23

Meili was found just after sunrise, the crew lifting a shout when they spotted her. Ben forced himself to walk up to the aft deck to watch Cheng's human crew lower a small vessel in the water so they could retrieve the wreck of Meili's body. He forced himself to watch as her friends and colleagues cried out in horror. He forced himself to see the shark bites that covered the evidence of vampire trauma.

He forced himself to watch it all and never forget who Meili had been and why she had died. She'd died because a vampire had been cruel and vicious. Her body had been wrecked to cover the evidence of their crime.

There was no diving or recovery that day. Professor Chou was forced to call the girl's parents and share the heartbreaking news. Meili must have fallen overboard and been unable to signal or shout for help in the night. It was tragic and she would be missed.

Meili's parents were stoic. Professor Chou was wrecked.

All the university students and divers gathered in the operations room and the mess hall where Cheng's crew cared for them. Mr. Lu arranged for the helicopter to come from Shantou.

Professor Chou would accompany Meili's body back to Shanghai while his colleague, Professor Yao, continued on the *Jinshé*.

Ben spent time with all the students that day, especially Lin, Delun, and Jon, who were Meili's closest friends.

"She was so excited to be here," Jon said. "And she was doing such good work."

"She'd never been on a ship this big before," Lin said. "She had quite a bit of seasickness the first few days. I wonder if that was what happened?"

Ben kept having to swallow his words. "It could have been anything. If she went out after dark and was walking along the rails, a sudden shift could have caused a fall."

"She was such a good swimmer though." Delun's hands were folded on the table, and he was worrying his thumb. "This is quite shocking."

"You know, I've had falls that knocked the wind out of me," Ben said. "If I'd been alone in the ocean..."

"We forget the ocean can be so dangerous." Lin's eyes filled with tears. "I will miss her so much. She was such a bright and cheerful person."

Jon and Delun both concurred, leaving Ben feeling like shit. She hadn't lost her balance. She hadn't been careless. She'd been attacked.

"Do you think Professor Chou will come back soon?" Jon asked. "When will they conduct a funeral?"

Delun kept his voice low. "Were her parents religious?"

Lin shook her head. "No, I do not think so."

"We should have a wake," Ben said. "Tonight. For Meili."

Lin frowned. "A wake?"

"We can get pictures of her and put them up in the mess hall. We'll all share a drink and everyone can share their favorite memories of Meili."

"I like that idea," Lin said. "We can invite the crew as well."

Leaving Meili's friends with a purpose, Ben walked down to the operations room to find Fabia, who was briefing Professor Yao on the status of the excavation so far.

"The rate of progress has been exceptional, but I am concerned that some of the measurements have been less than precise." Professor Yao pointed to several spots on a diagram. "There should be storage jars here, for instance. Where are they?"

"Perhaps lost or damaged." Fabia spread her hands. "I can only organize by what the divers note, and underwater measurements are notoriously hard to keep consistent."

"So true."

Fabia shot slightly panicked eyes to Ben.

"Fabi, can I talk to you for a second?"

She excused herself from the professor and walked to Ben, switching to Italian. "He might be more difficult."

"I thought Professor Chou briefed him."

"I thought he had too, but..." Fabia shrugged. "What should we do?"

"I'll pass the word along to Tenzin and Cheng tonight," Ben said. "Anything else I should be concerned about?"

"Other than a friend being killed?" Fabia's expression held the same bitterness Ben's did. "I guess not."

"I know."

"Do you?" She looked up. "Or are you accustomed to their way of thinking now, Nino?"

He clenched his teeth. "Not fair. I'm trying to keep everyone safe here."

"That's kind of the point though. We're not safe. None of us are safe."

"Are you quitting on me?"

"No." She settled her face into a resolute mask. "But this is the last vampire archaeology project I'll be working on."

She walked back to Professor Chou and continued comparing notes while Ben walked up to the bridge.

He felt like a punching bag that morning, hit by the students' grief, Fabia's anger, and his own guilt. Had there been something he'd missed? Did he need to contact Zhang about this? Would this be seen as a failing on his part? He had no control over vampires. Most days, he felt like he was herding cats just trying to get everyone to cooperate.

He opened the door to the bridge and waited for the proper announcements to be made. "Mr. Lu, good morning."

"Good morning, Mr. Vecchio." Mr. Lu looked as calm and competent as ever. "How are the young people this morning?"

"They're sad, of course. But also grateful to the crew for your thorough search of the ship and the water."

Mr. Lu nodded slightly. "That poor girl."

"They're taking the day off work."

"I understand." He glanced over and snapped an order to his first in command. "Mr. Vecchio, I would appreciate a word in private if you have the time."

"Of course." Ben followed Mr. Lu out the door and back to the map room.

Once they were alone, he asked, "What did you need to speak to me about?"

Mr. Lu said, "I know what happened to the girl, though not the details. Kadek told me."

"Do you think it was him?" Ben knew he was risking his safety by asking the question, but something about Mr. Lu inspired trust.

"I do not have an opinion about that. I believe it could be one of three people, but my speculation adds nothing."

"Then why did you ask me down here?"

"Because we have a saboteur on the ship."

Ben blinked. "Excuse me?"

"A saboteur is on the ship. There have been attempts to damage one of the remote vehicles the researchers use while they are diving, and I found an artifact hidden in the engine room."

"Have you shared this with Kadek or Cheng?"

He shook his head. "I discovered these things this morning. The attempt at damaging the ROV was clumsy. The person did not understand the technology."

"Vampire?"

"Possibly."

"And the artifact?"

Mr. Lu reached in his pocket. "It is small, but I am quite certain that it came from the *Qamar Jadid*."

It was a bar a little larger than the slim gold bars they'd found the day before. Only, this bar wasn't made of gold, but of glass. Mr. Lu handed it to him.

"Where did you find it?"

"In an isolated part of the engine room. It was wrapped in a rag and tucked behind a pipe."

"How—?"

"This is my ship, Mr. Vecchio. None of my sailors would leave a rag out of place."

"Understood. Is that..." Ben squinted. "Is it writing?"

"Yes, but I do not read Arabic."

"Oh, it *is* Arabic." He didn't read Arabic either. He wondered if he could video call Giovanni from the ship.

"I believe Tenzin could offer a translation," Mr. Lu said. "If you would be willing to consult with her."

"Right."

Right.

~

THE EXTERIOR of the glass had been corroded by saltwater, leaving the small tablet looking frosted. Luckily, the writing—which had been etched into the glass—was still legible.

Tenzin handed the glass bar back to him. "It's a manifest."

"A what?"

"A list of what was stored on the *Qamar Jadid*. It has a list of glass pieces. It also has a date and the name of the ship, which should be useful. Fabia will want it for her report."

"So it's nothing...?"

She rolled her eyes. "If you were hoping it said 'Watch out for that Zanzibari vampire,' I'm sorry to say it does not. I don't know why anyone would take it."

"So this could have nothing to do with Meili's death?"

"It probably doesn't. It is mostly likely that one of Cheng's human crew found it or thought it was interesting and pocketed it to keep as a souvenir. It's not valuable except for historical interest."

"Okay." Ben put the glass bar back in his pocket. "Why would a manifest be written on a glass tablet?"

"Because it's waterproof?" Tenzin shrugged. "I have no idea."

"Did Harun write it?"

She narrowed her eyes. "It's possible that he included a list of his pieces to distinguish them from the rest of the gifts Arosh was sending to Zhang. A glass tablet would be... a bit of a flourish, which would not have been out of character. He was very proud."

"Okay." He closed his hand over the tablet. "I'm going to keep this with me for now. Whoever hid it, I don't want them knowing who has it or who discovered it. The last thing we need is another vampire targeting humans."

"I don't think she was targeted, Benjamin." Tenzin's voice was sad. "I think she was simply convenient."

"Nope." He shook his head. "You're the one who taught me there is no such thing as coincidence."

"I don't think I ever said that."

"Pretty sure you did." He walked to the door. "If you didn't say it, you showed it. A hundred times over."

"Benjamin."

He stopped at the door and turned. "What?"

She sat on her pallet, cross-legged, with music playing from her tablet. "I do not understand your anger."

His chest felt hollow. "I'm not angry anymore." *I just love you.*

"I have tried to be honest with you."

"You tried?" He smiled. "That's an interesting way of putting it."

"Truth doesn't come readily to me like it does to you."

"What does?"

"Survival."

Ben nodded. "I know."

"I don't recognize the emotion I see on your face right now."

"I know." His voice was soft. "But... I can't really explain it to you, Tiny."

"Can't or won't?"

How could he explain what he barely understood? He loved her. He probably always would. But he knew she wasn't good for him, and he wasn't willing to sacrifice his life just to spend it on the periphery of hers.

"I can't." His voice broke. "I'm sorry, Tenzin. I can't explain it."

She nodded and turned back to her book. It was a thin volume and it looked like it was Italian.

"What are you reading?"

"Sixteenth-century Italian philosophy by someone named Tullia d'Aragona." She glanced up. "Fabia was finished with it and I ran out of books."

"Right." He waved. "I'll see you."

"I will see you, Benjamin."

FABIA AND BEN worked with the university divers for the next three days, trying to make up for the loss of Meili and the disruption to the excavation. The vampires had slowed down and were starting to search away from the main body of the wreck.

While the night crew had found jar after jar of fine glass-work, metal objects of unspeakable beauty, and gold bars and coins, not a single weapon had been found, especially not the sword that was the main goal of the expedition.

Ben and Fabia swam around the wreck site. Ben tapped Fabia's shoulder and switched his radio to a private channel. "Do you think it's lost?"

"We have no way of knowing." She shook her head. "It doesn't make sense." She stopped to watch Lin and Jon take a basket up to the surface. "Even if the blade has deteriorated, the hilt was supposed to be made of precious metal and gemstones. Those things would last."

"Is it possible someone stole it?"

"It's possible. Anything is possible." Fabia was watching the divers. "Have you noticed something unusual today?"

"Fabi, most of this stuff is a mystery to me. I only know a little of what you guys—"

"That area over there." She pointed to a section of the hull. "No one is working on it."

"Are there still storage jars?"

Most of the cargo jars had been collected, and the divers had moved on to looking for smaller pieces of the shipwreck puzzle. Looking for tools and personal items from the sailors. Things the vampires had little interest in.

"That section butts up to the reef, so it's been harder to sift through." Fabia swam over to Jon and Ben followed.

He saw her switch radio frequencies to the public channel, so he did too.

"That section by the reef." She pointed to it. "Has it been excavated yet?"

"Meili was working there," Jon said. "I suppose we haven't wanted to disturb it."

"Would you like me to examine it?"

"You may, of course. We would be grateful for the help. I would be happy to assist you myself tomorrow." He pointed to Lin. "Each section is a two-person job."

Lin pushed the button on her microphone. "I am taking tomorrow off."

"Good." Fabia pointed to the wrecked hull. "I'll take a look today, but I'll make sure I don't move anything without taking notes."

Jon gave her a thumbs-up and got back to his work. Ben and Fabia swam over to Meili's section of the wreck.

The whole of the wreck had been thoroughly photographed, but Fabia still took out her notebook and began diagraming each coral formation and outcropping of sediment. Ben watched a small yellow fish poke out from the coral and look at them with round eyes. The little creature darted away when they moved closer, churning up a small puff of sand that had gathered on the coral and revealing a glint that caught Ben's attention.

"Fabia?"

She moved closer. "Hmm?"

Ben held his finger up to his mask. Quiet. Then he took his hand and waved it over the section where the fish had fled. The water surged over the coral, revealing more of the color Ben had noticed.

Fabia held up a hand and moved her pencil rapidly over her notebook. She showed Ben where she'd made a note of the artifact before she gave him a thumbs-up again.

Ben pushed more water toward the lump. It had small growths on it that must have been various types of coral, but it wasn't secured to the reef. He reached under and grabbed the edge of the small glass bar, sliding it from under the piled rocks and corals.

He held it up, and Fabia reached for her pencil.

It's like the one Mr. Lu found.

What?

He found another bar like this with writing. Ben pointed to the wrecked hull and piled rocks. *We may find more glass in this section.*

And more glass means?

Harun worked in glass and metal.

Understanding, Fabia took the glass artifact from Ben and tucked it in the small net pocket on her belt before she gave him the sign to surface.

They swam up, then over to the ladder fixed to the side amidships. Climbing up, they handed up the notebooks on frames first, then took the hands of the crew who helped them on deck and removed their tanks and masks.

Once they'd dropped their equipment, Ben and Fabia walked over to the tanks where Fabia wrote up a tag and placed the glass bar in the correct tank.

"So you're saying there might be more glass in that section?" She kept her voice low.

"More important, that might be where the sword is," he

said. "Harun worked in glass and in metal. He made the sword. He made the glass pieces. Tenzin translated the other bar Mr. Lu found. It was a manifest of items from Harun's workshop. He wanted Zhang to know which things came from him, I guess."

Fabia rolled her eyes.

Ben asked, "Do you know what this means?"

"Artists have egos no matter what century it is?"

"No, Fabi—I mean yeah, obviously—but that means Meili was working in the section where Harun's glass tablet was found. Meaning—"

"Whoever killed Meili might have taken the tablet from her." Fabia's face went pale. "But why? It was a list. Just a list."

"I don't know," Ben said. "But I do know I'm going down there without the university team. Tonight. We need to figure out what Meili found."

24

F abia was helping Ben suit up. "I don't like the idea of you going down by yourself."

"You did three dives today," he said. "I did two. Also, I want you up here on the radio. I won't be able to avoid Johari, Cheng, and Kadek, but they won't be able to hear what we're saying. I don't trust any of them, and I want someone up here I can talk to."

"Four dives isn't out of the safety realm, Ben. It's not that deep. We can get Tenzin on the radio so I can go down with you."

"You're joking, right?" He adjusted his belt. "Tenzin on the radio? She'd break it."

"Night dives are no joke," Fabia said. "It's a completely different world down there at night."

"And we already have lights on the area," he said. "I have a headlamp. I'll stay down for thirty minutes, max. But I need to be able to dig in there when the other humans aren't looking. And I don't want to clue Cheng and Kadek in on it. They're the ones who have been swiping artifacts as it is."

"And Johari? You're going to need her help to move that rock."

He paused. "You've been working with her for weeks now. Have you ever gotten suspicious? She's quiet and hardworking. She's pleasant to the humans and respectful of the crew. Nothing about her says she's a thief."

"She turned a rock in to me the other day. She thought it looked like it might have had writing on it, so it could have been an artifact."

"Did it?"

"No. Just some odd scrapes, but I did have to check."

"See?" He glanced around. "I'm sure Kadek killed Meili. He's loyal to Cheng and no one else. He's annoyed by humans and only likes the ones who defer to him in everything."

"Be careful, Ben."

"I'm not going to be by myself. You'll be on the radio. Besides, no one is going to try anything with witnesses."

"Still—"

"Stop worrying." He took her by the shoulders, kissed her forehead, and picked up his fins. "Wish me luck."

"Good luck."

Ben walked to the edge of the deck and waited for the crew to open the railing so he could climb down and enter the water. He fixed his mask and pushed the microphone button.

"Fabi, can you hear me?"

"Yes."

"Going under."

Ben sank beneath the water and was immediately seized by the creeping cold that slipped along his spine. The water was warm, but far cooler than the air above. He immediately flipped on his headlamp and allowed himself to sink to the ocean floor where underwater floodlights marked the edges of the site.

The lights turned the water an eerie blue green; it rippled

like a living thing. Shadow and light were starker in the night-time, and among the fantastical corals and wrecked hull, the three vampires moved at speeds so quick watching them threatened to make Ben nauseous.

"Ben, you all right?"

He pushed his button. "I'm good. For some reason I assumed they'd be slower underwater. Johari's a little slower, but not Cheng and Kadek."

"What does it look like?"

"Honestly?" The comparison was too apt. "Sharks. Really fast sharks."

"You know, I was hoping you were going to say mermaids."

"Nope. Definitely not mermaids, though I guess Cheng has the hair for it."

Fabia laughed.

With the grace of apex predators, Cheng and Kadek moved with sinuous efficiency. While they were still removing artifacts, they were hunting as well, searching the perimeter of the wreck for signs of tossed artifacts or scattered debris before they returned to the hull.

Johari worked on the hull, continuing to coax sediment away from the cargo hold of the ship, using hand motions to alert the other vampires when a new section had been cleared. Watching her was astonishing. The sediment around each fixed object seemed to melt away under her hands, revealing perfectly intact objects that had been hidden for over a thousand years.

"I wish so hard I could video this," he said. "It's amazing."

"I wish I could see it," she said through the radio. "I may have to go down tomorrow night."

"It's pretty damn cool."

Ben headed for the end of the wrecked hull where Meili had been working. He swam down, focusing his light on the base of the coral, but it was far more compacted than he remembered. The coral sat atop a section of hull that had broken off, blocking the area beneath it and whatever might have been stored there. It wasn't a large portion, and if he hadn't been looking, he would have thought it was simply part of the reef.

"I'm getting Johari."

He motioned to Johari, who held up her hand in the universal signal to wait.

"Are you sure?"

"I'm not going to be able to move this without her."

"Okay." She sounded skeptical.

"I couldn't move this with a sledgehammer, Fabi, and I don't want to be that destructive if I can help it."

"Just be careful."

Ben had cleared some of the loose rocks and debris from the base of the collapsed hull by the time Johari swam over. He couldn't talk to her, but he motioned to the portion of the hull he wanted to lift, hoping she got the idea.

She nodded and began to slowly move the section of rock the coral had attached to, probably hoping to disturb the reef as little as possible. She waved at him to get back, so he moved and allowed her to work.

"Okay, you're not gonna be happy what we're doing here," Ben said. "But she's moving it."

"How many coral are you killing?"

"As few as possible." It was the truth. The rocks moved far more slowly than the sediment. Johari had her hands under them, and it almost looked like she was very slowly shifting a crusted-over Volkswagen.

"The hull is pulling away with the rocks," Ben said. "I can see what's underneath now."

"What is it?"

He swam down and managed to take a peek before Johari

whacked the back of his head with her hand. He looked up. She pointed to where Ben had been waiting.

Get back. Her glare was unmistakable.

"I need to wait until she's finished with the rocks."

"Okay."

He checked his watch. He'd already been under for fifteen minutes. He had enough air in his tanks for an hour, but he'd promised Fabia he'd only be gone a half an hour.

Five minutes later, Johari waved him over. Ben lowered himself to the sea floor and began brushing away the sediment with the tools Fabia had given him before Johari held her hand out and the sediment began to melt away from the dark lumps that had been hiding.

"Fabia, there are glass ingots."

"Colored ones?"

He grabbed the flashlight from his belt and shined it and his headlamp where Johari's hands moved. "Yes."

There was bright red and brilliant green. But more than anything, there was blue. Rich, cobalt-blue glass that winked at him from the bottom of the ocean like colorful cabochon jewels.

Ben's heart was racing. While nothing about the glass ingots was sexy, he was taken by the thrill of the hunt. He was uncovering something that had remained hidden for a thousand years. Glass ingots poured in the fires of Damascus, brought by caravan to be loaded onto a ship that traveled thousands of miles, only to sink on the bottom of the ocean floor.

Ben said, "So Meili was definitely on track to find Harun's glass."

"Do you think that's why...?"

"Why would that put her in danger?" Ben asked. "That's what I don't get. It's just glass. There are mountains of way fancier glass pieces all through the wreck."

Just as he turned his radio off, Johari's hand stroked through the water, moving a broad swath of sediment and rock to reveal...

Not an ingot.

Ben swam closer. *What on earth?*

From the outside, it looked like the other ingots, but instead of being one round lump, this was long. It must have been three feet at least. It looked like an enormous loaf of bread made of frosted red glass.

"Fabi, I found something weird."

"Tell me more."

"I don't know what it is. Maybe it's a few ingots fused?" He looked at Johari, who shrugged and shook her head. "Yeah, Johari has no idea what it is either."

She motioned toward the main part of the hull where Kadek and Cheng were working. Then she curved her arms and made a carrying gesture before she swam away.

"I think she's going to get a basket."

"Good idea."

Ben went closer to the glass object. He wished the glass wasn't so frosted, but maybe if he shined his light closer...

Ben turned his headlamp off and brought up his smaller flashlight. He pressed it to the surface of the glass and saw a shadow.

What the hell?

He moved the small flashlight around, trying to illuminate the ingot. It was fixed to the ocean floor, so he couldn't lift it. Ben put his flashlight on the far side of the object, propping it on the rocks and lying flat on the ocean floor to look through the other side.

The outline of a hilt was unmistakable.

Laylat al Hisab.

The sword was encased in glass, sealed away from the elements by the fire master who had forged it. Ben moved the flashlight down, seeing the shadow of a perfectly preserved blade.

He nearly cried with joy. It wasn't ruined. Despite everything, despite the years and the miles and a thousand years of corrosive seawater, it had endured.

He pushed the microphone button. "Fabi, you're not going to believe—"

The pain in his back was quick, silent, and unmistakable.

Ben gasped. Then everything went numb. He couldn't move his arms or legs. He couldn't push the button on his microphone.

"Ben?" Fabia's voice on the radio.

He felt an odd tugging in his belly, and he looked down to see a silver blade pinning him to the ocean floor. His body drifted in the tug of the current, and a black flower bloomed beneath him.

"Hey Ben, get back to me."

Johari swam in front of him. She didn't look at him at first. She methodically removed the sword case from the sediment that held it, then she looked up.

Her eyes weren't sad, but they weren't empty either, and Ben felt oddly grateful that she felt something as she killed him.

"Ben, what's going on? I need to hear your voice."

Why? He felt his lips form the words.

Her eyes were resolute. She mouthed, *I'm sorry.*

Johari lifted the sword case and swam away, leaving Ben in the darkness. Leaving him unable to move, drifting in a growing cloud of his own blood.

Would the sharks come?

Would the vampires?

"Ben!"

He let the tears come to his eyes, and he was grateful to feel their heat in the dark, cold water.

Tenzin.

∼

SHE WOKE from her meditation with a rapid burst of three heartbeats.

She sat straight up. "Benjamin."

She was stripped down to a pair of short leggings and a black tank top. It was too hot for anything else. She heard distant footsteps and the sound of panting.

Someone beat on her door and screamed, "Tenzin, you have to come *now!*"

The Italian girl.

Benjamin.

Tenzin didn't waste time with the door. She flew up and forced the forward-hold doors open with a punch of wind. She flew straight up and over the ship, immediately scenting his blood and flying straight for it.

No.

No. No. NO.

This. Would not. Happen.

Cheng was carrying him across the deck. "Get back! And get Tenzin right now!"

She saw it in the deck lights. The sword pierced his back, running straight through his spine to his belly. His limbs were limp and motionless, encased in the black diving suit he wore underwater. She could hear his heart beating.

Cheng laid him on his side, and crew members crowded around him. The ship's medic was running toward them with a white bag while two humans ran, carrying a stretcher behind them.

Tenzin landed in a crouch next to Ben and snarled at the humans. "Get. Back."

Cheng gently removed the mask. "His tank was still working. He's still breathing. He didn't run out of air. I smelled the blood as soon as I got in the water and swam straight for him."

Ben was pale, but his eyes were open.

The corner of his mouth turned up. "Hey, Tiny."

25

B en was drifting in and out of consciousness as Cheng and Tenzin fought.

"I'm calling the helicopter."

"They won't be able to fix him."

"He's not dead! Whoever meant to kill him failed. We can save his life."

Tenzin crouched next to Benjamin, stroking a hand over his cold cheek. "He will not die."

Cheng gripped her shoulder and shook it. "Do not do this. He didn't want it. You know he didn't want it."

The Italian girl was standing in the crowd, sobbing. "Someone do something! Take the sword out of him, *Madonna*, take it—"

"Do not touch the sword!" Cheng and Tenzin both roared.

Her eyes rose to meet Cheng's. He had been in battle. He knew exactly what kind of wound this was.

"He might not die," she said quietly. "But he'll never walk. He'll never climb a mountain. He'll never fly if the humans are allowed to heal him."

"He did not want this." Cheng shook his head slowly. "I won't do it."

She watched Ben's eyes. They were open, but he wasn't listening to them. He was in too much pain. "I'm not asking you."

Cheng reached for her wrist as Tenzin moved to lift Ben, but she snarled and bared her teeth.

He whispered, "He will not forgive you, Cricket."

She looked at Ben. Looked at Fabia crying. Looked at the panicked faces of the human crew. Looked back at Cheng.

"So be it." She picked him up, not thinking twice about the weight of his body, only cradling him carefully so she didn't disturb the blade that was keeping him alive.

Tenzin took to the air and flew. She emptied her mind of everything but the mental image of the courtyard where her father would be drinking tea and feeding her carp as they darted between the boulders and fountains in her garden.

"Tenzin?"

"Shhh." She glanced down. "Be calm. Be quiet."

"Don't change me," he whispered. "Don't you dare."

"I'm not."

Tears filled his eyes. "You promised me. Do you remember?"

The pain clogged her throat. She choked out, "I remember."

"So don't you dare." His voice was barely over a whisper.

"Ben, be quiet."

"I need to tell you something."

"Tell me later."

He laughed, and a drop of blood stained his lip. "I'm dying."

"No, you're not." She blinked at the red that filled her eyes. "You're not going to die."

"I don't feel anything." His voice was like a child's. "That's so weird."

"Benjamin, be calm." She forced back the scream that wanted to burst from her throat. "Just be quiet."

His eyes closed and he fell silent. Tenzin moved with inexorable purpose, her mind on nothing but her father in the courtyard.

He will be there.

He will be there.

He will do this for me.

"Tiny?"

"Ben, be still."

He forced his neck around so he could see her face. "You're crying."

"It's the rain." The storm had come on them swift and sudden. She could hear thunder in the distance.

"It's red though." He was starting to slur his words.

"Ben, be quiet."

They were halfway there. Over halfway. She could feel his blood dripping between her fingers. It had slowed but it hadn't stopped.

"Tenzin."

"I told you to save your strength."

"You were right about Johari."

Rage burned in her chest. "She did this?"

"We found the sword. It was with the glass like you thought." He started to slur his words again. "Glass ca-cash. Case. Like... bubble. Bread. Weird."

She didn't know what he was talking about, and she couldn't find it in her heart to care. She didn't care about the sword. She didn't even care about Johari yet. Soon she would, but for now all she could think about was her father in the courtyard. Drinking tea. Waiting for her.

"I feel I am needed."

Why else would fate have brought him to her? Why had

any of this happened? Why did she still live? Why had she survived? Why had he survived until this moment?

The tears and the rain mixed together. "Everything will be as it will be," she whispered.

"Tiny?"

"Shhhh. You need to be quiet."

"I need to tell you something."

"Tell me later."

"No, I n-need to tell you now." His voice took on a strange clarity. "I need to tell you now, Tenzin."

"Don't—"

"I love you." There was more blood staining his lips. "I love you so much. And I'm dying, so you need to know that. That I love you. I love you more than anyone I've loved in my life." He swallowed hard.

"Benjamin—"

The corner of his mouth curled up. "You never talk and now you want me to shut up, but I'm dying and you need to know..."

The rain lashed her face. She could see the lights of the city on the horizon.

"You're... lovely." He sniffed. "Lovable. You're... worthy of that." He started to slur again. "I am too, I think. So when I'm gone, don't kill anyone, okay?"

"Be quiet, Benjamin," she whispered. "Just be quiet."

"I wish I could kiss you one more time." Tears and rain wet his face. "I really wanted one more dance."

She put her lips down to his ear, and her tears mixed with his. "Shhhhh."

Something broke inside him, and he cried. His body was motionless, but harsh sobs burst from his mouth. "I didn't want to die yet."

"I know," she whispered. "You won't."

She pressed her cheek to his and let her amnis slip over him.

"Tenzin don't... don't... dooon't..." His voice trailed off as she put him into the deepest sleep she could risk. His heartbeat slowed. His temperature dropped.

"Be calm." She flew past the lights of Shanghai without even slowing. "Be calm."

She flew through the darkness. She didn't stop. She didn't slow. She didn't think of anything but her father in the court-yard of her house, feeding the fish. Drinking tea. Waiting to finally pay his debt.

He will be there.

He will be there.

He will do this for me.

Ben's eyes were closed, but his heart was still beating when she landed in the courtyard of her house.

Her father was nowhere to be seen.

Tenzin lifted her voice and screamed, "ZHANG!"

Jinpa came running. Mei came running. She ignored their cries of surprise and shock. They ran toward Tenzin.

"Stop!"

They halted, both holding hands over their mouths.

"Zhang Guolao!" she screamed again.

Her father stepped through the doorway of her house. His face was grim and his eyes severe. He took in the situation in an instant. He was old. He had seen battle. He would know the favor she asked of him before she opened her mouth.

Tenzin gently placed Ben's body on the ground, propped him on his side, faced her father, and allowed her tears their release.

She lowered herself to her knees and put her forehead to the ground. *"Aabmen."*

"Min zuvu." Zhang's voice was pained. "What have you done?"

Tenzin crawled on her hands and knees, her face turned to the ground, until she reached her father's feet.

She could smell the cooking fires and hear the stomping ponies. Taste the blood in her mouth as his sons laughed and kicked her as she passed through the gauntlet.

Tenzin reached Zhang's feet and put her forehead to the ground again, her ears tuned to Ben's slow heartbeat.

Thump. Thump. Thump.

She pleaded in his mother's tongue. "*Aabmen*, I ask this of you."

Zhang was silent.

"My father, I ask you—"

"Daughter, he did not want this fate."

She felt the blood in her veins rise. Felt her fangs lengthen.

She smelled the cooking fires and heard the ponies. The sound of laughter and the pain as they kicked her. She lunged toward the bronze blade in the soldier's hand, eager for a swift death. They laughed again. They slapped her. They broke her.

Until she broke them.

Ben's heartbeat steadied her.

Tenzin raised her eyes to her father's and spoke softly. "You will do this for me."

His face was full of compassion. Sorrow, even. But his eyes were resolute. "My daughter, he did not want—"

"*You!*" She flew straight up and looked her sire level in the eye. "You will do this. For *me*. For your only child. For the daughter who killed your sons. For the *warrior* who led your armies." She pointed at Ben, whose pulse was starting to fade. "You will do this for *me*."

Her sire was silent as a stone.

"Zhang Guolao, I killed your children one by one. Every child of your amnis was laid to the ground and the earth *drank their blood.*" She beat her breast. "I did that! And now I offer you another."

His eyes burned her. "If you are so determined, change him yourself."

Her breath stopped. "I cannot."

"Why?"

She screamed in his face.

"Tell me why, Tenzin." Zhang's voice was a whisper.

"You know why." Her voice broke. "You *know.*"

His face softened, but his eyes did not. "Daughter, I know this man. He *did not* want this."

"You will do this for me." Tenzin's voice was a low promise. "You will change him. You will give him your power and your life. Or you will be *nothing* to me."

He blinked.

"I will have no father in this life or in eternity. I will not see you. I will not speak of you. Your name will be dead on my tongue, and the language you dream in will never cross my lips again."

Zhang's eyes went wide. "You are my *daughter.*"

She gripped his collar. "I will have *no* father." Tears poured down her face. "Hear this now: if you deny me this, I will never speak your mother's words again." She made her voice the blade that would slay him. "And when the long night comes that your soul departs this body, there will be *no one* to sing the songs of your fathers that will lead you to your ancestors."

His face went blank.

"You will be lost. You will be *nothing.*" Tenzin swallowed the hatred that threatened to choke her and whispered, "So you will do this for me."

Zhang walked over and gently picked up Ben's body.

Tenzin waited.

And waited.

Zhang looked at Tenzin. Then looked at Ben. He put a hand on Ben's pale cheek. "I will do this for you."

She fell to the ground and put her face to the earth. *"Aabmen."*

"Send the humans away," he said. "And leave."

Her eyes flew up to his. "I will not."

"From this night forward," Zhang said, "he will be my child."

She put her head back to the ground. "I understand."

"Know that I will never command him to forgive you."

Tenzin felt her heart move. She closed her eyes and felt Ben's pulse inside her own body. Her heart beat in time with his. *Thump. Thump. Thump.* Her chest ached with the pain of it, but she welcomed that pain.

Then Ben's heart faltered.

She closed her eyes. "Do it now."

26

S he heard his heart struggling. She heard it fall silent.
And then nothing.

Tenzin sat frozen in the courtyard, under the light of a waxing crescent moon. She held her breath, lifted her face, and prayed to the moon once more. She prayed to the stars and the sky. She prayed until the thin, golden thread of new amnis wound its way through her house and into the courtyard where she waited underneath the tangerine tree.

She'd sent Jinpa and Mei away from the house for the next day. Zhang and Tenzin would fly Ben to Penglai at dusk the next night, only hours before he would wake and become aware of what she had done.

Tenzin clung to his amnis. It was warm. Golden. It grounded her and gave her focus.

An hour after Ben's heartbeat had gone quiet, Zhang called for her. He stood in the doorway of her home and allowed her inside. "He is as he will be."

Tenzin walked into the house, noting the changes even before she saw him. His scent was different. His energy, once so ebullient, had deepened to a low, thrumming pulse she could almost feel against her skin.

Zhang had cut the black diving suit from his body and washed him, placing him on a pallet in her meditation room.

Shining boy.

Tenzin knelt down and brushed his hair back from his forehead.

One day you will be infinite.

His skin was pale with only a shadow of the summer tan he'd carried from Italy. The bruise on his lip would heal by morning. Every injury he'd worn was healing before her eyes. The wound from the sword. The gash in his belly. The nerves in his spine were knitting back together, fed by amnis that had been on this earth for over five millennia.

Old scars would remain, but his body was durable now. His mind was eternal.

"I need to tell you something."

She had wanted to be the one to wash the seawater and blood off him. Wanted to care for him as his body transitioned from mortal to immortal.

"I love you. I love you so much."

Would he remember?

Of course he would. He remembered everything.

"I have let you see him," Zhang said. "Now you should go."

"He will forgive me." Tenzin didn't move. "If it takes a century, I will wait."

"A century?" Zhang's eyes were pools of sorrow. "Oh, my daughter. I have waited far longer for forgiveness."

She looked up at her father. "Do you compare my actions with yours?"

"I would not claim that." Zhang sat across from her, Ben stretched out between them. "You acted out of love. I acted with only self-interest."

"Yes." She combed her fingers through Ben's tangled curls.

"But I am sorry for my actions," Zhang said. "I have carried regret for millennia. And you will never be sorry for this. You will never apologize for taking his life."

"No." She stared at Ben, memorizing every inch of his skin. The angle of his jaw and the exact arch of his brow. The soft curve of his lip and the faint bruise where she had bitten him, angry, afraid, and confused by the surge of emotions he elicited. "I regret nothing."

"Then we will both wait," Zhang said. "And we shall see who is forgiven first. You need to go. His immortal life is my privilege and my responsibility now. We will leave at dusk for Penglai. I want him to wake on the island."

"Of course."

Ben's life belonged to Zhang now, though Tenzin would make good on any number of threats if her sire put pressure on Ben to be anything other than what he was.

You don't know what he is now.

He could be a threat.

He is a threat.

He is not.

He is a wish.

Tenzin rose and walked to the door, taking comfort in the waves of amnis she felt growing stronger by the hour. He would be strong. He would be so strong.

"Tenzin."

She turned at the door.

Zhang's gaze was like iron. "I have not sired a child in over three thousand years."

"I know."

"He will be powerful."

"Good."

"He will be angry with you."

She nodded. "I also know that."

Ben wouldn't be the only one. Tenzin walked to the library and opened a cabinet where Ben had stored a spare tablet. She propped it in against the bookshelves, pushed the button, and woke the device.

"Waiting for voice log-in." Cara's voice was a sharp reminder that life continued outside the walls of her house.

Tenzin took a deep breath, suddenly overcome by everything that had happened in only a few short hours. She put her head in her hands and breathed out. In. Out.

"You're lovely. Lovable. You're worthy of that."

He would not think so now.

Tenzin blew out a sharp breath and felt the air draw near her skin, brushing her back and neck, swirling softly against her face as if to comfort her.

"Waiting for voice log-in," Cara repeated.

"Log in Tenzin."

"Waiting for two-factor authentication."

Tenzin placed her face in front of the tablet camera, wondering if she looked the same as she had twenty-four hours ago. How could she? She had everything and nothing she had wanted.

"Identity confirmed. Welcome, Tenzin. You have twelve new voice messages and thirty-four new text messages."

She didn't have the energy to read. "Show voice messages on-screen."

One from Ben. She would save that for when she needed it.

Two from Fabia.

Three from Chloe.

Three from Giovanni.

Two from Cheng.

One from Beatrice.

"Call Giovanni Vecchio."

She waited while the encrypted video messaging system connected. She glanced at the clock. It would be nearly noon in Los Angeles. Would Beatrice answer or Giovanni?

Giovanni's worry-ravaged face appeared on the screen. Blue-green eyes went wide when they saw her face. "Tell me he's alive."

"My boy." Tenzin swallowed hard and tried to control her face, but it was useless.

Giovanni's voice was rough. "Tell me he is alive."

She closed her eyes. "He is alive."

The unspoken question hung between them.

Tenzin opened her eyes. "He is Zhang's now."

A pained grunt, as if he'd been punched in the stomach. "But he is alive."

She nodded.

"He is Zhang's." Giovanni's eyes narrowed. "The wound in his back—"

"Already healed."

A shadow of relief.

Tenzin lowered her eyes. "If I call Cheng, will you tell the others?"

"Yes."

Silence lay like a thick fog between them.

"He told me"—she cleared her throat—"he said he didn't want to die."

"No one wants to die." Giovanni's voice was cold. "But you take dying words as permission."

The screen went black.

He was wrong. She knew it wasn't permission. She had done it anyway.

She called Cheng. He was in his cabin and Kadek was with him. "Tenzin, what—?"

"Send Kadek away."

There was silence. A minor protest from Kadek, but she heard his footsteps departing and the door opened and closed.

"Tell me."

"Zhang did it."

He answered with a string of low curses. "Your father gives nothing without price," Cheng said. "What did you have to promise?"

"To continue being his daughter." She wiped a hand over her eyes. "Cheng, tell me what happened after I left."

"It was Johari. She is gone. I cannot tell you where. By the time we put everything together after you flew away, my men couldn't find any trace of her."

"She has the sword."

His eyes narrowed. "Are you sure?"

"Ben told me. They found it. She was waiting for the opportunity. She took it and tried to kill him."

"Did she?"

It was a fair question. If she had wanted Ben dead, she could have slashed his neck. She could have cut the hoses that let him breathe underwater.

What was in your mind, Johari?

Cheng's brow furrowed. "None of this makes any sense. She is Saba's daughter. Saba and Arosh are consorts. Why would Saba—?"

"What does it benefit Saba if Arosh and Zhang are allies?" She wiped an errant tear from her nose. "What does she care if one human gets in the way?" Two humans. Johari had killed Meili also. "For that matter, Johari may not be loyal to Saba. She may be working for someone else entirely. She abandoned her element, Cheng. She gave up her amnis to live a few more years. She. Has. No. Loyalty."

Cheng appeared to be surprised by her outburst.

"I need you to send men to find her," Tenzin continued.

"She's an earth vampire, not wind. Not water anymore. She won't be able to get far without help."

"Saba has connections in Asia."

"Not as many as you do." She lifted her eyes. "Send a message to Sina in New Zealand. Tell her I am calling in a favor and offering one in return if she finds her for me."

"Just finding her?"

"Find and hold only."

Cheng nodded. "You're going to Penglai."

"At first dusk before he wakes."

Cheng took a deep breath. "Are you sure you want to be there?"

"I have to be."

"Cricket—"

"*Wǒ péngyǒu.*" Tenzin held up a hand. "No matter what happens, I need to be there. He deserves that."

"I understand. Call me if you need me." Cheng's eyes turned calculating. "So after thousands of years, Zhang Guolao has sired a son."

"Don't get that look on your face." She reached to turn off the screen. "This has nothing to do with him."

"I think you're wrong, Cricket. This has everything to do with Zhang."

THE SUN ROSE.

Tenzin rested. She meditated. She read books he had left at her house. She took shelter in the stone garden house where her father usually rested during the day. Its austerity calmed her riotous mind.

The sun reached its zenith.

She knew her father had already sent word to Penglai.

There would be celebration on the island and preparations to feed and welcome the new immortal. The elder had chosen a son. The court would celebrate such an auspicious event. She looked at the calendar and noted the position of the moon. Predictions would be made based on the hour of his turning. There would be speculation. Gossip.

She steeled herself for the field of curious faces that would meet them.

When she felt the sun go down, she left the stone house and gathered Ben's clothes, stuffing them into the spare backpack he'd left in his room. She walked out to the garden to see Zhang with Ben wrapped in a white sheet to protect his sleeping body from the wind and rain.

"I'll be flying high and fast," Zhang said. "Can you keep up?"

"Haven't I always?"

Without another word, her father soared into the sky and out of sight.

27

His body hovered a foot over the bed with a single silk sheet draped over him. It was the lightest silk they could find, nearly transparent. His skin would ache. His throat would burn. He was in Tenzin's rooms, surrounded by luxury and protected by a cadre of her father's servants, but Tenzin would not leave him.

The first night of immortality was traumatic whether you were waking in a dirty tent or a palace.

She waited with fresh blood. Waited for Ben to open his eyes.

She would not apologize.

Tenzin saw the sheet begin to move first. His amnis was waking. It was confused. Chaotic. He drifted higher, and Tenzin gently tugged the sheet to keep him in place. His power was a tangible thing. She reached out and brushed against it, trying to bring him calm.

Tenzin sensed it a split second before it happened.

His back arched and he drew in a ragged breath—the first instinct of humanity—before his eyes flew open.

Tenzin darted toward him, holding his shoulders as he opened his mouth to scream.

"*No!*"

Her heart froze, but she held him.

His body bent in half; she knew the hunger was overwhelming. His stomach would cramp and burn until he fed it. She turned him on his side and pushed him as gently as she could down to the soft mattress. "You need to drink."

His eyes flew to hers and she saw them for the first time; her breath caught.

My Benjamin.

She swallowed the knot in her throat and forced her face to remain calm.

His eyes, which had once been a warm, rich brown, had altered in immortality. They were a silvery-grey shade with dark flecks of gold.

"Tenzin?" His voice cracked. "It hurts."

"I know," she whispered. "You need to drink."

She lifted a bag of blood and held it to him. The guttural snarl he let out should have been expected, but it still surprised her.

He grabbed her wrist to hold the bag in place as he bit, and she saw his fangs for the first time. They were long, thick, and lightly curved. She pushed back her instinctual reaction to seeing them and held steady as Ben tore into the plastic bag of blood.

Zhang had suggested a goblet, but Tenzin knew better. Ben would need to bite. Need to sink his fangs into something that gave way to quench the insatiable thirst.

And he would be insatiable the first night. He would drink roughly ten pints of blood through his first night and slightly less every night for the first month. Eventually, his body would regulate. His amnis wouldn't be quite so voracious.

But this night, he needed to feed.

He finished one pint of blood, and she quickly reached for another. He saw it from the corner of his eye and whipped around to grab her other wrist.

She couldn't touch him if she tried. He gripped both her wrists with hands so strong she wondered if he could actually break her.

He was anchoring himself, holding on to something familiar, but she took nothing for granted. She knew him—despite his new body—and she knew he was furious.

When she'd been human, she'd been a thin woman recovering from her second pregnancy in four years. She'd been strong but spare. Lean.

Ben was a human in prime physical condition. He fought. He trained in weapons. He'd forced himself to climb and jump in ways normal human beings couldn't, simply so he could keep up with the predators with whom he spent his nights.

After the second pint, his initial thirst was assuaged.

He dropped his legs over the side of the bed, still gripping her wrists, and put his feet on the ground, flexing his body and rolling his shoulders.

His immortal body was perfect and primed by amnis. He looked at his feet. Flexed his toes. He looked at his knees. His naked manhood, which was standing erect, like every hair on his body. Finally he looked up at her.

Their eyes met, and she saw the rims of his eyes were red.

"You did this," he whispered.

She swallowed. "Zhang sired you."

He shook her wrists, still gripped in his hands. "You. Did this."

She blinked hard. "I did this."

He roared in rage and shoved her away. He stood and

paced. The sheet slipped from his body and she felt him flinch. "It hurts."

"Your senses are heightened," she said, keeping her voice to a whisper.

He rolled his shoulders again. "What am I feeling? In my back, there's—"

"Your back was injured. Your spine. The nerves are still knitting together."

He reached his hands up to tug his hair—a blessedly familiar gesture—but quickly dropped them. "It hurts. Everything hurts."

"I know."

He started to laugh. It was a low, bitter sound that turned into a harsh groan. "You promised. You promised. You fucking promised, Tenzin."

She'd promised not to turn him, and she hadn't. But she said nothing.

He marched over to her, his silver-and-gold eyes furious, and backed her against the silk-paneled wall, slamming both hands against it. "You *promised!*"

As soon as he shouted, he covered his ears. Then he covered his eyes. Tenzin could see the red seeping from under his fingers where his tears now mixed with blood.

She put her hand on his shoulder, touching as gently as she could, and drew amnis around him to soothe his skin.

"What are you doing?"

"Trying to make it hurt less." She kept her voice at a whisper. "Until you can control your amnis—"

"Kill me."

She froze. Felt her fangs lengthen. "No."

He bent down and stared her straight in the face. "You didn't want me. But you didn't want to let me go. So you fucking did this."

~

Tenzin shook her head, but Ben could see the guilt in her eyes.

"You don't know what you're talking about," she whispered.

"Don't I?" He put his hand on her cheek, and it didn't feel cool anymore. She felt warm. How did she feel more human when she was such a monster? And why couldn't he stop wanting her?

Ben wanted her so much, every cell in his aching, hungry body cried out for her.

He wasn't an animal. He wasn't a monster. He refused. He *refused.*

But he couldn't back away. He felt like every sense was on fire. He smelled everything. The smoke from the single candle in the room. The scent of blood on his lips. The scent of jasmine blooming out in the garden. The pine forests and the sea.

Ben bent down and pushed his face into Tenzin's neck, inhaling the familiar smell of cardamom and honey. He leaned his temple against her cheek, and she tilted her head to the side, giving him room to smell her skin, her hair.

He heard a single low thump. "What was that?"

"My heart." She swallowed. "Ben—"

"My heart." He put a hand to his chest.

Silent.

You are not human. You aren't human anymore. Your heart isn't beating. Your body is fueled by blood and amnis now. He felt dizzy, but the air licked along his skin, soothing him and igniting him.

"You did this," he said again, "so I couldn't leave you. So I could never be free of you."

She didn't answer for a long moment. Finally she simply said, "Yes."

He slammed his hand against the wall again, and she flinched.

"What gave you the right?" He bared his teeth. Why did he do that? "Tell me, what gave you that right, Tenzin?"

Something in her eyes flared, and he recognized anger. In a split second, she rose up and bit his lip, exactly where she had before.

This time Ben bit back.

He reached for her and lifted her by the waist as if she weighed nothing, bringing her mouth to his and slamming their bodies together. It hurt. And it didn't. The ache of contact was soothed by his intense hunger.

She hooked her arm around his neck and molded her lips to his. He tasted blood on her tongue and he drank it. He bit her lower lip, and Tenzin let out a soft moan. She wrapped her legs around his waist, and he pressed his body into hers.

His erection was nearly painful. His body lay in the curve of hers, and she wasn't pushing him away. She wasn't draining him. She was holding his shoulders so tightly Ben thought he might bruise. Her lips ran over his skin and her tongue licked the blood from the scrapes her nails left in his shoulders.

His blood only seemed to stoke her hunger. Ben could smell the arousal rising from her body, and he ran a hand up her thigh, sliding his fingers under the robe she wore.

He brushed his thumb between her thighs and it came away wet. Ben put his finger in his mouth, tasting her as she lapped at his blood. Driven by both hungers, he tore the clothing from her body and threw it across the room.

He wanted to feel her. Wanted her bare skin and hard angles. Her nails moved to his neck and she scraped him again. Ben roared and threw his head back, only to have Tenzin bare her teeth and put her mouth to his neck.

Ben didn't think. He couldn't. He only knew hunger and

the means to sate it. He spread her legs and angled his neck to the side, entering her body as she pierced his throat.

It was so fucking good he couldn't even describe it.

Take me.

Take me.

Take everything.

He thrust her against the wall, and his body was on fire. Whatever he'd thought sex was, he'd been wrong. This was the only pleasure.

She drank from him, and he felt his newly woken amnis enter her blood. The sensation was so disorienting he nearly stumbled. He braced himself against the wall, pinning her body as he drove into her over and over again.

Air swirled around them, but Ben couldn't concentrate. He heard things falling. Something ripped through the air.

She surged and moved with him, her breath the only music he wanted. He could smell the blood in her veins and he hungered for it. He put his hand on the back of her head, gripped her thick hair, and pulled her mouth away from his neck.

Tenzin released him, licking his blood from her lips as her cheeks flushed with color.

You did this.

Ben couldn't stop moving. He didn't think about rhythm. He didn't think about bringing her pleasure. His mind had distilled to emotions. Desire. Anger. Hunger.

The room crashed around them, the air whipped into a frenzy.

His fangs fell, and his throat burned.

She lifted a hand to his mouth, stroked them, and it was as if she'd run a finger along the length of his cock. He bit down on her finger and tasted blood.

A satisfied moan left her throat, and Ben bit harder.

"Yes." She put her hand on the back of his head and caressed his neck, her body rocking as he drove back and forth. Her hair clung to the red silk walls. Her eyes were dilated, her mouth was open, and her breath came in sharp, panting pulses.

Something cracked and glass broke. A loud banging noise came again and again.

She leaned forward, taking his mouth with hers. She didn't bite him this time; she moved her lips with aching, thorough languor, and the sigh she breathed into him nearly made him come. The air crept up his body, licking in soft whispers like feathers against his skin.

No.

It was too soft. Too gentle. His hand went to her nape and he pushed her hair to the side, baring her pale neck to his fangs. Her breath caught.

Ben froze.

The air around them whirled and kissed them, teasing his skin and warming it. It was as if a thousand tongues licked up his body. Ben was poised on the edge of climax, Tenzin's vein under his lips.

She whispered, "Do it."

He bit, and she exploded around him. Her amnis blew his hair back from his face and her body convulsed as Ben drank her in.

Tenzin's blood was the perfect wine. It was heat and life and tears and the salty sea. It was blood, the essence of her. Her life in his. He felt her body shaking as he climaxed, but Ben couldn't understand where or why or how he knew, he knew, he *knew* she wanted him and hated him and feared him and needed him. She wanted more and she would take *everything*. Her blood was his and his was hers.

You did this.

You did this.

You did this.

He was crying inside, but it was her voice in his mind. Her anger in his heart. Her blood on his tongue.

I did this.

They came together, blood binding them as the wind caressed their bare skin, and Ben realized he wasn't even touching the ground.

BEN LICKED her blood from his lips and pushed away from the ceiling, floating to the ground with only a faint wobble. Tenzin watched him as he walked to the table and reached for another bag of blood. He bit into it as he'd bitten into her.

Tenzin watched silently, unable to speak.

He had destroyed her, and he didn't even realize what he'd done.

She felt shattered. It was not unlike the moment her blood mate, Stephen, had died. She and Stephen had exchanged blood, but he had never taken it from her vein. Tenzin hadn't let anyone drink from her vein in thousands of years.

You don't know him anymore.

He made no move to cover himself. Why would he? He was a perfect specimen of masculine beauty. His body was lean and perfectly formed. His legs were long and his body well proportioned. He had an innate grace and athleticism he had honed over fifteen years of careful study and practice.

He hated her.

Ben caught his reflection in the mirror and stared. He was seeing his eyes for the first time. Seeing the reflection of the creature she had made him. She hadn't forced her blood into his body to make him immortal, but she had taken him to her father, demanded his blood, and issued the direst of threats to make it happen.

She could have taken him to the human healers. He would have lived. He might have walked with enough human science. He could have had a full mortal life.

She hadn't done that.

Ben bit into another bag of blood and drank as Tenzin floated to the ground and retrieved the robe she'd been wearing. She'd worn deep plum, but he wouldn't have noticed. She wrapped the robe around herself and waited silently.

He tossed the empty bag to the side and swallowed, wiping all traces of it from his lips. "My eyes?"

"Will stay mostly as they are now."

"Did your eyes change?"

"I assume so."

"You assume a lot," he said quietly.

"I know."

Ben reached for the silk sheet and gingerly wrapped it around his waist. "We're in Penglai?"

"Yes."

"Am I in your father's quarters or in yours?"

"Mine."

"I'd like to move to Zhang's tonight." He walked to the bathroom and paused at the door. "Please leave."

28

B en held his breath under the bathwater until he realized he didn't have to breathe. He'd been subconsciously waiting for the burning in his lungs, but it never came. He sat up and wiped the water from his face.

The pressure from his own hands hurt.

His body—everything about this strange shell—felt wrong.

His throat burned. It was like the worst case of strep throat ever, but without the swelling or the ice cream. His skin ached. Even his hair hurt when it moved. He wondered if he could swallow ice or if his body would reject it.

He didn't feel the need to pee.

He was hungry again.

He was horny again.

Ridiculously, excessively horny. He'd come five minutes ago and was still hard as a rock.

You had sex with Tenzin.

It had been... He didn't have words for it.

He wanted her to be there when he got out of the bath, and he knew she'd be gone.

She was good at leaving.

You asked her to leave.

Ben was so angry with her he didn't know what to say.

I hate you.

I need you.

Don't leave me.

I can't stand the sight of you.

Among the tangle of thoughts in his mind, he kept coming back to three things: he'd had sex with Tenzin, he'd drunk her blood, and he didn't have words to describe it.

He needed a few years and a few barrels of whiskey to even begin to explain what he was feeling. In that moment, all he felt when he thought about her was anger. He wanted to hit her. He wanted to hold her. He wanted to scream at her.

He wanted to do it again.

Fuck, he was a mess.

Ben sucked in a harsh breath and rubbed his eyes. He wanted to go home to LA. He wanted to hide in his room at Giovanni and Beatrice's, eat a chicken burrito, and sleep for a week. He wanted to wake up from this nightmare.

He wanted his eyes to be brown again.

He didn't want blood to taste good.

He wanted to talk to Beatrice. He wanted to know what to do.

How am I supposed to feel, B? Because right now I can't think. Every time I think more than five minutes in advance, I feel so overwhelmed I want to cry.

Why did he want to cry? He was angry, not sad. He'd been stripped of his free will, his humanity taken from him, and handed over to a vampire not even Tenzin liked.

Okay, maybe he had a good reason to cry.

You can't stay in the bath forever.

Ben stood and reached for a towel, keeping his eyes fixed on the floor. He kept catching his reflection in the mirror and wishing he hadn't, wishing the old myth about vampire reflections was truth.

Sometimes it was worse knowing.

Kill me.

It was still an option. All Ben would have to do is park himself out in the sun and he'd burn up in the daylight. But there were two problems with that idea. He'd seen a vampire burning one time, trying to kill himself. It wasn't quick and it was incredibly painful. Also it was one thing to be faced with death and accept it, it was another to actively go looking for it.

He reached for a soft cotton towel and wrapped it around his body. He tried to dry off his shoulders, but rubbing his skin hurt. Not as much as Tenzin's fingernails had hurt, but—

He'd had sex with Tenzin.

Ben glanced at his shoulder, but all he could see where she'd marked him were faint red lines. The bloody marks had already healed.

You told her to leave.

He didn't want to see her. And he did. If anyone else had caused this—if he'd been turned against his will by another vampire—she'd be the *only* person he would want. He would crave her advice and her comfort. She would hold him. She would put her arms around him and watch him while he slept and he would know—he would *know*— nothing in the world would survive her fury or her revenge.

And eventually she would find something funny and make him laugh.

And they would be fine. He would be fine. They would figure it out together.

But instead, she'd been the one to do it. She hadn't put her blood in his body, but Ben knew without a shadow of a doubt that she was the reason he was a vampire.

"You did this."

She hadn't denied it and she hadn't looked a bit sorry. Guilty? Yes. But not sorry.

Why should she be? She had him exactly where she wanted him now, tied to her by a shared sire for eternity.

Maybe death was a better option.

Ben walked out of the bathroom, sat on the edge of the bed, and closed his eyes. A thousand images flashed before him. The sun setting over the beach in Malibu. The heat of midday in the rainforest in Puerto Rico. Free running at daybreak over the rooftops in Hell's Kitchen. Strolling through the streets of Rome with Fabia teasing him about his appetite. Catching Chloe in the park so they could grab a bagel, sit on a park bench, and talk shit about tourists in Midtown.

And everywhere in his memories, Tenzin. More Tenzin. Still more Tenzin. Training together. Working together. Playing games and cooking. Dancing in the moonlight.

You told her you loved her.

He'd been dying and he'd thought she needed to know.

What a mess. What a complete fucking mess.

Ben heard a tap on the outer door and stood up, looking around the shattered room. "Just a minute."

How did controlling air work? Clearly, something explosive had happened between him and Tenzin, but he had no idea. He could tell that something was happening, but he couldn't tell what. Mostly he felt untethered. If he stopped moving for too long, he had a tendency to float.

Really, really disturbing.

He opened the door and saw Zhang. A rush of unfamiliar emotions hit him.

Familiarity. Fear. Hunger. Affection. Humility.

He had the urge to bow, and layered over that was a keen and powerful desire to please this stranger standing before him.

Ben let out a hard breath as tears returned to his eyes. "I don't know..."

Zhang looked curious but said nothing.

He shook his head. "I don't know."

Zhang took a breath and let it out slowly. "I suppose that is not a bad place to start."

"Okay." Ben backed up and Zhang Guo, elder of Penglai Island, king of the Naiman Khanlig, general of the Altan Wind, ancient immortal—and father of the woman Ben had just had sex with—entered the room.

Shit.

The long-haired vampire looked around the battered room, looked back at Ben. Looked at the bed. Nodded. "It smells like sex in here. Let's go somewhere else."

Fuck. That was embarrassing.

BEN WAS WRAPPED in a fresh zhiduo of dark blue silk. His skin reacted to everything that touched it, but he tried to ignore the sensation. It wasn't pain. It was just sensitivity.

"What are you feeling?" Zhang asked.

"Physically?"

Zhang poured two cups of tea. "We'll start there."

"Everything hurts. But not really hurts, it's just... a lot."

"Intense."

"Yes."

Zhang nodded. "That is normal."

But nothing about this situation could be considered normal.

They were sitting in a room that was startlingly plain

considering the owner. Half of the roof was open to the sky, and the walls were plain wood paneling. No flourishes. No wood-work or painting. Plain wood. The floor was bamboo covered in woven mats. It looked more like a monastery than the quarters of an ancient king.

Zhang looked around, noting Ben's careful eye.

"I understand the theater of ruling," Zhang said. "Rulers need theater. It is a valuable skill I have used for thousands of years. But you are my son now—"

Ben tried not to flinch.

"—so theater is not for you." Zhang looked around. "These are my personal quarters. As long as you are in Penglai, you may ask to enter them."

"Thank you."

Two low benches with cushions sat on either side of a small table. There was tea, and Zhang had ordered a quiet vampire in the corner to bring noodle soup and more blood.

"As for the intensity of your feelings, Benjamin, you will find that the more you indulge your appetites, the more intense they become," Zhang said. "That goes for everything but blood. Right now you *need* blood. When the time comes that you do not need it and simply want it, we will begin your training."

"What kind of training?"

"I believe I will wait for your uncle's guidance on where we should start," Zhang said.

Ben looked up. "Giovanni?"

Zhang nodded. "Your aunt and uncle are in route to Penglai right now. They immediately sought permission of the elders to visit you."

"Thank you." Ben felt like crying again, but he managed to take deep breaths to contain his emotion.

Zhang slid a cup of tea to Ben. "I have no desire to separate you from your uncle or aunt. One, they are valuable allies I respect and noted scribes here on the island. Two, they are close friends of my daughter. And three, they are your family. I respect family."

"Thank you."

"Nevertheless, you will not be permitted to return to them right now," Zhang said. "Or anytime in your first year, at the very least. They are skilled and capable vampires, but you are not a water vampire or a fire vampire." Zhang sipped his tea. "You command the air. And you are already very powerful."

A year? "I'm going to be isolated on Penglai Island for a year?"

"Of course not. This is a court. There are too many humans who have reason to be here, and having a newborn vampire on the island for an extended period of time would be an intrusion on my fellow elders' ability to conduct business. You and I will go to my fortress in the Khentii Mountains. You will be isolated there and no threat to humans."

"The Khentii Mountains?"

"Mongolia," Zhang said. "You will learn to harness your power, and I will train you in the ways of a warrior of my line."

Ben stared at his tea. "Your line?"

"Tenzin has never chosen to sire a child." The corner of Zhang's mouth turned up. "Or none that she has told me about. It would not be unpleasing to me if you did not follow her example. Currently, my line has only myself, Tenzin, and now... you."

Ben had to ask. Maybe he would be punished for it, but he didn't care. "Why did you do it?"

Zhang lifted his chin, and Ben felt immediately humbled.

He looked down, but he didn't regret asking the question. "I need to know."

"No, you *want* to know. You will learn the difference between need and want when you train with me."

Ben forced his eyes up to Zhang's. "Fine. I want to know."

Zhang's eyes softened a fraction. "You have a strong spirit. And someday I may tell you, but not tonight. Right now everything in your mind and body has been pushed to the limit. You need to feed."

As if on command, the quiet vampire who had been waiting on them appeared at the door with a large goblet of fresh blood.

"You will learn to drink from the vein in time," Zhang said. "For now, a cup will do."

He felt like a child with a sippy cup, and yet he didn't care. As soon as the vampire entered the room, all Ben could think about was the blood he carried.

Ben tipped the goblet back and drank the blood down as if he'd just found an oasis in the desert. He drank every drop and had to restrain himself from licking the goblet.

"Tai will get you more blood." Zhang waved for Tai to leave the room. "He will also be accompanying us to Khentii."

"But he's not your son?"

"No. Tai is the son of an old rival."

"What happened to his sire?"

"I killed him."

Ben wasn't shocked. "So now Tai works for you?"

"Trust me, he is quite grateful."

Zhang could have been telling the truth. Some sires were horrible to their children, though Zhang didn't appear to be with Ben. Was it because he was Giovanni's nephew? Or was it because Zhang, like the rest of the vampire world, somehow thought Ben belonged to Tenzin?

Zhang poured more tea in his cup and Ben's. "You may not realize it, but you are showing admirable restraint for a newborn."

"Thank you."

Zhang angled his head to the side and examined Ben's neck. "Ah."

"Ah?"

Zhang looked at Ben but said nothing else.

Ben realized what Zhang was seeing. He hadn't really looked in the mirror after seeing his eyes because he was avoiding his own face, but his new sire likely saw the marks Tenzin had left in his neck.

Awkward.

Ben pulled the collar of his zhiduo up. "When do we leave for Khentii?" Ben had the crazy wish that maybe he and Zhang could sneak away before Tenzin thought about finding him again. Maybe he could be the one to disappear this time. He could feel her at a distance—he didn't know how—and he sensed she was impatient.

That might have been her blood, or it could have just been that he knew her. Tenzin was always impatient.

Zhang said, "I am glad to know you are eager for this journey, but we will not leave Penglai until the matter of the Laylat al Hisab is finished."

That fucking sword.

Ben sipped his tea. "I saw it. It was on the ship."

Zhang's eyes gleamed. "So my daughter told me. What did it look like?"

"Intact. Astonishingly intact. I can't tell you more than that. It had been enclosed in..." Ben struggled to describe it. "Like a glass bubble or a case. The glass was thick, eaten away on the outside, but it wasn't cracked. I saw the outline of the sword when I..."

When I shined my flashlight through the case and Johari speared me to the bottom of the ocean like a putting a toothpick in a sausage.

"Harun must have created a special glass case for the sword, not wanting it to be damaged by water," Zhang said. "Clever,

clever vampire." He chuckled. "Now we simply have to retrieve it from the immortal who stole it."

"Saba's daughter," Ben said. "She won't be an easy target."

Zhang's expression could only be described as amused. "Saba's daughter will never be a match for mine."

29

On the second night after Ben had lost his mortal life, Tenzin cleaned up the wreckage of the room they had destroyed, folded the sheets he had slept on, and washed the bathroom he had used. Then she ate a bowl of noodle soup before she walked out of her rooms in Penglai Island and took to the sky.

Her father was waiting in the air. "The Laylat al Hisab is in an oblong glass case. Ben says he thinks it is red, but he was underwater and his memory of that night is incomplete."

"Understood." She kept her face expressionless and her thoughts to herself.

"He is doing well. His thirst is being sated by the typical amount of blood. He has no pain or memory of his injuries."

She nodded.

"He has not asked about you."

Tenzin kept her eyes on the horizon. "I understand."

Zhang reached down and lifted her chin, turning Tenzin's head until he could look her in the eye. "The truth is not always beautiful."

"I learned that centuries ago." She would not think of him.

She would not think of anything but her mission. "I will find the sword, Father. I will kill Saba's daughter."

"Is that what you think I want?" He stared at her. "My daughter, if you resist change, you will never be who you were meant to become."

She looked at him, the familiar planes of his face. The arched eyebrows and wide mouth. He was a man who had learned to laugh and smile when he was in company. He was a chameleon in a way she had never been.

"I know who I am," Tenzin said. "I will return when it is done."

Zhang released her, and Tenzin turned south. She flew over the ocean that guarded the sacred island and the fields on the mainland. She flew fast, marking landmarks as she passed them. She flew over Shanghai and didn't stop. The flight to Cheng's ship would take her most of the night.

Tenzin didn't think about Ben. She didn't think about the Laylat al Hisab or her desire to kill Johari. She opened her soul wide and absorbed the dark night around her, drawing strength from the emptiness of the sky.

I am as old as the wind I walk upon.

She dropped lower when she reached Fuzhou, blowing through the mist from the ocean and through the city air until she reached the ocean.

Murderer.

Liar.

Lover.

Thief.

Hero?

She could never be a hero. What she could be was a blade.

Tenzin dropped to the deck of the *Jinshé* and walked past Kadek, who was ordering men moving the tanks.

"No, no! You're going to tip— Tenzin?"

She didn't stop. She marched straight to the bow of the ship and looked for him. She could already scent his amnis.

Cheng turned when she rounded the corner. He held out his arms and she walked straight into them. She allowed herself to feel, just a little bit, as he embraced her. Cheng knew not to push too far.

That was the difference between Cheng and Ben. Ben *always* pushed too far.

"Cricket."

She said nothing because there was nothing to say.

"You came back for the sword?"

She nodded.

"Very well." He kept her wrapped in his arms. "We only have a few more nights of recovery. I am responsible for the human crew, but if you want me to send someone I trust—"

"I don't need anyone," she said. "I will need to see her quarters."

"Done. I haven't let anyone in."

"And I need a place to rest."

"Of course. The hold is waiting for you. The men already repaired the doors."

Tenzin was tired. She couldn't remember being tired before. Weary? Perhaps. But tired? It was a foreign sensation, one she hadn't felt in millennia and one she did not care for.

You have taken his blood.

One night. One bite. It was hardly significant. She stepped away from Cheng and rubbed a hand over her neck. "Is Fabia still here?"

"Yes, but she's leaving tomorrow." Cheng looked confused. "Someone is coming from California to pick her up in Fuzhou. Who—?"

"Giovanni and Beatrice will be on their way to Penglai."

Cheng's eyes went wide. "She won't be able to see him. She cannot see him."

"She won't. They're not idiots. But after they see Ben, they'll return her to Rome."

"I would have assumed they'd be taking Ben back to Los Angeles or one of their other safe havens."

Tenzin cocked her head. "Why?"

Cheng frowned. "He's their *son*, Tenzin."

"No. He's Zhang's son now."

"Is he?" Cheng took a step back. "You made whatever deal you made with your sire, Cricket. But Giovanni Vecchio is the son of an ancient, just as you are."

She scoffed. "His sire is dead."

"But his sire's sire is not. And Kato is as old as you and Zhang. Perhaps older."

"It doesn't matter. Giovanni is a fire vampire who belongs to a water clan."

"You think they don't have wind vampires loyal to them?" Cheng said. "Of course they do."

Tenzin thought about all of Giovanni's connections. While he might not be as old as Tenzin, there was a reason she'd once chosen him as a partner when she'd been an assassin. What he lacked in power, he made up in political connections, discipline, and sheer ferocity.

"What are you trying to say, Cheng?"

"I'm saying that Ben might not be in Penglai by the time you get back with your father's sword. Be prepared for that."

Tenzin stared at the horizon, watching as the sky lightened to a dark, pearlescent grey.

"I am prepared for Ben to hate me quite thoroughly. In fact, I expect it."

"So why—?"

"I did what I had to do, Cheng." She turned and walked to

the stairs that led belowdecks. "Ben is alive, and I will not regret it."

~

SHE WAS STARING at the painted white bulkhead, drifting in a heightened level of consciousness. She saw the room from above, floating over her body. Saw the neatly stacked books, the spinning basketball, and the young girl cowering in the corner.

Wait.

She blinked awake, came back to her body, and stared.

What was that?

The basketball was between her palms and she was pushing the current of air around it, spinning it in an endless spiral. She heard footsteps approaching and knew who would open the door by the rhythm of the steps.

She didn't knock. Impertinent. Then again, Fabia was trying on wrath for a change.

"You should not have come back here." Fabia stood over Tenzin, putting her hands on her hips. "How could you do it? You *knew* what he wanted."

"To die?" Tenzin said quietly. "Do you really think he wanted to die?"

"No one wants to die"—tears filled her eyes—"but you knew he didn't want to be a vampire. You *knew* it, Tenzin."

"I know he didn't want to die." She turned back to the corner where she'd seen the vision of a girl. "Go away."

"You should go away!"

Tenzin looked back at Fabia. "You're young and you love him. But don't test me."

"You called him your friend"—tears were running down her face—"but you are the one who killed him."

"Johari killed him." Her patience was wearing thin. "I saved his life."

"You ended it." Her voice broke. "Don't you know why he didn't want this? He worked every day and every night to prove he wasn't like them. And you've taken that away."

"Now you are being foolish." Tenzin rose and walked to Fabia. "Go away before you try my patience."

"You think you know him—"

"No," Tenzin said firmly. "I do not think I know him. In fact, I know I do not." She walked toward Fabia, who backed up to the door. "Your mistake, Fabiana Teresa Salvadori, is thinking that you do." She shut the door in Fabia's face and leaned against it.

Why was she so tired?

She locked the door and walked back to the soft pallet where she'd been meditating. She lay down on her back and closed her eyes.

And then Tenzin fell asleep.

SHE WOKE WITH A GASP, confused and uncertain where she was. She looked around and locked eyes on the one thing that made sense.

Basketball.

Metal room.

Benjamin.

She reached for the shirt she'd taken from his room and put her face up to inhale the familiar scent. She took a deep breath and let it out.

Ship. She was on the ship, and she would need to search Johari's compartment that night when the sun went down. She glanced at the battery-powered clock on the box by her books.

5:41 p.m.

Tenzin blinked. "Cara?"

"Welcome, Tenzin."

"What time is sunset in... wherever I am right now."

"Sunset was at 5:40 this evening."

She sat back on her knees. She'd slept for over an hour. An *hour*. And she'd woken at sunset. "How did this happen?" she whispered.

"I'm sorry," Cara said. "Can you repeat the question?"

She'd slept. She had closed her eyes and lost time that hadn't been spent in meditation or zoned out doing another task like weaving or playing music.

What was happening to her?

You took his blood. He took yours.

Once. She'd taken his blood once.

You took from the vein. He took from yours.

"That shouldn't matter," she muttered.

She rose and smoothed a hand down her clothes, straightening the tunic and leggings she'd put on the night before. She needed to visit Johari's room. She needed to find out if Sina had any news about the sword or the vampire who had sealed Ben's fate.

That was you.

"Cara, call..." She stopped before she finished the question. "Cara, call Andrew Leu."

"Calling... Mister Stuffy."

"Who—?" Oh, that's right. That's what she'd nicknamed her father's friend in her address book. "Cara, he can't see his nickname when you call him, can he?"

"No, Tenzin. Nicknames in your address book are private."

"Probably a good thing."

A few rings and Andrew picked up. "Hello, Tenzin."

"Andrew. I am assuming my father has told you."

Andrew's voice was cautious. "He has."

"There is no need to express any personal thoughts. I will likely need to speak to Benjamin later tonight once I go through Johari's room. Please make sure he is in the phone room at the palace."

"I will convey your message to Zhang."

"Thank you. End call." Better to not let Andrew express opinions. He tended to be far too insightful. Not unlike Cheng's annoying butler, Jonathan. Or Giovanni's Caspar.

What was it with the men in her life all having world-weary, insightful servants with charming English accents? Was Ben going to get one in a few years? Or was every vampire in her life slowly turning into Batman?

Tenzin turned off her tablet and packed what she could into the backpack she'd brought on the ship. She would likely be leaving after she searched Johari's quarters, and she needed to travel light. She left the backpack in the hold and walked up the stairs to Cheng's office.

He opened the door before she could knock. "Good evening, Cricket."

"I need to see her room."

"First you need to see this." Cheng opened the door and gestured for Tenzin to enter.

Sitting at the desk, Kadek was writing in a notebook. He glanced up, grunted, then went back to work.

"Friendly as ever, I see." Tenzin walked over to the long table where a bright blue tarp had been laid; a dozen or so plastic buckets sat on top.

"Kadek believes you should not have changed Benjamin."

"I didn't change Ben." Tenzin started looking through the buckets. They contained artifacts. Glass lamps and platters. Porcelain. More glass.

Cheng coughed slightly. "It would be more correct to say he thinks you shouldn't have *had* Ben changed."

Tenzin looked up at Cheng. Then to Kadek, who was glaring. Then back to Cheng. "Is there a reason I am supposed to care what Kadek thinks?"

"Shouldn't have happened," Kadek muttered. "Boy didn't want it."

"I suppose you could try to kill him," Tenzin said, looking in one bucket that held what looked like old-fashioned glass floats. They weren't round; they were flattened and pocked from age and saltwater. "He is more powerful than you, Kadek, and he is only two nights old." She glanced at Cheng. "He's more powerful than Cheng too."

"More powerful than you?" Cheng leaned against the table. "Tell the truth."

"No."

Kadek asked, "No, he's not more powerful than you? Or no, you won't tell the truth?"

"Either," Tenzin said. "What are these?"

"They're boxes," Cheng said. "This is what I wanted you to see." He walked over and lifted one glass piece from the bucket, carefully inspecting it and holding it in two hands. "It looks like an ingot, doesn't it?"

"Yes." The color was brilliant, but the glass was pockmarked from hundreds of years of soaking in seawater.

Cheng twisted the glass, and the two halves split apart, a seam appearing out of nowhere.

"How—?" She gasped. "Oh. Clever, clever."

He held it up to her. The glass inside the box still shone. "Harun made glass boxes with seams so fine they lasted a thousand years and protected the objects inside." He walked over to the desk where Kadek sat. "Look." He placed an object in her hand. "Do you know what that is?"

"Prayer beads? They're beautiful." Tenzin turned them in her hand. "They're wood and lapis lazuli. Beautiful. I can't determine their origin."

"The wood is ebony," Kadek said. "And we found them in one of the boxes."

Tenzin looked up with wide eyes. "Impossible."

This was what her father had said. *The sword is in an oblong glass case.* Now Tenzin understood what she was looking for.

"Look at the inside of this one." Cheng lifted another from the bucket and handed it to Tenzin.

She looked for a seam but couldn't see it. But she held the glass in both hands and twisted. With some effort, the glass fell into two pieces with a perfect seam. She held the glass up to the light and saw that the inside of the box was a work of art in itself. The interior was inscribed with flowers and pomegranates, filigreed words from an ancient Syrian poem.

Cheng handed her a necklace made of wrought gold and rubies. "This was inside the box."

"He sent treasures stored in treasures." They were so beautiful her heart hurt. "Take pictures and send them to Ben. He has to see this. Also, everything in glass must go to my father. This was the true gift. Everything else was simply filling the boat."

"I would not think of keeping it," Cheng said. "Though I may request to buy some of these pieces for my collection."

"Understandable." She wanted the ruby necklace for herself.

"Do you realize what this means, Tenzin?" Cheng said. "If your father's sword was in a case like these, the Laylat al Hisab could be in nearly perfect condition."

"Yes. But that's not all it means."

"What else?"

She remembered Ben's words exactly. *"We found the sword. It was with the glass like you thought. Glass ca-cash. Case. Like... bubble. Bread. Weird."*

Ben hadn't known what he'd been looking at. Not at first. And Tenzin would never have imagined it without seeing these pieces. But Johari had known immediately what they had found, because she wasted no time eliminating her competition.

"Johari knew exactly what to look for," Tenzin said. "That means whoever sent her knew exactly what Harun packed in that caravan a thousand years ago."

30

Tenzin was staring at the day quarters of a vampire she didn't know. She didn't know Johari's history or connections. She didn't know anything about her training or her power. She was a vampire who had changed elements. She had switched loyalties, which meant she was not to be trusted.

She looked for clues in the things left behind. Johari'd had no opportunity to take her belongings after she stole the sword, leaving a few clues to where she might go.

There was a book about Taiwan and another about Macau. There was a map of the region with no markings on it. There was another book of nonfiction written by an Indian journalist. It was about refugees surviving in East Africa.

Interesting. And unexpected.

Tenzin picked up the book and paged through it, looking for pages that had been read, minute marks on the paper, and creases. The book might have been random, or it could offer a clue about who Johari truly was.

A picture fell from the paperback.

She stopped it before she lost the page, opening it to the beginning of a chapter entitled "The Good Doctor."

She skimmed the pages of the chapter detailing the work of one man in Uganda, a doctor who focused on women and children in the refugee camps, but nothing stood out as unusual until she came to one paragraph.

Dr. Zuberi, born of an Arab father and an East African mother, sees it as his mission to help these women in need, though a rare skin condition keeps his clinic operating almost entirely at night. Nevertheless, he manages to...

Manages to be a doctor and a vampire at the same time. Tenzin flipped over the picture, which was yellowed with age. A tall, attractive man in a formal, long-sleeved *thobe* stared back at her. The long, off-white robe contrasted sharply with the man's dark skin. His bearing was regal, and he did not smile. The picture was taken in a studio, no doubt at night using artificial light if it was the same ageless man. She looked at the back of the picture.

Zuberi in Lamu, 1934.

So this Zuberi was important enough to Johari to keep a picture of him, and also a book.

Interesting.

She searched the rest of the quarters, but there was nothing else of importance to note. Tenzin took the book and the photograph back to her hold and brought out her tablet.

"Cara, call Penglai."

"Calling."

The phone started to ring. Tenzin pictured it in the small room off the palace. The old landline was the only telecommunication off the island for the vampires who resided there, and the room was staffed by humans most of the time, polishing and cleaning the old rotary phone to keep it shining.

The ringing stopped and there was silence.

"Hello?"

She closed her eyes when she heard his voice. Tenzin

couldn't think of a single thing to say. She saw his face. His fine, graceful fingers holding the phone handset to his ear. His lips waiting to speak.

"Tenzin, you wanted me here, so I am. I've been waiting for an hour and a half. What do you want?"

She swallowed hard. "Did Johari ever mention a man? A doctor in East Africa named Zuberi? He is a vampire."

"No."

Damn.

"But she did mention a lover. He was the reason she changed, but they weren't together anymore."

"Did she say where he was? Did she tell you anything more?"

"No." His voice turned hard. "Is that all?"

No, that wasn't all. "Benjamin, I am going to find her. I am—"

"I don't care." The line went dead.

Tenzin sat frozen. A minute later, her tablet buzzed.

"Incoming call from... Penglai."

"Answer."

He didn't wait for her to speak. "If you're still on the ship, have Fabi pack up my stuff so she can give it to Gio. If she can't do it, I'll have Zhang contact Jonathan."

She took a breath. "I can—"

"Just pass the message along." The line went dead again.

BEN SAT IN THE HARD, straight-backed chair in the telephone room. His throat was on fire. Zhang and Tai stood over him, watching his every move like he might fly out of control at any minute. Ben didn't feel out of control—he felt numb.

She'd left, just as he'd anticipated. But then she called.

And all she cared about was finding the sword.

Ben didn't give a shit about the sword. He'd slept a dreamless sleep the day before, falling asleep like an exhausted child. He didn't dream. He didn't wake until the sun went down, but when he opened his eyes, her scent surrounded him and he ached for her.

The aching only led to anger. She was in his blood, and he wanted her desperately. Almost as much as he resented her.

"Are you ready to go?" Zhang said. "I will have Tai wait here. If she has any more questions, he can relay them to you."

"If she has any more questions, she's out of luck," Ben said. "I don't know anything more about Johari than what I told her."

That wasn't strictly true. He'd chatted with Johari on and off, but he didn't want to think about that because it was probably all lies. He'd thought they were friendly. He'd thought she was a good person he could trust, even if she was a vampire.

But no, Tenzin had been right.

Again.

Which was just fucking annoying.

Instead of allowing himself to feel the anger that burst out every time he thought of Tenzin, Ben had taken Zhang's advice and focused on the mechanics of existing as a vampire, especially a wind vampire.

Feed on blood, which wasn't as gross as he'd imagined. Oddly enough, it tasted a little bit like warm milk now, only a little saltier. Describing it wasn't easy. Ben couldn't say the blood tasted *good*; he could only say it was satisfying.

And it was very, very satisfying.

Pull his amnis around him like a shield, but don't let it make him float away. That one was harder. He wished there was some kind of button he could push to turn it on or off, but all he could do was work with his mind. The level of awareness in his body was at an all-time high.

He had to focus on the weight of his body against the ground. Going barefoot helped, but his feet were cold all the time. If he used amnis to heat them up, he started floating again. He felt like a kid learning how to ride a bike that was actually a unicycle, and by the way, it also had no brake.

Ben walked out of the phone room and around the palace, marveling at the night sky. It was astonishing in ways that he couldn't even describe, greater than any stargazing. Better than the pictures NASA posted online. It was as if he'd been wearing sunglasses his whole life and he'd just taken them off. Colors were more vivid; the dark wasn't dark at all.

A voice in the back of his mind told him that he'd miss the sun eventually, but for now he was enjoying the many changing shades of the moon.

"Once you're off the island," Zhang said, "you'll be allowed to have a voice-operated phone that is more familiar. There is no reason for you to be isolated from your friends or family as long as they are supportive."

A warning tossed out, but Ben understood. As long as no one gave him a hard time about being a vampire—or allowed him to vent his misgivings about Zhang—he could speak to them. Ben thought about all the people he wanted to speak to. Chloe. Gavin. Fabia.

Tenzin.

No, he didn't want to speak to Tenzin. He couldn't.

"Ronan," he said. "I'd like to speak to my friend Ronan when it's possible."

"Of course," Zhang said.

If anyone could understand, it would be Ronan, who had recently transitioned from mortal to immortal. Or would he? Ronan had chosen to be a vampire. He hadn't had it forced on him by violence.

Who did he know that hadn't made the choice?

Giovanni, of course. Though he'd been expecting it. That was complicated.

Brigid.

Brigid would listen to him. Brigid would help. She was a fire vampire and not always the best at control, but she was mated to Carwyn, one of Giovanni's best friends—a vampire Tenzin didn't particularly like but Ben trusted implicitly.

But he'd talk to Ronan first. Besides being a friend, Ronan was a bit of a gossip. If Ben wanted to spread the word quickly that he was no longer among the strictly living, Ronan was the man to tell.

He walked back to his room in Zhang's wing of the palace and thought about the previous night. It was a little past dusk, and Giovanni and Beatrice would be picking up Fabia in Fuzhou soon. After that, they would make their way to Penglai and arrive just before dawn.

Until then, he would wait.

He refused to think about the treasure in the ocean or the Night's Reckoning or Johari and her crimes. If he did, he'd drive himself mad. He had to focus on making it through each night and becoming familiar with his body again.

He'd stared at his reflection in the mirror until the blood-stained tears dried and he could look at his eyes without raging.

Persian eyes.

He didn't know what that meant. What did any of it mean? Why had his eyes changed but Beatrice's hadn't? Why did he feel sharp pinpricks in the soles of his feet at times? Would that sensation go away? Zhang thought they were echoes of the injury that would have left him paralyzed if he'd not been changed.

Ben tried not to notice the pinpricks and focused on controlling his amnis. He couldn't fly yet, even though Zhang said the ability was entirely up to him. He had the power, he just didn't have the control. Floating while he slept wasn't really flying.

Gavin once told Ben that it had taken years for him to have the ability to fly. Logically, Ben knew that having Zhang as his sire meant that he would be very powerful. Right now, however, he felt like a clumsy child that cried too often and didn't know how to control his emotions.

Ben read a book of poetry Zhang had given him as they walked barefoot through the garden. It was in Mandarin, which was easy for him to speak but difficult for him to read. This poet wasn't anyone Ben had heard of, but his writing was spare and used easy characters, which made the exercise challenging but not impossible. Focusing on the characters soothed his tumbling thoughts.

He'd once thought he'd have to be content speaking Mandarin well and only reading a little. But now Ben realized he had time.

He had a lot of time.

Ben had so much time before him, it threatened to drive him a little insane.

Focus on the now. Focus on the characters.

Once he understood the literal meaning, then he could think about the metaphorical meaning. Ben suddenly realized why Giovanni loved reading poetry so much, especially poetry he had to translate. Keeping his mind focused and occupied was difficult with so much new stimuli.

A female vampire approached the garden from the Hall of the Elders and stopped at the edge of the grass.

"You may approach," Zhang said.

The woman stepped forward and bowed. The slight current of air that gusted toward him smelled of aromatic resin and anise, which meant she'd been working around incense. The closer she came, the more Ben caught hints of gardenia flowers.

No one told you that when you became a wind vampire, the whole world was composed of scents. Good ones. Bad ones. Some truly horrendous ones. The wind had been blowing off the ocean when he woke earlier, and the overwhelming scent of seaweed—which he'd once enjoyed—had almost made him puke. It was incredibly potent.

There was a whole wing of Zhang's palace that smelled of honey and cardamom, the two scents he associated most with Tenzin.

Don't think about her.

If he thought about Tenzin, he would want... He would just want.

The vampire approaching them walked slowly, no doubt not wanting to startle the newborn. "Zhang's son, you are looking well this evening."

"Thank you." He tried to smile at the sweet-faced woman, but it probably looked more like a grimace.

She smiled back but spoke to Zhang. "Your guests have sent word that they will arrive in two hours, Elder. The boat will be waiting for them at the dock."

"Thank you," Zhang said.

She bowed and backed away, probably to avoid turning her back on the newborn.

"How long are people going to be afraid of me?" Ben asked.

"Does it bother you that they're afraid of you?"

"Yes." Ben had spent his life trying to be inconspicuous, trying to set people at ease so they would give him what he wanted or needed. "I really hate it, actually."

"Then there is good news and bad news for you," Zhang said. "The bad news is that for the rest of your immortal life, there will be some—possibly many—who see you as a threat. This is because you are dangerous and you will be very powerful."

"Great."

"The good news is that your attitude pleases me. Too often men seek this life because they want to be feared. That you do not means that my daughter was correct."

"Oh?"

Zhang turned and looked him in the eye. "Yes. She told me years ago that you would make an extraordinary vampire, Benjamin Vecchio. I believe she was right."

Ben didn't know how to respond to that.

"Of course," Zhang said, "we don't need to tell Tenzin she was right. She already thinks she's omniscient. No need to encourage her."

31

Tenzin conveyed Ben's message to Fabia, dismissing the girl's obvious anger so she could focus on finding any trace of the doctor or Johari.

If Tenzin's suspicions were correct, Johari would be feeling lost, literally out of her element. The man she probably still loved was in a refugee camp across the ocean, she had been sent on a deadly assignment with little hope of success by her new vampire sire, and she hadn't had any time to plan.

What would be Saba's play? What was the plan? They could not know when or how the Laylat al Hisab would be found. How was Johari supposed to get it back to her sire? Who would she meet? Where?

How did an out-of-place earth vampire get an ancient sword from the East China Sea to the Mediterranean, particularly when her sire had few connections in East Asia and Pasifika?

A ship. Obviously, it had to be a ship.

She waited in Cheng's office for him to see Fabia off on the helicopter, staring at the large map he'd posted on his wall.

Taiwan.

Hong Kong? No, still ruled by Penglai, though it had its own regional lord like Cheng controlled Shanghai.

Would she have gone south?

The Philippines.

Hainan.

Once she reached the South China Sea, all bets would be off. Power in that region shifted constantly. If Johari reached the Indian Ocean, she and the sword would be lost. The ocean was too big. There were too many ports in Southeast Asia as it was, and Tenzin had connections there. She had to stop Johari before she reached the Indian Ocean.

Cheng entered his office and caught her staring at the map.

"Tell me Sina has something," Tenzin said.

"I don't think she went that far south." Cheng sat on the corner of his desk.

"So we have nothing?" Tenzin cut her eyes to Cheng. "How can we have nothing?"

"Think, Tenzin. Johari once drew her strength from the water, but she's an earth vampire now. She's comfortable in the ocean, but swimming will eventually drain her energy."

"So she can't have gone far."

Cheng toyed with the cuff of his shirt. "I sent a message to Jimmu. I had a feeling he might know something."

"Jimmu doesn't owe me any favors," Tenzin said. "How much does he want?"

"Don't worry about it; Jimmu owes me a favor."

"Cheng—"

"I was hired to do a job, and I'm going to do it. Jimmu gave me a tip. A yacht owned by a Kenyan businessman docked in Taipei over a week ago. The businessman's name has been linked to a company that is vampire-owned. They were there for about a week, and no one presented themselves to Jimmu's daughter, who runs the island."

Taiwan was an independent human state, but in the vampire world it was a prefecture under Jimmu's control.

"Taipei." She glanced at the clock. "It's what? An hour to fly?"

"If that."

"Johari could have swum there in one night," Tenzin said. "Especially if she was desperate."

"You can see the lights of Taipei in the distance. Even without a water ability, she's still a vampire. She wouldn't have to surface. She wouldn't have to worry about predators. She could have swum to the north end of Taiwan from here before dawn."

"Is the boat still there?"

"No. The yacht departed last night. Since whatever immortal was on the ship never disembarked, Jimmu's daughter didn't pursue it. Their human crew bought fuel and supplies only."

"The name of the ship?"

"*Arion's Flight*," Cheng said. "I'm already asking."

"They took on supplies in Taipei?"

"Yes."

"How far could they get?"

Cheng was clearly frustrated. "Jimmu didn't give me enough information about the ship, and there are too many factors to even guess. We don't know how many or where—"

"They'll be headed to the Mediterranean," Tenzin said. "They're taking it to Saba."

"Why would Saba want this sword?" Cheng said. "It makes no sense, Tenzin."

"It does if you're her." Tenzin rose and started for the door. "I'm flying to Taipei tonight. Find me a place to sleep. I'll call you before dawn."

"Good luck," he said quietly. "And be careful."

BEN WAITED in his room while Zhang greeted Giovanni and Beatrice in the Hall. The arrival of two world-renowned scholars meant that every elder was in the Hall, particularly when those scholars were the adoptive parents of Zhang's newly sired son.

The drama and tension on the island were palpable.

He heard footsteps approaching and rose just as Beatrice opened the door to his room.

"Ben?"

He couldn't say a word. He rushed to his aunt, who opened her arms to embrace him. Ben fell on her, wrapped her in his arms, and held on tight. He could feel the silent tears running down his face, but he didn't think about them. He didn't think about anything but the comfort of her embrace, her familiar scent, and the sure and steady sound of her voice.

"It's okay," she whispered. "It's okay, Ben. You're going to be okay."

Ben hid his face in her neck and allowed a wave of carefully repressed sorrow to break free. He heard the door slide closed, and something fell off a table. Wind whipped around the room, and Giovanni's hand brushed over Ben's head and neck, soothing him.

"Calm down," his uncle said. "Be calm, Benjamin."

The wind died down and Ben lifted his head, wiping red-tinted tears from his face.

Beatrice put her hand on his cheek and forced his eyes to hers. She froze for a second, then her thumb brushed his cheek. "I figured you'd be even more handsome after. Look at those eyes, Gio." She smiled. "See? Now he'll never get the girls to leave him alone."

Ben let out a laugh that was halfway to a sob. "Everything is so weird, B. I can't even look at my face anymore."

"I know, kiddo." She took a breath. "But you're gonna get through this."

"Come here." Giovanni took Ben by the shoulder and drew him into an embrace. "We love you so much. You will master this. You are going to be fine."

"Have you talked to her?" Ben didn't know how Giovanni reacted to the question, but he saw Beatrice's mouth flatten to a tight line.

"No," she said. "Our priority was getting to you."

"You are the only thing on our schedule right now," Giovanni said. "We're here for as long as you want."

"Fabi? Wait— Sadia!" It suddenly hit Ben that he wasn't going to be able to see his adopted sister for at least a year. She was human. He wasn't going to be able to play hide-and-seek with her or push her on the swings. "Where's Sadia if you're here?"

"Sadia is fine," Beatrice said. "Don't worry about her. She and the nanny are at the hangar with Fabia. The pilot can take them all on to Rome if we need to stay here. But Fabi wanted to hear from us about how you're doing before she left. Everyone knows they can't see you right now.

"Let's sit." Giovanni kept his arm around Ben's shoulders and led him to a low sitting area in the corner. "Would you like tea?" he asked. "I think tea is an excellent idea."

"Sure." Ben sat next to Beatrice, keeping her hand in his. "Tea sounds good."

Giovanni went to look for a servant, leaving Ben with Beatrice. He felt an instinctive pull toward her, while also an instinctive caution. He supposed it was because he was a predator now. He could sense her amnis in an entirely new way. He felt how powerful she was. He could feel his amnis poking and prodding hers like a child testing its limits.

"You don't know what you're doing yet," she said quietly. "So I should tell you that it's quite aggressive."

He drew his hand back. "What?"

"It's okay." She grabbed his hand and didn't let go. "You have very little control right now. Just be aware that the way your amnis is testing mine, if I didn't know you, I'd consider it aggressive."

"I don't know anything," Ben whispered. "I am so confused right now."

"And you aren't a man accustomed to being confused, which makes it harder. You've probably counted on knowing how things work since you were old enough to tie your own shoes."

Ben thought back to a childhood running around the sidewalks and alleys of the Bowery, pulling petty cons on unsuspecting tourists. He could read a mark. He could read a room. And he knew the streets of his neighborhood like the back of his hand. "Pretty much, yes."

She took a deep breath. "Just focus on drawing your amnis in. Can you feel it? Like a second skin. Focus on drawing that close to you. Make it snug. It'll keep your skin from hurting so much too."

He nodded and focused on drawing his wild amnis back to himself. It felt like trying to grab a handful of water. Every time he drew it close, it dissolved and re-formed in a new way.

"You'll get it," Beatrice said. "It'll get easier every night. After the first month or so, you won't even think about it."

"Is that how long it took you?"

"Yeah." She narrowed her eyes. "I think so."

"Your eyes didn't change."

"Nope." She brushed her thumb over his cheekbone again. "But yours did. There are rules, Ben, just like in human biology, but there are probably more exceptions than there are rules. I always assumed Tenzin's eyes had changed, so maybe it's something about Zhang's blood." Her mouth fixed in that line again. "How has Zhang been?"

"Good," Ben said. "I guess. I mean, I'm still getting to know him. I don't know much about him, because it's not like Tenzin was ever chatty about her sire. Do you know much about him?"

She took a long time to answer, which told Ben that yes, she knew things about Zhang, and they weren't good.

"I can't tell you who he is now," Beatrice said carefully. "I only know some of Tenzin's history with him. But that was a long time ago, and it's not my story to tell."

"To me he seems... fair."

"Fair is good."

Ben looked down at their joined hands. "He wants to take me to a place in the middle of nowhere. Somewhere in Mongolia, I think."

"Mongolia?" Beatrice took another deep breath.

"Yeah."

"For how long?"

"A year at least, he said."

"So just for training?"

"I think so?" He lifted his shoulders. "B, I really have no idea."

"We should talk to Gio."

"About what?" Ben felt defeated. "He's my sire now. He can make me go wherever he wants."

"Is that why you're so angry?"

Ben swallowed the burn in his throat. "I'm not angry."

"You are furious." Beatrice smiled. "I can see it in your beautiful eyes."

I don't want beautiful eyes. I want my eyes.

"I'm not furious," he said carefully.

"Not even at Tenzin?" Her voice was odd. "Because I am."

"You're furious at Tenzin?"

"And grateful at the same time." She wiped her eyes. "I'm sorry, Ben."

He put his arm around her shoulders. "You're such a crier."

"I know. Gio says he's not letting me watch any Christmas movies this year."

"Blasphemy." He rubbed her shoulder. "I'm going to miss Christmas this year."

"No you won't. Gio already bought you a Nocht-compatible phone and tablet. Top of the line. He knew you'd go crazy if you didn't have your phone."

"I love you guys."

She smiled a little. "Because we brought you a smartphone?"

"No. Because you're my parents—my real ones anyway—and you know me better than anyone, and you're here." He hugged her again. "I love you."

GIOVANNI WATCHED through a crack in the doorway while Beatrice comforted their son. Because Ben was—no matter his biology—their son.

In Giovanni's fondest dreams, Ben asked him or Beatrice to sire him. He chose a safe place to turn when he was ready, away from prying eyes and the curious immortal world. Someplace he could spend time in the sun before he said goodbye. Someplace he could spend time with family and friends. Someplace he loved and was surrounded by love.

Cochamó. Giovanni had wanted Ben to change in

Cochamó, protected by Carwyn's clan, in the house where he'd spent so many summers and holidays. A place away from the world, a place that felt like a second home.

Zhang walked down the hallway, carrying a tray of hot water and teacups.

"You didn't have to bring it," Giovanni said. "I forgot your human servants would be gone."

"It's fine." Zhang said. "Tai is still waiting by the phone if Tenzin needs to call us. And no host should ever be ashamed to serve guests in his home."

Giovanni tensed when Zhang said her name. "Where is she?"

"Looking for the vampire who killed your son." The corner of Zhang's mouth turned up. "Or did you think that was me?"

Giovanni waited to answer. He wanted to make sure he didn't disrespect the eldest elder of Penglai Island, but there was something he needed to say.

"Many years ago," he started, "we had a conversation."

"Yes," Zhang said. "When your ward and my daughter began working as partners. I remember this conversation."

"If you remember it, why did you ignore my wishes?"

Zhang didn't look offended. He lifted his chin and watched Ben and Beatrice where they sat on the couch. "He is your son in all ways but blood."

"He is."

The elder turned his gaze back to Giovanni. "What man is there, who if his son asks for bread, will give him a stone?"

Giovanni's heart hurt. It was more than sorrow he saw in Zhang's eyes; it was understanding. Recognition.

"You could have told her no."

"No," Zhang said. "I couldn't have."

"And what did she offer you in exchange?" Giovanni knew

it wouldn't be nothing. That might have been how his and Ben's relationship worked, but that wasn't Zhang and Tenzin.

"In exchange?" Zhang turned his eyes back to Ben. "What my daughter offered is between her and me. But know this: she sacrificed far more than you could ever understand."

32

Tenzin called Cheng when she arrived in Taipei and confirmed that Jimmu and his daughter knew she was on the island for the day but wouldn't be staying long. All Tenzin wanted to do was question some humans about *Arion's Flight*, find as much information as she could, and take off again.

Normally Tenzin didn't worry about her security during the day. No, she couldn't be in the sun, but she didn't sleep. She could protect herself. But since her short spell of sleep the afternoon before, she knew she could take no chances. She wanted a room with multiple locks and an entry completely exposed to the light. And she didn't want anyone's humans to know where she slept.

The small room Cheng recommended suited her perfectly. She secured multiple locks and moved large furniture in front of the door before she took the sheets from the bed to make herself a pallet on the floor of the narrow closet.

Tenzin felt the dawn come, but she didn't tire. She checked the time and realized that it was night in New York, so she called Gavin. Gavin knew more about getting information online than she did.

The Scotsman's face came on the screen. He was already frowning. "Tenzin?"

Tenzin spoke plainly. "I know Chloe probably isn't speaking to me right now, but I thought you might."

"Was he dying?"

She didn't hesitate. "Yes."

"Then there's no problem between you and me."

Tenzin felt a weight on her heart lighten. "Chloe knows?"

"Aye." Gavin cleared his throat. "She doesn't hate you, Tenzin. No one does. We all knew what Ben said, but—"

"Ben hates me." She tried to keep her voice and expression even, but she didn't know if she succeeded.

Gavin's voice was soft. "No, Tenzin. He can't. Not really."

She cleared her throat. "I need information if I'm going to find the vampire who did this, and I'm not sure how to get it. I would usually ask Ben, but he won't talk to me, and he's in Penglai, so he doesn't have a computer anyway."

"What do you need?"

"Information on a ship called *Arion's Flight*. I can see that it's registered in the Seychelles, but other than that—"

"Give me about twenty minutes," Gavin said. "I'll call you back."

He hung up, and Tenzin placed her tablet in the far end of the closet. She took shelter in the darkness, focusing on the smell of sea air and the dull sounds of the busy street by the waterfront.

It was twenty-three minutes later that Gavin called back.

"Incoming call from Gavin Wallace," Cara said.

"Accept call."

Gavin's face popped on-screen, and he looked almost cheerful, which Tenzin took as a good sign. "*Arion's Flight* belongs to a Kenyan businessman—"

"I knew that."

"—who works with an Egyptian multinational—"

"I need to find it, Gavin. Just tell me what the range is. Do you have the specs?"

He looked irritated to have been interrupted twice, but Tenzin didn't care. "I'll send you an email with the full specs, but assuming they're running at a typical cruising speed, I'd say you're going to be looking at ports three to four days apart. It's going to have to refuel in that time."

"Three to four days."

"Assume three if they're being cautious. You never want to stretch your fuel at sea."

"Three days then." She pulled up a mental map. "Which ports would be within three days of Taipei? I don't know the oceans by sea."

"Where is the vessel heading?"

"To Alitea."

Gavin didn't speak.

Tenzin looked at the screen. "It was Saba's daughter who did this."

"No."

"Yes." Tenzin shook her head. "Why does everyone assume that Saba is some kind of benevolent earth mother? She nearly destroyed an entire island because her son got a cold. She has roughly the same level of human morals that I do."

Gavin said, "So... almost none."

"Human morals change all the time, Gavin! They make no sense. None."

He held up his hands. "I'm not going to argue with you. I was just surprised Saba was behind this. If they're headed to the Mediterranean, they'll be going south. Think... Manila. Hong Kong, obviously. Hainan. Brunei is too far. Singapore is too far."

"Manila, Hong Kong, Hainan." Tenzin nodded. "It will be one of those."

"Which one is the least likely? They know people will be looking for them."

"Possibly. They might not care. Saba's people are arrogant."

"What are you going to do? The ocean is a big place."

"I'm going to catch them before they can enter the Indian Ocean. I may not catch them in their first port, but I'll catch them in their second."

"Whoever did this—"

"Trust me." She met Gavin's eyes on the screen. An ocean separated them. They had never been particular friends. But they were linked by one person. "I will end them all."

SHE WENT OUT that night at dusk, walking among the sailors and crews of the luxury yachts that filled the marina. There were two types of lives in every port. The lives of people with money and the lives of people who worked. Tenzin was interested in the latter.

She went directly to the first fuel station she could find and walked up to the man in the fanciest uniform. Before he could even register what was happening, she grabbed his hand and drew him to the side.

"What—?"

"Shhhhh." She let her amnis wash up his arm. She could see the dizzy expression in his eyes when her influence reached his mind. *"Arion's Flight.* A boatload of mysterious and wealthy East Africans. Tell me what you know."

"They didn't buy fuel here." He muttered some disgusting racist epithet until Tenzin squeezed his wrist so hard he winced.

"Be quiet. Where did they buy fuel?"

"At Bristol. I think." His words were starting to slur.

"Where is that?"

He pointed in a general direction and Tenzin let him go. "Sit on the ground right now."

It would serve him right to dirty up his spotless white uniform. Humans could be idiots.

Tenzin walked outside and headed the direction the human had pointed. She spotted a sign in the distance that looked right and walked down the stairs leading to the smaller fuel dock where a man in blue coveralls was working.

She didn't use amnis. For now.

"I need information on a boat called *Arion's Flight*."

The man in blue narrowed his eyes. "I know it. Not here. Left two nights ago."

"I know that. Did it buy a full tank of gas?" Did they call it gas if it was for a boat? "Fuel?"

The man crossed his arms. "Why do you need to know? They weren't causing trouble for anyone."

"I'm trying to contact a person on the boat. Family emergency."

The man still looked reluctant, so Tenzin stepped closer, making herself look as innocent as she could. She tucked her hair behind her ears and smiled sweetly. That usually set human men at ease.

"I promise." She got close enough to feel his body heat and smell his blood. "I'm really trying to contact them for a good reason. They don't have a satellite phone and—"

"If you know the family, there must be a way—"

Tenzin grabbed his arm, gripping her fingers around his wrist and letting her influence work up his skin and into his mind.

"I didn't want to do this," she murmured. "But tell me everything you know about *Arion's Flight*."

"Strange people," he murmured. "Never saw the owners.

Crew disembarked. They had only been hired in Hong Kong. Flying back."

"They hired new crew?"

"Yessss." The man began to slur. "Short trip to..."

"Short trip where?"

"Phil...lippines. Good money. Flight back."

"They were going to the Philippines? To Manila?"

"Not Manila. Mm..."

"*M* what?"

"Mm-indoro. R-right across from... Batangas. Bay there. Weather coming."

Ah yes, the unpredictable storm season in the South China Sea. If there was a natural bay in the Philippine Islands, the boat would have to take shelter there. Not even vampires were invulnerable to typhoons.

Well, except Tenzin.

"Thank you." She let go of his arm. "You've been an enormous help."

THE STORM SYSTEM moved across the ocean like a slow-moving shroud. Tenzin flew above it, watching the billowing grey clouds bunch up like a mountain range, battering the sea beneath them with the power of the wind and rain.

She waited in a cloud of calm air, having spotted the bay the night before. There weren't many yachts in the harbor, and most of those would have been protected and anchored while the humans aboard took shelter on land.

But *Arion's Flight* wasn't an ordinary luxury yacht. There would be humans and there would be vampires. They were carrying a symbol that could bring peace or spark war. Protecting it was the only option they had.

Tenzin flew down into the storm, letting herself whip through the torrent and twist in the roiling power. She was soaked to the skin, but that didn't matter when the wind was so intense. She was hooked up to a live current, her amnis growing bigger and bigger, nearly bursting through her skin.

She halted in the middle of the storm, pushing her hands outward and creating a bubble of silence in the midst of the typhoon.

She closed her eyes and saw butterflies—every wing the color of blood—in a riot surrounding her, spiraling up and over the typhoon, thrown by the wind across the endless sky.

"You blew on that. Doesn't count."

Tenzin exhaled, adding her own breath to the storm. She hovered over the churning bay as boats rocked in their moorings and the humans huddled in their caves.

"You blew on that. Doesn't count."

"It's the only thing that counts. A butterfly flaps her wings and all your preparation and work mean nothing."

"So what's the point of playing the game? What's the point of any game?"

"The point"—she spotted a single lit boat in the distance —"is winning."

Tenzin speared down toward the water, circling the bay in silence as she scanned the terrain. The deep bay was surrounded by mountains and shielded from the worst of the typhoon, but it was still on the ragged edge. Boats bobbed like toys; every vessel but one was deserted. She approached silently, shielded from the wind and rain by her amnis.

All the guards had retreated inside. She made one circle. Two. There were two vampires visible through windows. Two humans above them on the bridge. Another human leaned against an outside door, trying to smoke a cigarette in the gusting wind.

No sign of Johari, but Tenzin knew she had the right boat.

Wet hair plastered to her cheeks, Tenzin landed on the railing across from the human who was trying to smoke. He looked up and his eyes went wide when she crouched down to eye level and bared her teeth.

"Run." She snarled, and he jumped to the deck, running toward the rear tender. Tenzin lifted her hand and forced the wind through the door. It broke with a giant crash, and she strode inside.

She stepped onto the relative calm of the bridge, water streaming from her clothes. She lifted a hand behind her and slammed the door shut with another spear of wind.

One of the humans dropped to his knees and began to pray.

Tenzin ignored him and looked at the other. "Where are they?"

"Below." He whispered it, cleared his throat, said it louder. "They're below." He pointed toward a staircase in the corner.

"Stay here." She walked to the stairs. "If you leave this room, I will kill you."

Tenzin began to descend. She could hear the water dripping below, hitting the floor under the spiral staircase like notes plucked on a harp.

Plink. Step.

Plop. Step.

Ting. Step.

The two vampires she saw when she reached the room at the bottom of the stairs didn't look afraid, but they weren't cocky either.

Tenzin walked toward them, already gathering the air in the room to her fingers. "Do you know who I am?"

"No." The female was more nervous than the male. "And you are trespassing—"

"Liar." Tenzin waved a hand and pinned the vampire to the far wall with the strength of her furious wind. "She told you I was coming."

The male didn't waste time talking. He reached into his belt and pulled out a gun. He raised it and fired at Tenzin before she had time to gather enough air to stop it. She ducked to the side, and the bullet clipped her neck.

She hissed and pulled the bronze blade she carried with her. She spiraled in the air, the blade held before her. The man darted to the side and pointed the gun again.

Fighting with one vampire took her attention off holding back the other. The woman fell to the ground and crawled toward them.

Tenzin spun and kicked the gun from the man's hand. It flew across the room, and Tenzin hooked it with a gust of wind, bringing the firearm to her hand.

The black metal handle slapped her palm and the gun was hers.

Tenzin saw the woman reaching for something under a seat. She pivoted toward her, raised the gun, and fired.

Something of Ben's many lessons must have stuck, because even though Tenzin had never fired a gun at a vampire before, she hit her target square in the back.

"Kendra!" The man screamed her name and ran toward her.

Tenzin pointed the gun at him and fired again. This time she missed, so she threw the gun away and lifted her sword.

The man wasn't paying attention. He ran to Kendra and knelt down, baring his fangs at Tenzin. "You monster!"

"Yes." Tenzin plunged the sword into his side and twisted. "This won't kill you." She pulled the sword out. "Neither will her injuries."

Kendra was on the floor, blood pouring from her wounds, but none of them had pierced her spine.

The man looked relieved for a second, until he saw Tenzin raise the blade again.

"But this will." Tenzin brought the sword down, severing Kendra's head from her body. Blood splashed up, and she could feel it hot on her cheek. She turned to the man, who was screaming and trying to stand, one hand clutching the bleeding wound at his side. He searched the ground, probably looking for the gun.

Foolish vampire.

Tenzin walked over to him, rose in the air, and swiped her sword across his torso in one swift motion.

Blood poured down his chest.

"Tell me who sent you," she said. "And I will make your death swift."

He shook his head. "None of this makes sense."

"You were very foolish to try to use a gun on me. So that is not an illogical sentence."

Tenzin brought her blade up again, and this time she removed his head in one sweeping stroke. The body fell, and Tenzin didn't wait. She knelt down, cleaned her blade on the man's jacket, and rose again.

Scanning the room, she noticed another staircase in the corner. Moving silently, she spiraled down from the upper deck, not even touching the rails, only to be met by two more bullets that missed their mark.

She made herself small and looked for where the shots had originated, swiftly gathering air in her hands. Her amnis was still rich with the typhoon's power. She was in a kind of hallway. It was carpeted in red, and doors branched off on either side, six doors in all, with a reading nook at the far end.

Tenzin stayed completely motionless, crouched under the stairs and watching the room.

"I can smell you, Saba's daughter."

She saw movement from the corner of her eye. A fraction of a second later, Tenzin flung a torrent of wind in that direction. The wind knocked paintings off the walls, vases off shelves, and pinned Johari to the wall behind the bookcase where she'd been hiding.

The vampire struggled to break Tenzin's hold, but Tenzin only pushed on her amnis harder, doing her best to break Johari's ribs. Doing her best to hurt the vampire who had ruined everything. Tenzin heard a quiet snap, and Johari shrieked in pain.

Satisfaction flooded her body.

Tenzin smiled. "Hello, Johari. Where is my father's sword?"

"I don't understand this!" The vampire struggled to speak. "We only... we did as you asked!"

33

Tenzin was so shocked that she loosened the wall of wind holding Johari to the wall. "What was that?"

"I was doing... what you asked!" She struggled against the wind and managed to work herself back down to the ground.

Tenzin walked over, shoved the bookcase across the room, and put her hand around Johari's throat. "Who told you that?"

"Saba." Johari choked out the words. "She told us... you didn't want him dead. Just wounded so he would have to turn. She said... said it was what you wanted."

Tenzin had heard the phrase "stone-cold bitch," but she didn't think it had ever described anyone as well as Saba. She loosened her grip on Johari's throat. "What else did she tell you?"

"You wanted the sword gone." Johari rubbed her throat. "But you needed cover for your sire. She said you didn't want peace between Arosh and Zhang any more than she did."

"She told you I said those things?"

Johari looked confused. "She said... it was what you wanted."

A fine distinction Tenzin would have to examine later. "Where is my father's sword?"

Johari didn't say anything, but her eyes went to the right and Tenzin followed. She kept one eye on Johari as she walked to a chest that was acting as a coffee table for the cozy sofa. If looked like the kind of thing Chloe would have bought for the loft and filled with soft blankets and maybe a pair of slippers.

Tenzin flipped open the chest and saw the pockmarked red glass still flecked with sand and mud. She lifted it and carried it to the upended bookcase. She tried to open the case, but it was stuck shut, the seam too packed with dirt and debris.

Johari shook her head. "We tried, but we couldn't—"

Tenzin still held the bronze blade in her hand. In one hard crack, she brought the hilt of her sword down onto the glass case, cracking it in the middle.

Johari's eyes went wide. "What—?"

"The point"—Tenzin smashed it again—"is the sword." The case broke into several large pieces and a hundred tiny ones. One shard flew up and struck the side of Tenzin's jaw. Another flew into Johari's face, leaving a red gash across her cheek.

Tenzin wiped the glass away with a swipe of wind, and a torrent of tiny blades flew up and struck Johari across her torso. Blood wept through her clothes, and Johari flinched but didn't move.

The Laylat al Hisab, last great work of the swordsmith, Harun al Ilāh, was cradled in a bed of cracked leather, nearly as perfect as the day it had been finished.

Tenzin lifted it in her hand, the gold hilt set with rubies for the Fire King and sapphires for Zhang. A whirling firebird was etched on one side of the blade and a coiled dragon on the other. The finish was dull but the edge was unmarred by corrosion. With even a little care, the blade would shine again.

The sword's deadly beauty caused an aching deep in

Tenzin's chest. Though the decorations on the hilt were rich, the Laylat al Hisab was no ceremonial blade. The balance and weight were perfectly calibrated to a warrior of her father's elemental ability and strength. It was, in all ways, perfect. And perfectly deadly.

Tenzin looked at Johari, the thief who had stolen everything. Blood and tears streamed down the vampire's face. She was standing against the wall, eyes locked on Tenzin, though nothing but her own fear held her.

"You didn't ask Saba for help?" Johari asked.

Tenzin raised the sword, leaving her bronze blade among the shattered glass, and tested it against her thumb. The steel edge was lethal, and blood welled in a fine, straight line.

"Why would I ever ask Saba for help?" Her eyes cut to Johari. "You have seen what conditions come with Saba's help."

Johari was wrecked. "My sire sent others first. She hoped to avoid my involvement. She wanted Benjamin Vecchio gone from the beginning so neither of you would be on the ship. There were supposed to be men in Shanghai who injured him."

The two vampires who went after Ben near her house. It felt like so long ago, Tenzin had nearly forgotten.

"But he fought them off," Tenzin said. "He was too smart for them."

"I don't know what happened, but she sent me a message. Injure the young man—do not kill him, no matter what—and take the sword. When he found it..."

"You could fulfill both tasks at once." She thought about another broken body. "And the human, Meili?"

Johari shook her head. "I panicked. She'd found the glass, and I was terrified the humans would bring up the sword during the day. I had to get it from the ocean before anyone saw it. I couldn't let others know it had been found. As long as it was never found—"

"You could avoid any suspicion. It would just be one more mysterious artifact, lost to the sea. And we would never know Saba had taken it."

Johari nodded. "The human was unfortunate."

Tenzin felt the wind whipping around her. The boat rocked to the side, the storm drawn by her fury. "And what about Ben?"

"He is alive, isn't he?" Johari looked confused. "He was to be changed. She said he would be changed."

"He is changed," Tenzin said quietly. "But not by me. Zhang has a new child now, one far more powerful than any of Saba's countless progeny."

Johari looked pale but resolute. "Nevertheless, I am glad he is alive."

Tenzin held out the sword and walked toward Johari, pointing it at her throat. The blade shone dull in the flickering lights of the hallway while waves rocked the yacht back and forth. Tenzin floated above the floor, steadied by the air around her.

In her mind, she saw the sword piercing Ben's back, the pain and torment as she flew him to her father. The pointed cobblestones against her knees as she begged. The taste of his blood and the ecstasy of his bite. The cold hatred on his face.

"You escaped your fate once." She put the blade to Johari's throat. "Tell me why I should let you escape again."

Johari's face was bleak. "You shouldn't."

The whispers came like a swirling typhoon, building and building in her mind.

Kill her! She is nothing.

She wants to die.

Her eyes beg for it.

He hates you because of her.

"I will find the sword, Father. I will kill Saba's daughter."

"Is that what you think I want?"

Her father's words came to her, louder than the whispers.

"Is that what you think I want?"

What did he want? What did Ben want now? What did Tenzin want? Did she even know anymore?

"My daughter, if you resist change, you will never be who you were meant to become."

She glanced over her shoulder at the curving bronze sword she had carried for thousands of years. The blade was stained with the blood of enemy and lover, friend and family, murderers, rapists, defilers of the weak. Those who were weak. Those who were strong.

Tenzin looked from the bronze blade, back to Johari.

Kill her.

She is nothing.

Thief, they whispered. *Liar and thief.*

"So am I," Tenzin murmured. "All that and more."

Her feet dropped to the soft red carpet, and she loosened the backpack she carried, still holding the sword on Johari. She withdrew a book in a clear plastic bag. "You know what this is."

Johari's face froze.

"I found your book. And the picture of your Zuberi."

"Please." Her breathing came faster. "He has nothing to do with this."

"Why do you keep his picture?"

"Because I love him." She blinked hard and held out her hands. "I have only ever loved him. But I was a fool. Please. Give it to me. If you kill me now, at least let me hold his picture when I die."

"I'm not giving you the book." Tenzin slipped it back in her backpack and stood straight, leveling the blade on Johari's neck. "But I will not hurt this man. This vampire who helps women the powerful have forgotten."

"Thank you." Her face fell in relief. "Zuberi—"

"I am going to find this kind doctor you love," Tenzin said softly. "And I'm going to tell him about Ben. And about Meili. About everything you have become."

Johari's chest heaved. "You would be more merciful to kill me."

Tenzin cocked her head. Looked at Johari. Looked at the sword in her hand. "It was only ever a symbol."

She rose again as waves crashed against the cabin, throwing everything in the hallway off-balance. Paintings crashed and glass broke. The smell of seawater was everywhere.

Johari held out her arms to steady herself. "The sword?"

"It was only ever a symbol. It was death captured in a beautiful vessel. Your sire and Arosh, they never understood. Zhang Guo never *needed* a sword, because he has me." Tenzin reached for Johari's hand, gripping her fingers and stretching her arm forward. "I *am* the Night's Reckoning."

Tenzin lifted the blade and swung down, severing Johari's hand at the wrist. She screamed in pain and crumpled to the floor, blood pouring from the empty stump on the end of her arm.

She tossed Johari's hand in her backpack and slung the bag over her shoulder. "There is my mercy, Saba's daughter. Your hand will grow back eventually, but your mother will know what it means. Tell her I know. Tell her I know everything."

Tenzin bent and retrieved her bronze blade, keeping both swords in her hands as she floated up the stairway, past the bloody dining cabin, and onto the bridge. She needed to leave the ship, which was beginning to list dangerously as the storm grew stronger.

The two humans on the bridge were desperately trying to keep the ship steady, but Tenzin knew it was futile. They turned with wide, terrified eyes when she stepped onto the bridge.

"You should go," Tenzin said. "Get the rest of the crew and take shelter in the lifeboats." She looked down the stairs as the men stared at her. "There's no one left to protect."

She pushed open the door with a gust of wind and walked into the storm. Once she was far enough away from the bay and hovering over the storm, Tenzin threw Johari's hand into the sea.

She flew a little farther and a little higher, her heart racing as she clutched the Laylat al Hisab in her right hand. She was heading north, back to her father. Back to Benjamin. If she was lucky, she'd make Cheng's ship by nightfall.

Somewhere past the storm, along the north end of the South China Sea, Tenzin held out her left hand and let the bronze blade slip from her fingers.

34

Tenzin lay motionless on the couch in Cheng's cabin, staring at the sword. Cheng had put it in a beautiful leather box lined in silk. Because it had never been exposed to saltwater, it didn't need to be desalinated. With only a little polish, Cheng had returned it to its original glory.

"Your father will be pleased." Cheng placed another blanket around Tenzin's shoulders, but she still felt cold.

He sat next to her on the couch and draped her legs over his knees.

"Look at it, Cricket. Focus on what we have accomplished— what you accomplished—finding the sword. Be proud of that right now."

Counting all the treasure found in Harun's clever glass boxes, Tenzin would be returning to Penglai Island with one sword, a pair of jeweled throwing daggers, five gold necklaces of intricate beauty made in the Sassanian style and set with polished jewels, a richly decorated headband with braided silver and gold, eight gold goblets decorated to honor the Eight Immortals, and various pieces of precious metal and polished stones.

The treasure of ninth-century Arabic glass that had been

recovered would need to be treated at the university laboratory and would likely go into a museum collection of some kind, along with all the research and video footage obtained from the wreck, but the treasure in Harun's boxes was for Zhang and his fellow elders alone.

Tenzin stared at the sword and the treasure, searching for the satisfaction she would have felt if Benjamin had been beside her. They would have opened champagne and played music. He would have made her dance, and he would have sung when he became drunk.

If they were in New York, he would have stumbled out the door with Chloe at midnight, forcing Gavin and Tenzin with them as they went to search for their favorite late-night street food. They would have eaten waffles with chocolate or french fries or shawarma from the vendor near the park.

"Tenzin." Cheng shook her shoulder. "Stop."

"Do you know his story?" Tenzin asked Cheng. "Do you know Harun's story?"

"Not really."

"Harun al Ilāh was a master of fire," she began. "Steel, glass, or gold, he could work with them all. He created crowns for ancient kings and mastered every style of weapon. It is said that the genius of Damascus steel began with him. That he was the first to order his steel from India, and he searched the whole continent to find the finest and most flexible metal to forge his weapons."

"And he shared that technology with the humans?"

"Eventually, yes. But he was the first. He created weapons so strong they could win any duel. In the hands of wind vampires, they could lay waste to armies. He designed blades specifically for our kind."

"Was he from a wind clan?"

"No one knows who his sire was or where he came from. He

was very old, very powerful, and had no enemies, because who would make an enemy of the man who could forge the finest blades?"

Cheng chuckled.

"But he wasn't kind. He was unmerciful to his human assistants. He could be a brutal craftsman and was known to kill those who didn't work to his exacting standards."

"And humans still came to him?"

"Oh yes." Tenzin sat up and rubbed her temple. "They came and they learned his secrets when they pleased him. He did beautiful things. Impossible things like these boxes."

"He sealed them somehow," Cheng said. "I still can't figure out how not a single one leaked, despite how long they were in the water."

"He was a magician," Tenzin continued. "Fire, glass, and metal were his obsession. He lived in the mountains alone, and he had no mate, no sire, no family at all. Only a few human apprentices and a woman from the nearest village who cooked and cleaned for him."

Cheng asked, "What happened to him? Something happened, because he is no longer living. Everyone knows Harun is dead. Unless it is a myth like Arosh's death."

"No, I am quite certain he is dead." Tenzin remembered the long night with the old man in a caravanserai near Samarkand. She remembered fire and tea and dates stuffed with walnuts. The human who told her the tale was an old Sogdian trader. He had a dagger and Tenzin wanted it. "I wanted to buy a piece in a man's possession—a double-edged dagger with a jade hilt—but the gold I offered was insufficient to convince him to sell."

"How much gold?"

"You don't want to know. The money meant nothing. I wanted one of Harun's blades. The old man forced me to pay him with an exchange of stories. Well, the gold and the stories. I would tell one of mine and then listen to one of his. And the story he told me was the tale of Harun al Ilāh."

"And you believed him?"

Tenzin said, "There are stories to tell a history and those to tell a story. This was a history, and I believe every word."

Cheng brushed a hand over her hair. "So what happened to Harun al Ilāh?"

"The old woman who cleaned and cooked for him died after many years, but as was the tradition of her family, her grand-daughter came and learned Harun's secrets so she could carry on keeping house for the immortal.

"The granddaughter came and learned all her grandmother taught her. Learned how to cook Harun's favorite meals and tend the fires in the house to please him. How to make his tea and keep the home cool. She knew that, like Harun's appren-tices, she would have to offer her blood once every month, but she would be rewarded for her devotion and secrecy.

"So the woman came to work for Harun, giving up her plans to marry a boy from her village and hoping only that, like her grandmother, one of Harun's apprentices might consider her a good wife. Her name was Layah. She was plain-faced but had hair so beautiful she wore it covered so no one could see and remark on it, because she was a quiet woman who didn't care for attention."

"The perfect housekeeper for a vampire," Cheng said.

"Harun took no notice of Layah at first. She was only another human. Another servant. She cooked his meals the same way her grandmother did and kept the house clean. She was so quiet some of his apprentices would joke that she couldn't speak at all.

"But she could speak, and in fact, she could sing. She sang as she worked, and while Harun slept he could hear her. He was an ancient vampire and did not sleep deeply. He heard her sweet songs in his dreams, and he asked her to sing them when he woke. When he was in a bitter mood or frustrated with a difficult job, he asked her to sing to soothe his temper."

"And she did?"

"Always." Tenzin shifted her gaze to the dark windows outside Cheng's cabin. "One night Harun realized that he didn't hear Layah when he woke. He went to her room and saw that she had a fever. She burned so hot Harun feared she would die. He called a human healer from the village and the healer came, but Harun would not leave her. The healer took the veil from her beautiful hair, and Harun was transfixed by its beauty, for her hair was a blend of gold and silver and unlike anything he'd seen in his many years."

"Did he love her?" Cheng asked. "It is one thing to be fixed on a beautiful object, but another to truly love."

"Faced with the prospect of losing the human who had given him peace for the first time in his immortal life, Harun realized he did love the woman. Her beauty was revealed by far more than her hair."

Cheng ruffled Tenzin's hair. "But beautiful hair always helps."

Tenzin felt a smile growing. "Layah grew healthy again, and Harun began to give her gifts. He moved her to a richly appointed room in his house, gave her jewelry and fine clothes, and hired another girl to help her tend his house. Eventually Layah told him that she would need to return to her village and her mother's house because she was no longer his servant. All her work was taken up by another, and all she did was sing and make his tea. Harun demanded that she stay—"

"Demands are a sure way to convince a human woman you love her," Cheng said. "Or so I've been told."

"—but he asked her to be his wife and not his servant." Tenzin turned to Cheng. "Asked. Not demanded."

Cheng's smiled was sad. "But would he have truly let her go?"

"I don't know." Tenzin turned back to the treasure. "She stayed. He created the most beautiful jewelry after he and Layah married. Her hair inspired him to blend gold and silver in many of his pieces." She pointed. "Like that headband. They were together for many years, and she bore him seven children."

"Vampires can't father children."

Tenzin shrugged. "Harun did many impossible things. Why couldn't he have fathered children too?"

"Did she turn?"

Tenzin's heart hurt. "No. She never did. And he never left her. Layah grew old and died, surrounded by their children and grandchildren. Harun buried his wife and finished all the swords he had promised to make. Then he walked into the light to join her."

Cheng took a deep breath and slipped his arm around Tenzin's shoulders. "You were never going to be Harun, Cricket."

"No." She stared at the gold-and-silver headband fashioned for a queen who would never die. "I am not so generous."

CHENG LEFT Tenzin at the dock with four richly carved boxes bearing Arosh's treasure. He bent down and kissed her forehead. "You know how to find me."

"I do."

She was dressed in her finest court clothing. Embroidered red silk adorned her body, and gold and jade combs decorated her hair. She would walk onto Penglai Island as the daughter of Zhang Guolao, head unbowed, a warrior returning with honor from battle, laden with treasures too long lost.

She didn't know if Johari had made it back to Alitea yet, but she had no doubt the vampire would eventually deliver her message to Saba. It could take years, but Johari had the eyes of a survivor.

"Tenzin." Myung was Penglai's boatman, someone Tenzin rarely encountered. He bowed and gestured to the front of the ship. "Welcome, daughter of Zhang."

"Myung." She stared at him. "You know I hate the bowing people."

The vampire grinned. "Why do you think I always greet you with a bow?"

"Irritating ant." She boarded. "My thanks for safe passage."

"The daughter of Elder Zhang is always welcome on my boat."

They set sail across the water, and Tenzin pushed a little wind into Myung's sails, making the water vampire laugh. As they approached the island, the fog parted and the shining jewel of the immortals rose from the sea.

It was spectacular from the water, just as the elders intended. She rose and disembarked, overseeing the transfer of the treasure from the boat to the carriages. Once they reached the top level of the island, eight servants appeared, each ready to help carry a chest. Tenzin took the leather sword case that Cheng had made for the Laylat al Hisab and carried it against her breast as the servants brought each chest with them, two by two.

She followed them through the garden and immediately sensed Ben's amnis. She looked around but did not see him. He would likely be locked in Zhang's quarters. There were too many humans running around the palace grounds for a newborn to be on the loose.

Tenzin walked through the jeweled doors and into the Hall

of the Elders, scanning the room for familiar faces as she walked toward the front.

There. Giovanni was in the Hall, watching the procession of treasure and filial devotion. Tenzin locked eyes with him and was relieved to see no hatred. The familiar blue-green eyes followed her as she walked.

As one, the elders rose and Tenzin stopped at the steps of the Hall. She bowed toward her father and placed the sword on the ground before his feet.

"Zhang Guolao, elder of Penglai, Eternal Ruler of the Naiman Khanlig, High General of the Altan Wind." She took a breath. "My father and immortal sire, as you have blessed me with the gift of eternal life, I humbly present the gift of Arosh, Fire King of the Western Mountains. In accordance with the Treaty of Kashgar, I bring you the final gesture of peace between your house and his." Tenzin rose to her knees, opened the box, and lifted the sword from its silk bed. "Crafted by Harun al Ilāh, the Laylat al Hisab, the Night's Reckoning, was recovered from the East China Sea, and has finally come to your hand."

Tenzin rose and walked up to her father's throne, holding the sword before her.

She could feel Giovanni's eyes on her back, among the throngs of the curious and suspicious. "Aabmen," she said quietly. "Your sword."

Zhang's eyes met hers. "No finer weapon has ever been given to me. You are welcome at my side."

Tenzin bowed her head, handed over the sword, and took her place to the right of Zhang's throne.

Zhang spoke to the assembly. "Let the rest of Arosh's gift be presented to the court of the elders, that we may convey our gratitude to the Fire King in turn and thank him for his offer of peace at last."

As the servants opened the rest of the boxes of treasure and lifted each item from their glass cases, the murmurs of amazement swept through the crowd. Even in Penglai, the richness of Arosh's gifts and Harun's brilliance could not be diminished.

"I also have documented reports from Benjamin's assistant Fabia that detail the rest of the excavation," Tenzin said quietly. "The glass pieces will need extensive desalination to ensure they are preserved. I'll make sure Tai receives the details and the inventory."

Zhang waved a careless hand. "It's fine, Tenzin. I am pleased the scholars at the university will be recognized for their work. I look forward to seeing an exhibition one day." He lifted the sword. "This really is an extraordinary blade."

"It is."

"Will you take it to my armory, daughter? Tai will find the perfect place for it."

"Of course."

She left the Hall via the antechamber where Ben had first met Zhang. She took to the sky, her heart moving slowly as she approached her father's house. She entered through the front door, only to be met by Tai.

Ben's amnis was everywhere—golden, warm, and even stronger than before. She looked around, but though his amnis and scent were everywhere, she didn't see him.

"Tenzin." Tai smiled. "It's good to see you."

Tai and Nima had once nurtured a deep and respectful friendship that saved the wind vampire when the previous elder, Zhongli Quan, had betrayed the council and been executed along with most of his children. It was Nima's testimony that had saved Tai, along with his reputation for honesty. Tai had become devoted to Zhang, who had spoken in his defense and taken him into his household.

"It's good to see you too," Tenzin said. "How is he?"

Tai smiled. "I know you don't inquire about Zhang."

"No."

Ben wasn't far away, probably in private rooms where he couldn't be tempted by the smell of human servants.

"Benjamin is well and healthy," Tai said. "I look forward to knowing him better when we leave for Khentii."

"I see." So her father was taking Ben to Mongolia. "He's not accustomed to cold weather, so make sure—"

"I can speak for myself."

Tenzin schooled her expression before she turned to face him. In the few short days she'd been away, he'd already grown in power and grace. His new eyes still startled her, but his body moved with the quickness and fluidity his human body had augured.

"Hello, Benjamin."

"Tenzin." His expression was as blank as hers.

Tai reached for the sword. "May I—"

"Let him see it first," Tenzin said. "If he likes."

Ben walked toward her, lifting the sword from her fingers. He gripped the hilt and raised it, stepping back and testing it with expert handling.

"It's beautiful."

"And beautifully made."

"Yes." He examined the hilt. "It looks like it was never lost."

"Immortal like Zhang."

His voice was cold. "Like us."

She had once been able to read his heart in his voice. In his expression. No longer. Perhaps the secret of Benjamin had been in his eyes, which were no more.

"Yes," she said. "Immortal like us."

"Did you kill her?"

"No." She swallowed hard. "Death would be too easy."

Ben handed the sword to Tai, who left them in Zhang's

entry hall, standing across from each other like the two wary predators they were.

"Is death easy?" Ben stuck his hands in his pockets. "I don't remember it feeling easy."

Tenzin took a deep breath. "When we were flying, you—"

"I remember what I said that night." Ben's eyes stayed on her. "But I'm not that man anymore. I'm not a man at all. I don't know what I am."

"You are still you." How could she make him see? "The man you were—"

"Is dead." His voice was flat. "And this vampire is pretty damn confused."

She stayed silent and waited for him to speak.

"See, I lost my human life." His voice was rough. "And I also lost my best friend, because she betrayed me in a way she promised that she never would." He cleared his throat. "But I'm not going to kill myself. I wouldn't do that to my family. I'll figure this out. I'll make the best of it."

"I am pleased to hear that."

"But some things didn't change." He lifted his chin. "I'm still done. I'm not going back to New York. I mean, I'm flying to fucking Mongolia for a year."

"After that—"

"After that, I'm still done." His face was like stone. "I told you, Tenzin, even if I had an eternity, I wouldn't spend it waiting around for you. So... goodbye." He turned and started to walk down the hall.

"Benjamin."

He stopped, but he didn't turn. "What?"

"We have both been changed." The realization was new and delicate, like skin revealed when a scab fell away. "More than you know."

"Tenzin..."

She waited for him to speak, but he said nothing more than her name.

Tenzin watched his back, the strong line of his body standing poised in the hallway, halfway between one place and another.

"I will wait," she murmured.

"What?" Ben turned, and his eyes were narrowed with suspicion.

"You said you wouldn't waste your eternity waiting for me, but I will."

"You'll... wait?" He looked confused. "For what?"

"Yes." She nodded and stepped toward the open door. "I'll wait."

"Tenzin!"

She turned toward him, and his expression was finally one she could read. He was exasperated.

"Yes doesn't answer my question."

She couldn't stop the smile. "I know."

Pushing back the temptation to linger, Tenzin walked out the door and flew away.

35

Giovanni sat in her rooms in Penglai, sipping tea and avoiding her gaze.

"It's fine." Tenzin poured tea. She'd changed out of her dress clothes and into more comfortable leggings and a tunic when she reached her rooms. "I knew he wouldn't want to see me anymore."

"He's hurt and angry. You remember how all your emotions are heightened during that time."

"Not really." She lifted her cup. "I was regularly traumatized and abused for the first few hundred years of my life, so I don't remember much. I choose not to."

Giovanni paused lifting the tea to his mouth. "I didn't know that."

"You always suspected."

"Yes, I suspected." He set down his tea. "Tenzin—"

"I'll go to the mountains, if that's what you're wondering. I'm overdue for a visit. There are still matters with some of Nima's family that need to be settled."

She had needed quiet and time to think after everything that had happened in Puerto Rico. She really needed it now.

Giovanni said, "Something has changed."

Tenzin thought about the desperate flight to her father, her helplessness and her fury. The taste of Ben's blood in her mouth and the inevitable explosion of their amnis colliding like winter storms over a mountain.

His lips leaving hers as surely as he'd left her body and walked away.

She remembered sleep. And dreams.

And over and above all, the sensation of a curved bronze blade slipping from her fingers and falling to an ocean grave.

"Yes, something has changed." Tenzin sipped her tea. "I wanted to see Beatrice before I left. Has Sadia already left for Rome with the nanny?"

Giovanni said nothing.

She set down her cup. "I see."

"She's angry, Tenzin. You knew how he felt—how he's always felt—and you ignored him. He's her son and she's angry right now."

"I understand." A different ache grew in her chest, and Tenzin let out a bitter laugh. "Tell her I don't expect her to thank me."

"She won't."

"Even though I know she's grateful." Tenzin looked Giovanni square in the eye. "You both are. Because you don't have to be the villain now, do you?"

His eyes narrowed. "If you think—"

"What would you have done, Giovanni Vecchio? This isn't Caspar growing old peacefully in his home, surrounded by his family and the woman he loves." She leaned forward. "This is Benjamin, bleeding out in *your* arms, his human body paralyzed by the blade of *your* enemy, telling you '*I didn't want to die yet.*'"

Giovanni said nothing.

Tenzin sat back and lifted her chin. "Don't tell me what you would have done, because I know."

"What did you give Zhang?" he asked quietly.

"I will never tell you that." Tenzin picked up her tea. "You haven't earned the right to my secrets. I love you deeply, my boy, but some things you will never know."

THE FORTRESS in the Khentii mountain range was a low, four-sided castle with two forward towers facing a broad, grass-filled valley. The castle surrounded an open courtyard where a large bonfire burned. The structure had to be at least five hundred years old, but the floors were polished, the walls were in perfect repair, and a bathroom had been added.

Just one, but Ben didn't have to use it as often lately. So far it was the only convenient thing about being a vampire.

His throat burned all the time. He was constantly hungry. He still couldn't control his amnis enough to make himself warm, so he was always, *always* cold. Of course, the frigid Mongolian autumn weather probably didn't help. He was starting to think fur wasn't just a fashion statement.

The land was bleak but stunningly beautiful. The skies were clear, and no human settlements spoiled the night sky for miles and miles around them. The wilderness that protected the humans from Ben also protected Ben from the temptation of the humans.

"I will teach you." Zhang ushered Ben to the north wing of the fortress that butted up against the mountains. "For the next year, you will be my student in the ways of survival. I will teach you how to best your enemies, how to protect yourself, and how to find purpose in eternity."

A hundred times a night, Ben wondered whether these were

the same lessons Tenzin had lived through when she'd been a new immortal. It had been a different time and there hadn't been a fortress, but Zhang's wisdom was eternal, right?

Ben walked along the far wall of the training room, eager to try the many weapons in his sire's collection. He was starting to see that Tenzin had inherited her obsession.

"You will have to fight differently now." Zhang spoke behind him. "You will have to think differently. Move differently. Your enemies will not strategize in months or years but in decades and centuries."

There were countless swords and daggers from every corner of the globe. Shields and maces. Staffs and battle-axes. Bows and crossbows. Every weapon Ben could imagine.

"Your body is both a weapon and a liability. You are stronger than most, but your control is still developing. You are vulnerable during the day. Guarding yourself in daylight will be your greatest challenge and your first priority."

The wall of swords gave way to a corner full of training dummies, blocks, wooden staffs, and even a few devilish-looking whips. Ben felt like he'd been cooped up for months instead of weeks. He desperately wanted to flex his new power and beat the stuffing out of a few of those dummies.

Zhang continued. "But most of all, you must come to understand your amnis, for the air is both surrounding us and within us. It is not matter but space that forms the tapestry of all things. And when you truly understand and are the master of space, you will be more powerful than a vampire of any other element."

Ben ran his hand along a straight-edged *jian*, reaching for the leather-wrapped hilt.

Zhang said, "Let us begin."

Ben turned and squared his shoulders at Zhang, only to see his sire sitting in the middle of the training room, cross-legged on the ground, with a small table and a board game set in front of him.

Ben blinked. "Wh-what is that?"

"The game is called abachee, and it is a general's game. My father, who was a great warlord, taught the game to me, and I will teach it to you. This"—he pointed to the board—"is the true beginning of your education."

Ben's shoulder fell. "But..."

Zhang's eyes were all amusement when he glanced at the sword. "The sword comes last, Benjamin. Right now we will work to train your mind."

Ben let out a long breath.

It's going to be a very long year.

Two NIGHTS after she'd left Penglai Island, Tenzin came to rest in the cave of the Eternal Goddess, high in the Himalayan Mountains. The air was crisp and turning colder each night, but prayer flags whipped in the wind, flapping their petitions to the heavens and to her.

She checked the altar in the cave where she had once spent centuries resting, and took the time to taste and appreciate the food that had been left for her, knowing it was a gift of the people in the valley and she should not ignore it.

Tenzin gathered the food and left the prayer scrolls, flowers, and candles behind, flying to her home higher in the cliffs that overlooked the broad, sweeping valley where a river cut through the mountains, creating a fertile pocket in the middle of the wilderness.

Green fields and birch forests filled the river valley, and arching bridges and narrow passes connected the small village to the outside world.

Spare white lights marked where each stone house stood. Some of them had radios and televisions now. A wireless tower had been built only a few years before, putting mobile phone technology within reach for the village. Tenzin could use her tablet in the valley, though the signal didn't reach up to her home in the mountains, for which she was grateful.

YouTube was simply too addicting.

Despite the incursions of modernity, her home remained unchanged. It was the stone house she'd built with her own hands centuries before. The home she had shared with Nima. The place where her soul rested most quietly. The place where she found peace.

Now she was more grateful for it than she'd been in a millennium. Her mind felt new and burgeoning. She was a snake shedding her skin. A blade emerging from the tempering fire.

She was her sire's weapon, newly forged, lying in wait for the time when she would rise and touch the heavens.

Her fifth life was upon her.

For the first time in thousands of years, Tenzin lay down in the mountains and dreamed of flying. Through the forests of red birch trees. Over wide oceans of grass and across the midnight desert.

Tenzin slept and she dreamed.

EPILOGUE

"I don't think you're putting the door together correctly," Tenzin said. "Did you read the instructions?"

"I don't need any bloody instructions," Gavin muttered. "It's a fucking glass house, not a nuclear reactor."

"If you can't put a glass house together, I think a nuclear reactor is a bad idea."

"I'm not getting— Just hand me that screwdriver and be quiet!"

Tenzin handed him the screwdriver, stepped back, and looked at the large glass structure she and Gavin had constructed on the roof. It was nearly complete—the door was the last piece—which was a good thing because her plants were starting to take over the loft.

Once the door was finished, they could turn on the heater and move the plants that had been living in the apartment all winter into the glass house. Tenzin had watched numerous online videos and was satisfied that she was nearly an expert.

She knew how to use the roof panels to allow air in during the day and close them at night, trapping the warmth in the glass house so it created a tropical paradise like Ben had loved in

Puerto Rico. She had installed fans and humidifiers that would keep the plants from overheating in the sizzling New York summers.

Plus the birds would be much happier in the glass house among the trees than stuck always in their cage in the loft.

"Do you think he'll be annoyed that we built this without him?" Tenzin muttered, "Actually, I don't think I care if he's annoyed."

Gavin huffed. "You took him to your sire to change him into a vampire without his permission, Tenzin. If he manages to forgive you for that, I really don't think the glass house is going to be much of a stretch."

"Good point." She refused to think about Ben not forgiving her. He would. Eventually. "I should have gotten a bigger one."

Gavin uttered one of the long and delightful Scottish curses that sounded like complete gibberish to her. "No, you fucking shouldn't have. This one is complicated enough."

"But you didn't even need to read the directions."

Gavin couldn't hold in his laugh. "Woman, you're a menace."

"I know."

He closed the door, and Tenzin listened for the click.

She turned to Gavin and grinned. "You did it."

"Thank fuck, we did." He pointed to the glass tiles on the ceiling. "I'd have never figured out the roof panels on my own."

"You're becoming more modest," Tenzin said. "Is it because you're in love with Chloe?"

"Fuck if I know," he muttered, using one of Tenzin's favorite American curses. "Probably."

"Did she talk to him this week?"

"We both did." Gavin cleared his throat. "He told Chloe about learning how to fly better and how he didn't have to use his hands to close doors now. She warned him about getting a fat arse because he was turning lazy."

"And what did he tell you?"

Gavin hesitated for a moment. "He hunted last week. First time with a human. Zhang was with him. No one was hurt, but he's feeling conflicted anyway. He asked Zhang about animal blood."

"Not as healthy for his amnis, especially when he's so young."

"I know. He knows too. I talked to him."

Tenzin nodded. It was those harder lessons she wanted most to talk with Ben about, but in the months he'd been in Khentii, he hadn't asked to speak with her once, even though Chloe had told Ben she was back in New York.

Gavin walked inside and closed the glass door before he turned on the heater, giving the house a few moments to warm up before they started moving the plants from the loft.

"Hey, Tenzin?" Chloe walked out on the roof and clapped her hands. "It's so great! He's gonna love it." She ran into the glass house and looked around. "It's huge."

"It won't feel so big when all the plants are inside." Tenzin spotted a thick envelope in Chloe's hand. "What is that?"

"Oh right." Chloe walked over and handed the envelope to Tenzin. "This came to the pub today. Nearly forgot about it."

Tenzin glanced at the wax seal and lack of postage. "Courier?"

"Yes. Didn't recognize her, but she had an accent. Maybe Russian?" Chloe shrugged. "I'm not sure. Just asked for Ben's assistant and dropped it off."

Tenzin had already spotted Ben's name on the front, but she was pretty sure she recognized the seal too.

"Gavin?" She held it so he could see. "Recognize that?"

Gavin frowned. "I think so. But why would he be sending a message to Ben?"

"Remember when I told Ben to send a courier to Bucharest and have that courier get lost for a year or so?"

"I have a vague memory." Gavin took the envelope and looked at Ben's name on the front. "But what does Radu want with Ben?"

"To hire him."

"He hasn't heard the news?"

"Maybe he sent it before he heard," Tenzin said. "Maybe he doesn't care Ben is Zhang's son. As far as the vampire world knows, Ben and I are still partners and we're still for hire if the price is right." Tenzin reached for the envelope again and felt the weight. "And judging by the gold in this envelope, the price is probably right."

"So that means Ben..."

"Isn't going to be able to relax in the mountains forever." Tenzin handed the envelope back to Chloe and picked up the last ficus plant. "Put it with his other mail for now. Radu will have to wait. Besides, it's nearly springtime."

"Why does that matter?" Chloe asked.

Gavin said, "That means Radu will be impossible to find unless we can magically figure out how to find his damn caravan."

Chloe looked confused.

"I'll explain later, dove." Gavin walked into the loft and came back holding the birdcage with the two singing lovebirds. "Do you want to do the honors, Tenzin?"

She smiled and reached for the cage, taking the birds to the far side of the glass house. "I should probably just leave them in here until they get used to it."

"Why?" Chloe crouched down next to the cage and fed the male bird a sunflower seed that he snatched up and took to his mate. "They've been in here for weeks. They're probably dying to stretch their wings."

Tenzin double-checked the door, the roof panels, and the windows to make sure the glass house was completely sealed before she sat on the ground next to the birdcage. "Okay, let's see what you think."

She held out her finger for Layah first. The bright yellow bird with a soft orange blush hopped on her finger. Tenzin lifted her from the cage and closed the door before Harun could escape.

She carefully set the little bird on the branches of a small lime tree and watched as she hopped up and down the branch until she took to the air and flew across the room to an upright palm.

Her partner was clearly outraged to be left behind.

"I hear you, *tseetsa*." Tenzin opened the door, and Harun immediately shot from the cage and arrowed over to Layah, his green feathers blending in with the shadowed palm as he settled next to her and groomed her neck feathers.

"Look at them!" Chloe was almost dancing. "They're so happy. This is perfect, Tenzin."

"Job well done." Gavin reached for her hand and shook it. "We should celebrate."

"Good idea." She pointed to the table she'd put together. "Sit. And watch my birds."

While they sat down to watch the birds explore their new home, Tenzin carefully opened the door and slipped out to grab the bottle of champagne she'd bought on impulse from the bodega the night before.

She walked in the kitchen, grabbed the bottle and three glasses before she paused at the counter.

Taped to the cupboard above the bar was a picture Gavin had taken with his phone and sent to Chloe just before they'd left for Puerto Rico. A picture of them before, when everything was golden and full of promise.

Ben's warm brown eyes caught her. His right arm was slung around her shoulders and his left arm was around Chloe's waist. He'd been teasing Gavin about kissing his girl, and his face was flushed with life and laughter.

Tenzin leaned into him, unconsciously drawn to his warmth and life.

"Smile, Tiny. Just one picture."

She'd relented, but she hadn't smiled. Her hair covered half her face, and she'd kept her mouth firmly closed, intent on hiding her teeth.

Tenzin grabbed one more glass and carefully opened the bottle of sparkling wine. She set the glass on the counter and poured, the wine fizzing up to the rim and then settling down to bubble happily under Ben's picture.

"Let's dance, Tiny."

Always. Always. Always.

Tenzin left the sparkling glass with Ben and picked up the other wineglasses, grabbed the bottle of champagne, and walked back into the night to celebrate with her friends.

THE END

Continue reading for a preview of
VALLEY OF THE SHADOW
an Elemental World novella.

"I'm sure of you. Everything else,
we'll figure out along the way."

For eight years, Baojia and Natalie have pursued their goals: family, career, friendship and love—trying to carve out an ordinary life in an immortal world. And for eight years, they've been mostly successful, save for a world-bending adventure every now and then.

Except that their life was never ordinary. It was never going to be.

Natalie and Baojia may have made plans, but when ordinary life comes crashing down, they'll have to turn to the family they have chosen, vampire and human, for help keeping their world together.

Five couples, four kids, three weeks, two paths... and a partridge in a pear tree? Return to the Elemental World for a Christmas reunion of old friends and forever loves.

For Natalie Ellis, it's time to come home.

Valley of the Shadow is a novella in the *Elemental World* series by USA Today bestseller, Elizabeth Hunter, author of the *Elemental Mysteries*, the *Irin Chronicles*, and *Love Stories on 7th and Main*.

~

CHAPTER ONE

Baojia lived his immortal life from sundown to midnight. He and Natalie had decided as a family that midnight was as late as two small children could be allowed to stay awake, even if they had a non-traditional school schedule and slept until noon. Though his security work sometimes interrupted, the primary focus of his life from sundown to midnight was his children and his wife.

He carried his squirming daughter under one arm and nudged his son with the other. "Bed."

Jake yawned loudly. "I'm not ti-ired."

"Clearly." He mussed the boy's dark brown hair. "We can finish the game tomorrow."

"But not until you wake up," Jake whined. "I don't want to wait that long."

His daughter Sarah did her best impression of a boiled spaghetti noodle and flipped backward in his arms.

"It's good to want things." Baojia wrangled Sarah upright. "It teaches you patience. Don't play dead, monkey. You're going to hit your head."

Sarah's lively brown eyes were not tired in the least. "I'm not playing dead. I'm playing vampire!" She patted her father's cheek. "Let me see, let me see."

He forced himself to snarl and allowed his fangs to fall. "Rawr."

Sarah squealed in delight and nearly twisted out of his arms again. "Rawr, rawr, rawr!"

Jake looked up with adoration. "I'm gonna have really big fangs when I grow up."

"That" —Baojia nudged him into his room— "is a very mature decision that you cannot make until you are very old."

"How old?" Jake hopped into his bed.

Baojia slung Sarah over his shoulder to keep her from

crawling out of his arms. She truly was their monkey. She crawled and climbed on everything in sight. "Hmm... let me think."

Jake wasn't budging. He crossed his arms over his skinny seven-year-old chest. It was a gesture he'd recently began copying. "When can I decide I want to be a vampire?"

Baojia went with his gut. "When you're forty-seven."

Jake's mouth dropped. "What? No way, Dad. I don't want to be an old man."

"Forty-seven isn't old."

"It's *really* old." Sarah grabbed Baojia's head and pulled herself up to sit on his shoulder. "That's almost a hundred, Dad."

He laughed low and long. Nothing made him laugh more than his children. They were the light and life of his eternity, and words could not express how grateful for them he was.

Even when they were being restless.

"Bedtime, Jake."

He swung Sarah onto his back and sat on the edge of Jake's bed while they said goodnight prayers. It was a habit Natalie had begun with both the children, and while Baojia wasn't religious, he appreciated the habit of gratitude it engendered.

"And thank you for our house," Jake said. "And thank you for my bike."

"And my bike too," Sarah whispered.

"Thank you for Sarah's baby bike."

"Jake." Baojia's voice was a warning.

"And thank you for fishing. And thank you for Ariel and Miss Olivia."

Baojia murmured, "Wrap it up."

His son could be very grateful. For close to an hour if he didn't want to go to bed.

"And thank you for Uncle Lucien and Auntie Mak and for cousin Carina and also for Butch, amen." Jake finished his prayers and opened his eyes, his lips pressed together.

Baojia raised an eyebrow. "Butch?"

"He's out there, Dad. We just haven't found him yet."

Jake was bound and determined to have a dog. He'd been begging for two years. Natalie and Baojia had resisted. They already had enough people in and out of their house simply to help take care of two active children. A dog seemed like another thing to keep track of.

"I know it." Jake yawned loudly. "When Butch finds us, you'll know too."

"I'll keep my eyes open." He bent over and kissed Jake's forehead. "Goodnight. I love you."

"I love you too!" Sarah sang. She giggled when Baojia stood and swung her from his back into his arms.

"Love you, Dad." Jake punched his pillows to get them exactly as he wanted. "Tell Mom I hope she's feeling better."

"I will." He held Sarah in place as she tried to crawl up his shoulder and onto his head. "Sweet dreams."

He walked out of Jake's room and into Sarah's. A bathroom connected the two rooms, but while Jake's bedroom was decorated plainly with dark green trim and dinosaurs scattered everywhere, Sarah's was an explosion of purple.

Purple curtains. Purple bed. Purple painted monkeys crawling along the top of each wall. Baojia tossed Sarah onto her bed and smiled when the little girl erupted in giggles.

"Do it again." She held out her arms.

"No." He sat on the edge of her bed and tried to settle her down. "I'll read you a book and then you need to sleep."

"I want Mama to read it."

"Mama is not feeling well," Baojia said. "So we're letting her sleep."

Sarah pouted. "I want to go say goodnight."

"You already did that."

"I want a glass of water."

Baojia pointed to the water bottle by her bed. "Done."

"I want..." She huffed out a breath. "I want... a stuffie."

"Sarah." Baojia stood and gave her the look she had to recognize. "Seriously?"

Sarah looked at the line of stuffed animals decorating her bed and shrugged helplessly. "Someone is missing."

He stood and watched her from the corner of his eye as he walked over to the hammock of stuffed animals in the corner. "Lion?" It was an adorable fluffy thing that had no basis in reality, but she loved it.

Sarah shook her head.

"Unicorn?"

Eyes wide, she shook her head again.

"Snake?"

She considered it, but it was a firm head shake. Not the snake, but he was on the right track. His smallest child had a warped sense of humor and a fondness for the macabre.

Not unlike her mother.

Baojia lifted another one. "Bat?"

She cocked her head and considered it. "Mmmm. No."

Baojia sighed and picked up the one he should have grabbed first if he hadn't wanted to go through the mock trial Sarah loved so much.

"Vampire?"

Eyes wide, Sarah grinned and held out her arms.

Baojia sighed and tossed her the ridiculous joke his wife had bought the Christmas before. It was a stuffed cartoon vampire with a purple cape and felt fangs. It looked like it belonged on a cereal box.

Sarah absolutely loved it. Just as Natalie knew she would.

You married an evil, evil woman.

"Okay book, then bed." Baojia sat next to his little girl as she snuggled under the purple blanket, hugging the ridiculous vampire and sucking her thumb. "And remind me what the silly vampire's name is?"

Sarah took her thumb out of her mouth. "Giovanni."

Baojia smiled. "That's right."

~

He pulled his shirt off before he slipped into bed next to his wife.

"Hmm?" Natalie rolled toward him, her face pale and her long red hair piled on top of her head. "Hey, handsome. Kids in bed?"

"Yes." He scooted next to her pulled her into his chest. "How are you feeling?"

"I'm just overtired." She yawned and snuggled in. "I had those two deadlines last week and I've been running on empty."

"You need to sleep more." He stroked a hand over her hair. "Maybe the kids' schedule—"

"Shh." She put a finger over his lips. "The schedule is fine. I'm fine. Just working too much. Thanks for putting the kids to bed."

"It was my turn anyway." He kissed her hand. "Did you want to sleep more?"

"Maybe." She drifted a little, still drowsy. Her hand traced the lines of muscle on his chest. "Give me a minute."

If she wanted to sleep, Baojia didn't mind laying with her. His wife was his favorite person. He could sit all night just listening to her heart beat and hearing her breathe.

He loved watching Natalie, seeing the changes in her face

and her body as the years passed. They'd been together over eight years and Baojia felt the privilege of witnessing her mortal years, because she had chosen *him* to be a permanent part of her life.

Natalie had transformed during pregnancy, a fascinating and frightening time for a vampire unaccustomed to change. Her belly swelled and marks appeared on her skin. Her lips and breasts were fuller. Her feet grew bigger. Her dark red hair had thickened and even her heart sounded different. Her blood tasted richer and he had to be very careful when he took her vein. She'd protested when he tried to abstain.

During the first pregnancy, he'd been more than a little alarmed. Then it happened again, and he wasn't alarmed, but their three-year-old son had been.

Family life, Baojia had decided, was the greatest and most unexpected adventure.

"Is Sarah sleeping?" Natalie murmured.

"Hopefully."

"With her vampire?"

He grunted. "Yes."

She let out an evil laugh. "I'm going to get Sadia one for her next birthday."

Baojia smiled. "What an excellent idea." He loosened her hair and began playing with it.

"Ugh." She batted his hand. "It's dirty. I need to wash it."

"I don't care if your hair is dirty." He spread it out and feathered it over his skin. "It's still sexy."

She lifted her head from his chest and wiggled her eyebrows. "My dirty hair is sexy?"

He ran his hand down her shoulder, under her arm, and along the side of her breast. "Everything about you is sexy."

"Mmmm." Her eyes turned from sleepy to playful. "I see someone doesn't want to leave the bed."

He smiled and scooted down so he could kiss her. "Why would I want to leave the bed when you're in it?"

She met his lips in a long, languid kiss, sighing into his mouth. "Don't know. Thought you might have..." she stroked her tongue out and flicked the tip over his already-extended fangs. "...work or something."

"Something." He sank into her kiss, ran his hand down her thigh, and hiked her leg over his hip. "I do have something... to do."

"Oh yeah?" She ran her hand along his nape, playing with the short ends of his hair that needed to be trimmed. "What's that?"

"I need to debrief you about..." He played with the lace trim on her panties. "...something very important. This underwear has to go."

"Just the underwear?" She bit his chin. "I mean, I can leave the pajamas on, but you might have to get creative."

"Ha ha." He began tugging. "I could rip these off."

"You better not. This is my last clean pair of pjs."

She quickly shoved her sleep shorts and underwear down her legs, kicking them down to the foot of the bed. Baojia lifted her shirt up and teased her breasts, making her arch her back and sigh happily.

He was just pulling her shirt over her head when the door creaked open. "Mom?"

Nooooo.

"You forgot to lock the door?" she hissed.

"Stay." Baojia poked his head up from the covers. "Sarah, go to bed."

"I'm thirsty."

"Uh uh." His voice was sharp. "Bed. Now."

She pretended to sniff. "But I miss Mom."

Natalie shoved the tangled hair out of her face and lifted her head. "Sarah, honey, what did Dad say?"

"But—"

"I said goodnight to you earlier."

"But—"

"I'm gonna use amnis on her," Baojia muttered. "Don't think I won't."

"Shhh." Natalie was trying to bite back a laugh. "You are not." She raised her voice. "Sarah, I already said goodnight. You're not getting in bed with us. What did Dad say?"

Sarah sighed.

"What was that?"

"Stimefrbed," she mumbled. She let out one last pitiful sigh before she closed the door.

Baojia waited to hear her little feet walk back to her bedroom, shuffling the whole way. Her door creaked open. Shut. He could hear her muttering under her breath as she got back into bed.

He looked down at Natalie, whose lips and cheeks were still flushed. "We are the worst."

"The meanest parents ever."

He smiled and settled back down in bed. "Horrible and rotten."

"Come here." She hooked her arm around his neck. "Let me show you what I do to horrible, rotten, mean vampires as sexy as you."

"Hold that thought." He slipped out of bed. "And let me lock the door."

Baojia woke the next night in the small room they'd built into the farmhouse where they lived on the Northern California coast. He took a moment to orient himself, listening for the voices he expected beyond the thick, cement walls of his day chamber. It had been built to withstand storms, earthquakes, explosive concussions and gunfire. In it, there was a small bathroom and enough provisions for four humans to survive for thirty days.

His day chamber also doubled as their panic room, which was necessary when you were a senior security chief for the immortal in charge of the Pacific Northwest, much of Canada, Alaska, and a not-insignificant part of Russia.

Baojia listened for the expected sounds of life beyond the walls of his day chamber.

But the sounds were unexpected.

"Mom?" His son sounded scared.

"Are they awake yet?" It was the nanny, and her voice was panicked. "Natalie, would Baojia be awake yet? The sun is down. How about Lucien and Mak?"

He didn't wait another moment. Pulling on a pair of sweatpants, he unlocked the deadbolt that secured his room and rushed toward the voices, which were coming from the kitchen and dining area. "Natalie?"

He forced himself to remain calm when he saw her lying on the kitchen floor. Sarah was crying. Jake was sitting next to his mother on the floor, and Ariel, their children's nanny, was on the phone.

She spotted him. "I'm on the phone with Lucien."

"Tell him to come." He bent down and looked in her face. Her eyes were open. She wasn't unconscious. "What happened?"

"Just..." She tried shaking her head, but her pupils were abnormally dilated. She blinked. "Dizzy. I just got dizzy. I laid down on the floor so I didn't fall. That's all."

"Did you eat today?"

"Had breakfast with the kids. Snack an hour ago. Something like that."

That should have been enough. He performed a basic physical exam. She didn't have a fever. Her skin was cool and clammy. "Jake, take Sarah into the family room."

"I wanna stay with Mama!" Sarah wailed.

"Sarah." Baojia gave her a steady look. "Mama is going to be fine. She's just a little sick. Remember when you got the flu and threw up last winter?"

Sarah stuck her thumb in her mouth and nodded.

"Mama is sick like you were." Mama was *not* sick like Sarah had been. Natalie had no fever. Her pulse was normal. Something else was going on. "I know it's scary when Mom gets sick," he continued, "but Uncle Lucien is going to come over and give her a check-up, so you and Jakey need to go play so there's room in the kitchen."

Ariel held out her hand. "Come on, guys. Let's go do a puzzle, okay?"

Jake was giving him suspicious eyes.

"Jake," Baojia said. "I need you to take care of Sarah."

"Okay." His voice was small. He stood and held his hand out for his sister. "Come on, Monkey. Dad'll take care of Mom."

"Can I get up now?" Natalie's lips were pale. "I'm not dizzy anymore."

"Stay put." He put a hand on her cheek and spoke quietly. "Just... give me a break, okay Red? Stay here until Lucien can examine you."

Red like firecrackers. Like chili peppers. Like her hair. Natalie didn't look like her nickname just then. She looked tired and wan and unwell.

Baojia clamped down on the creeping terror that lived in his heart. Every night, he had to control his fear and pretend like the world was a safe place. That he could keep the monsters at bay. That his children would be protected. He had to, or he would go insane. But kneeling next to Natalie in the middle of the kitchen, the fear crept out and would not be contained.

Something was wrong with his wife.

Valley of the Shadow
will be available December 10, 2019
and is available to preorder at all major retailers.

Want to read more about
Ben and Tenzin's adventures?

Obsidian's Edge
is now available at all major retailers!

For the first time ever, all three origin novellas in the Elemental Legacy series are available in one volume, along with a bonus novella, *The Bronze Blade.*

In **Shadows and Gold**, driving a truck full of rotting vegetables and twenty million in gold across mainland China wasn't what Ben Vecchio had in mind for summer vacation. If he can keep Tenzin's treasure safe, the reward will be worth the effort. But when has travel with a five-thousand-year-old wind vampire ever been simple?

In **Imitation and Alchemy**, all Ben wanted was a quiet summer before his last semester of university. All Tenzin wanted was a cache of priceless medieval coins that had been missing for several hundred years. And some company.

In **Omens and Artifacts**, Ben needs a job. A *legendary* job. Finding the lost sword of Brennus the Celt would make his reputation in the vampire world, but it could also draw dangerous attention. The Raven King's gold isn't famous for being easy to find. Luckily, Ben has his own legend at his side.

OBSIDIAN'S EDGE is an anthology of novellas in the Elemental Legacy series by Elizabeth Hunter, USA Today Bestselling Author of *Midnight Labyrinth*, *Blood Apprentice*, and other works of fiction.

~

> *He's a human in a vampire's world,*
> *but she's the reason he's not sleeping at night.*

MIDNIGHT LABYRINTH

Benjamin Vecchio escaped a chaotic childhood and grew to adulthood under the protection and training of one of the Elemental world's most feared vampire assassins. He's traveled the world and battled immortal enemies.

But everyone has to go home sometime.

New York means new opportunities and allies for Ben and his vampire partner, Tenzin. It also means new politics and new threats. Their antiquities business is taking off, and their client list is growing. When Ben is challenged to find a painting lost since the Second World War, he jumps at the chance. This job will keep him closer to home, but it might just land him in hot water with the insular clan of earth vampires who run Manhattan.

Tenzin knew the painting would be trouble before she laid eyes on it, but she can't deny the challenge intrigues her. Human laws mean little to a vampire with a few millennia behind her, and Tenzin misses the rush of taking what isn't hers.

But nothing is more dangerous than a human with half the story, and Ben and Tenzin might end up risking their reputations and their lives before they escape the Midnight Labyrinth.

MIDNIGHT LABYRINTH is the first full length novel in an all-new contemporary fantasy series by Elizabeth Hunter, author of the Elemental Mysteries and the Irin Chronicles.

> *If you're a human in a vampire's world,*
> *nothing goes according to plan.*

Blood Apprentice

When a map to the mysterious fortune of notorious privateer Miguel Enríquez falls in the lap of Ben and Tenzin, only one of them is jumping at the opportunity. Tenzin can't wait to search for a secret cache of gold. Ben, on the other hand, couldn't be less excited.

All Ben knows about Puerto Rico is what he hears on the news and a few lingering memories of his human grandmother. Going back to his roots holds zero appeal for the carefully constructed man he's become.

But in the end, the lure of hidden gold can't be denied.

Ben and Tenzin head to Puerto Rico where the immortal world is ruled by *Los Tres*, a trio of powerful vampires commanding the wind, the waves, and the mountains that make up their small island in the Caribbean.

To find Enríquez's treasure, they'll have to walk a fine line between flattery and secrecy. To leave the island might mean a bigger fight than either one of them foresaw.

Blood Apprentice is the second novel in the Elemental Legacy, a paranormal mystery series by Elizabeth Hunter, author of the Irin Chronicles.

∼

Sometimes falling is the safest step to take.

The Devil and the Dancer

Chloe Reardon has a problem, and his name is Gavin Wallace.

Okay, Gavin isn't exactly a problem, unless you consider a highly attractive wind vampire with dubious intentions a problem. Especially if that vampire is your boss. With an affinity for kilts and excellent taste in music.

But none of that matters because Chloe Reardon has had enough of dangerous men. Danger is overrated. Danger is the opposite of sexy. So Gavin is the last man—or vampire—on earth she needs to let into her heart.

Except what if the most dangerous man you knew was also the one who made you feel the strongest?

The Devil and the Dancer is a paranormal romance novella in the Elemental Legacy series.

~

Darkness comes for everyone,
and some fates are inescapable.

NIGHT'S RECKONING

For over a thousand years, the legendary sword Laylat al Hisab —the Night's Reckoning—has been lost in the waters of the East China Sea. Forged as a peace offering between two ancient vampires, the sword has eluded treasure hunters, human and immortal alike.

But in time, even the deep gives up its secrets.

When Tenzin's sire hears about the ninth century ship-wreck found off the coast of southern China, Zhang Guo real-izes he'll need the help of an upstart pirate from Shanghai to retrieve it. And since that pirate has no desire to be in the middle of an ancient war, Cheng calls the only allies who might be able to help him avoid it.

Unfortunately, Tenzin is on one side of the globe and Ben is on the other.

Tenzin knows she'll need Ben's keen mind and political

skills to complete the job. She also knows gaining Ben's coopera-tion won't be an easy task. She'll have to drag him back into the darkness he's been avoiding.

Whether Ben knows it or not, his fate is balanced on the edge of a thousand-year-old blade, and one stumble could break everything Tenzin has worked toward.

Night's Reckoning is the third novel in the Elemental Legacy series, a paranormal mystery by Elizabeth Hunter, USA Today bestselling author of the Elemental Mysteries.

∼

COMING SPRING 2020
Dawn Caravan
Elemental Legacy Book Four

Please subscribe to my newsletter for more information about the Elemental Legacy series and other news and updates about my books.

AFTERWORD

Dear Readers,

Thanks for returning to the Elemental Legacy series. I hope you enjoyed reading *Night's Reckoning* as much as I enjoyed writing it. The core of this book has been planned for over six years now, so it felt really great to finally get it down on paper. I truly hope you enjoyed.

The next book in the series will be **Dawn Caravan**, which will be coming in Spring 2020. In the meantime, I'll also be releasing a holiday novella in the Elemental World series called **Valley of the Shadow**. There is a free preview at the end of this book.

I hope you take the time to sign up for my newsletter to receive a free short story, or subscribe to my blog at ElizabethHunterWrites.com. Those are the best ways to keep up with all the latest news, teasers, and contests happening for my books.

And of course, honest reviews at your favorite retailer are always very welcome and help a writer out!

Thanks for reading,

Elizabeth Hunter

ABOUT THE AUTHOR

ELIZABETH HUNTER is a *USA Today* and international best-selling author of romance, contemporary fantasy, and paranormal mystery. Based in Central California, she travels extensively to write fantasy fiction exploring world mythologies, history, and the universal bonds of love, friendship, and family. She has published over thirty works of fiction and sold over a million books worldwide. She is the author of Love Stories on 7th and Main, the Elemental Legacy series, the Irin Chronicles, the Cambio Springs Mysteries, and other works of fiction.

ElizabethHunterWrites.com

ALSO BY ELIZABETH HUNTER

Blood and Sand

The Bronze Blade

The Scarlet Deep

A Very Proper Monster

A Stone-Kissed Sea

Valley of the Shadow

(December 2019)

<u>The Irin Chronicles</u>

The Scribe

The Singer

The Secret

The Staff and the Blade

The Silent

The Storm

The Seeker

<u>The Cambio Springs Series</u>

Long Ride Home

Shifting Dreams

Five Mornings

Desert Bound

Waking Hearts

<u>Contemporary Romance</u>

The Genius and the Muse

<u>7th and Main</u>

INK

HOOKED

GRIT

Made in the USA
Columbia, SC
08 August 2022